4 Angels! The story is wonderful: filled with intrigue, suspense, romance, psychic powers and an evil bad guy that will stop at nothing to get his way. I enjoyed the story and loved the ending...

—Stephanie, Fallen Angel Reviews

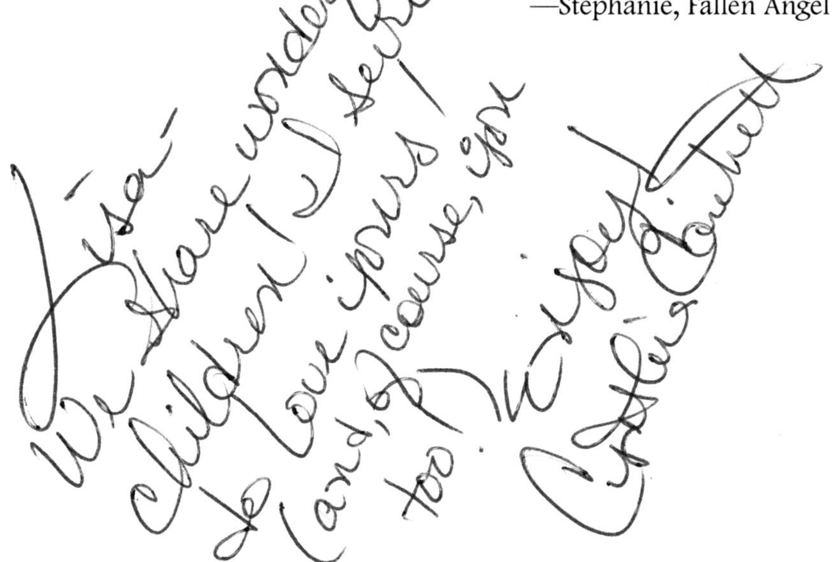

Novels by Cynthia Cantrell
Published by Mundania Press

The Wolf Series

Flame's Ghost
(Book One)

Wolf's Shadow
(Book Two)

The Vampire Series

Kat
(Book One)

Other Books

The Curse of Amun-Re

Flame's Ghost

Cynthia Cantrell

A Mundania Press Production
Mundania Press LLC
6470A Glenway Avenue, #109
Cincinnati, Ohio 45211-5222

To order additional copies of this book, contact:
books@mundania.com
www.mundania.com

Cover Art © 2008 by SkyeWolf
SkyeWolf Images (http://www.skyewolfimages.com)
Book Design, Production, and Layout by Daniel J. Reitz, Sr.
Marketing and Promotion by Bob Sanders

Trade Paperback ISBN: 978-1-59426-709-3
eBook ISBN: 978-1-59426-708-6

First Edition • May 2008

Production by Mundania Press LLC
Printed in the United States of America
10 9 8 7 6 5 4 3 2 1

This book is dedicated to my family.
Especially to you, Mom.
You told me
I could and I did!

I love you!

Chapter 1

She is standing in the meadow, arms outstretched at her sides, waist length, sun-kissed, red hair blowing wildly around her. The most beautiful woman they have ever seen. A goddess.

Even from this distance they can see her enormous green eyes, very angry green eyes. Two very large wolves stand on either side of her. At least five more can be seen coming through the knee high grass toward her.

They hear her speak calmly, but very clearly. "You will leave this land! There will be no killing done here! I will not allow it! If there will be death here it will be your own!" This goddess declares to them with a soft southern drawl.

This said, the wolves start moving, surrounding the woman, never taking their eyes off of the men, teeth bared and growling.

"Lady, we just came here to hunt! We saw a big moose come into the woods up the road aways and we followed its tracks here!" states one of the men. He turns to the others and in a quiet tone says, "Boys, come on. Let's get the hell outta here. We're on private property and we all know it. That moose ain't worth this kind of trouble."

They all nod, but one.

This one tells them, loudly, "I came here to kill that damn moose and I ain't lettin no woman with a bunch of damn dogs scare me off. What the hell do you think she can do? We have the guns. We'll just kill a few of those overgrown dogs and she'll move off!"

The other men shake their heads and turn to leave.

Before they move very far the one speaks again, this time to the woman. "Lady, I been trackin that damn moose all day, and I aim to kill it. I don't care what you say! If those damn dogs don't back off I'm gonna kill a few of them too!"

The others protest, trying to make him leave with them. He refuses.

"You will *not* kill anything on this land! You will leave now!" states the woman, raising both arms toward the heavens. The wolves start moving toward him.

He turns to see that his friends have all left the stand of woods. He is now standing alone. He pulls his rifle to his shoulder and shouts, "Call em off lady!"

As he says the last word, from behind him, the wolf attacks. It has crept upon him from behind. The wolf hits his arm, biting deep, and the rifle goes off. The wolf turns him loose and runs toward the woman.

The man sees that the rifle shot has hit the woman. He sees blood on her shirt as she falls to the ground. He turns and runs after his buddies, hearing the wolves howling behind him. He slows as he reaches the trucks, telling his buddies, "It ain't worth it. I told her we'd leave em be. Let's get outta here."

One of them says, "We heard the shotgun go off. What were you shooting at?"

"Just one of them damn dogs! It snuck up behind me and bit me! I tried to shoot the damn thing, but it got away." He shows them his arm.

The others never knew he had shot her.

As the woman falls to the ground she thinks back to the day, a week ago, that she had found this meadow, deep in the forest. She thinks she is dying and her life is flashing before her. She seems to be seeing herself as if in a movie; her memories coming to life.

She sees herself...*finding the small dirt track that led to this clearing in the forest trees. It's so late and I'm so tired, but as soon as I see them run into the trees,* I know *this is my place. The place of the wolves. The place I've been looking for, longing for, all of my life.*

They lead me to this wonderful clearing in the trees. This small meadow of such beauty, and even though it's too dark to see its full beauty, I can feel it. Deep inside, in my secret heart; the place of my dreams.

There's a small brook. I know, because I can hear its voice calling out to me.

The small meadow is knee high in deep green grass. There are petals of Indian Paintbrush reds and Daisy whites flying through the air all around me. The ancient trees surround this meadow of beauty in silent watch, making me feel safe and loved for the first time in my life. I'm welcomed here.

I spend this first day with joy in my heart. Joy of freedom, hard won. Now, I'm sitting on the rocks by the brook watching the squirrels and birds flit from tree to tree. Fussing and arguing among themselves. They remind me so much of the small children from the orphanage, always fussing over one thing or another.

I close my eyes and I hear a soft growl. I glance up quickly to see them standing there, only feet away, watching me through the trees. They're the same ones that I'd seen from the road. The ones that led me here; the alpha pair.

They're watching me with beautiful eyes of gold. I smile and feel the most intense sense of joy I have ever felt. They know me and I know them. I belong to the wolves. I've known this in my heart since the first time I ever saw one. I remember that time very well.

The teachers had taken all of us, the orphans, to the zoo. A treat, and the only time I'd ever been taken to see the animals. Yes, the first time, and the last.

I remember seeing the wolves there. I cried because I could feel their pain. The pain of being in a place where they could no longer run, play, or have the life they were born to. Just like me.

I knew their fear and loneliness. They knew mine too, I could feel that. I knew their hearts, and they mine.

The teachers had tried to comfort me. They'd tried to tell me that the wolves were taken care of, but I knew what the wolves felt. I lived the same life. Never loved and never free.

The wolves saw me there, crying. They came to the very edge of their enclosure and whined while clawing at the bars. I was drawn to them, even then.

I was able to break away from the teacher's arms and flew to bars of the enclosure. I wrapped my arms through the bars to hold onto the neck of the closest wolf. He nuzzled me and I loved it.

Then, suddenly, I was seeing through the wolf's eyes. I knew his thoughts. I saw the children there, through him. I could see myself standing there. My eyes were running with tears, but empty, because my heart, my very soul, was within the wolf. I vividly remember going back into myself.

The teachers grabbed me and pulled me away, all the while screaming at me. I was hysterical. They were taking me away. It was as if they were taking me from my family.

The wolves went wild. They howled, throwing their bodies full force into the bars of the cage. Then they fell back, dazed and bruised.

It took all three of the teachers to get me back into the bus. I was never again allowed to go on trips with the other orphans. But, that was just as well...I didn't want to. I wanted nothing to do with this cruel world that I was forced into.

Now I'm in the meadow, by the brook again. I look into the eyes of the largest wolf. He's huge, weighing at least 150 pounds, with gray fur and golden eyes. The female is smaller at about 130 pounds and solid black.

It was the female, I know, that had watched me from the woods the night before. She had waited until I saw her clearly before walking into the woods next to the dirt track with her mate. They waited for me to follow them.

For six days I've camped here, making a fire at night, sitting and watching the wolves. They come and go, but stay close to me, especially at night. I talk with them, as if to children. I tell them of my days and nights, alone and afraid. They cry their mournful song to the moon as I cry and heal my broken heart.

Now it's all changed. I'm dying here, but I am with my wolves. Will they miss me?

Chapter 2

The wolves are frantic, rushing to Flame. She does not realize her full power yet. She knows she is different, can do things that others cannot, but she doesn't know the full force of it. They know. She is a leader among them. They know of one other like her, the old man.

It is the other one that they have to get to now. They must go to the old man, for only he can save her. He is a healer. One gifted with vision. He is also a good man and they trust him. He is old, but still very strong. Strong enough to save Flame, they hope. He lives in the forest. He has a small home here.

The female stays with Flame. She covers Flame's small form with her own body, thinking only of protecting her while the male runs to the cabin. It is not far, but the old man will have to follow him back to Flame.

The male knows he must hurry; that guns can kill. Men like these have been in this forest before. He runs as fast as four legs can carry him.

Joseph Wolf has lived on this land all of his life. He owns many hundreds of acres of this forest land, all connected to the small rural town of River Valley. His small cabin is old, but it is all he needs. His life has been long and one he has treasured.

His family is all gone now. His grandson, Joe, is all that is left and even he is now gone. He lives in the city. Not too far, but a whole world away, as far as his grandfather is concerned.

Most people do not even know his full name. They just call him Grandfather, for he is just that, grandfather to all. He is Sioux, and born at a time when the Sioux had kept to themselves. He loves his home and will protect it and its land from all harm.

Grandfather knows the wolves. He knows them well. This is also their home and he will always help them to protect it. He watches over his land, many times through their eyes. He walks with and sometimes *in* the wolves.

He knows of the girl-child called Flame also. He had seen her in his dreams before she came onto his land. Perhaps it was a vision, a Sioux belief, one of a big change coming into his life.

He also knew when she entered his forest. He has seen her through the wolf's eyes and knows her gift is like his. He has been watching her for many days now. He senses that her gift can be even greater than his, though she doesn't know it yet.

He knows that she has been shot. He has been watching through the alpha male, the same one that comes for him even now. He felt the bullet, too; his chest hurting as if he, too, had been shot.

Using the mind link Grandfather tells the wolf to return to Flame's side, that he will meet him in the meadow. He takes the few things that he will need with him. He cannot take one of his horses. The horses are still scared of the wolves, even after all this time. He knows he will have to get Flame back to his cabin in his truck. His truck is very old and rusted, but it will run.

He knows that he must be quick if he is to save Flame, for she is losing a lot of blood. It will be hard on her. She will have to be very strong to live through this, but he has a feeling she is very strong, not only of body, but of mind and of gifts.

He drives as quickly as possible over the old dirt track. This track runs over most of the one thousand acres. He uses it often, watching and protecting what is his. It was cleared of trees by his father, who had owned this forest land before him. He keeps it clear so he can watch over this land and its occupants.

This is prime Montana land. Many times over the years men have gone to great lengths to buy this land. He will not give it up and they will not take it. He makes sure of that.

Oil fills this land. The earth here is full of it. He knows this, as his father before him knew it. Unfortunately, so do others.

He owns more land. Land filled with more oil, but that land is located far from here. He has three oil wells that have been producing for many years, but this land, his home, will not be drilled on. Mutilated.

His grandson, Joe, will see to that from now on. He is a lawyer now. Grandfather paid for his education after his mother and father had been killed in an automobile accident. Joe does not want to live on this land, but he knows how much Grandfather loves it. He is a good man. Though he does not carry the gift of vision, like Grandfather, he knows of it.

Grandfather reaches Flame's campsite. The female stands, shakes her body, and whines her worry to him. He pats her head, giving the alpha couple a treat of prime beef steak that he has brought with him. He often brings them treats since they have helped him many times when he uses his gift of vision. He tells them he will take Flame to heal her.

They move off to the side and Grandfather goes to work. He checks the wound. It is located just above her right breast. He applies pressure to the wound and binds it by wrapping a strip of cloth around her upper torso.

The bullet has gone straight through, thankfully not hitting any vital organs or bones. He must get her to his cabin to clean the wound properly though. He also has a variety of medicines, as he cares for all of the animals here that are hurt or wounded.

Grandfather has a friend that is a veterinarian. He has given Grandfather the medicine and continues to give him what he needs. He knows Grandfather cares for all the forest animals and it is easier to give the medicines to him than to go to his land every time an animal is hurt.

Grandfather can approach any animal without fear of harm to himself or to the animal. The vet cannot. Nor it seems can anyone else, until now. Until Flame.

Flame murmurs, crying out as he settles her into the truck. She weighs next to nothing. He thinks, *Almost like a child, but this is no child.*

She is a beautiful woman, but still very young. Already he loves her. She is his family now. One that carries the gift. This makes her family. She is very special and he *will* heal her *and* train her.

As they go back to his cabin the wolves keep pace with the truck, following closely. They will go back to their den soon to care for their pack. They will be back though. He knows they will not leave her unprotected. Wolves protect their own.

Flame is dreaming. She must be dreaming. She seems to hurt all over, but on the right side of her chest there is a sharp, fiery pain.

She is dreaming of an old Indian man. He is talking to her in soft, concerned tones. She notices the strangest thing about his speech… he doesn't use contractions. For some reason this strikes her as funny. She wants to smile, to laugh even, but not *at* him, just to laugh for the joy of it. He has kind eyes and a beautifully, wrinkled smile. She trusts him.

He talks about the wolves. He loves them and she knows it. He loves *her* and she somehow knows this too.

Grandfather enters her mind. He sees her thoughts, her worries, and her dreams of the past.

She thinks she must be delirious…or dying. *Is this what happens when you die? Is he an angel?*

Now she is a shadow, watching as a stooped man in an old tattered coat lays a basket at the top of the steps of the orphanage in Tennessee, where she had spent her childhood. He tucks a note into the basket, turns away, and leaves.

The basket moves and she hears a child's high pitched cry. She waits and sees a woman, a maid, open the door and exclaim in a loud cry that someone has left a baby on the steps again.

Then she watches from the shadows as the head of the orphanage, Miss Hodges, picks up the child. The baby is naked, except for a blanket that has been loosely wrapped around her. As Miss Hodges picks her up the note falls out, hits the floor, and the maid picks it up. She exclaims that the child has a name. Flame.

Miss Hodges says that the baby is a girl. She says that from now on the girl's name will be Flame Warren, using the orphanage's name, Warren House, as a last name, like so many countless others before her.

She watches as, in the way dreams do, the years float by. Now she is a child of five and she sees a young couple that has come to the orphanage to find a girl child. They see her, a beautiful young girl, and think she is perfect. They want to take her home to see how she will fit in.

Flame watches as Miss Hodges looks from Flame to the young orphanage teacher that is assisting the couple. Miss Hodges shakes her head and turns away. She knows Flame will be back. She is always brought back.

The couple is so excited. So is Flame. She wants a mother and father so badly. This couple is nice. Flame is a smart child. Some would say too smart.

When they get to the couple's home Flame is immediately drawn to their large mixed breed dog. She loves all animals, and this dog loves her at first sight. The couple is thrilled, as they had thought it might cause a problem, since most children are afraid of the dog. They do not know that Flame can feel the animal's thoughts and memories It is almost like looking at the picture books she loves so much, though these pictures are not very pretty.

That evening the couple leaves Flame playing in her room, which was their daughter's before she had died. They want to talk to one another about adopting her. They notice that the dog stays with Flame. He will not let her out of his sight.

Flame sees herself sitting with the dog, but then she is suddenly inside the bedroom of the man and woman, a ghost among them, as they talk about their child, Misty, who had died of a sudden and unexplained illness a year earlier. The lady cries and the man seems upset, but he does not cry like the lady.

The lady worries that if Flame ever gets sick they would not know her medical history and they could lose her too. She cannot bear losing another child. They talk of all sorts of things that grownups talk about when thinking of adopting a child. Flame feels as if she is intruding, even though she is not really there… she is only dreaming and it has been many years since this actually happened.

Then she watches as they go to talk to Flame, the child. They wanted to find out if she likes them, but she is in the room crying when they walk in. The lady rushes to her and quickly picks her up to comfort her.

Flame tells them that she is sorry that Misty had died. She tells them that Misty had not been sick, but she wants to know why Misty's daddy had hurt her. She tells the woman that the reason Misty died was because her Daddy shook her too hard, causing her death. She wanted to know why he would shake a baby.

The lady is shocked. She screams and cries, and little Flame feels so sorry for her, but she is afraid of the man, Misty's daddy. He looks at her the way the teachers sometimes look at her when she asks them questions. His face is all red and Flame is afraid he will shake her too.

This is when the dog attacks the man. He bites the man all over, until he is bleeding all over everything. Blood now covers the room. Flame's fear causes this, as the dog is only thinking to protect her. She never finds out if the man lived or died. Flame is taken back to the orphanage by a policeman that same night.

Now, Flame is a child of six and the teachers are taking all the kids on a trip. Miss Hodges says that Flame can go, which is unusual, since they normally do not like her to mingle with the other children. She talks to Flame about not asking personal questions of anyone, but Flame does not understand why

She always knows who did something wrong and, at first, when the teachers asked who did the wrong thing, she would tell. That made the other kids get punished and they blamed Flame. This also made them shun and dislike her, though she was too young to really understand it.

She even knows when the teachers do bad things. Nobody, not even the teachers, want to be around Flame very much. They are afraid that she will know their secrets. She has only to touch them and she knows all kinds of things about them; their rights, wrongs, and sometimes even their immediate futures. She soon learns that people do not really want to know the answers to some of their questions. Some do not want to know their futures either. They are afraid of it, and of her.

This is the day when the teachers take them to the zoo. All of the kids are excited. Flame is too. She has never been to a zoo.

She knew that the animals were there, but she did not understand why they were in cages. At her young age she had no concept of what cages were for, but she did know what it felt like to be trapped. She feels extreme sympathy for these animals.

Animals always do what Flame wants them to do, all animals, except humans. She does not even have to tell them, they just seem to be able to *feel* what she wants. She does not understand that they don't do what others want them to. She is heartbroken to see the animals in those cages.

While the other kids laugh and talk about the animals, she cries. The other kids tease and laugh at her, so she stays to herself until they get to the wolves.

Suddenly she can see through the wolves' eyes. At first she is excited by this, but then she feels what they are feeling. She feels their despair. They have no freedom, just like her, and she realizes she has her own cage. The orphanage. That is when she sobs.

The scene plays out just like it did earlier in her mind. She is seeing it all again. She cannot seem to *stop* seeing it. In parts of it she is like a shadow, seeing herself as a child, but in others she is the child again. She does not realize that it is Grandfather making her remember these things. Through her memories he is learning about her. About her past. About her gift.

After they take her back to the bus the other kids are relentless in their scorn of Flame. They are cruel, as only kids can be to other kids. They nickname her the "wolf_girl" and make howling sounds to tease her. She has never felt so alone, scared, or hurt, and her emotions explode. She screams for the kids to stop, to leave her alone, and suddenly all the windows on the bus explode outward.

She never makes friends with the other kids. They are all afraid of her. The teachers and aides do not want to take her places, or be with her at all. Miss Hodges has finally stopped bringing her down when someone comes to the orphanage for a child. People stop trying to meet her. She is all alone.

Now she is a young lady of fifteen, finding a small puppy in the alley behind the orphanage. She tries to save some of her measly dinner for it every day. She feeds the little thing more than she is eating herself. She loves this little puppy.

One of the teachers sees her sneak out one night with her dinner for the puppy. She is caught and punished. Miss Hodges calls the dogcatcher to pick up the puppy and makes Flame hand over the puppy when he gets there. Then she asks the dogcatcher to talk to Flame and to tell her what will happen to this little puppy at the animal shelter when nobody comes to adopt it.

The dogcatcher is a nice man. He does not like the way Miss Hodges talks to her. Not at all. He is furious, but does not show it. He tells Miss Hodges that he will tell Flame all about the animal shelter. He even asks Miss Hodges if he can take Flame to see it. She smiles and tells him that it is a great idea.

Flame's afraid, crying, but the dogcatcher takes her hand and smiles at her. It is a real smile and she knows it. She can *feel* this man's anger at Miss Hodges, his real concern for Flame, and his love for animals. She cannot help but like this man immediately. She is eager to go with him now.

On the way to the shelter the dogcatcher, Mr. Allen, tells her all about the animals in the shelter. He explains that sometimes when the shelter becomes too crowded they have to make room for other animals. That means finding homes for some and for others it means that they have to die.

She begins to cry, silent tears falling unheeded down her cheeks. She cannot bear the thought that her puppy might die. She does not like that fact that any of the animals must die, but foremost in her mind is her puppy.

Mr. Allen tells her that they will not put her puppy to sleep. He explains that is what they call it when they have to kill them. He promises her that even if he has to take the puppy to his own home, it will not be put to sleep. This makes her smile for the first time in a very long time.

She loves the animal shelter and thinks it is a wonderful place. She loves the idea of caring for all of these animals that need someone. She is so enthralled by the shelter that Mr. Allen asks her if she would like to come to work for them. He says he will pay her to work there after her classes and on the weekends.

She is so excited that she can hardly hold it in. She loves the idea, but she is afraid that Miss Hodges will not let her do it. When she tells Mr. Allen of her fears, he says to leave Miss Hodges to him. This is when Flame gets her first job.

She works every day that they will let her. She even goes to the shelter on days that she isn't supposed to, just to help out, and see the animals. She gets to keep her puppy there and she names him Lucky, as because of him, she feels she has a place in the world. They never try to find him a home or put him to sleep.

She does not like the days when they have to put one of the animals down, but she learns that there are times when it is a blessing to the animals. They are able to find homes for most of them though, and she is happy for the first time in her young life.

When she is not working, she researches wolves and their habitats. She goes to the library and reads everything she can find on them. Fact or fiction, she reads it all. She knows that she will find the wolves one day. Soon. It is what she wants most of all. They have become her family, in her heart, and in her mind.

She finds out through her research that many places have almost killed off the wolf population. This is because people have so many misconceptions about them. She reads that they are being reintroduced in some places though. Montana is one of these places. This is where she will go when she gets old enough and she *will* find her wolves.

Mr. Allen opens an account for her at the bank and she saves all but a small amount, her own spending money, of her paycheck every week. He tells her that when she is eighteen she will be able to leave the orphanage and will have enough money saved by then to move out of there and take care of herself. She cannot wait.

On the very day she turns eighteen Miss Hodges comes into her room without knocking, and gives her the note that was found in the basket on the night she was left in the orphanage. She tells her that it is time for her to move on. She offers no further help, almost throwing her bodily out into the street.

Flame didn't care. All she had ever wanted was to leave this place. It was not her home and never had been. She draws out all of her money at the bank, goes to a cheap hotel and rents a room for a week. She knew Mr. Allen would be upset that she did not come to him, but she did not want to impose.

As soon as she could she went to the courthouse to have her name changed to Flame, dropping the "Warren" completely, not just from her name, but from her life. It is the name she was given at birth and the only name she wanted. She wanted no contact with the orphanage, or the people that worked and lived there.

The next thing she did was to buy her old VW van. It was used, but to her it was more than she had ever hoped for. It would be her home when she left Tennessee and searched for her wolves. She supplied it with a sleeping bag and the items necessary for her trip to Montana.

The hardest part of leaving Tennessee though was leaving the animal shelter. She cried as she hugged Mr. Allen tightly He promised that he would take care of Lucky. She knew he would. He was the closest thing to family that she had ever known. She will never forget him or Lucky, but she had to find the wolves. She never looked back.

Chapter 3

Grandfather is with Flame, in her mind, in her memories. He sees all of her dreams, feels her pain, and knows her small joys. His heart breaks for the small child and worries for the young woman. She is a fighter. She was named for fire and it fits her well. She is as strong as the hottest flame, but right now she is still very, very weak.

She has lost a lot of blood. Grandfather has to use all of his skill as a healer when he enters her mind and then her body, in the form of energy, working his way to the area where the bullet entered her body. He works meticulously, mending her from the inside out, all the while seeing her memories and knowing her heart.

After he is done working on her this way, he comes back into his own body, breathing a weary sign. He thinks to himself that he is getting too old for this, though he is not done yet. He carefully stitches the skin that was torn from the bullet, and then he gives her antibiotics to help to fight infection. He will continue to give it to her until he is sure the infection will not become a problem. He could not heal the skin in the same way as he healed the inside of her body, as he was much too weak to do so. He calls on all of his strength and hers too, during the healing.

While Grandfather is in her mind learning of her, he is also giving her his knowledge, his vision, his gift. He is a skilled warrior, whether it is for fighting man, animal, illness, or death. He leaves his mark in her mind.

She will remember this gift. She has only to call upon his memories and they will be there for her. She will know things that it takes many their whole lives to learn. She will be a gifted healer, gifted in many ways that she has never dreamt of. She already has the gift of vision, and now of healing, but she will have to learn how to use it properly.

What he would have given to have had the opportunity to raise this young woman, to train her. Grandfather would have filled her world with laughter, love, and *such* knowledge. She believes her difference is a thing to hide. She had no one to tell her what a gift it truly is. It is not too late. She will have his knowledge and his love.

He cannot wait to see her face light up with wonder and laughter. Her memories are heartbreaking. It will be his honor to watch her face light up with joy. What a gift she will be to the world, and to him.

He can hear the wolves outside. They howl during the night and pace the porch during the day. The whole pack has moved under his porch. It is not the first time they have done this and it won't be the last. They are very faithful.

They know that Flame is one of them. She can run in their minds, even while she is dreaming, and Grandfather runs with her and them. They run together.

She is beautiful, running with the wolves. She feels the joy of being a pack, of loving, of the simple pleasures. She thinks it all a wonderful dream, this Indian man and his wolves. Her wolves. They are one. One heart and one body. He is the grandfather, in her heart, in her soul. She does not want to wake from this dream, but Grandfather knows she must, and soon.

Grandfather takes a much needed nap, but wakes to find Flame gone from her body. She is not dead. No, to most they would think her still sleeping. But he is in her mind and she is not there. His mind moves to the wolves and he finds them sleeping under the porch.

He wonders, *Where is she?* He goes deeper into her mind and finds a sliver of light, her soul, and rushes toward it.

She has more power than he had ever thought possible. She is amazing. She is riding the sky with the hawk. He has never, ever, heard of one who can do both, run with the wolves *and* fly with the hawk! It is almost more than his old heart can take. He is filled with awe and wonder.

She pulls him to her, taking him through the night. Now she is teaching him.

Does her power know no bounds? he wonders

They fly through the night until the sky turns pink with the sunrise.

Grandfather is sitting in the chair next to her bed. She is still sleeping, but she will wake soon now. He has been giving her a sedative to help her to rest and she is healing quickly. She will sleep for a few more hours and he needs more rest also. He is exhausted.

He falls asleep listening to sounds of the wolves waking and nursing their young. He sleeps with a smile on his wrinkled face. There is a small smile playing at the corners of Flame's mouth also. She dreams sweet dreams now, not troubled dreams of the past.

When Grandfather wakes he places a pot of homemade vegetable soup on the stove. Leaving it on a low flame it fills the room with a wonderful homey smell that makes your mouth water. He knows she will be hungry when she wakes.

It has now been two days since she had been shot. She has had nourishment only through the broth that he can make her swallow while she sleeps.

They will both need to rebuild their strength from this long ordeal.

A while later, Flame wakes to find herself in a small bed covered with an Indian blanket so soft and worn that it feels like satin. She is hungry and so very thirsty. She feels like she has been run over by a truck. She is sore all over and her shoulder and chest ache.

She slowly raises her head and sees the bandage wrapped around her chest. All the memories come flooding back. The hunter. The wolves. Her dreams. It is then that she turns her head and sees the old man.

She thinks, *Grandfather. He's real! It's all real!*

More real than her life has ever felt. She can remember Grandfather running with her inside the wolves. She also remembers the joy of gliding on the wind drifts, of taking Grandfather with her. She remembers his feeling of shock and hers of pride. Pride in being able to teach him. He has taught her so much; to go inside the body of others, animal or man, and to heal their bodies. So real. *Can it be possible?*

She realizes that she knows this man. He is Sioux. He has a grandson who is a lawyer, Joe, and Grandfather's name, too, is Joseph. Joseph Wolf. She knows he had a wife who died many years ago, as did his only son and daughter-in-law.

Grandfather had raised Joe. Did he tell her all of this? Is that it? But then, why does she know so much? She has vivid memories of his life. Memories of healing both man and animal.

She studies him while he sleeps. She knows his memories, but not what he looks like. He seems to be very old. He is stocky, with long gray hair pulled into a long braid down his back, and smile wrinkles around his eyes and mouth. She knows his eyes will be so dark brown that they will look black.

Grandfather wakes to the sight of Flame staring at him. Her eyes are wide and her mouth open. She quickly closes her mouth when he smiles at her. She smiles back shyly, but she feels foolish. It was all a dream, or she *is* crazy. He just keeps smiling at her, knowing the war that is raging in her mind.

Flame has never met anyone else who is like her, that can talk to the animals and be inside them. It is a shock to her. Maybe she isn't as strange and alone as she has always believed herself to be.

"I am so glad to see you awake, young lady." Grandfather tells her with a large toothy smile.

He has a beautifully kind smile, just as she knew he wouldm and she says softly, "Thank you. May I have a drink of water and, if it's not too much trouble, maybe a little bit of that soup I smell? I'm embarrassed at how hungry I am!"

Grandfather is taken aback at her lovely southern accent. She is a treasure. What a gift she will be to the right man one day. She is so amazing. He almost wishes he were sixty years younger, at least.

Her smile lights her whole face and those eyes, he is not prepared for those big green eyes. How in the world had anyone ever been so cruel to her? He cannot understand it, but he knows that humans can be so cruel. Animals kill quickly, but humans usually kill the spirit first.

He gets up, pours her some of the tea brewed with strengthening herbs, and hands the cup to her. She quickly drinks the cup dry.

He goes back into the large living area that has a combined kitchen. She can see him through the door. He puts on some water to boil for more tea, takes two soup bowls from the cabinet and fills them both with soup. He brings one to her and sits down in the chair next to the bed with his own.

She tries the soup and her eyes widen in appoval. It's wonderful and is nothing like the canned soup that the orphanage had served them. She is lying in a very large comfortable bed with a small bathroom off to the side of the room. She wonders if he has given her his bed, and he smiles as if he knows what she is thinking.

He does. Not because he is in her mind, but because he knows her so well after spending so much time in her mind and memories. Though she was treated so cruelly, she is still a thoughtful and caring young woman.

"No child, this is my grandson's room. I have the other one, next to you. I have been staying right here in this chair though, to keep an eye on you. You had lost a lot of blood. The bullet went through your chest but hit no vital organs or bones.

"I repaired the damage from the inside out. You are healing nicely, though you still need antibiotics for awhile longer. I also have medicine for the pain, should you need it." Grandfather tells her while they eat.

"You've been so kind to care for me. How did you find me?"

"The wolf called to me. I knew where to find you. I have known of you being in the meadow since you arrived, but you already know this, Flame. Think. You will remember it all, if you try." He stops speaking and looks toward the door.

After a moment of listening, he says, "The wolves are here. Do you hear them? They give you their strength, as do I. You will come to understand this."

And, she does. She hears the whine of the wolf cubs and knows he is telling her the truth, but it doesn't seem possible.

He watches her, knowing she is fighting the truth.

Finally, he gets up, goes into the living room, and opens the front door. He does not need to call them, they are waiting.

The alpha male and female walk in first and behind them comes four others. Two are gray like the alpha male. One is a very dark gray with black around the head and ears and the other is solid white. It is the white one that comes straight to Flame. Flame knows that she is female.

Grandfather watches her reaction. It goes from troubled, to brilliant and glowing. When she smiles her eyes light up, and go from emerald, to a much darker green. He knows what she is feeling. It is one thing to be near these majestic animals, but another to have them against you, loving you. He is smiling from ear to ear with tears in his old eyes, just as they are in hers.

Flame cannot believe this is happening. She feels the warm fur, the warmth of the tongue licking her face, and knows it has all been true. She knows them *and* Grandfather. Also, she knows that this female has cubs. She remembers that she has been with her while she was nursing, in her mind, the feel of the cubs warm against her body. She also remembers that Grandfather was there, inside one of the males. She had felt him there and had even known his thoughts when he was inside the wolf.

Reading her thoughts, Grandfather says, "See child, she knows you just as you know her. It is all the truth. You are special, Flame. I have the gift of vision, just as you do, but yours is so much stronger than mine. You taught this old man, who thought he was beyond the age of learning, many things.

"You flew with the hawk, taking me with you. I suspect that you can enter the mind of many other animals, though not most humans. You can read their thoughts through touch only. There will be a few exceptions. You will be able to read those that carry certain gifts. Gifts like ours. Usually the person with these gifts does not even realize that they have it.

"They feel what they think is a warning or premonition. What they might think is a gut feeling. They can be read and you will know these people's gift only through touch. After the first touch you should be able to hear, or speak, telepathically with them. This is difficult and you usually have to know this person very well to understand the way their mind works, but I will teach you more about this later. Since we both have the gift we should be able to do it with each other. It is harder to do this when great distance is involved, but as strong as your gift is it will just take more energy. I think we will both learn a lot from one another."

Without hesitation Flame tells him, "Yes, Grandfather, I believe you and all you tell me. It's just so hard to accept that I'll be able to do all of these things. I think this is what I've been looking for all of my life. I felt different and was shunned for my gifts, but you accept me and I know that. I'm so grateful for this opportunity. I love you already and I love them. Thank you so very much. It's strange, I've never trusted *people* before, but I can feel in my heart that you're one to trust."

He smiles gently and tells her, "You will stay here with me until it is time for you to go into the world. You have a wonderful life to live…and you will *live* it. You will never feel ashamed of your gifts again. You will be proud. You will be like the wolf, full of pride and cunning. Not being afraid to use your gift. Use it carefully, Granddaughter, for good and never bad."

"I'm so happy, Grandfather. Thank you. Thanks to all of you. I feel like a have a real family here." And, with this said, she hugs each one of the wolves and then Grandfather. This is a bit awkward for her, as she has to use her left arm.

The wolves take their leave, but the alpha female stays at the foot of Flame's bed. She will stay to watch over and protect her.

Chapter 4

Flame spends her days and nights learning all that Grandfather can teach her. They run with the wolves and she takes him on flights with the birds. She can fly with any of the birds, but prefers the hawk or eagle because of their amazing eye sight.

She learns the boundaries of the land belonging to Grandfather. She loves it all. She is accepted, even loved, something she had never thought possible for herself. She is ecstatic with this new life. That is how she feels, like she has been given a whole new life.

Grandfather teaches her how to open her mind to other humans with the gift. He shows her how to read them through touch. He also teaches her how to *talk* to people with the gift. This is more difficult. She takes to reading through touch very easily, but she has learned most of this herself, when she was very young.

When Flame was younger she avoided the touch of others. Through touch she would feel things, *know* things that the person had in their mind. She knew if they were going to be hurt, killed, or even if they were lying. She had avoided their touch, as most did not want to know these things about themselves. Knowing these things scared her.

While a child, both children and adults called her a witch. Now she knows her gift is not wrong. She is not a witch. They just didn't know or understand her gift. At that time, neither did she. She learns how to hone her gift and focus it.

It is during this time that Grandfather tells her about his grandson, Joe. Joe is not interested in Grandfather's forest home. He loves the animals, but is not like her. He does not have the gift. Joe wants his life in the city and all that comes with living life in a large city. He loves being around other people and working in the hustle and bustle of the city. Being a lawyer was always his dream.

Grandfather tells Flame that oil is on this forest land. That many have tried to buy him out, to take his land. They have done this legally, and some not so legally. They have tried to force him out, many times.

Only his grandson, Joe, has kept the land from being taken from him, by using his legal expertise. He tells Flame that no matter what happens, even after he dies, he wants this land free of humanity. Those same humans that do not care for the forest, or its animals, but that just want more...more money, more everything. He knows they will tear out the trees, take the oil, and then build on his land.

Flame understands what Grandfather means, but she cannot imagine anyone not loving this forest land. She does not understand his grandson not wanting to live here. It is a perfect life.

She tries to understand his feelings, but they are foreign to her. She hopes to meet Joe one day, to find out more about this man. Grandfather obviously loves and trusts him very much. He must be a good man.

Flame spends a lot of time with the wolves, even when she is not in their minds. She plays with the cubs and, eventually, names them. She names them by what they remind her of, or by their color.

Grandfather laughs at this, telling her, "Flame, these are not dogs. They come to you without a name, each knowing which one you are talking to, but I guess there is no reason they cannot have one."

She knows that he is partial to the smallest cub and she baits him by saying, "I've named them all, but I can't think of a good name for this small one. Can you name him, please?"

"Ah, Granddaughter, you are learning to be as cunning as they are!" he chuckles. "This little one will be smart and overbearing. One day he will be an alpha, I can see that. Since he looks so much like his father, I shall name him Prince." And, of course, this one becomes a regular around the cabin. He is a gray.

Flame has a favorite also. He is the largest cub and solid white, like his mother. She names him Ghost, and he is with her everywhere she goes. He becomes hers, like no other. He seems to know her so well, even as young as he is. They spend so much time together that she cannot stand the thought of leaving him, Grandfather, or the rest of the wolves, but it is inevitable. Grandfather has made her understand this. She has to know what the real world is like.

Grandfather knows it will soon be time for her to spread her wings. She needs to live, really live, outside in the world. He has special plans for her, but she will not know this until the time is right. He also has a special gift prepared for her. He will show it to her when it comes time for her leave.

She spends many weeks learning and teaching. She doesn't ever want to leave them, but she knows Grandfather is right. Soon she must, but not quite yet. She can wait just a little longer.

One afternoon she decides to go get her old van. She knows it will need some small adjustments, to be ready when it comes time to leave. Ghost follows, as does his mother. She spends several hours walking, laughing, and frolicking with them over the well worn path.

As they get to the meadow, she clears all signs of her camp, putting everything into the back of the van. She wonders how the wolves will take to riding inside the van for the trip back. She hates leaving this meadow behind, just as much as she hates leaving everything else, except leaving Grandfather and Ghost. This she hates most of all.

Ghost is very happy to ride in the passenger seat. He sits in the seat as if it is his own throne.

Flame laughs at his haughty expression and tells him, "What a proud one you are, my Ghost!"

When it comes time to start the van his mother will not get inside. She whines and paces.

Flame tries giving her pictures of riding inside, but she will have nothing to do with it. Finally, she gives up trying. "I'll just have to go very slowly, my friend, so you can keep up," she says to her.

As she gets close to the cabin she has the strangest feeling that something is wrong. The wolves are there as usual, but they are bristling with anger. She gets out of the van and helps Ghost out, as he is too small jump that far.

She stands close to the van looking at the cabin. This feeling is not coming from Grandfather, for she can hear him trying to calm the wolves with an ancient song. The sound is beautiful, but haunting. The words are in the Sioux language.

Suddenly, one of the hawks swoops in and lands on the hood of the van. He looks right into Flame's eyes and she knows immediately that he wants her to fly with him. She slips from her mind into the mind of the hawk. They quickly take off toward the entrance to Grandfather's land.

There are men coming onto Grandfather's land. Two cars full of them. One group of them has suits on, with three of them riding in an expensive sedan. The other group, four men, is wearing fatigue type clothing. There are large guns visible in their old jeep.

The hawk lands on a branch over the heads of this last group of men. Using the amazing senses of the hawk, Flame smells gasoline. These men are not here for a friendly visit.

The group of men in the sedan motions for the driver of the jeep to come forward. She can hear every word spoken, for the hawk's hearing is much better than any human's.

The man in the suit calls the other man by name. "Otis, you boys stay here until we come back. We'll try this the easy way first. It probably won't make any difference, it never has. By the time we get back, if the old man doesn't sign, you boys be ready. We'll get this land, one way or the other."

The man named Otis agrees and goes back to wait in the jeep with the three others.

Flame immediately sends the hawk into the air. She must return to Grandfather now. There has to be some way to stop this. They have very little time to prepare. Flame does not know what will happen once these men leave and the others come, but it cannot be a good thing.

She sends both male wolves into the forest to watch the men in the jeep. They will know if they are coming here to the cabin, or if they will start the forest burning. They will link with her if this happens. There will be nothing she can do if they burn the forest, except try to stop them.

She bursts through the door of the cabin to find Grandfather preparing his ancient rifle. "There are men coming, Grandfather!" she screams, and adds, "They're coming here, but there are others waiting in the driveway, near the entrance, and they're planning to burn the forest, or maybe your cabin!"

Grandfather knows the men are on his land. It is a well remembered feeling. It has happened many times. He always knows when someone enters his land, but he is not prepared for the others with them, with their thought to burn the forest, or his home.

She tells him, "I sent the males to watch the ones waiting at the entrance. They'll fight them, but, Grandfather, they have guns. What will we do?"

"We wait. They will come here first to try to get me to let them buy my land. We can handle these men, but I do not know what to think of the others. This has not happened before. I have been shot at, but never has the land or my home been threatened." He is angry, but still worried.

"Grandfather, they don't know I'm here. I can use one of your guns. You've shown me how to use it. I'll take one of the horses and wait until they get their orders. The males will be there waiting for me. The females will be here with you. They can protect you here. Between us we won't let them burn the land, or your home!" She's frantic to do this.

"I cannot allow this! I cannot let you be placed in this kind of danger! *No*, Granddaughter, do not leave here. Let me take care of this, please?!" He gives her a pleading look as he moves toward the door.

She hears the men coming. While Grandfather goes outside with the rifle, she grabs up one of his pistols, putting it into her waistband and running for the back door. She has only ridden the horse a few times, but she knows she has to do it now. She runs to the barn, bridles the horse, and climbs onto it bareback.

She spurs the horse as fast as it can go and, while doing so, calls to all of the birds in the forest. She knows the male wolves are there already. She also knows that the females will protect Grandfather with their very lives.

Before the car comes to a complete stop, Grandfather knows that he remembers this man. He has been here before. His name is Stokes. He carries a briefcase and wears a fake smile.

Grandfather waits until he and his two men come onto the steps of the porch. He knows Stokes from his coming here to try to buy the forest from him before. He thinks Stokes is a lawyer, but has no idea who for, and doesn't really care. He is prepared, and he holds the rifle loosely at his side.

"Hello again, Mr. Wolf. I hope this is not an inconvenient time for you. I have some things to discuss with you. I think you will find it quite interesting," says Mr. Stokes.

It is quite obvious that the other two are some kind of body guards, for their size gives them away. They each place one hand into their jacket, moving the fabric aside so that their guns show.

Grandfather already knew they would be carrying them. He says, "Ah, Mr. Stokes, I have been through this many times with you. I will not sell my land to you, sir. You know this, yet you keep coming. The answer is no, and it always will be no. Please do not bother me again with this."

"Mr. Wolf, you'll find, if you will permit me to come inside and show you the contracts, that the offer has greatly increased. I'm sure even you won't want to turn this offer down."

"No, you will not come inside. I do not want to see your offer, or hear it. Now, please, take your friends here, and leave my land."

"Mr. Wolf, I think you should reconsider this. You know, anything could happen to you all the way out here. You have no one, and it would be a shame if something should happen to you, or to your home. I wish you would reconsider my offer."

At this threat the wolves come onto the porch, one from one end, one from the other. Their hair is raised in a high ridge along their backs, their teeth are showing, and growls come from their throats.

Mr. Stokes is clearly scared of these animals and his men pull hand guns from their coats. Grandfather will not let anyone threaten these wolves. His shotgun goes off into the air and then it is suddenly pointed at Mr. Stokes' heart.

Mr. Stokes exclaims, "I'm leaving, Mr. Wolf! Men, put your weapons away. Keep those dogs back Mr. Wolf! We're leaving."

"Do not come back here. I will not be so friendly next time. And, those are not dogs, Mr. Stokes. They are wolves and there are more close by. It would serve you well to remember that. They will not let you onto my land again. Leave while I can still see to your safety!" Grandfather says boldly, with a grim smile on his ancient face.

The men hurry to their car and, when they get inside, Mr. Stokes cracks his window just far enough to speak to Grandfather. "You'll regret your lack of hospitality, Mr. Wolf. You won't have a home to live in soon."

With this said, they back up to turn around, and Grandfather shoots out the back window of the sedan with a loud blast from his shotgun.

"Humph...threaten *me* again you sorry shit! Next time I will blow your damn head off!" and Grandfather steps into the cabin.

He sees immediately that Flame has not listened to him. She has left, taking one of the small pistols. He is frantic in his worry for her. He thinks, *She must not be harmed!* He grabs up the shotgun, taking off for the barn.

Flame watches the men in the jeep. She ties the horse to a branch close to the small creek and far enough away from the wolves so that it won't spook. She tells the horse, by mind link, not to make any noise.

The wolves are waiting for her. The men have no idea that they are being watched. She knows that Grandfather has now entered into one of the wolves and watches over her. He watches the men too.

She watches the sedan fly up to the jeep, with small rocks and dirt shooting out behind them, and sees the man give Otis a nod. The sedan flies out the entrance and onto the main road.

She knows it will happen soon and she calls to the birds, to all of them in the forest She sends out a plea for them to go to the cabin, to help to protect this land.

One of the men gets out of the jeep carrying a can of gas. He heads into the forest on the other side of the dirt drive. He does not carry one of the guns.

She nods at the alpha male and watches him go quietly forward, knowing the man will never be able to use the gas.

The jeep continues on toward the cabin. Flame sends the other male to follow behind the it. She rushes to the horse, bolting onto its back, and races through the woods to get to the cabin first.

She hears the call of the birds as she goes. She knows they will be waiting for her signal and will attack on command. She is scared for the forest and Grandfather's cabin, but thrilled by the excitement.

She cuts through the trees and, when she reaches the cabin, she sees the jeep coming around the bend. She must get to Grandfather. She jumps off the horse telling it to go to the barn. As she does, the wolves come to her.

Thinking that Grandfather is inside the cabin, she runs to the front porch. She doesn't know that Grandfather is in the barn. She stands there, with the pistol in her waistband, waiting for the men to get out of the jeep. They haven't seen her yet.

One of the men jumps out of the jeep with a can of gas, heading for the barn. Flame nods at the other male then. He slinks toward the barn too. She knows he will not let the man burn the barn.

There are two men left. They get out, coming toward the cabin with their guns drawn.

As the men get closer to the cabin they see Flame standing on the porch with her hair whipping wildly around her and her arms outstretched at her sides. There is a gun in her waistband and she stands looking directly at them with her eyes shooting sparks.

The man, Otis, laughs and says, "This will be more fun than we thought boys, looky here...we have a welcoming party. Nobody'll miss this little injun lover. We'll just take her with us and have us some fun when we get done with the old man."

Flame hears every word and her anger increases. How dare these filthy pigs speak of her like this? She is no weakling now. She will never let anyone hurt those that she loves, not the wolves nor, especially, Grandfather.

"Put down that gun right there, little lady. We have a few nice surprises for you here. We just have to get rid of that flea bitten old man and burn out that nasty cabin first. Then you and us'll have more fun than you'd ever have with that old injun!" says Otis, with a sneering laugh.

She speaks commandingly, "No! You will *not* come near Grandfather, or his home!"

The men laugh loudly.

There is a shotgun blast from the barn and the man who had gone to burn it runs out quickly, yelling to Otis that he is out of this. He runs down the road, yelling something about wolves and Indians.

This infuriates Otis. He moves closer to the porch, but before he can step onto it the female wolves rush him from both sides. The man behind him aims his gun at one of the wolves. Before he can shoot the male comes up behind him and takes him down by throwing his full weight upon him.

Otis pulls out his gun and aims for Flame. He shouts, "Little lady, call off those wolves now! There's no need for all this! We just came to do a simple job and we aim to get it done!"

Flame raises her arms higher and calls out to the birds, "Come now! It's time! Rid us of these pests!"

With this, an army of birds hit both men, pecking at their eyes and flocking their faces. Then, the wolves attack.

Grandfather sees it all. He is amazed. She is something standing there with the wind blowing her hair, sparks shooting from her eyes, and commanding all. He stands there with a large grin on his face.

The men are trying to fight off both the wolves and the birds.

Grandfather walks to where the men have thrown down their guns and gathers them up. He will be sure to keep these tokens, he thinks to himself.

When Flame sees this, she puts her arms at her sides. The birds fly into the trees and the wolves move to her side. She stands there with a small smile upon her face.

The men are rushing to the jeep with their faces and arms bloody. They speed out, onto the dirt track as fast as they can, with the jeep swerving from side to side in their haste.

Flame mind links with the hawk, flying to find the men who ran. She finds the first man as he is jumping into the jeep, screaming about wolves, with blood coming from several bites.

Flame, in the hawk, reaches the entrance to the forest in time to see the last man. He is high in a tree, waiting on the jeep, screaming his head off. The alpha male is at his feet and has a large, toothy grin on his face.

She laughs to herself and sends her call to the wolf. He heads for the cabin just as the jeep reaches the entrance. The last man jumps from the tree, running for the jeep.

As they leave, Flame, within the hawk, flies close to the jeep's window. She can hear the men talking about the witch woman. They will not be back anytime soon. They do not dare.

Chapter 5

It is time for Flame to go out into the world and it will be the hardest thing she has ever done. She doesn't even know where she will go. Grandfather says that she will find her way, that it is time for her to travel and see the world on her own.

"Granddaughter, I know you will miss your friends here, but it has to be. You must learn about things outside of this land. You are always welcomed here, you know this. You will be able to contact me anytime. We have a mind link and it cannot be broken. I will always know if anything happens to you, because we are so close.

"You can also call me anytime you want and always call me collect. Do not ever hesitate to do it." he tells her, with a sad smile. He hates to see her go too.

"I know it's time for me to leave, but it's so hard. How do I say goodbye to you? I love you, Grandfather. I know it's been such a short time, but you're in my heart, as are the wolves. I can't bear the thought of not having either of you!"

"Child, I am always with you. Always in your heart."

Then, they hear scratching on the door. As Grandfather opens it he has a smile on his face. In comes the white female with Ghost. Flame cannot bear the sight of him for she knows she is losing him, but then the most amazing thing happens.

The female picks Ghost up by his scruff, carrying him to Flame. She places Ghost at her feet, looks directly into Flame's eyes, and her thoughts enter Flame's mind. She shows Flame that Ghost is now hers. That he will go with her. She wants him to protect and love Flame, always.

At this, Ghost gives a yelp and jumps on Flame. She picks him up, cradling him to her with tears rolling down her cheeks. She bends and hugs the female to her. She thanks her for this great sacrifice. It is more than she could ever wish for.

Now, in walks the cub, Prince. He goes to Grandfather and sits proudly at his feet. He will stay with Grandfather.

Grandfather is overwhelmed. He cries openly, knowing that this small

Prince will be his comfort in letting Flame go.

With a last glance at her cubs the female walks proudly out. She has given her children to the humans she loves. She is happy with what she has done.

Now Grandfather tells her, "Granddaughter of my heart, you are prepared for your journey. I, too, have a small gift for you. It is not as wonderful as the gift you have given me, just by being here, and it does not come close to being so great as the gift of your Ghost. All the same, it is yours."

With this said, Grandfather motions for her to follow him. He goes into the barn with Flame, Ghost, and Prince on his heels. He opens the large storage room that holds the hay for the horses, and inside stands a small travel trailer. It is a home on wheels! It has everything Flame will need to make it her home.

He grins and tells her, "I am hoping you will travel and see many places. In this way you will have your home with you wherever you go. I hope you like it."

He sees her tears of happiness and continues, "I have already attached a hitch onto your van, so you are ready to go. I filled your small refrigerator with plenty of food. It has a kitchen and a small bed. Though it is small, the kitchen has everything you need to cook with. I have placed a few hundred dollars inside a small lockbox under your bed. It is yours, to help get you started, Granddaughter. I hope you like your gift."

"Oh, Grandfather, what a wonderful gift! I love it! I can travel anywhere and always be at home! I love you! You are my only family and I will always be in your debt." She has tears running down her beautiful face.

"No, child, you owe me nothing. This has been the best few months I have had in many years. I never thought to have a granddaughter in my old age. I do now, and I love you as if you were born to me.

"Do you see this necklace that I wear? It is a wolf's tooth necklace. It has been handed down to me from my grandfather, from his grandfather. It holds the power to be master of this land. One day it will be yours. Go, with the blessings of this old man, and the love from all of us in your heart."

The next morning she sets out. Saying goodbye is the hardest thing she has ever faced in her young life. Ghost sits proudly in the passenger seat and howls his puppy howl at the gathering of wolves and Grandfather.

The birds are even there, watching it all from the safety of the trees. Together, birds and wolves alike, they make a tremendous racket. Grandfather waves as she leaves his land. She pulls away with tears rolling down her cheeks.

Chapter 6

3 Years Later

Flame is setting up her booth at the latest site for the carnival. She began working for the carnival over two years ago. She loves moving around from one town to another. It is always something different and new.

She has her own little booth, paying a fee to the carnival owner after every move. Her booth, when broken down and not in use, goes into the back of the old van. She uses the trailer that Grandfather had given her to travel and live in. She is her own person with no one to answer to, except Ghost.

She has even made some friends here at the traveling carnival. The carnie workers are unlike most people. They are accepting of people, no matter their differences. Of course, there are some that are not so appealing, but overall they are wonderful and very caring, trying to help her fit into their small family. That's what they feel like, a family of sorts.

Flame's best friend is Frankie. He owns a traveling food booth, making all sorts of treats, the like found at any moving carnival or circus, everything from cotton candy and funnel cakes to corndogs. He keeps Flame and Ghost very well fed, much to Ghost's delight, and Flame's chagrin. She worries that Ghost isn't eating right, though she supplements them with vitamins, even Frankie.

This week they are on the outskirts of a city that she has heard of from Grandfather. Munson, Montana. This is where Joe, Grandfather's grandson, has his law office.

She has promised Grandfather that she will be in touch with Joe and try to get together with him while she is here. They have yet to meet, but have gotten to know each other by phone, quite well. She finds that she likes him very much. He is so much like Grandfather that she cannot help but like him, even if he doesn't want to live in the forest.

She keeps in touch regularly with Grandfather. She calls him at least twice a week. She worries about him and about the people always trying to take his land. So far, he says, no one has threatened his life again, though they have been consistent, as ever, in their plots to talk him into signing the land over to them The same man, Stokes, being the most persistent, though he swears he didn't have anything to do with the men that had tried to burn Grandfather out.

Both Flame and Grandfather know this is not true. She prays daily that he, and the land, will never be threatened again. She knows that people like Mr. Stokes do not give up easily.

She has done a lot of growing up over the last three years. She is a beautiful woman, with shining red hair reaching well past her waist, enormous green eyes, fringed with long black lashes, and full, beautiful, naturally rosy lips.

There have been many opportunities to date, but that is not something she wants, at least right now. She is happy just living her life with Ghost and her friends at the carnival. She still doesn't trust people. They have hurt her too many times over the years.

Ghost has grown a lot over the last few years also. He's now over 165 pounds of muscle and teeth, and very protective of Flame, as always. He trusts only one other human. Frankie. Flame is not sure if that's because of the food or for the simple reason that Frankie is no threat to her. There are many here that Ghost will not tolerate coming too close to her though.

Ghost stays with Flame as she sets up her booth. She is a fortune teller at the carnival. She reads palms, telling the future of those who pay a handsome sum, and she is excellent at what she does, drawing more customers than any other booth, except the dancing horses. That large tent is always full, but rarely is there standing room around her booth either.

Ghost stands beside her while she reads some customer's futures. Others just want to know things about their love interests, such as; whether so-in-so will fall in love with them, if they are going to get that new job, or if they should open their own business.

Only when children are present does Ghost show off. He loves children and if their mothers aren't fearful of him, he will let them pet him. He eats up the attention from children, but most parents won't let their kids near him. He has a way of smiling that doesn't quite look like a smile. It is always very large and very toothy. Also, he is not hesitant to show his teeth, or even growl, when he feels someone is getting to loud or pushy around Flame. Though, so far, he hasn't had to bite anyone.

Some men have been known to get a bit forceful with her, thinking that since she works at a carnival, more than getting their fortune read might be for sale. Though she always makes it clear that she doesn't want that sort of attention, it is not always clear to the men asking. Ghost makes sure that they listen, and listen well.

This morning, as she sets up her booth, Frankie comes sauntering down the midway in his usual cocky manner. He asks her, yet again, if he can help her "style that silly booth." He has a flair for the dramatic, always wanting to paint her booth with pictures of flames and wolves, though she is happy with her own artwork and sign stating, "The Amazing Flame - Fortunes and

Fantasy!"

"Frankie, I don't think I'd be very comfortable sitting here with flames all around me!" laughs Flame, yet again.

Before Frankie can speak, the horse trainer and rider, Gregori, is leading one of his horses into the large tent. It is a very large, white Arabian named Trixie. There are five white Arabians that dance in the large tent nightly. Gregori is very tall, handsome and muscular. He knows it too. He is drooled over by all the women paying or working at the carnival.

As he makes his way down the midway to the tent, he calls out to her, "Flame, will they all perform at their best tonight, or are any of them going to give me any trouble?"

"They're all in fine spirits today, Gregori, but watch out for Trixie. She's in a feisty mood. If you put her in front of Sage, she'll kick him just for the fun of it! Oh, and check on Samson's left foreleg again, it's still hurting him." This is a normal conversation for the two of them as she can read these animals too.

Gregori doesn't quite believe her when she tells him how she does it. He has been around the carnival for most of his life and believes that all fortune tellers are just alike; good story tellers. He is beginning to come around though, as she has been right every time. He's begun to ask her daily if his animals are well, and she respects him for this. He cares for his horses better than some people care for their own children.

"Thanks, Flame! If it weren't for you these damn nags would be the death of me!"

She calls back, "You'd be lost without them and they know it!"

He laughs and slaps Trixie's flank playfully, but doesn't disagree.

"Humph, that man. I swear, Flame, he knows 'bout them damn animals. He just wants your attention. Acts like he's all that and a sack of curly fries too." swears Frankie.

"Yeah, and so do you!" Flame snickers, while Ghost watches Frankie expectantly.

"Well, hell yeah. Just look at that butt! It be a shame you let that fine thing go on droolin day after day, just a wantin you...and he won't even give me the time of day!"

"Frankie, he's not gay! You know that. But if you keep after him maybe he'll eventually give in." she says, with a wink at Ghost.

Ghost just puts his head down, with both front feet over his eyes, and gives a large cough, sounding very much like a laugh.

"And *you*, Mr. Wolf, won't be gettin no more of those corndogs if you don't watch your mouth either! Don't you be a laughin at me!" Frankie shakes his head from side to side, giving Ghost a look of disapproval.

Ghost politely looks up and grins his big wolf-grin for Frankie. He knows he can win him over. He always does.

"Now, don't you go tryin to play me you sneaky damn dog! I knows when you be playin me!"

At this Ghost rolls over, exposing his belly for his usual rub.

"I swear that sorry wolf is just a damn baby. He sure knows how to play this old black boy." He bends down and rubs Ghost's belly, just as they knew he would, then says, "You know, if you keep up that laughin at me, I'm gonna turn your wolf butt in to one of those animal rights people and they'll take you back to them woods!"

Frankie is only joking playfully, but both Ghost and Flame know that if anyone ever find out that he is a full-blooded wolf, he will be taken from her. Wolves aren't allowed to be kept as pets, but most people think him an overgrown Shepherd.

When Frankie sees their expressions he feels like a jerk. He says, "Awww, come on you two, you two knows I love you's like my own. Shoot, you two's the only family I got. Ain't many people wants a gay black man 'round and you two're everything to me. I'd never turn your butt in, Ghost."

Ghost stands, puts his front feet on Frankie's shoulders, and gives him a large, wet kiss right across the face.

"And that goes for me too, Frankie!" Flame laughs.

"Guess I better start up the grease and get ready for all these local yokels." Frankie makes his way back down the midway to his stand, his large butt moving from side to side in what he calls a "seductive sway".

The first day of the carnival goes wonderful in Munson. Flame and Ghost do very well this night, as usual. Ghost shows off during breaks in customers, howling and then smiling as people walked by. He is a natural for the carnival. He brings in as many customers as does Flame's accurate fortunes.

Flame had called Joe that afternoon. They are going to meet for a late dinner tonight. He has a girlfriend that he is anxious to show off. Flame can tell by the tone of his voice that she is special. Joe and Flame already feel like true family from their many conversations over the phone, so meeting him face-to-face is special for her.

It is almost time to close up shop for the night. Flame is trying to get her booth cleaned up and closed. She has to meet Joe and his girlfriend in an hour and she wants time to change out of her fortune teller getup. She has to get Ghost fed and settled in for the night also, though she hates leaving him alone. She usually stays in, or goes to Frankie's, but Ghost is always welcomed there.

Her van and trailer are parked in the nearby parking lot. She locks up the booth and then goes to her trailer and changes clothes. She wants to look her best when she meets Joe and his new girlfriend.

She feeds Ghost before placing her lockbox on the small kitchen counter.

She has made a good haul today, almost five hundred dollars, a lot for the first day in a new town. Usually it takes a couple of days before she brings in that much money, as word of mouth is her best advertisement. She hugs Ghost, turns on the small television for him, and locks the door behind herself.

She noticed a few young men standing around in the parking lot as she went into her trailer and, when she comes out, there are still a couple of them hanging around. She thinks nothing of it. It is fairly normal for some kids to hang out after the carnival closes up for the night. They make a few calls to her, the usual crude stuff, laughing as they do it. She ignores them and keeps walking.

She reaches the restaurant, noting that it is a very nice place. It's close enough to the carnival that she is able to walk it easily. It seems to be a very nice city from what she has seen so far. She can see the river running behind the restaurant and the skyscrapers towering in the night sky, making it seem as large as some of the major cities they have been in, though in truth it is not that large.

Joe and his girlfriend, Mercedes, are waiting for her at the entrance to the restaurant. Joe is just what Flame had expected. He looks very much like Grandfather, though he is a bit taller and his hair is much shorter. His hair is raven black and pulled into a short ponytail in the back, which is not like any lawyer she has ever seen, but it fits him well. His eyes are sharp and very dark, almost as dark as Grandfather's. He has high cheekbones and a beautiful smile.

She is surprised when Joe turns around and pulls another man forward. He introduces the man as Shay Larson, a detective for the local police department. He seems to be a very nice man, but Flame lets Joe know, subtly, that she is not interested in a date.

She wonders why he would do this to her. She is here to meet *him*. First he brings a girlfriend, and then a blind date for her. She is clearly not comfortable with this, and she hates to be rude, but she was taken completely by surprise. She tries to pull herself together, not wanting to hurt anyone's feelings, but she knows she's not pulling it off.

As they take their seats, Shay leans close and with a shy smile says to her, "I'm so sorry. Joe told me you knew I'd be here. I'm not up for a blind date either, but since we're here let's try to make the best of it. I promise I won't get drunk, I won't try to make a pass, and I'll be on my best behavior." He flashes her quick smile.

Flame cannot keep from laughing. He is really very nice and, she notices, quite good looking. His very dark brown hair is a bit long, but she likes it. He has the most beautiful light blue eyes, high cheekbones, and a dimple on one cheek that she cannot seem to quit watching. He is broad shouldered, tall and lean. Maybe it won't be such a bad blind date after all.

Shay too is very surprised, but also very pleased. He thinks, *Damn Joe, for doing this to me. He tricks me into coming and the lady is clearly not interested. Well, I'll be sure Joe gets paid back for this. But I have to admit, this woman* is *gorgeous. Those beautiful green eyes and that smile she gave me almost knocked my socks off. I wouldn't have believed I'd ever want a date with someone with a name like Flame, but damned if it doesn't fit her perfectly. I just wish this had been done on the up and up. Damn Joe anyway!*

Joe watches it all. He is very pleased with himself. He knows, from Grandfather, that Flame has not really dated at all and as far as he knows, Shay hasn't been out with a woman in ages either. He and Shay have been friends since college and he feels that Shay works too damned hard, always putting everyone else's needs before his own. Working double shifts and trying to take over the whole job of police protection in Munson. Mercedes had thought it would be a good idea for Shay, too, and that sealed the deal.

Flame and Mercedes hit it off very well. Joe and Flame talk about Grandfather and his worries over his land. Joe promises Flame that he will never let anyone take the forest from Grandfather. He also tells her that he has something to talk to her about, but that she needs to come by his office the next day, if she will.

She has no idea what it could be, but agrees to meet him in the morning before the carnival opens at noon. They have late nights and even later mornings at the carnival. It is nice to be able to sleep in after the long days of reading fortunes. She is also able to spend some time walking and exercising with Ghost. They both need a lot of exercise to keep off the pounds from Frankie's corndogs.

She asks Mercedes to come by the carnival and let her read her palm, saying it will be a gift. Mercedes seems anxious to do it. Flame cannot help but notice how beautiful she is. She is a petite woman, with long auburn hair and beautiful, large, amber colored eyes. It turns out to be a very enjoyable time for all of them. Both Flame and Shay enjoy their conversation and easy banter with Joe and Mercedes.

"Okay, little sister, come by my office in the morning around eight. I'll take you to breakfast and then we'll go over a few things, okay?" Joe tells Flame.

"Sure, that's fine, Joe. Oh, and Mercedes, if you can come by the carnival about noon, I'll give you the works! Past, present, *and* future!" Flame smiles gently at her.

"I can't wait, Flame! I am so glad we met. I hope you get to spend a bit of time here after the carnival leaves. We can have so much fun. Of course, a girl always needs to shop and I know all the right places!" Mercedes beams.

She obviously comes from money. She is impeccably dressed and wears large diamonds at her throat and ears, though Flame does notice that she wears no rings, only a gold watch.

"I'm so sorry, Mercedes, but I leave when the carnival leaves. We have until the end of the week and then it's on the road again, as the song goes, but one day soon I'll be taking a bit of time off. I plan on visiting Grandfather this fall. That's only a month away and it's only a couple of hours from here to Grandfather's, in River Valley. I could probably spend a day or two here then. Maybe you and Joe could come to Grandfather's too! I know he'll want to meet you."

Mercedes looks completely forlorn when she says, "Oh, I'd hoped you'd have a bit of time off, but I understand. I'd like to see you in the fall too, but I'll definitely see you tomorrow. It was so nice to meet you. I think Joe's planning for me to meet his Grandfather very soon anyway." She glances at Joe as she says this and they share a small smile.

"Yes, Flame, you're all Grandfather says you are; smart, sweet, and very beautiful. I'm proud to call you family." Joe grins when he tells her this and Flame's face turns slightly red at the compliment.

"Flame, may I walk you home? I know you're a big girl, but it's just the cop in me. You're a beautiful lady and some of the good old boys in this city don't know how to treat a real lady. May I, please?" Shay has to ask. He finds himself wanting to get to know her better and for all the right reasons. He agrees with Joe, she *is* gorgeous. He could listen to her sweet southern accent all night.

"Thank you, Shay. Yes, you may. There were a few of those good old boys hanging around the parking lot when I left. Since I don't have my body guard with me tonight, I'd be honored if you would." She smiles at Joe who, knowing her body guard is Ghost, can only stifle a laugh.

Shay and Mercedes give them a bewildered look, then Mercedes smiles at Shay and shrugs her shoulders in confusion. They leave after their mingled hugs and goodbyes.

Flame and Shay walk in comfortable silence. The night is beautiful, with the moon full and bright. All at once Flame stops, unconsciously grabbing Shay's arm in a tight grip, her eyes wide.

He exclaims, "Flame, what it is? What's wrong?"

"We have to hurry! Someone's in my trailer. Ghost is hurt! Hurry, Shay!"

At once she takes off, running quickly, with Shay right on her heels. He has no idea who this Ghost is, or how she knows someone is in her home. He thinks she must know something though, because she is beginning to cry.

She sobs as she runs. She feels Ghost's anger and his pain. There are two men in her trailer. They came in after the lockbox she had carelessly left on the kitchen counter. She knows it could be seen by looking through the door's small window.

She thinks, *How could I have done something so stupid!? Ghost's hurt and it's all my fault! I'll never forgive myself!* She is in a blind panic.

Chapter 7

"I tell you, Sammy, it's a damn *wolf*! It bit me too! Look!" whines Buck.

"OH SHUT UP YOU DAMN WIMP! I killed the damn thing. It won't be after you no more." shouts Sammy.

"It ain't dead, Sammy. I seen it movin in there. You got the money, so let's get the hell out of here before the damn big ass wolf comes after us again!"

"I TOLD YOU TO SHUT UP! That stupid woman had to have more in here somewhere. I'm gonna find it too."

"I'm outta here, Sammy. I might already be sick from that damn wolf bite!"

"I told you, you dumb ass, that ain't no wolf. It's just a *dog* and it's *dead*."

But, Buck is already out the door and running for the car.

At the same time, Flame and Shay are upon him. They have seen him running from the trailer. Flame sees Shay pull his gun from his ankle holster and throw the man against a car. She runs on. She knows Ghost needs her. She feels his pain.

"Flame! *Stop*! Wait for me! You don't know who else might be in there or even how many!" Shay shouts, trying to stop her from getting hurt.

She just keeps running. She barrels into her trailer, running straight into the other man, Sammy.

"Hey, little lady. You sure are prettier up close than you were from across the parking lot. I'd like to get to know you…" his thoughts are interrupted as she flies at him.

She attacks him with all she has, her nails raking his face, and kicking him as hard as she can. It doesn't even faze him.

He pulls his gun, puts it into her face and tells her, "Now that's enough. I got what I came for and even put a bullet in that damn dog of yours. Now move out of my way! But, maybe one of these days I'll come back for some more… You'll enjoy that, won't you?"

It is then that Ghost, even hurt to the point of death, lands on the man's back. Ghost takes him down, ripping at his throat. The man, mortally wounded, is screaming at the top of his lungs.

Flame is knocked sideways when Ghost hits the man and his gun is lying at her feet. She can hear Shay calling her name and then he bursts in the door. He runs straight to her, but seeing Ghost tearing the man's throat out, stops him.

Flame can hear Shay yelling at her, but it seems as if it is coming from very far away, for she is in Ghost's mind, and in his body. She is trying to keep him alive, giving him her strength and feeling him tearing out the man's throat at the same time.

Shay is yelling at her, "Flame! Call off the dog! He's killing him!"

As Ghost releases the man he starts to lunge toward Shay thinking he, too, is an enemy. Flame, finally realizing what is happening, thinks, NO, *GHOST! He is a friend. Rest now.*

Ghost is very weak. It has taken all his energy to protect his beloved Flame. He falls sideways and crawls to her.

She can only sob, hugging him to her when he gets to her. She tells him mentally, *You must use your strength, Ghost, and mine too. You must fight death!*

He is very close to dying and she cannot bear to lose him. She is so hysterical that she cannot use her gift to heal him. She cannot even think straight, let alone enter his body to heal him.

Someone from the carnival had seen what happened when the man ran from Flame's trailer and called 911. An officer rushes into the trailer and sees the man on the floor bleeding profusely and looking like his throat has been torn out. Then he sees Flame with Ghost wrapped in her arms.

Shay starts giving orders to the officer, "Take this bum out of here and to the hospital. I doubt he'll make it with a wound like that. It's damned hard to feel pity for him though. There's another one cuffed to the door handle of the old Nova out there. Book him. Book this one too, if he makes it. Take the lockbox and gun as evidence. I'm sure their prints are all over them."

"Sure thing, Detective. Should we call an ambulance for the lady too? She looks like she's in shock."

"*NO*! I won't go anywhere until Ghost is taken care of! Shay, please help me get him to a vet. He's losing so much blood. That man shot him. Oh please, Shay, help me!" She is sobbing, hugging Ghost to her, and rocking back and forth.

"Come on, honey. I have a friend here in town that's a vet. He's close by. He's retired, but he's still the best. He'll fix your dog up in no time." Shay responds, though he doesn't really think the dog has much of a chance.

He was shot in the chest and he has lost a lot of blood. It's everywhere. It covers the dog and there is another large puddle of blood where he has lain. Shay doesn't understand how the poor thing had the strength to attack that man, but he sure is thankful that he did. Shay gently picks up the now unconscious Ghost and carries him to the back of his van, lying him gently down inside it.

They leave before the police are done. Shay tells them that he will take Flame to file a report in the morning. He calls his friend, Doc Butler, from a phone booth in the parking lot next to the carnival. He tells Doc Butler that they are coming, giving him the details of Ghost's condition.

Flame insists on riding in the back of Shay's van with Ghost. She cradles him, talking to him like a child, all the way to Doc's.

Doc Butler is just a couple of miles away and he lives alone. He is old, but he has a way with animals. Shay notices, as they pull into the driveway, that Doc has turned the lights on. He knows Doc will have the room he uses for surgeries ready too. He hopes the dog makes it, for Flame's sake.

He carries Ghost inside and Doc puts him in the operating room, telling him and Flame to wait outside while he works. He stops long enough to tell them that Ghost is in bad shape, that he has rarely seen worse injuries and have the dog live through it

He is surprised when Flame insists on being in the room with Ghost. She will not take no for an answer. Doc reluctantly agrees and Shay stays in the room also to lend his support to her.

Flame seems to go into herself as Doc works. Shay has never seen anyone so still. Her eyes are glazed over and unblinking.

He doesn't know it, but Flame is in Ghost's mind. She is encouraging him, keeping him fighting for his life, and aiding him with her strength to get through this ordeal. She mentally tells him, over and over, *Please Ghost, don't leave me. I can't go on without you. You're all I have. I love you.*

She is speaking to him, but she can only find a small pinprick of light in him. He cannot die. She won't let him. She stays and speaks to him, using their mind link throughout the operation.

She has never used her healing gift on something this serious. Grandfather told her that she was a natural healer, so she has to try. She expands her thoughts, searching Ghost's body with her mind.

She finds the damage from the bullet in Ghost's lung. He is drowning in his own blood. She knows that he will die long before the doctor can stop the bleeding if she cannot repair it now. She moves her energy to the damaged area, using only her thoughts and the healing gift, as she works at repairing the hole in his lung. It's very draining, but she has to do it. She is in his body, moving through his chest, willing the damage to heal. She sees it working, but she is beginning to grow weak.

Shay feels her sway into him and he catches her, noticing how pale she is. She will not respond to any of his questions. He picks her up, carrying her into the living room. She gives no sign of protest as he moves her. The healing has worn her out.

She knows that the hole in Ghost's lung is repaired. Doc Butler finds the bullet and removes it. He is in quite a state of shock himself after finding what the damage from the bullet has done, or rather has *not* done. As he comes into the living room, he tells them both Ghost is going to make it.

"I can't understand it. I removed the bullet, but it was close to his heart. The bullet entered from his side, so would have *had* to pass through his lung, but I found no damage *at all* to the lung. It's damned impossible! I even had to drain the blood from his lung. It's the oddest thing I've ever seen, and believe me, I've seen it all. Though I did have to give him quite a bit of blood, he'd lost so much."

Flame knows Ghost is going to recover. He will have to rest and build his strength back, but now she knows he *will* live. He will come home to her again. *Thank God.* Flame thinks to herself.

Doc wants to keep him for a few days, just until his strength returns and Flame knows it will be best for him to stay. She asks if she can see him for a moment, alone.

"Of course. It'll do him good to see you. He seems to be looking everywhere for you anyway." Doc says, and watches the emotions run across her face. This animal is more than a pet to her and he understands that. He has been close to many of his own animals over the years. Sometimes they are better friends than humans.

As Flame leaves the room Doc turns to Shay and tells him, "Shay, I know you said that was a dog, but I've got to tell you…that's *no* dog." He lets that sink in a moment, and then says, "That's the biggest damned wolf I've ever seen! And, I've never seen one that fit either. There's not a scrap of fat on him. He's 165 pounds of muscle! It's more than a bit scary how that bullet didn't kill him. Never seen nothin' like it in my life.

"You keep an eye on that little lady. She seems to have plenty of protection, what with that wolf, but she needs a bit more of the human kind." Doc slaps him on the back.

"Doc, did you say that he's really a *wolf?*" asks Shay.

Doc nods.

Shay runs a hand through his hair and says, "*Damn*, you know that she can't keep a wolf as a pet."

"Boy, leave her and that wolf be. I've never seen anyone tied to an animal like that little lady is to him. She needs him and he needs her. He's so weak he can hardly open his eyes, but all he did was look for her. I thought I'd have to sedate him to keep him still."

Flame is rubbing Ghost's head and telling him how much he means to her. He is so still, but he is alive and healing. She tells him, *Ghost, you must stay here with the doctor for a few days. I promise that I'll be here to see you every single day. The doctor's a good man and I trust him. Shay helped us both, Ghost.*

She gives Ghost a mental picture of Shay and continues, *He'll care for me; watch over me, while you're getting better. You know I can hear you when you need me to. You can hear me too. If anything happens, and you need me here, just tell me. I'll come right away. I promise. Please remember how much I love you. I'll be back tomorrow morning to see you.*

It breaks her heart to leave him here, but he needs the rest and the doctor's care. She knows he will get better care here than he would at the carnival, with all the people and germs there, but she hates being without him.

She goes back to Shay and Doc with tears in her eyes. She hugs Doc, telling him she is so very thankful. She also wants to know how much she owes him.

Shay looks on with admiration shining in his eyes. She is a strong woman and she's a beauty, inside and out. It shines in her eyes and in her smile. He is in awe of her. All of her.

"Little lady, you don't owe me a thing. You forget, I'm retired. Besides, I can't afford to start paying those taxes again now!" he chuckles and continues, "I've never worked on a wolf before and that's the biggest damned wolf I've ever seen!

"To tell the truth, it's more a miracle that saved him than me. I just removed the bullet, but somehow his lung wasn't punctured, or he would've died before I ever got to that bullet, though how it was filled with blood and *not* punctured I'll never know!"

"Thank you so much, Doctor Butler. Yes, he's a wolf, and I've had him since he was a small cub. I couldn't bear losing him. He's all I have. Being on the road all the time he's just about the only friend I have too." She hugs Doc again while giving Shay a pleading look.

She tells him, "Shay, I know you're a cop, but please don't let anyone take Ghost from me. I know I'm not supposed to have him as a pet, but don't you see...? He's not a pet. He's my best friend and I'm his. He willingly left his mother for me. I can't lose him, and he can't lose me."

How can he do anything but give her a reassuring smile? She is standing there with tears in her eyes and her heart on her sleeve. He would have to be the biggest cad in the world to hurt her like that. All he can do is to pull her into his arms, telling her not to worry, that her secret is safe with him.

He thinks, *Damn, I hope my heart's safe with her, because she's got a grip on it. What the hell am I doing? I'm doing the one thing I always said I'd never do, falling, and falling hard. How can I possibly feel this close to her already?*

He just continues holding her, but says, "Don't worry, honey. No one will take your wolf from you as long as I can stop it. He's safe with me, and so are you."

She has never felt this close to a man. Sure, she has her friendship with Frankie, and her love for Grandfather, but never this feeling of tenderness. It is so new to her. She isn't quite sure it is a welcome feeling. He has been so good to her tonight, and she knows she will never forget it, but she doesn't believe in love at first sight.

Love at first sight? Am I nuts? I've never even been kissed, or had a real date! Not that I couldn't have, but still...

Chapter 8

When they get back to her trailer Flame asks Shay inside, forgetting about the blood. It seems to cover everything. Immediately, Flame starts shaking all over just remembering.

Shay can hardly bear seeing the way the blood affects her. "Flame, I have enough room at my place for you. Please? I promise this is no come on. I really mean it. I just want you away from this right now. We'll both come over tomorrow and clean it up. Or, even better, I'll clean it for you while you work your booth. I'm used to this sort of thing, and I can see you won't be able to handle it. Please, say you'll stay with me."

She trusts this man. She has been in his arms and she knows his heart. He is a good man, and he is just what he seems, nice, honest, and trustworthy. She feels his emotions clearly. He is clearly attracted to her, but he will never hurt her, as least not intentionally. If she says no, he won't push it.

She also knows something that he seems not to know; that he is gifted too. His gift is not strong, but it gives him the intuition that he probably uses on his job. It would be what most would call a gut feeling. She will be able to talk to him mentally, but he will have to learn of his gift first.

She tells him softly, "Yes, Shay, I'll stay with you. Thank you so much. I really don't think I could sleep here. Also, I've never had to be without Ghost. Not since I moved into this trailer. He's always been my companion, friend, and protector.

"Before we leave I'll need to grab some clothes. Also, I should go to Frankie's trailer to let him know what's going on. He'll be frantic if he comes by and finds me gone. We usually have our morning coffee together."

Shay is relieved, but wonders who this Frankie is. He actually feels jealous, something he always despised in others.

I've got it bad. If I have it this bad now, after only one night, how will I feel after really getting to know her? he thinks, and then he asks her, "Is Frankie a boyfriend? If he is, should I be prepared to defend my honor?" He laughs and wiggles his eyebrows.

She actually laughs out loud and he thinks it is the most beautiful sound he has ever heard. It's like a beautiful song.

"No, Frankie's not a boyfriend. Not like that, anyway. I think he will like you just fine." She gives him a very large grin, and continues, "You'll just have to see for yourself."

She gathers her clothes and toiletries. Then, they head out the door. Shay tosses her small bag into his van as they pass it heading for Frankie's trailer.

They walk hand in hand. It is just past midnight and she knows that Frankie will be up, probably watching the Late Show, one of his favorites.

Shay is a bit shocked when he actually sees the trailer. It has "Frankie's Buns" printed in bright red letters across its side. He thinks it's a little bold, even for the carnival.

Flame knocks and Shay is so surprised by the sight of Frankie that he has to cough and cover his mouth with his hand to smother the sound of his laughter.

Frankie is a *very* large black man, not just tall, but around. He is dressed in a pink silk nightgown and robe, has big, pink, furry slippers on his feet, and his face is covered in thick, white cold cream.

Flame turns to Shay, smiles that big beautiful smile and says quietly, "He thinks his wrinkles are starting to show."

At this, Shay lets out a whoop of a laugh, not even trying to hide it. The laugh is cut short though when Frankie pulls his .357 Magnum out from behind his back.

He gives Shay a slightly crooked smile and says, "Sorry you two, but you's never know 'bout the people comin round here this late. Me and my buddy here will put a hole the size of Montana in their ass. But come on in!

"Hey, I didn't mean to scare you there big fella. And hello to you too, girlfriend! You're just in time for the jokes. Flame, who *is* this gorgeous man? I hope he's for me, cause you keep promisin' me a nice big fella, but I don't think this one's quite got the gay thing down yet." Frankie tells her, in his usual boisterous manner.

Then he stops, looks out the door for Ghost, and his eyes grow huge. He asks emphatically, "*Where's Ghost?!*"

Flame reaches out, takes his hand, and smiles gently, telling him, "He's okay, Frankie."

Frankie breathes a great sigh, leans against the door, and fans his face. He steps back and motions them inside. They step into the door and take a seat at the small kitchen table.

Once everyone's seated, Flame says, "Frankie, this is Detective Shay Larson. A couple of thugs were waiting for me at the trailer tonight." And she tells Frankie the whole gruesome story.

Frankie gets tears in his eyes when she tells him about Ghost being hurt.

"Shay has kindly offered me a place to stay until I can get all the blood cleaned up. I have to meet Joe in the morning for breakfast and then I want to go to see Ghost, so I probably won't be here until I have to open my booth at noon."

Shay speaks up, "Frankie, I hope you have a permit for that cannon of yours. Do you?"

Frankie just grins at him.

"Never mind, I don't want to know. I think Flame needs to carry one herself. At least it'll make *me* feel better. Do you know how to use one?" Shay asks, as he turns to Flame.

"Of course, I've just never had the need to carry one until now. Ghost was always there for me, but Grandfather taught me how to use one. I even have one that he gave me put away at the trailer. I guess it might be a good idea to start carrying it, I just hate to do it." she admits.

Frankie shows them to the door a few minutes later, leans close to Flame and whispers, "Damn, girlfriend, keep that package 'round. Don't be lettin loose of him. That be one fine hunk of meat. I think he likes you too." He grins, a predatory look on his face and asks, "Is there anymore where he come from?"

Flame laughs and quietly says, "I can always count on you to lift my spirits, Frankie. I think he's quite a hunk too, but we'll see about the hanging around part later. Much later."

While riding to Shay's, in his van, she suddenly sits straight up, exclaiming loudly, "Grandfather!"

Shay cannot figure out what this is about, but then she continues speaking, "I'll call you, don't wear yourself out! You know the distance is too great for this!"

She had forgotten the strong mind link between herself and Grandfather. She should have realized he would know something was dreadfully wrong. He has to use very strong mental thought to speak to her at this distance, and it will drain his physical strength doing it, but he knows her anguish is great.

He has also known Ghost's pain. She is so used to being alone that she speaks out loud, without thinking about Shay hearing her.

Shay gives her a concerned look and asks, "Flame, what in the world are you talking about? Are you sure you're not in shock?"

"I'm sorry, Shay. I forgot. I'm not use to being with others. You must think I'm nuts." She gives him a small sample of her laugh and tells him, "It's Grandfather. He knows something's wrong and he's anxious for me to call him. I know you don't understand, but we're able to communicate through a form of telepathy. AND STOP LOOKING AT ME LIKE I'M NUTS!"

Shay cannot even speak for a minute. He knows she is a fortune teller for the carnival, but this? He knows people claim this sort of thing really happens, but damn, he has never been confronted with it.

"You have to know this is what I do! This is how I make a living, Shay! You knew that! *What*? Did you think I was a fake?" She actually looks hurt.

He breathes deeply, calms his voice, and says, "Flame, calm down. It's been a very long night and I know you're upset. I don't doubt you, but you have to give me a minute to get this down. I mean, I've never met anyone who can do this sort of thing.

"No, I'm *not* saying you're a fake, so please don't put words in my mouth. I just need time to understand it and you'll have to help me with that. We'll just have to trust each other. Okay?"

She thinks this over a moment, realizing he is right. She cannot expect him to just accept it. Not without showing him the gift. She would never have believed it either, once. Now she knows, but it took a lot for her to get here too. He still has no idea of his own gift.

She thinks, *Boy, he thinks this is hard to swallow… just wait until he has to accept his own gift!* She giggles out loud, and says, "Sure, Shay. I already trust you. Afterall, I've never gone home with a man before!"

"And now you're laughing at *me*?" he asks her jokingly and teases, "Okay, woman. Let's get there then, so you can call your grandfather. I'm anxious to hear *that* conversation!"

"I don't recall you asking if you can hear it." she says, smiling.

"*Women*!"

She can only laugh the harder.

He, too, breaks down and laughs right along with her.

When they arrive at Shay's home Flame is amazed at how nice it is. He has wonderful taste. His apartment is filled with antiques, soft leather furniture, and the most beautiful landscape paintings she has ever seen.

Though the apartment is not especially large it does have two bedrooms. There are beautiful handmade quilts in both. He sets her small suitcase in the smaller of the two rooms.

She exclaims, "Shay, this is the most beautiful quilt I've ever seen! I love the furniture. I especially love the paintings!"

"Thank you. My grandmother made the quilts for me years ago hoping, I think, that I would find a wife to put them to use. The paintings are my favorite also. My father painted them. He was a very sought after artist."

"I can see why! They're all so lovely. Doesn't he still paint?"

"He and my mother were killed almost ten years ago. They were caught in the crossfire of a bank robbery. That's why I dropped out of law school and became a cop. I went to law school, with Joe, before the shooting."

Shay's eyes take on a haunted look and it breaks her heart. She never knew her parents, but she does know what being alone is. She tells him, "Oh, Shay, I'm so very sorry. I can understand you wanting to avenge their deaths though, that becoming a cop was your way of doing something about it. Was the shooter caught?"

She wants to wrap her arms around this man. To comfort him and to take comfort from him. She tries to not show her loneliness to others, but with this man, she wants to tell him everything. It shakes her deeply and she fears getting too close, way too fast.

"Yes. There were three robbers involved and all were captured. Two were killed while running from the police and one was sent to prison. He'll be in prison for ten more years, and the one who did the shooting was killed.

"I just couldn't go back to law school afterwards. I think I was born to be a cop. I enjoy putting the bad guys away. I don't think I could defend someone accused of crimes that I know they probably *did* commit." he confesses.

She automatically puts her arms around him without even thinking about it.

He holds her to him. He hasn't talked of his parents in a very long time. He tries not to think of the pain their deaths caused him, but here, with this lovely woman, he is close to tears. He doesn't understand the hold she has on him.

She breaks the embrace, a bit embarrassed at herself, hoping he doesn't think she is being too forward. To cover her embarrassment she says, "Shay, I need to call Grandfather. He's waiting. Very impatiently, I might add, for my call. You're welcome to listen if it'll help you to understand the gift we have. Do you mind if I use your phone? I'll pay for it."

"Thank you, Flame, but I won't intrude, and no, you cannot pay for it! You just talk as long as you want. I can afford it." he says with a smile. "You go into the living room and make yourself comfortable while I put some tea on. It might soothe your nerves a bit."

She settles herself on the soft brown leather couch, picks up Shay's phone from the end table, and dials Grandfather's number. He answers almost before the first ring is over.

"Flame! What has happened to Ghost? Are you okay?" Grandfather exclaims, before she can say a word.

"Yes, Grandfather, I'm fine. Ghost was shot, but he's doing well. He's at a vet's office here in Munson. Doc Butler's, and he'll be fine. You were right, my gift for healing seems to be working just fine.

"Doc thinks it was a miracle because the bullet went through Ghost's side, through his lung, barely missing his heart. He removed the bullet, but he couldn't figure out why the lung wasn't punctured. Grandfather, I went into Ghost and repaired the lung while Doc was working on him."

"Granddaughter, I knew your healing gift was strong, but even I am amazed. I think it is the love you share with Ghost that gave you the strength to save him. I have been so worried. I knew your fear and I felt Ghost's pain. He was more scared for you, than for himself. Please, tell me, what happened?"

She tells him all that has happened, even about her dinner with Joe and Mercedes. Then she tells him about meeting Shay. She even tells him that she is with him now. She explains about the blood in her trailer and that Shay has brought her to his apartment.

He gives a small chuckle. He knows that she doesn't trust easily. He also knows that Joe would never leave her to someone that is not suitable for her. It could be that this is just the right thing for her. He worries about her being alone, save for Ghost, all the time.

"Grandfather, I heard that! What are you laughing about?! I'm staying in his guest room! Besides, I'm a full grown woman!" She looks up to see Shay standing in the doorway, his mouth twitching suspiciously at the corners. She waggles a finger at him, mouthing *"don't you dare!"*

Grandfather tells her that all is well in the forest. The wolves have had another litter, born this past summer, and all of the cubs are healthy. He chuckles and tells her, "They have moved the whole den under the porch now. I think they are getting very spoiled. Of course Prince is now the alpha and his mate is a beautiful black, just like the last alpha female.

"The older ones are now staying in the woods and have formed their own small pack. It is most unusual for two separate packs to live so closely, but here nothing is normal, as you know."

He tells her, "I love you, Granddaughter. Give my love to Ghost. I have sent him my own message telling him how proud he has made me in defending you. Tell Joe that I hope to meet this Mercedes very soon. I have dreamt of a wedding. I just wonder if it is Joe's or yours!" he says and chuckles again.

"Grandfather! Stop that! You're such a pest! I love you, too, and Ghost and I will be seeing you this fall. Maybe Joe and Mercedes can come at the same time. I mentioned that to them already. I can always stay in my trailer, so they can have the room.

"Oh, and Joe and I are meeting for breakfast. He has some mysterious papers to go over with me in private. You wouldn't know anything about them would you?" she asks him, suspiciously.

"Joe will go over it all with you, Granddaughter. I am sure we will have a wonderful reunion this fall. Please call me and let me know how Ghost is holding up. I know your gifts are great. Do not forget to use them well. Know well what is going on around you. Do not put faith in people that do not deserve it. I am not talking about your young man. There are others out there to watch out for. Maybe it is a good thing, this young man. He can help to keep you safe. My dreams have been troubling lately, except, of course, the wedding one." He chuckles again and says, "Goodbye, Granddaughter of my heart."

She hangs up with tears in her eyes.

Shay immediately comes to her and asks, "What's wrong? Is he okay?"

She smiles sadly and says, "Yes, it's just that I miss him so much. I haven't been able to see him for over three years now. I know I'll see him soon, but I miss him so much. He's the first family I've ever had. There's a lot you don't know about me, Shay."

He sits down on couch beside her and tells her, "Here, honey, drink this. It's chamomile, and it should help to calm you down some. I hope to get to know you, by the way. I want to know everything about you. I feel like I've known you for a long time already, though you're right, I don't really know much about you.

"I do know that you're very brave, strong, and have this *gift*. I'm not lying, Flame. I *do* believe you. Please know that." Shay looks her in the eye when he speaks, so she can know he is telling her the truth.

She believes him, and says, "You're not like any man I've ever met. I've always found it hard to talk about myself. I don't feel that way with you. I do want to tell you everything, but just give me a little time, okay?

"I have to be up early to meet Joe. I also have to open my booth at noon. Maybe, if you're not busy, we could have a late dinner tomorrow night. Of course, I must check on Ghost in the morning, and again tomorrow night. Then we can go to dinner. Is that okay with you?" She looks at him hopefully.

He feels like he has won the lottery and tells her, "That sounds wonderful. I'm off tomorrow too. I'll drop you at your van in the morning so you can meet with Joe. While you're gone I'll get that trailer cleaned up for you. Then, I'll take you to see Ghost, before we go to your trailer, and tomorrow night, after dinner, we can see him again. Okay? I think he'd better get to know me. I want him to know that I'll watch over you while he's away."

"Thank you, Shay. You've been wonderful. I know Ghost will like you. The tea tastes just right, and it's already working. I'm so tired. Maybe tomorrow I can read your future for you."

He stands, reaching for her hand to help her up. "Come on, let's get you all tucked in. I'll set the alarm and wake you in the morning. We'll see about the reading tomorrow. I'm not sure I want to know the future, unless it's filled with all good things!" he says and chuckles.

Flame lies in the big comfortable bed staring up at the ceiling. She is so tired, but she cannot seem to turn off her mind. She thinks of Ghost and sends him a goodnight while checking on his wounds.

He is healing, but very sore. Doc has given him some pain medication and a sedative. He acknowledges Flame's goodnight and reassurance of her safety before the drug takes effect. He will sleep heavily.

Thoughts of Shay run around in her head. She wonders if he is really as good as he seems. She has never really had romance in her life before and the way she feels about him already has her a bit scared. She wonders, *Will he break my heart?*

She falls asleep with Grandfather's laughter echoing through her mind. Her dreams are full of weddings and wolves; the forest, and Grandfather's smile.

While Flame lay in the guest room thinking of him, Shay lies in his bed, thinking of her. She is special. He knows that already. He wants to protect her from all the hurts the world can give her.

He can feel her attraction to him, just as he feels his for her. He cannot get the feeling of having her in his arms out of his mind. She fits so perfectly. He knows he has to be careful, for she is leaving again with the carnival when the time comes. That doesn't give them much time, only a few days in fact.

Chapter 9

Flame wakes to the smell of coffee brewing. It smells so good. She has no idea what time it is, but she trusts that Shay wouldn't have let her oversleep. He knows she is to meet Joe at eight.

It is nice to have someone to be able to trust in. She has never had anyone to count on, except Grandfather. Their time had been so short, but so full.

That's it! That's how I feel about Shay. Trust. Like Grandfather. But then again, so not like Grandfather. I've never trusted anyone else. She realizes she has been trying to figure out something that has no explanation. It is felt, not rationalized and she thinks, *Hmmm...I guess I'll have to go with the flow, as Frankie would say.* With this thought she gets out of bed with a sunny smile on her face.

Shay is pouring her coffee when she walks in to the kitchen.

"One lump of sugar." he states, as he pours her cup full. He cannot help but notice that she is even more beautiful in the morning with that sleepy eyed, tousled hair thing. He thinks she is the most beautiful woman he has ever seen, let alone met.

He adds, "I hope you slept well. I know it's hard to sleep in a different bed sometimes." He feels like he is rambling.

He had a very hard time sleeping last night himself. He could not get her bright smile, huge green eyes, and flame red hair out of his mind, but the hardest part to forget was how she felt in his arms.

She gives him that big smile again and his heart melts. She says cheerfully, "Good morning, Shay. I actually slept very well, thanks! I hope you don't mind, but I couldn't resist the smell of the coffee...I must look terrible. I didn't even take time to brush my hair yet. I can't believe you remember how I like my coffee. We only had one cup at the restaurant."

"I don't think it's possible for you to look terrible. You look beautiful. Sure, I remember how you like your coffee. My mother always told me, "it's the little things you have to remember" and I guess I took that advice to heart."

He actually blushed! Shay blushed! Damn, but he's so good looking, and so thoughtful...what the hell am I doing? she thinks, but says, "Shay, you're a very thoughtful man. Your mother would be very proud of you. What time is it?"

"It's only seven. Would you like a bite to eat? I know you're supposed to meet Joe for breakfast, but first we have to go down to the station and file a report. I'm sorry, but it's got to be done.

"I called Joe at home and told him what happened. He says that he's so sorry and that he's very glad that Ghost is doing okay. He also says to bring you by his office when we get done. I hope you don't mind."

"No, I don't, and thank you. I'm fine. I really don't have much of an appetite right now anyway. I do want to stop over and see Ghost though, if that's okay. Can we go file the report, and then check on Ghost? He's never been without me and it breaks my heart." she says, and looks at him hopefully.

"Sure. I know how much he means to you. Joe will be okay. It shouldn't take us long at the station anyway. I can make a mean omelet though. Please eat a bite with me." He worries about her. She has circles under her eyes this morning. It doesn't take away from her looks at all, but he can tell that she is under a lot of strain.

"No, Shay, really, I'm fine." she says and smiles, but she feels drained. She knows a lot of it is worrying over Ghost, but most of it is being so weak from the healing. It really does take a lot of energy. Grandfather tried to tell her it would, but she had no idea how much.

"So, tell me about yourself. I think it's time for us to get to know a little about each other." Shay says, and watches her eyes go so sad as a haunted look clouds them. This look changes his mind and he immediately amends, "Okay...I'll go first. Well, I told you about my parents last night. They were the best. I really miss them a lot. My Grandmother died just a year after they did. She took their deaths so hard. It just broke her heart.

"I was so tied up with trying to get justice for my parents that I didn't even see it coming. I should have. She was so good, Flame. It breaks my heart to think that I might have been able to help her. Truthfully though, I don't think anyone or anything could have made a difference.

"My parents always wanted me to be a lawyer, but I just couldn't finish school after they died. It didn't mean anything to me anymore.

"As I said, I went to school with Joe. He was my roommate for those few years and he was always so good to me. He really cares, you know? Not like some of the other kids. They could have cared less. All they cared about was partying and the opposite sex. Not Joe though. He cares about his friends and he doesn't have many.

"If you haven't noticed, Joe's being an Indian makes him stand out a bit. I never cared, but there are so many people that are still so prejudice. He still has a hard time. He made better grades than anyone I ever knew, though. He's very smart, Flame. He's the best damn lawyer I've ever met and, also, the best damn friend I've ever had.

"He stood beside me, even when I wouldn't let anyone near me. He understood. I guess, because he'd lost his parents so tragically, too. He took their deaths hard from what I understand. I know his grandfather was great to him though.

"He told me that his grandfather had paid for his schooling. From what Joe has said to me, his grandfather's very wealthy. You'd never know it by Joe though. Except for his schooling, he never really shows off the money. Shoot, he even still drives that old Toyota truck that his grandfather gave him for his high school graduation.

"I'm twenty-nine years old, getting up there, with not much to show for it. I made detective a few years ago. It doesn't pay all that well, but I do okay. I have quite a bit of money put away, since my dad left me everything. I sold the house after they died, too. I just couldn't live there anymore. Grandma's too.

"I've lived here, in Montana, all my life. I have traveled a little bit, but someday I hope to be able to do a lot more of it. As a kid I always had my nose in a book. I guess all the girls thought I was a nerd. I never really dated much back then. I still don't. That blind date with you last night was Joe's way of telling me that I need to get out more!" he says, and laughs.

Then, he says, "Okay, now it's your turn." He has watched her eyes go from sadness to laughter. He can read her emotions as well as his own. It is amazing to him that he feels so close to her. He thinks, *Well hell, I've never met anyone like her. She's strong, sweet and oh so gorgeous. And, that southern accent...hell, I'm lost.*

She tells him, "Oh, I'm so sorry that you've been so alone since your parents and grandmother died. I know what that's like. At least you had Joe. Okay…I've never told this to anyone except Grandfather, and I really didn't tell him, but maybe you'll understand more about that in a little while.

"Grandfather, and now Joe, is the only family I've ever had. He knows me better than I know myself.

"I was raised in Tennessee, just a little town that had an orphanage. I was *in* that orphanage, Shay. I lived there until I was eighteen. I got out of that town, shoot, that state, as soon as I could. Tennessee's beautiful, don't get me wrong, but I could never be happy there. Not after that orphanage.

"I'm twenty-one. I met Grandfather that first month after I left the orphanage. He saved my life. I was camping on his land when I got shot by a hunter. He found me, and healed me." She doesn't know if Shay can handle the truth, but she has to be honest with him. "I've always been closer to animals than humans. They know me and I know them. You might not believe me, but I can get into their minds." She stops and looks at him a moment.

Then she continues, "No, not just know them by looking, Shay. I mean I can actually *enter* their minds." She cannot even look at Shay while telling him this. She has never told anyone this. No one knows it except Grandfather, and he understands because he can do it too. She is so afraid that Shay will wear that same look that Miss Hodges and the others used to give her, that half-scared, half-disgusted look.

She finally says, "Grandfather has this gift too. Joe doesn't. That's why Grandfather claims me as his family. We're very much alike. He loves the animals, the wolves especially, as I do.

"Ghost was given to me by his mother. He was just a cub. He protects me, and I him. We're very close. You can't possibly understand how close. I can see through his eyes and sometimes, I think, though I don't know for sure, he can see my thoughts. Since we're always together, I haven't used the gift much in the last couple of years, except with the people that pay for their reading at the carnival, and I read them through touch.

"I guess I do use it with Ghost, after thinking about it, but it's so natural for us now that I don't notice actually doing it. I use it on the horses in the carnival sometimes, so Gregori will know how the horses will perform, but he doesn't know how I do it. I used it last night to say goodnight to Ghost and tell him I love him. I also told him about you. Please believe me...I won't lie to you…ever." She still hasn't looked up at him. She holds her coffee cup, twisting it slowly in her hands.

He doesn't say anything, so she continues, "I also have the gift of healing. This is something new for me. Grandfather taught me how to use my mind gift to heal, from the inside, Shay. I was in Ghost last night. The bullet went through his lung. He was dying. I *had* to. That's why I was so tired afterwards." she says, finishing, and looks up at him.

She looks scared, like he will not believe her, but she holds her head high and looks him in the eye. She will not be cowed. Not anymore. Not by anyone. She is no longer a child, and she will not let anyone see the pain it causes her to see the look on their faces when she shows her difference. Not even Shay.

Shay is befuddled about halfway through her story. He doesn't know what to think. It is taking him awhile to wrap his mind around what she tells him.

He remembers Joe talking about Grandfather being a healer, and something about his wolves. He remembers Joe saying that Grandfather's wolves are the only reason that he wouldn't sell the forest land that so many have tried to buy. He says that Grandfather talks to the wolves.

Then Shay also remembers what Doc Butler had said about the bullet.

That it had to have passed through the wolf's lung. That the lung had been full of blood, but had no hole in it.

He's amazed and thinks, *She's telling me the truth. I can't believe it, but it's true. It has to be. Nothing else explains it. I thought Joe was just superstitious when it came to the things his grandfather does. He was telling me the truth. Flame is too, I can see it in her eyes.*

She waits. Shay just keeps looking at her. She wants so badly to try to enter his mind, as Grandfather said she could with others that have a gift. He doesn't even know he has a gift, she has to remember that. She has to take it slow with him.

She thinks, *He doesn't believe me. He thinks I'm crazy. I can't bear for him to see me the way the kids use to.* but, she says, "I'll get dressed now, Shay, then we can go. You can just drop me at Joe's later. I'll take care of the trailer. Don't worry." She jumps up from the table, almost knocking over her coffee cup.

"Flame, stop!" he shouts and rushes to take her arm. As he pulls her around to face him, he sees the tears in her eyes, and says softly, "Oh, honey, please don't cry. I'm so sorry. Forgive me, Flame. I'm not doubting you. Never. Not you. I'm just tying it all together. I believe you." He pulls her close, kissing her tears away.

He thinks, *God, she's something. Coming from anyone else I'd call them the worse kind of liar, but, Lord help me, I believe her.* He can't resist it. He kisses her.

For a moment, after the kiss, everything is quiet. They simply look into each other's eyes.

She finally smiles, touches her lips, and says embarrassingly, "That was my first kiss. I mean my first *real* kiss."

He laughs heartily and exclaims, "Now I *don't* believe that!"

She, too, laughs saying, "It's true, Shay. I've never had a boyfriend, or even a date, until last night."

He smiles even bigger, saying, "Good! I was wondering if this, Gregori, was going to be a problem!"

They both know a moment of relieved laughter before preparing for the rest of the day. She quickly showers, dresses, and dries her hair. She is as ready as she is going to get, but puts off going out of the room for just a moment.

She touches a finger to her lips again and thinks, *He believes me! He even kissed me! Grandfather, do you hear me? He kissed me!*

And, Grandfather, though hours away, smiles.

Chapter 10

Shay and Flame walk into the Munson City Police Station holding hands. This leaves a lot of sly smiles and raised eyebrows in their wake. They never even notice. They have eyes only for each other.

"Flame, this is Sergeant Marty Diener. He'll take your statement while I go type up my own. I won't be long." Shay tells her reassuringly.

Sergeant Diener is in his late thirties. He is a nice looking man, and his smile makes her comfortable immediately.

"Hello, Ms. um...Flame?" asks Sergeant Diener, making it an obvious question.

She hesitates momentarily, then smiles, and Sergeant Diener forgets all about her last name for a moment. She says softly, "Hi, Sergeant Diener. It's Flame. Just plain Flame."

But, Sergeant Diener thinks there can be nothing plain about her. He could see immediately that she is pretty, but when she smiles she becomes jaw dropping beautiful.

Thirty minutes later Shay returns. Flame and Sergeant Diener are just finishing up.

As she gets up, Sergeant Diener leans over and says in Shay's ear, "Larson, you are one lucky S.O.B. She's a real beauty."

Shay smiles, and says proudly, "Damn right."

When they get to the door he stops, looks at her, and says, "Flame, wait a second. I forgot all about calling Joe. He doesn't know we're stopping off to see Ghost. Come on, it'll just take a minute, and I need to leave a number for the chief anyway."

He pulls her along with him into the room full of cops. He asks her to wait just a second as he steps into an office. He had found out the guy that Ghost attacked had died. He doesn't want her to know that yet. He leaves his report on the chief's desk and comes right back out and takes her to one of the desks.

He tells her, "Sit down right here, hon, and I'll call Joe."

She notices his name on the desk nameplate and thinks, *So, this is his desk. Hmmm…very neat, and everything right where it should be. Says some-*

thing about the man, I would think.

Shay sits behind the desk and dials Joe. After a brief hesitation, he says with a smile, "Hello, Debbie. This is Shay. Do me a favor…tell Joe that I'm bringing Flame over to sign those documents in about forty-five minutes. We have another stop to make first."

He smiles into the phone a moment more and says, "Sure, Debbie. Tell him I said no problem...but only for a little while!" He laughs, hangs up, looks at her and says, "Seems Joe thinks I should let you loose for a bit. He thinks I'm monopolizing all your time." He winks.

As they are getting into Shay's van a phone call is being placed from inside the station.

"Morning, boss. Thought you'd want to know about this. That new sister of Wolf's is going over to his office this morning to sign some sort of documents."

"Do you know what kind of documents, Sergeant?"

"No, but I thought you'd like to know they have something brewing."

"Yes, I want any information you can find about her. Try to find out more and let me know as soon as you can."

"Yes, boss."

While Shay and Flame are on the way to Doc Butler's office, he turns to her and asks, "Flame, since you can see, or rather, talk to Ghost while you're not with him…how is he this morning?"

She glances quickly at him, thinking that he is doubting her again, but she sees no doubt on his face. She only sees curiosity. She cannot blame him if he does doubt her though, it *is* a hard thing to accept and believe.

She says, "I know that you're curious. I would be, too, in your place. First, I don't see Ghost, I see through him. I enter his mind. Let me try to show you. I'll tell you what Ghost sees. Okay?" She wants him to know it is the truth.

"I don't doubt you. You don't have to prove anything to me, but, yes, I am curious. I've never heard of anything like it. Please show me."

She smiles and relaxes into her seat, going into Ghost's mind. He is well and missing her terribly. She lets him know that she is on her way to him and then she tells him that she wants to look around. He is in a large outdoor enclosure in the back of the home, but there is not much that would stop him from any task that she asks of him.

With her help—telling him what to do—Ghost opens the gate of the enclosure. He is slow in moving, as he is sore, but he is not endangering himself. He knows she would not ask him to do anything that would hurt him.

He goes to the doggy door that leads into the kitchen and enters. She tells him to go quietly, not to scare the doctor, and to act very friendly if he sees anyone. She doesn't want to endanger Ghost by having him scare someone unnecessarily.

He goes into the front room slowly and sees that the front door is open, but the screen door is not. He looks out and sees the doctor talking to a man in a suit. The man shakes the doctor's hand and then opens the backdoor of his large black car. Out comes a very large dog. They all start walking to the front door.

Flame tells Ghost to go back into the kitchen, but to stay and listen.

As the men enter the house the dog gets excited. She smells Ghost and breaks from the man, running straight into the kitchen, and almost barrels over Ghost.

She is the largest dog that Ghost has ever seen, but she is not trying to attack. He realizes that she just wants to play. She seems to know that he is hurt though, and doesn't try to get rough with him.

The man and the doctor rush into the kitchen behind the dog.

The man in the suit stops short and forcefully calls out, "Sadie! Sit girl. Stay." Then turns to Doc and exclaims, "Damn, Doctor Butler, is he yours? He's beautiful!"

Doc is stunned. He knows that he had shut Ghost in the fenced-in yard and he is in no shape to dig his way out. He glances out the kitchen window and sees the gate open. He says almost reverently, "No, Mr. Holst, he's not mine. He's a new patient of mine and a damned smart one at that. He was in that gated fence out there just a few minutes ago. I guess he got lonely, but, yes, he's a beautiful dog, isn't he?" Doc grins, knowing that this man can never know that Ghost is really a wolf.

Flame hears it all and smiles when Doc grins. Shay was right. Doc is a good man. He will never intentionally hurt Ghost, or her.

Ghost gives her pictures of the old vet petting him and talking to him.

She tells Ghost that she will soon be there and leaves his mind. She turns to Shay and realizes that he has stopped the car.

He is calling her name and looks extremely worried about her.

She had forgotten to tell him that when she is in Ghost she cannot hear or see what's going on around her body. He must have been frightened. She tells him that she is fine, not to worry, and then explains to him why she couldn't answer him. She then tells him all that she saw and heard.

"Damn. Mr. S.R. Holst. You have quite a gift there, darling! Mr. Holst is one of the richest and most powerful men in Montana. Not many people even know what the S.R. stands for. I've heard that it's Scott Randall, or something like that, but everyone I've ever known calls him Sir.

"He has a few oil wells, quite a bit of holdings in our city, and others all over the state. His dog's one big assed dog. She's been trained as a guard dog and goes with him everywhere. I've never seen him without her. Oh, and he's also Mercedes' father." he says and grins at her.

"Well, Sadie took quite a shine to Ghost." she tells him and laughs remembering how Sadie looked at Ghost.

Then she asks, "That man's Mercedes' father? No wonder she had on all those diamonds! Truthfully, I wondered if she was squeezing Joe for money...but I hate to admit that. I don't have much trust in people. I was hoping to learn more about her today when I read her."

"Speaking of that…how do you *read* people? Do you enter *their* minds too?" he asks curiously.

"No, Shay. I can't enter a human's mind, well… not really. I can read them through touch. I know their thoughts while I'm touching them. People that come to the carnival think I'm reading their palm, but I'm not. It's their head, or mind, that I'm reading. Don't give my secret away." She smiles, but he can tell that she is very serious.

He thinks, *It frightens her to trust me, and it's all connected to her past. Damn. I'd like to get my hands on whoever hurt her so badly. It won't happen again, not if I can help it.* but, he says aloud, "Flame, never worry about me telling anyone. I will *never* hurt you. I swear that on my life."

"I believe you, Shay. I really do. I trust you and that doesn't come easily to me, but I guess I just admitted that when I told you about reading Mercedes." She gives him a small laugh.

He tells her, "I can't say as I blame you. I'm sorry your past was so hard, honey. I swear, I'm going to do my best to make your future much happier."

She doesn't say anything in reply, but regrets that she will be leaving in a few days. It is going to be almost as hard to leave him as it was to leave Grandfather, but in a much different way.

They arrive at Doc's home to find Mr. Holst and Doc coming out the door with Sadie. She truly is a beautiful dog. She has to weight nearly the same amount as Ghost, but in a much different package. She is solid black and her fur has got a healthy shine.

As Shay and Flame get out of the van, Doc smiles and says, "Mr. Holst, here comes his owner now. Flame, this is Mr. S.R. Holst. He's been admiring your dog," he winks, "and so has Sadie here!"

Mr. Holst holds out his hand to Shay first saying, "Hello, Detective Larson. Nice to see you… and this lovely lady is Flame? Mercedes talked about you just this morning. She's so anxious to get her palm read." He smiles, a tight, forced, fake smile. He reaches out to shake Flame's hand and Sadie picks this moment to jerk away from him and knock Flame down.

When Flame goes down Sadie is straddling her, with Shay and Mr. Holst both grabbing for her collar. Sadie is not to be pulled off her though, and at that moment Ghost barrels through the screen door. Instead of going for Sadie, Ghost goes straight for Mr. Holst, teeth bared and growling. It all happens in a split second. Shay and Doc are stunned into instant immobility.

"GHOST, *NO*!" yells Flame.

Ghost backs off, still baring his teeth. Flame finally sits up, telling Sadie to back up. Sadie sits down beside Flame and gives her a big wet lick right across her face.

She giggles and says, "I think she likes me! Ghost, calm down."

Ghost sits beside Sadie and gives Flame his own form of love by laying his head on her shoulder.

"Well I'll be damned! If that's not the strangest thing I ever saw!" exclaims Doc.

"Sadie, get over here! Bad girl! Go to the car! That's twice today you've acted up! I'm going to punish you if you do it again! I'm sorry, Flame, Larson." says Mr. Holst, and he nods once in their direction, never taking his eyes off of Sadie as she mopes to the car. He tells them, sounding almost apologetic, "I don't know what's gotten into her today. She's very well trained, but today seems to be her off day." And, he smiles that fake smile again.

"No problem, Mr. Holst. Dogs seem to like me. I guess they know I like them more than most people." Flame gives him a wide eyed, innocent look.

Shay and Doc are behind Mr. Holst, so he doesn't see the grin they give each other.

"Please tell Mercedes I'll be waiting for her. Nice meeting you." *Not!* And, Flame turns her back on Mr. S.R. Holst.

Once he is in his car and Flame, Shay, Doc, and Ghost, are behind the closed door of the house, they all erupt in uncontrollable laughter.

"Shay, I didn't even have to touch that man to know I don't like him." she says, and gives a little shiver.

"You're not alone on that count, honey. I think you put a kink in his chain though. Did you see his face when Ghost burst through that screen?! I've never seen anything like it! Although, I have to admit, when that big assed dog knocked you down my heart was in my throat." he admits, thinking again to the sight of Sadie standing over her.

"Mine too, son. I thought the little lady was a goner. Then her wolf just about gave me a heart attack for the second time today!" exclaims Doc.

"He knew Sadie was no threat to me. I did too, she just took me by surprise. She's a big baby, but that baby weighs a ton! Ghost just didn't want Mr. Holst's hands on me. He's got a great sense of people. I don't know if he got the vibes from me, or if I did from him." she admits to them both.

"Well kids, that's my excitement for today. You have a nice visit. I have to do a few things." Doc pats Ghost on his head and tells him, "And I don't blame you, Ghost; I don't like that man either. I think Sadie will be okay though, and she's going to teach that man a lesson one day, I'll bet. Young lady, you can take Ghost home tomorrow, if you make him stay close and *if* he stays in the fence tonight!" He actually shakes his finger at Ghost.

Ghost gives him the same grin that he always gives Frankie.

"Well, I'll be damned. That wolf is a man is fur suit!" Doc says to them both, shaking his head on his way to the back of the house.

Shay is staring at Ghost with a slack jawed sort of look.

"Shay, close your mouth before you catch a fly in there!" Flame giggles and says, "Ghost, quit that now, you're freaking them out. Shay doesn't realize how smart you are yet, but he will."

Ghost stops grinning and nudges Shay's hand.

"Flame, I have to agree with Doc. I admit I've never actually met a wolf before, but isn't his brain a bit on the large side?" Shay is watching Ghost with awe.

"Yes, he's very smart. He hasn't been with any other wolves since he was a cub and I've spent a lot of time with him, and *in* him. I guess he's just a quick learner. He never forgets anything. He's thanking you right now."

By now Shay is rubbing Ghost's head and scratching in just the right spot on his ears. He says, "Ghost, you're very welcome. I promise that while she's with me nothing, and I mean nothing, will happen to her. I'll keep a good eye on her." He adds, "And I'm glad we'll finally have a chance to get know each other. I think you and I have a lot in common."

"You have more in common than you know." Flame tells them both.

Chapter 11

Shay drops Flame off at Joe's office at nine-thirty. He asks her for the key to her trailer, telling her that he was serious about her not seeing it like that again.

"Thank you, Shay. You can't imagine how grateful I am. Will you still be there when I get home to change for work?"

"I wouldn't miss the chance to get another kiss, now would I?" He leans over and places his mouth on hers. This kiss lasts longer than the one before it.

Finally, she climbs out of the car.

Shay tells her, "I'll see you soon, honey. Make Joe buy you a big meal. He needs to pay for making me give up any of our time together!"

Flame smiles, nods, and walks into the building.

Shay can tell that she is distracted. Something about this is bothering her, but he has no idea why. He figures it must have something to do with whatever Joe wants her to sign. Joe loves his grandfather. Flame loves him too, and surely if he asks her to do something it will be good for her. Something is making her uncomfortable with it though and he wishes he knew what.

She does have misgivings. She trusts Joe and Grandfather, but she has a bad feeling. She doesn't know why. She just feels like it is something that will change her life, but she isn't sure that she wants it changed. She is finally happy with her life. Well, up until today she was.

For the first time since she joined the carnival, she is having doubts about staying with it. She knows it is because of Shay and probably being so close to Grandfather and the forest too. She really wants to see him before she leaves town again. She is so close to him and the forest that it would be a shame not to. And, she has to admit to herself that she doesn't want to leave town. Not yet.

She takes the elevator to the third floor. Joe's office takes up the whole floor. It is decorated beautifully, with soft, dark leather furniture. There is a petite blonde sitting at a dark Cherry wood desk. Flame likes her as soon as she looks up and smiles.

"Hi. I have an appointment with Joe. I'm..." and, before she can finish, the woman holds up her hand, stopping her.

"No...don't even tell me! I know who you are! You've got to be Flame. I've heard so much about you! Oh, I'm sorry! I'm Debbie Daly, Joe's secretary, but you can just call me Debbie, everyone does. I'm so glad to meet you." says the woman, Debbie, in a rush.

Flame opens her mouth to speak, but before she can utter a word, Debbie continues, "Oh, I was *so* hoping you'd bring your wolf! Oops! I'm sorry. I mean your *dog*, Ghost, is it?"

Flame speaks quickly, to be sure she can get it in. "It's nice to meet you, Debbie. Yes, I'm Flame. I'm sorry, I couldn't bring Ghost, he was hurt last night He'll be back with me tomorrow. I'll make sure that you meet him before we have to leave."

She notices a picture on Debbie's desk of two beautiful children. They both have dark hair, and are about thirteen and eleven years of age. She asks Debbie, "Are these your children?"

"Yes, they're my whole world. The oldest is Tessa and the younger one is Kayla. I would love for them to meet you and I'm sure they'd just love meeting Ghost. That would be such a treat for them. I don't get to spend enough time with them as it is. I'm a single mom and it's hard at times." Debbie smiles, and reaches for the intercom button, but before she can push it Joe comes through the office door.

"Flame! I'm glad you finally got away from Shay!" He laughs and continues in a more somber tone, "I'm so sorry, little sister, that I wasn't with you last night. Thank God that you're all right. I've said a few prayers for Ghost too. He'll be fine, won't he?"

"Yes. Thank you for saying those prayers for Ghost. He means so much to me and it was awful to see him like that. He's doing great though. I just left Doc's and he said that I could bring him home tomorrow." she tells him happily.

"Now, where are you taking me to eat?" She grins, rubs her stomach, and says, "I'm starved!" She really isn't a bit hungry, but she doesn't want her trepidation to show.

"Well, do you think we could talk for a minute first? I want to show you these papers before we go. Then I'll take you to get anything you want to eat! I'm taking the rest of the day off. I thought I'd go back to the carnival with you since Mercedes is coming to get read. Is that all right with you?"

"Sure, that's fine with me. Now, let's see what you have. I must admit, curiosity is killing me." She doesn't want to tell him that she has a bad feeling about this. It could just be everything that has happened since yesterday, but she doesn't think that is it. Something is not right and she cannot figure out what it is.

"All right. Debbie, please set the phones to take messages, then take the rest of the day off. Okay?" he says, as he moves toward his office.

"Sure, Joe, that's great. Thanks! Flame, it's been my pleasure to meet you. I can't wait to meet Ghost. Would it be okay if my girls meet him too?" she asks, with a hopeful look at Flame.

"It was great to meet you too, Debbie. I'd love for you all to meet Ghost. I promise that we'll get together before I leave. Ghost loves children and he's very good with them." she says and smiles at Debbie as she walks into Joe's office.

Joe's office is very spacious, with the same soft brown leather furniture as the front office. His desk is very large and made of teak. It is gorgeous. She notices that he also has two beautiful Indian landscapes on the wall. One depicts a buffalo hunt and the other an Indian dance.

"Joe, those paintings are beautiful! Did Shay's father paint them?" she asks immediately.

"You have a good eye, little sister! Yes, he painted them just before he was killed. I was still in law school and rooming with Shay. He gave them to me for a Christmas present. I spent a lot of time with Shay and his parents. I had no family, except Grandfather, and they treated me like their own son. They were good people. So is Shay. I take it you two are getting along pretty well?" he asks, with a sly smile.

She chuckles and tells him, "You're more like Grandfather than I ever would have believed. Yes, he's wonderful. I can't believe we've only known each other since last night. I was planning to have a word with you about setting me up last night, but I have to admit, I changed the word...thank you, Joe."

He cannot help rubbing it in by saying, "I knew you two would hit it off. I only wish the circumstance you were in last night had been different. Now, let's get down to it, sis" He has a serious look now.

"Grandfather's asked me to do this. He wants you to have the forest land. He knows how much you love it and he knows you'll take care of it *and* the wolves. He's leaving it to you. He's also leaving you enough money to take care of the land, two million dollars." He sees that her eyes are filling with tears, but she just looks at him, saying nothing.

"Flame, what's wrong. Surely you suspected this would happen. He loves you. You're truly like a granddaughter to him and like a sister to me. We both love you. I know that we've only just met face to face, but, little sister, you must understand, once you're part of this family, you stay that way. I know you through him and, also, I know of your great gifts *and* your huge heart. I'll always be here for you, and Grandfather will too. Even after he dies, Flame. His spirit will live on in that forest land. Surely you realize that."

Finally, she speaks, "Joe, I know all of that. I just don't even want to consider the idea that anything could ever happen to Grandfather. Oh, Joe...don't you understand? I've never had real family. I just got this family and I can't bear the thought of not having him, or you!" She has to stop at this, as she is so overcome that she cannot continue speaking.

She thinks, *This is what's been bothering me. Grandfather knows this too. He's feeling it. I'm losing him. Something's wrong. Joe doesn't understand! He doesn't realize what Grandfather's doing. He's setting everything up; he knows that he's going away soon. I can't bear this!* She jumps up, running from the room.

Joe follows her, wondering what in the world brought this hysteria on.

She runs into the bathroom with Joe right behind her. She slams the door in his face and he hits his open hand against the door, his worry for her palatable.

He shouts, "Flame, please calm down! Everything's all right! Grandfather only wants to make sure that the people and the land he loves is taken care of. He's only doing what he thinks is best…for you, *and* for the land." He listens a moment, but hears nothing.

He continues after a moment's silence, "You know I don't want the land. I would have taken care of it for him, but he knows that I wouldn't live there. He's left me so much. Flame, please understand, I don't want it." He tells her all this hoping that she will believe him. He feels terrible, and he *is* telling her the truth.

The land should belong to her. She is its next keeper because she has the gift. From the first, he knew it would be hers. It has been handed down by his ancestors for many generations. His father would have been next in line, but he had carried the gift. Joe doesn't. It belongs to those with the gift.

Flame cries herself dry. She knows all he says is true. It's just the shock of hearing it. She has never imagined anything happening to Grandfather, but Joe is right, he is only doing what Grandfather wants him to do.

She finally says, "I'm okay, Joe. I'm coming out." And, she does.

He takes her into his arms and holds her tight, and then he brings her to arms length and looks into her eyes. He tells her, "God, Flame, I know a lot's happened to you. You know, I never thought I'd be comfortable seeing anyone else on that land. At first, after you came along, I thought maybe it was all a set up. You know many people want that land. I wondered if Grandfather was making a mistake, but, sis, now I know you.

"You're what's been keeping Grandfather going over the last few years. He told me once, a long time ago, that there was "one out there looking for us", and I thought it was a bunch of hooey. He was right though. You *are* part of us; a part of that land. Please understand *why* he's doing this." he says, looking at her pleadingly.

"I do, Joe. I know he's doing what he thinks is best. I love him so much.

You too. I've never had to deal with all these emotions before. I don't think I can bear losing him! He's so special and he's taught me so much, but I'll do as he wants. Let's go back into your office now. I need to sit down." She gives him a watery smile and they walk back into his office together.

When they are both seated once more, she tells him, "Okay, Joe. I'll do as Grandfather wishes, but you know that you're always welcome there. We'll always be a family."

"Yes, I do know that. Now, there are some points here we need to go over. First of all, the land will be yours when Grandfather passes on. The money too.

"He's already opened an account in your name, here in Munson. He has also already put five hundred thousand dollars into it. That money's yours now. It doesn't come out of the two million. It's purely a gift to you."

Flame opens her mouth to speak, but Joe puts up his hand to stop her, and continues, "Now...he's left everything else to me. He left me a lot, sis. I'll never spend it all, it's so much. There's more coming in every day from the oil wells. I'll be fine. So will my family, one day.

"There's one stipulation, even if we both marry. If anything happens to me everything goes to you, even if I'm married. My wife would, of course, get a small amount to take care of her, quite well, I might add. If I have kids, then my inheritance would become theirs once they're twenty-one years of age, with you as executor of the estate. The same goes for you.

"If something should happen to you, I'll get your inheritance. It works the same way for both of us and our separate families. If, for some reason, anything should happen to both of us, everything will go to our next of kin. If neither of us is married, then the land, the oil wells, and the money, will go to the Sioux Indian Tribal Unification Institute.

"Now, do you understand all that I've told you?" Joe asks, as he finishes up.

Though she is taken aback, she nods. She had no idea that Grandfather was so well off. She is slightly dazed by this.

He asks her to read the Will over and make sure she understands everything he has said.

She does, and nods to him.

He folds the paper, puts into his jacket pocket, and says, "Okay, sis, we're almost done. The bank that holds your account's on the first floor here. We'll stop in there and get your checkbook. While we're there we'll get this signed and notarized. Then you're all set and we can go eat. Deal?"

"Deal. Let's go."

CHAPTER 12

Shay stops off at the nearest hardware store and buys a deadbolt. He knows if anyone really wants to break into Flame's trailer they will. No lock of any kind will keep them out. He is glad Ghost will be back tomorrow. He will do his best to take her back to his apartment again tonight. He couldn't get a wink of sleep if she was in that trailer alone, gun or not.

When he arrives at the trailer he notices the door is open. He jumps out of his car, running toward the trailer. Just as he gets to the door Frankie pops out of it with a big grin on his face.

"Well, hello again, big boy! Didn't mean to make you jump! Seems like I keep doin that to you!" Frankie gives a big laugh and adds, "Where's my girl?"

"Hi, Frankie. Yes, you *do* seem to get me every time. She's at Joe's office. He'll bring her back here in awhile. I just want to put this lock on her door and try to clean the place up a bit for her. I don't want her seeing this place until all that blood's gone."

"You're a good man, Shay. I knew right aways that I'd like you. That girl gonna keep you awhile?"

Shay grins and shrugs.

"I bet she does. She's a smart little gal. I got a feelin that she won't be hangin round here much anymore. I'm pretty good at predictin' things too, ya know. She thinks she's the only one can do that, but I do good at it too. I sure will miss those two. I love em both a whole hell of a lot. That bad assed Ghost's like a kid." Frankie says, lost in thought for a moment.

Then, he says, "I done cleaned up most of this crap. They sure did bleed, huh? Ghost's really okay, right?"

Shay finally gets to speak, "Yes, you know one of us would've called you otherwise." He winks at Frankie and decides he really likes this guy. He is different, but he has a big heart, just like Flame said. Then he adds, "Frankie, the guy Ghost attacked died, but don't tell Flame. I don't want to add to her distress over all of this."

Frankie says, "No problem. I agree, she don't need no more on her. Damn guy deserved it though.

"Come on in! See what you think. I done real good at gettin' the blood up. I went to Gregori and told him what happened. He came by and fixed that glass in the door. He's pretty good at stuff like that. I like to kid Flame about Gregori, but he's really not all that bad. He just thinks he's somethin else, and damn if he's not." Frankie grins.

Shay thinks, *That's a predatory grin if I ever saw one!* But, still, he likes this guy. The trailer does look really good. There are a few stains in the carpet, but overall Frankie has done a great job and he tells him so. "Frankie, you did great. I was worried that I wouldn't have time to get it all done before Flame gets back here. Thank you very much. She was so upset over Ghost, who, by the way, can come home tomorrow." He shakes Frankie's hand.

"Well, hell. I'd do 'bout anything for that girl. I'm so glad Ghost's okay too. I'd best be goin. I gotta get a few things done myself. Shay, you take care of my girl. Tell her that I'll be stoppin by the booth later."

"Will do, Frankie, and thanks. You're a good guy. I think we'll get along just fine. But, do me one favor, okay?"

Frankie stops walking, turns to him, and asks, "What's that?"

"Keep Gregori real busy for me, okay?"

Frankie gives a barrel laugh, rolls his eyes, and exclaims, "Damn straight!"

Joe and Flame are seated in the front booth of the local Italian restaurant eating a huge plate of pasta each.

She says, "This is great. I'm so glad we were finally able to get together. I see so much of Grandfather in you. You're a good man, Joe."

"I'm glad too, Flame. I've thought about you often. I'm so glad that you and Grandfather have gotten so close. He missed my parents so much. Dad was like you and Grandfather. He was *so* gifted. Grandfather tells me stories about him a lot." he tells her.

She says, "Yes, I've heard quite a few stories about you both. He loved your mother too. I'm so sorry that you both lost them. It's so sad that you and Shay, both, have lost your parents. I wish I'd gotten the chance to meet them all. I think you and Shay are very much alike also."

"Shay's a great friend. He's a good cop too. I wish he'd finished law school, because he'd have been a great lawyer. He keeps saying that one of these days, when he settles down a bit, he'll think about returning to school. I pray that he does. He's good, Flame. He has great instincts."

"Joe, you know that Shay has a gift, don't you?" she asks, catching onto the meaning of his statement.

"Well, yeah, I guess I do. I've thought so ever since I met him. I've never mentioned it to him because he doesn't understand it. He has no idea. Most people who're gifted don't know it, from what I've learned. I only picked up on it because I've been around Grandfather, my dad, and now you. I can see it."

"I noticed it last night. I think he has the gift of precognition. He seems to know what's happening just before it happens, but, you're right, he doesn't know. I don't know if he'd even believe us if we told him." she says, as she takes the last bite of her pasta.

"I'm stuffed! How about you? Dessert?" he asks.

"Lord no! I'm stuffed too. I really didn't think I was hungry," She looks down at her empty plate, shrugs, and admits, "but, I guess I was hungrier than I thought!" She laughs, giving him that beautiful smile.

"Looks like you were pretty much running on empty there, little sister!"

"Oh, my gosh! Look what time it is, Joe! It's already 11:30 and I haven't even changed yet! I have to get my booth open! Mercedes will be there at noon and Shay's waiting at my trailer!" She jumps up, grabbing her purse and his arm.

When they climb into Joe's truck, Flame remembers what Shay had told her about the truck. She realizes he has taken great care of it and she tells him, "Joe, this is a great truck. Shay tells me that you've had it since high school, that it was a gift from Grandfather, right?"

He grins and says, "Yes, I think I'm going to retire it soon though. I'm looking into a family car."

"Joe! *Really*?! Have you talked to Mercedes about it?" she asks, giving him that big beautiful smile with her whole face lighting up.

"Well, yes. I wasn't supposed to tell you, so don't tell Mercedes. I asked her last night, just before we met you and Shay at the restaurant. She said yes! We've been dating for about six months now, and Flame, I really do love her and she loves me. I know she comes from a whole different world than ours, but she's a great person and I think we really do have a future. I just hope her father agrees with us." he adds, with a slight frown.

After meeting S.R. Holst, she completely understands what he means. He would not be an easy man to deal with and she tells him so. "I do understand, Joe. I met her father today. He was at Doc's when I stopped by to see Ghost. I have to admit, I didn't take to him very well. He seemed a bit...stuffy? I guess that's the word I'm looking for."

"Yes, he is. I've never understood why he even let Mercedes go out with me. He's made it no secret that he doesn't care for people of a different race. Truthfully, he's a bigot. He's bought up a lot of land for cheap prices and then made bundles on it. Most of it belonged to Indians. He treats them like they have no rights and no need for the money. I don't like it and I don't much care for him.

"When I first met Mercedes, I didn't know who her father was. I have to admit, once I found out, I was hesitant about seeing her again." he says and smiles, remembering. "But, if you get to know Mercedes, you'll see that once she has her mind made up, well...there's no changing it. She's like her father in that respect.

"I think she only wanted to see me in the first place to make him notice her. Then it changed for her and, I admit, me too. She's wonderful, Flame. She only wants his love and attention but has never gotten it.

"Her mother died when she was ten years old and he pushed her off to boarding schools and nannies. He's a real hard man. I hope he doesn't give her a hard time about us getting married. I don't need or want his money and neither does she." He frowns, looking determined.

"I understand, but if Mercedes loves you as much as you love her, you'll be fine. Trust her to take care of her father, Joe. I'll know more about her feelings after today though." She grins at him and says, "Really, have faith. If it's supposed to be, it will. I'm so happy for you. I know Grandfather will be too. When is this going to happen? I want to be here!"

"That's something I've wanted to talk to you about. We decided that we want to do it as soon as possible. Like, next week." he says, glancing over and laughing at her wide eyed stare.

He adds, "I'm calling Grandfather tonight. I'm going to ask Shay to be my best man and I believe Mercedes wants you to be her maid of honor, but don't you dare tell her that I told you! She'll divorce me before we even get married, if you do! Next Saturday is the day we want to do it. Will you stay a little while longer, sis?" He gives her a pleading look.

She giggles and tells him, "Joe, you're a mess! Yes, I'll stay. I have to admit, I was thinking of staying a while anyway." She looks away, with a small smile playing on her face. She cannot wait to tell Shay. He will be happy, she knows.

"Yep. I knew it! You can't hide from me, sis! You and Shay are getting along great. I was hoping for that. Please, give him a chance." Joe begs her.

She heaves a great sigh, turning to look at him, and admitting, "I know he's wonderful. I've just never dated before and I don't want to scare him to death. I'll try to take it slow. Besides, I also want to see Grandfather. I'm so glad to get all this worry about leaving taken care of. I've been debating with myself over it since last night. I'd really like to spend a week with him in the forest, too, since I'm already staying awhile. I can always catch up to the carnival when I'm ready."

Chapter 13

When they arrive at the trailer Flame jumps out, rushing to get inside She opens the door, invites Joe in, and finds Shay sitting at the small bar with a cup of coffee, two corndogs, and a large, powdered sugar covered funnel cake in front of him.

He looks up, grins at her, and says, "Hello you two! I hope you both had a great lunch. Frankie made sure I had my grease for the week! Lord, Flame, that guy's strange, but I really like him."

She gives a great laugh and tells him, "I hope you're real hungry and that you're cholesterol isn't too high. Shoot, if it's not now, it soon will be! I'm glad Frankie brought you something because I forgot to tell you that my cupboards are bare!"

"Who is this Frankie?" Joe looks at them both, in confusion.

They just look at one another and grin.

Joe says, "Never mind, I guess I'll find out sooner or later."

Flame tells them quickly, "Boys, ya'll gotta go now. If you haven't noticed I don't have anywhere to dress, privately, with you two in here. You can go to my booth, open the locks, and get the thing opened for me though, if you don't mind. Shay, here's the key to the locks. I'll see you two in a few minutes."

Shay takes the key and hands her back the keys to her trailer. Then he tells her, "Here you go, honey, that's your door key and the new key is to the deadbolt I put on. Please use it. Frankie had this place all cleaned up before I got here. I only had to put in the deadbolt. Oh, and Gregori put the new glass in your door."

He gives her a sheepish grin and admits, "Though I still don't know about that guy… Gregori, I mean."

She laughs and he shakes his head from side to side.

Joe is looking between the two of them like they are talking a different language.

Frankie has done a good job, thankfully. This is just like him too. He's the only person that she has ever given a key to, until today.

He must have talked Gregori into helping. She owes Frankie a huge hug.

He is so good to her. Also, he is the first real friend that she has ever had. Gregori did a great job too and she will be sure to tell him so later. She will even let Shay go with her.

She tells Shay, "Thank you, and I'll be sure to thank Frankie and Gregori in a bit. Go on you two! Get!"

She shoos them out the door and then reaches into her purse to take out her copy of the Will that Joe had notarized for her at the bank. She places her new checkbook and the Will together, and then puts them both into a small lockbox that she keeps under her bed. The other lockbox is still at the police station.

Shay and Joe laugh all the way out the door.

On their way to the front gate of the carnival Joe asks Shay, with a huge grin, "So, you and my little sister are getting along well I take it?"

Shay punches him lightly on the shoulder, grins, and says, "Knock it off, Joe! You know damn well that we're doing great. I admit, I have to thank you for asking me to come last night. Honestly, I was going to tell you no, but I had this feeling that I should come.

"I think I was just curious to begin with, because I've heard you talk about her so much. I sure didn't expect it to be like this though and I don't think she did either. I can't believe I found the perfect woman...*on a blind date*!"

Joe grins, but doesn't say anything. Not that Shay would have noticed if he had, with that dazed look on his face.

He's a goner, for sure. Joe thinks, still grinning from ear to ear.

Shay smiles brightly, thinking of Flame. "She's really something. I thought it was load of hogwash...you know, the *gift* thing that you always talk about?"

Joe stops walking, turns to Shay, chuckles, and asks, "You mean she actually made a believer out of you? What did she do...tell your fortune?" He can't help it, he chuckles again.

"No…she did even better than that. She healed that wolf, right in front of me. Then, while we were driving to see her wolf this morning, she told me everything that was happening at Doc Butler's *before* we got there and she was right! It was the damnedest thing I ever saw!"

Joe is shocked. He cannot believe she has shown him so much. She is a very reserved, untrusting little lady. This does not sound like the Flame he has heard Grandfather talk so much about, or even the one he has known from their calls.

Wow, this is even better than I thought! Joe thinks, but says aloud, "Damn, Shay! You sure are doing something right. I know I don't have to tell you this, but I'm going to anyway. You know that you're my best friend, and I trust you with my life, but I have to trust you with my family now. Please don't hurt her."

He holds up a hand to stop Shay from saying anything, and continues, "Grandfather told me about her childhood and it's not pretty. I don't want to have to hurt you if you mess this up. I'm honestly shocked that she trusted you with all that information. She's never even talked about that with me. Grandfather is the only one she has ever opened up to. Until now."

Shay's very pleased with that tidbit of information and he gives Joe a reassuring smile, saying, "Don't worry, Joe, I won't hurt her. I think I'd kill anyone who did. I'm even taking her back to my apartment tonight, if she'll agree. And, don't look at me like that. I've only kissed her a couple of times." He grins, thinking about it.

Then he says, "She stayed in the spare room and she's going to do the same tonight. I don't want anything to happen to her. Ghost will be back tomorrow, so until then she's staying at my apartment where I know she's safe."

They continue walking. They didn't think to ask her where her booth was located, so Shay, seeing Frankie, asks him where it is.

Frankie walks with them, to the booth, then turns to look critically at Joe. He looks him up and down and then exclaims, "Well, this has to be my girl's big brother! I have to say, you don't look much alike!" He laughs and holds out his hand. "I'm Frankie. You wouldn't happen to be gay would you?"

Joe has that wide eyed, run like a rabbit look, but he shakes Frankie's hand. He reddens as he says, "Nice to meet you, Frankie. No, I'm *not* gay. Little sister and my best friend here should have warned me about you though!" Then, he grins at Frankie.

"Well, hell. Just my luck. Cain't find no good looking gay guys anywhere round here!"

Joe looks a bit uncomfortable with this conversation, but Shay and Frankie have a good laugh at his expense.

Joe ends up with a sheepish grin, and says, "I do want to thank you, Frankie. Shay told us that you cleaned Flame's trailer for her. I'm glad that she's made such a good friend. Grandfather and I worry about her."

"Don't you be worrying about my girl. Between Ghost and me, we keep her safe as possible. I've acted like a jealous boyfriend lots of times! Here's her booth, fellas. I'll be round here, don't worry." Frankie grins, turning to go back to his stand.

"So, *that's* Frankie? Damn, Shay, you could've warned me!" Joe says as they both turn to watch Frankie make his way to his own booth.

Shay laughs watching Frankie wiggle down the fairway. He tells him, "Nope, you had to see that guy for yourself. I don't think anything that I could have told you would have done Frankie justice."

"Yeah, you're right on that one!"

When Flame gets to her booth she gets a whistle from Joe and a large sunny grin from Shay. She looks the part of a fortune teller. She has on a bright turquoise colored, full, long skirt and a white, puffy sleeved blouse that is worn over the top of the skirt. It is bound to her waist by a large silver and turquoise belt. She wears several silver and turquoise necklaces, long matching earrings, several bangle bracelets, and rings on every finger. Her hair is worn loose and flowing down her back, past her waist.

"Damn, little sister, you sure look the part! I can see why Ghost sits here with you. Somebody has to keep the men off you!" Joe looks her over, smiling.

Shay is flabbergasted. He thinks she is the most gorgeous woman he has ever seen. He didn't think it was possible for her to look better every time he sees her, but she just proved him wrong again.

When he finds his tongue, he says, "Flame, you're something else. I'm glad I'm off work today...cause I'm not letting you out of my sight! Does Frankie have an extra chair down at his stand? If he doesn't I'm going to have to get one from your trailer, cause I'm going to sit right here and beat the guys off of you myself!"

She gives them both her huge, straight from the heart, smile. She feels herself blushing under Shay's scrutiny. She has taken a little extra time while getting ready today hoping for a good reception, but she didn't expect it to be this good."Thank you. Both of you. I never have to worry about the men, or rather, never before now. Ghost smiles quite frighteningly when anyone gets too close.

"Shay, you really don't have to stay. I'll be fine. I know you have more to do than to sit here being my bodyguard." she says, secretly hoping he will, but she doesn't want to push him.

"Honey, I'm not leaving your side. There's nothing more important to me than keeping you safe. Besides, it'll give me a chance to watch and learn." He doesn't want to leave her. Nobody has ever made him feel so protective. He is truly besotted. He knows that Joe is going to give him a really hard time, but he could care less.

Joe speaks, breaking the uncomfortable silence, "It's time for Mercedes. I'm going to hang around long enough to see her and get her reaction to your reading." He sits on the edge of the small table that she uses for customers.

The table is covered with a red tablecloth and a crystal ball sits in the middle of it, but it's just for looks. There is a stool on the front side of the table. Flame sits on the back side of the table in her padded, folding chair.

Shay looks around the booth and sees another stool in the corner. He pulls it out, places it a few feet away from Flame and Joe, and says, "This will be my new body part for today." He laughs and adds, "I'm going to have to have help getting it off me later though. I think I'll be stuck to it before the night's out."

Flame grins and tells him, "Go on down to Frankie's stand and tell him to give you my extra chair. It's just like this one I'm sitting in. It'll be much more comfortable. I tried using one of those stools a few times and it just about killed my rear end! I bought two of these, and he keeps the extra one in the storage compartment of his booth."

She waits until he is halfway down the midway before she asks Joe, "Are you and Mercedes going to tell Shay today, or do you want me to wait to before saying anything about the wedding?"

"I'm going to tell him today. I want to ask him to be my best man, but I don't want Mercedes to know I've told you. I thought you'd be better at acting surprised, because Shay's feelings can always be seen on his face. She'll know right away that I told you guys. Let her surprise him. He'll be all over the place, since it means that you'll be staying here for a bit." Joe grins and winks at her.

He can see that something special is happening between the two of them, and he is so proud of himself for fixing them up. He knew it was a good idea, even if they both got mad at him last night. It was worth it.

Shay comes back with the chair and a sheepish look on his face.

Flame raises one brow at him, wondering what Frankie has done now.

Shay admits, "That crazy man wouldn't stop laughing at me. He said that I was better than Ghost as a bodyguard since I carry a gun."

Joe and Flame look from Shay to each other, and crack up.

Flame tells him honestly, "I think he likes you, Shay. I've got to find him a boyfriend." She turns to Joe and asks, "Do you know any gay men, Joe? You're so good at fixing people up, maybe you can be on the lookout for one for Frankie."

He just laughs and says, "I can't think of one right off hand, but I'll keep an eye out for one. Mercedes has some really strange friends maybe she can help."

They all laugh and Joe points out, "Here she comes now."

Mercedes is walking down the midway.

Flame thinks Mercedes looks like she is glowing. Her eyes light up when she sees Joe. She can see, even without reading her, that she really loves Joe. She cannot wait to read her though, just to see if she is serious about this marriage. Flame loves Joe and only wants him to be happy.

Mercedes greets them all with a huge hug and an enthusiastic smile. "Hi you guys! I can't believe you're all here to see me! Or, is it that you're all here to hear what Flame has to say?" she says, and laughs jokingly.

Joe kisses her and says, "Hi, babe. Shay was here when Flame and I got back from lunch. He's off today and is standing in for Ghost." Joe winks at Flame and adds, "I just thought I'd hang around to see you. You know I can't pass up any opportunity to do that!"

"I'm so glad you did. Can we tell them now? I'm about to burst! I want to yell it to the whole world!" She is actually hopping from foot to foot in excitement.

Flame likes her even more for it, thinking she is like a kid getting a present. She is obviously very excited.

"Sure, babe, you tell them." Joe says, grinning, but he holds up her left hand for them all to see.

The ring is beautiful and the stone huge. The diamond is at least two carats, set in gold, with a smaller diamond on each side.

Mercedes has a huge smile on her face as she asks Flame and Shay, "Want to come to a wedding, you two?" She continues on too fast for either of them to comment on the ring, or the wedding, "Flame, I need a maid of honor!"

Joe adds, "And, Shay, will you be my best man?"

Shay grins from ear to ear, and says, "Hey! That's great you two! Sure, Joe, I'd be honored to! When's this wedding?" He is truly happy for them. He knows them both well enough to know that they truly are in love.

"Next Saturday! I'm calling Grandfather tonight. I want him to be here and Mercedes and I are only inviting a few friends; Grandfather, her father, and about ten of our friends. It'll be a small wedding." He looks at Mercedes and leans over to give her a chaste kiss.

"But, Flame, I thought you were leaving this coming week? Are you going to be able to stay awhile?" Shay immediately asks her, hoping for the answer he's looking for. He desperately wants her to stay. He cannot stand thinking that they only have a few more days together. He knows he will never get enough of her.

"Oh, Joe...I can't stand it; I have to tell the truth. You know me...I'm not good at secrets!" Flame grins at Joe, hoping he won't be mad at her for telling the truth.

She says, "Mercedes, Joe's already told me about it. He's just as excited as you are and couldn't help himself. He told me over lunch. I'm so happy for you both. I told Joe that I'd stay." She glances at Shay, blushes, and adds, "Actually, I'd already been thinking of staying awhile longer anyway. I want to spend some time with Grandfather too. I thought I'd take a few weeks off." She is hoping that Shay will be happy about her decision.

Shay is so relieved. He has really been getting depressed thinking that she is leaving soon. He grins and exclaims, "I don't know who to kiss first! Joe and Mercedes, I am so happy for both of you, but I think I'll give Flame that kiss."

He does, wrapping his arms around her, he holds her close, looks into her eyes, and continues, saying, "I am so, so, happy that you're staying. I was beginning to think that I was going to have to kidnap you and I wasn't sure that Ghost would like that too much." He chuckles.

It is just the reaction that she was hoping for. She gives him that very large, very sunny smile, and says, "I think Ghost would understand. Thank God that he's coming home tonight. He really has to get to know you better."

Joe had told Mercedes this morning about the incident at Flame's trailer. She says, "Flame, I'm so sorry about your trouble last night. I wanted to meet Ghost so badly. I will have to stop over here tomorrow and meet him. I'll bet he's gorgeous and, besides, I've never met a wolf before."

Then she grins and adds, "Also, we need to look at some dresses! I have a book I'll bring with me. Do you think Ghost could be our flower wolf?" Mercedes grins at them all now.

They all get a chuckle out of this and Flame tells her, "I'm sure he would be honored. He can wear a headpiece of flowers around his head. I hope it doesn't embarrass him though!" Picturing that, she burst into laughter, asking, "Can't you just imagine it?!"

The others join her, laughing, all of them imagining a wolf with a flowered headband.

Mercedes tells them, "And we have the most romantic honeymoon planned! We're going off to a small island bungalow. It's all alone on the beach, but we'll have servants to see to our food...if we eat…!" She looks to Joe and blushes, realizing what she has just said.

"Okay, I want to hear this reading *now*!" Joe states, bringing them all back to the moment. He looks at Mercedes and tells her, "You just sit right down in that chair."

They all take their seats and Flame wonders if she should make the guys leave for a few minutes. She doesn't want Mercedes to be uncomfortable when she reads her. She asks, "Mercedes, do you want to do this alone or with the guys looking over our shoulders?"

Without hesitation she answers, "No, they can stay."

Flame nods, glad that Mercedes seems to have nothing to hide. Or maybe she just doesn't believe Flame actually *can* read her, but she is definitely going to read as much from her as she can. She tells her, "Okay...give me your right hand, Mercedes. I won't say anything to you, except perhaps to ask you a question or two, while I read you. I'll tell you what I see after the reading."

Mercedes places her right hand in Flame's.

Flame immediately starts seeing images. Mercedes is either easily read or she is showing only what she wants seen. Most people are harder to read. They keep a block up, but Flame is almost always able to get around it. A few, though, are like Mercedes, with the images and thoughts coming through easily, almost too easily.

CHAPTER 14

Flame sees Mercedes as a child, crying over her mother dying, her father giving her no consolation at all. The images of her mother are very vivid. She looked very much like Mercedes, and died much too young.

Mercedes suspects that her father had something to do with her death. Her mother had committed suicide, slicing her wrists in the bathtub. Her young daughter, a ten year old Mercedes, finds her. Mercedes closes herself off from everyone, but wants so badly to be held by her father, as she is missing her mother desperately.

Next, Flame sees; Mercedes' father sending her to boarding school, alone and terrified. Not even going home for Christmas break, but going instead to her roommate's home, growing closer to a few young friends.

Only one friend has stayed faithful, still being very close to her, living here in Munson, but married now and with children. Since that friend has married, Mercedes has not had anyone close to her, getting to know her, doing things with her, until this year, with Joe.

Now Flame sees Joe. He is portrayed in Mercedes' mind as if he is a prince. She loves him deeply, growing closer and closer to him. She sees Mercedes' father, at first against the relationship. She sees him yelling at Mercedes, telling her that he will not allow her to date an Indian.

Mercedes, for the first time showing her anger to her father. Telling him that she will see Joe no matter what his feelings are. She sees her throwing and breaking things all over the house, very unlike anything she has ever done before.

The house is tremendous, a mansion. She sees Mercedes tell her father that the money he goes through like candy had all belonged to her mother. Then blaming him for her death, and finally telling him that the house is in her name. Mercedes' mother had left it to her. It had been placed in her name by her mother's lawyer when she was twenty-one years old, and now...Mercedes threatening to throw him out.

She sees Mercedes' father telling her to date Joe, that he doesn't give a damn. She sees him stomp out of the house, yelling for Sadie to come with him and Mercedes thinking that he gives the dog more love, more attention, than she has ever gotten from him.

Now Flame sees Joe, in Mercedes' mind, asking her to marry him, and her happily agreeing. She sees the love that Mercedes has for Joe. He has held her, loved her, and she has given him her heart. She loves him more than life itself.

She sees Mercedes imagining their children, hers and Joe's, and living in the mansion. She plans to ask her father to move out after the wedding to Joe.

Flame sees Mercedes, telling her father about the marriage this morning and then sees his reaction to the news. Mercedes bracing herself to face his wrath. His face turns red, his eyes and mouth look harsh, but then, he surprises her by smiling, and telling her that he is very happy for her. Mercedes feels great relief, thinking that he will object to the marriage.

Flame recognizes what Mercedes' doesn't. Mercedes' father is furious. He is saying what she wants to hear, but it is all an act. He does not like the idea of the marriage at all, but for some reason he is lying, hiding his true feelings. He has the same tight, fake smile on his face that Flame has seen herself, this morning, at Doc's.

She wonders why he is lying, thinking it could be because of the house. Maybe he doesn't want Mercedes to make him leave the house, but she feels there is more to it than that. Something else is causing Mercedes' father to agree to this wedding, because she knows, he has not changed his feelings toward Joe.

She gets a sense that Mercedes has her own darkness inside. Something is causing a blank area in her memory. She is either blocking something, or there is something that she actually doesn't remember happening.

She has read Mercedes' past, but wants to see some of the future. Usually she doesn't do this. She cannot really *see* the future, but she can feel if there is going to be happiness, danger, or even death coming to the person she reads. Usually it's oncoming grief that she feels through others, but sometimes she gets flashes of things to come. The future can always be altered though. Fate is fickle.

She closes off all sense of what is around her, going deeper into Mercedes' mind. Feeling what Mercedes is feeling. She feels great joy, anticipation, and a longing for her dreams to be fulfilled. She also feels danger. Something is going to happen that will place her, or someone she loves, in terrible danger.

She feels a sense of grief, anger, violence, and determination. Something is going to happen that will turn Mercedes' world up-side down, but she also sees happiness and a house full of children. She doesn't see how many, or if they are girls or boys, she only has the sense of fulfillment; children, a loving family, and security. A sense of Mercedes' life dream being fulfilled, but she must come through the darkness first.

She pulls herself back into her own body and opens her eyes, looking first at Shay, then at Mercedes. She smiles reassuringly, squeezing, and releasing Mercedes' hand. She tells her, "Mercedes, I'm so sorry about your mother. You know that you look very much like her, don't you?"

Mercedes' eyes widen at this statement. She had no idea that Flame would be able to *see* her thoughts. Then she smiles and tells her, "Yes, I know. My father likes to tell me that, especially when he's angry. For some reason he's still mad at my mother.

"At first, I thought it was because she committed suicide. That he blamed her for leaving us too soon, but over the last few years I've begun to think it's because she left me the house. I don't know why he's so angry at her, but I think I must remind him of her so much that he takes it out on me." A forlorn look briefly passes across her face.

Joe looks surprised at this revelation. He tells her, "Honey, I'm so sorry that man has caused you so much grief. I didn't know the house is yours. Are you planning for us to live there with your father?" He doesn't look very happy with the idea.

"No, don't worry, Joe. I haven't told you before because there was no reason to. I love the house because it was my mother's gift to me. I plan on asking my father to move out after the wedding.

"I'd honestly had planned on surprising him. I don't want to just throw him out. I want to find a condo for him. I'm planning on buying it and then giving it to him as a surprise. I don't want him to think that I would just ask him to move out with nowhere to go. I was planning to talk with you about it tonight. So, what do you think?" she asks, the worry still in her eyes.

Flame and Shay are obviously uncomfortable with the conversation. They feel as if they are intruding.

Joe just looks at Mercedes and smiles. Then he turns to Flame and Shay, accurately reading their expressions, and says, "Sorry, you two. We didn't mean to make you uncomfortable. I wouldn't normally talk about these things in front of anyone, but you two are family." Then he turns back to Mercedes, smiles, and tells her, "Honey, we can do whatever makes you happy. That's all I want, for you to be happy.

"But, I must admit, I wasn't prepared for this. I've never considered living in that house. Don't get me wrong, it's beautiful, but it's so…*large.* I hope this means we will have enough kids to fill it up!" He wiggles his eyebrows and grins.

Then he places his hand on her shoulder and tells her honestly, "Honey, I'll be glad to help you look for a condo for your dad. I'm afraid that he won't like the idea of giving up his home very much though"

She nods, then looks at Flame and says, "Okay, now…what else did you see? Do you know how many kids we'll have?" She grins, the light back in her eyes, and exclaims, "I hope it's ten! That should help to fill the house!" She laughs and cuts her eyes to Joe.

Flame grins and admits, "I don't really know, but I did see that you'll have quite a few of them. I know that you're very happy. I can sense that your dreams will be fulfilled, eventually.

"Also, and I don't want you to worry, but I think you should know this to help you to be more careful and to keep your eyes open for it...I *do* see that there will be something in your near future that will cause you grief. I'm sorry that I can't tell you what it is, or even who it's concerning. I only know that I see pain and danger to you or to someone you love. I'm sorry I can't tell you more.

"I do see that Joe makes you happy and that's very promising. I'll try to read you again after you two get back from your honeymoon. Maybe I'll be able to tell you more then. Your excitement for your wedding may be clouding the future, or what I can feel, so we'll try again after you're an old married couple." She smiles brightly, hoping to take Mercedes' mind off of the warning, or to at least lighten the mood.

Mercedes' face has taken on a haunted look. Joe, too, looks worried.

Flame looks at Shay, seeing that he is taking all of this in, that he obviously believes her warning is the truth and that she is honestly worried for Mercedes.

Mercedes looks at Joe with a worried, frightened look on her face. They have all taken the warning seriously. She turns to Flame again and asks, "Do you see anything that will help me watch for it? I mean, do you see if it's my father, or is it Joe, or myself?"

Flame wants to reassure her that everything will be fine, but she cannot. She knows that something will happen to Mercedes that will alter the rest of her life and she tells her honestly, "No. I can only tell you that whatever it is, it will change your life forever. I don't want to scare you, not now, when you're so happy. I wouldn't have said anything at all, but I want you to be careful. Watch those around you and listen too. Keep your eyes open for anything that doesn't sound or look right. I'm sorry I've spoiled your happiness. I feel like a real jerk." She lowers her eyes, a rush of sadness enveloping her.

"No, *never*! You're the best and we're going to be great friends. I love you already! Please don't feel bad about telling me. I'm so glad you did so I can be prepared to stop it, if I can. I'll do as you tell me too. Please, Flame, don't be upset, I'm okay. Don't feel bad for me. I'm happy and nothing can take that away from me. Okay?" she tells Flame, taking her hands and reassuring her.

Flame feels terrible. First she has doubts about Mercedes, wanting to read her just so she can see if she really loves Joe. Then reminding her of the worst thing that has ever happened to her; her mother dying, and then telling her that something bad will happen, but not knowing what it means or who it would happen to.

She, also, cannot believe that she has doubted and hurt this young woman. She wants Mercedes to be happy. She deserves it. She has had a very hard, sad life. Having money does not mean that happiness or love is guaranteed. She looks Mercedes in the eyes and tells her, "I'm so sorry. If I can do anything to help, please, just let me know. I feel like I've ruined this for you. I want to see you happy again, not so sad and worried."

"Flame, honey, you did the right thing. She can be watching for it now and you've helped her to be more careful. You know Mercedes needed to be warned. That's better than letting something slap her in the face when she least expects it." Shay says, pulling her up out of her seat and hugging her to him.

Joe, too, reassures Flame that she did the right thing.

Then, they get to their feet and Mercedes tells her, "I'll be by tomorrow to meet Ghost and look at those dresses. Please, stop worrying. I'll be fine. Nothing can spoil this for me."

They leave arm in arm after reassuring Flame repeatedly that everything will work out, but she still feels like a heel for upsetting Mercedes, and doubting her in the first place. She realizes that her distrust in people can hurt them almost as much as she has been hurt herself, in the past. She is determined to try to change that in herself.

The rest of the day goes by quickly. Flame and Shay laugh, talk, and enjoy each other's company in between readings. They close the booth a bit early because she wants to get ready for their dinner together and she is very anxious to see Ghost again. They walk to her trailer hand in hand.

CHAPTER 15

Flame is happy to see Ghost. He is feeling much better and whines terribly when it's time for her to leave him. She tells him that she will be back the next morning to pick him up, that he is coming home with her then. He finally lies back down, trusting her to keep her word.

Shay has convinced her to stay the night at his apartment again. She is actually relieved to do so. She doesn't like the idea of going home to an empty trailer. Besides, she wants this time alone with him. She knows they have something very special and hopes to show him how she feels tonight.

They have had a wonderful evening. Dinner together had been great, though she couldn't even remember what she had eaten; she was so tied up in him. She cannot seem to concentrate on *anything*, but him. It is no different for him, as he cannot seem to get enough of looking at her, touching her.

They are on their way back to his apartment now. She has butterflies fluttering all throughout her stomach and cannot stop looking at him. She is so excited, but not really nervous, as she had expected to be. She trusts this man and knows that she will give herself to him tonight, heart, body, and soul. She knows it's right, that they are right together.

He feels her watching him and knows that he would be looking at her, also, if he didn't have to keep his eyes on the road. They don't need words; they are comfortable in the silence. He wants her so much, but he is afraid it will scare her off if he lets her know how much. He wants to make love to her all night long. He is going to take it slow with her, if he can. He has doubts, not knowing that if once he touches her, he *can* take it slow.

Once they reach his building, he takes her small bag out of the back of his van and they walk, hand and hand, through the building and to his apartment's door. They enter, never speaking, and once inside he sets the bag down. They turn to one another immediately, embracing, holding on for dear life. They kiss, and when they come apart they can only look into each other's eyes. He finally reaches down, picks her up, and carries her to his bedroom.

He sits her on his bed and whispers to her, "Are you sure?"

"Oh, yes, I've never been more sure of anything in my life."

He sits beside her, once more taking her in his arms. She fits so perfectly.

He thinks, *Lord, I love this woman. It's so early to feel that, I know, but I do. I love her so much. She's perfect. I never want her to leave and I'll do everything in my power to keep her with me. Forever.* But, he knows he must take it slow with her.

She has never been with a man before, he knows that. She is so innocent, in so many ways, yet so knowledgeable in others. He wants her to enjoy every moment of this.

She is tied in knots, wanting so badly to please him, but having no idea what to do. She thinks, *I want to be your everything, Shay. I want you so much. I* love *you so much.* She wants to tell him all of this, but her mind doesn't seem to be connected to her mouth at the moment.

She reaches up and places a hand on each side of his face, a small caress. Looking into his eyes she finds the words, "Shay, I love you. I know it's so soon to say that and I hope it doesn't scare you off, but I have to tell you, I do. I want to make you happy. Please…make love to me."

He looks into her eyes and says softly, "Oh, Flame...I love you too. I was so afraid to tell you that. Afraid I'd scare *you* off. I know it's fast, for both of us, but, honey, it feels *so* right. *This* feels so right. We were made for one another. You do make me happy. *So* happy." He kisses her again.

He removes her shoes and then he stands, pulling her gently to her feet. He pulls his shirt over his head all the while looking into her eyes. He takes off his shoes, unbuckles his belt, and finishes taking off the rest of his clothes.

He takes her breath away. He is so much more than she had ever imagined. He is gorgeous, with his toned muscled chest and stomach. The curly black hair running down from his navel intrigues and fascinates her. Her hands itch to touch it, to see if it feels as soft as it looks.

She unbuttons her blouse and pulls it off her shoulders. He turns her around, unhooks her bra, and it slides off her arms to the floor. When she turns to face him, his breath catches in his throat.

He thinks, *God, she's beautiful! So beautiful. And, she's mine.*

She unhooks her skirt, letting it slide down her legs and to the floor. Then she melts into him, going pliant, wanting him to hold her. She wraps her arms around his neck and her fingers find his hair. She gives herself to him fully.

He feels like there is no oxygen left in the room. She is unbelievably more beautiful than anyone he has ever known, or ever will. She is a beautiful temptress, a gorgeous innocent. He gasps, and almost whispers, "Flame, you are so very beautiful. I'm the luckiest man in the world."

He takes her in his arms and they tumble to the bed. He traces her body with his fingertip, sending chills up her spine. He loves this woman more than life and he tells her so, with his body.

He loves the way she gives herself so generously. She has no hesitation in touching him, tasting him, with the same urgency he has for her. He loves her again and again.

She has never imagined making love could be this special, almost reverent. There is brief pain at first, but he treats her so gently that it lasts only a moment. She knows that she could never feel this way with anyone else. Only Shay.

He loves her well. She pours her heart into him, gives him everything she has, and more. She knows she'll always want him this way. Forever.

He knows her body as well as his own and touches her in all the right places, as she does him. They are made for one another, fitting together like pieces of a puzzle, becoming one, one heart, one body.

When she reaches climax, he is with her, filling her with an explosion of his own. Their loving is complete, body and soul, they're one. They make love for hours, never tiring, never getting enough of one another.

Finally, she falls asleep wrapped in his arms, snuggled to his side. He is so happy, never knowing such joy. Loving her is the best thing that has ever happened to him. He falls asleep with the thought of telling Joe how appreciative he is for the blind date madness.

They wake early when the alarm goes off to wake Shay for work. He immediately turns it off, telling Flame to go back to sleep. He decides to call in and tell them he will be late. He wants to take her to pick up Ghost and get them settled back in her trailer before he goes in to work.

He calls, telling them that he will be in about two hours late. He figures if he is going to be late that he might as well do it right. He makes coffee, scrambles eggs, fries bacon, and makes toast. He pours her coffee, makes her a plate of breakfast, adds some orange juice, and places it on a tray. Then he takes it into the bedroom and wakes her by saying softly, "Flame, honey, wake up. Breakfast is served."

She opens her eyes, sees his broad smile, with his hands holding the tray and says cheerfully, "Good morning! What's this? Umm...I think I *have* worked up an appetite! Or, should I say, *we* have worked up an appetite?!" She chuckles, blows him a kiss and gives him her sunshine filled smile.

He is so relieved to see that smile as he was worried she might have regrets about last night. He is so happy that she doesn't or at least she doesn't seem to. He answers, "Good morning, honey. I figured you'd be ravenous. I know I am. Here's your plate. I'll just run and get mine and we'll have breakfast in bed. How's that sound to you?"

"It sounds like heaven. We'll eat this breakfast, and then I'll have you take care of my *other* hunger...I hope that's okay with you." She gives him a sensuous smile, looks at her plate, and says, "Umm...Wow, great sex and you can cook too! I think I'm moving in!" She laughs.

He enjoys the sight of her in his bed, with that sun filled smile lighting up her face. He says honestly, "Honey, you can move in today if you want to."

When she just smiles, he adds, "I'm serious. I don't ever want to let you out of my sight. I'm afraid you'll disappear if I do. I would love having you here. I don't know how the neighbors would like Ghost though." He chuckles, but he is very serious.

She doesn't answer right away, so he lets the subject drop as he watches her take a bite of egg.

He asks, "Do you need anything else?"

"Only you." she says with a seductive smile, but adds, "This is great, Shay! Go on, get yours and hurry up and come to bed."

She could tell that he was serious about her moving in. She doesn't know how she feels about that yet. She has barely had time to get used to the idea of loving him and she doesn't know if she is ready to give up the life she has made for herself with the carnival and moving every other week. She has to think about this and talk it over with Grandfather and Ghost first.

He comes to bed with his plate and they eat, glancing at each other frequently. After eating their breakfast, she puts his plate on top of hers then gets up to go wash the dishes.

He gives her a sly grin and takes the tray, placing it on the floor. He pulls her back down onto the bed and they make love again, slowly and beautifully.

Chapter 16

It's time to go get Ghost. Flame is so excited to see him. She has missed him so much and, even though she has seen him everyday, it's like a piece of her has been missing.

Shay is taking her to get Ghost and then back to her trailer. She knows that Shay needs to spend some more time with Ghost too. She will have this afternoon to tell Ghost all about him, but he understands her so well that she knows he will understand her feelings for Shay.

They arrive at Doc's and Ghost is waiting at the front door for her.

Doc comes to the door and tells Flame, "I gave up trying to keep that rotten boy in the fence. Once he learned how to open the gate I couldn't keep him out of here. He stays with me everywhere I go. Not that I mind, he's great company. I swear he understands everything I say.

"That's the smartest animal that I've ever seen in my life, and that's a lot of animals. He was with me this morning while I was with Officer Johnson and his cat. I told John that I'd forgotten my stethoscope in the front room and that crazy damn wolf ran out of the room and came back with my stethoscope! How'd you teach him all this stuff?" he asks.

She laughs and looks at Shay, giving him a knowing little smile, and telling him, "I told you he was smart." Then she turns back to Doc and says, "Doc, I didn't teach him. He's been with me so long that he just learned. I've never treated him as a pet. He's my friend. I guess he just does what he thinks you expect from him."

Doc doesn't look too convinced.

Ghost comes into the room, walks to Flame, and puts his leash in her hand.

Shay laughs and says, "I think he's telling you that he's had enough time away from you."

She smiles down at Ghost and tells him silently, *I told you I'd be here. I've missed you so much. You'll never be separated from me again, if I can help it. I love you, Ghost.*

And, Ghost tells her, in his way, that he loves her more than life.

Flame, Shay, and Ghost, pile into the van after Doc says his goodbyes. He would not take any money for keeping or healing Ghost. He said it was an experience he would never forget and that he would not take anything for it.

Shay doesn't want to go to work, but he must after dropping Flame and Ghost off at her trailer. He cannot stand being without her for even the few hours he has to work. He looks down at the dashboard noticing, for the first time, he is almost out of gas. He shakes his head from side to side and says, "Damn, I've let myself get so wrapped up in you that I've even forgotten to check to see if we have gas. I'd better stop and get some before we end up on the side of the road." He glances over at her and she grins.

He quickly pulls into the nearest convenience store and they both get out.

She tells Ghost to stay in the car and tells Shay, "I'm going in too. I need a cup of coffee. Okay?"

"Sure, honey, but make me one too and I'll pay."

She nods and they walk into the small store together. She goes to make their coffee as he gets in line to pay for it and the gas. She smiles at him and tells him she will be in the van. As she walks out the door, a man coming inside bumps into her.

When they touch she gets flashes of violence and a gun. This man is not in his right mind. He is high on drugs and very dangerous. He will kill for money, if he has to. She inhales quickly, holding her breath until she gets back in the van.

She thinks quickly, *Ohmygosh! He's going to rob the store! I have to warn Shay. Ghost, go to Shay! Stay in the aisles of the store. Don't let the man see you. Go now.*

She slips back out of the van, all the while watching the window of the store. The man, the perpetrator, is in the aisles acting like he is shopping, waiting for some of the people to leave.

There is a pay phone on the side of the store she will use to call 911 while she sends Ghost into the store. She opens the van's back door for Ghost to get out. He slips out, moving low and staying out of sight.

He knows what to do and will follow her directions to the letter He pushes the door to the store open with his body and slides inside. He moves to the back of the store, keeping his eyes on the man. He will protect Shay, just as he would protect Flame, because she has asked him to, and because he knows she loves him.

The man is waiting for his opportunity. The only other people in the store are the clerk, an older man, and Shay. Ghost waits. The old man pays and leaves.

Flame dials 911 and lays the phone down, keeping the line open. She knows they will trace where the call comes from and send the police directly to the store. She cannot wait to tell the operator what is happening because she must keep her eyes on Shay and Ghost.

She watches the old man leave and sees the perp pull his gun out of his jacket. She can wait no longer. Shay must be warned. She uses the only option left to her...she must talk to Shay, telepathically.

She sends, *Shay...don't turn around, keep the clerk busy! There's a man coming up behind you. He has a gun! He's going to rob the store. Ghost is in the store with you. He'll help. Please stay safe!*

As she warns Shay, Ghost is coming up behind the perp.

Shay hears her warning, but he is not prepared for this voice, this surprise. He jumps without even realizing what he's doing. He automatically looks around for her. When he does, the perpetrator runs to him, shoving the gun against his head forcefully.

He yells at the clerk, "DON'T MOVE OR I'LL SHOOT THIS GUY! PUT ALL THAT MONEY IN A BAG MISTER, OR I SWEAR, I'LL SHOOT HIM!"

In a split second Shay realizes what has happened. Flame has tried to warn him. He hopes that Ghost doesn't try anything right now. This guy is wired so tight that the smallest thing could get Shay shot and killed.

Shay tries to stay calm, but tells the perp, "Don't worry mister, you'll get your money."

"*SHUT UP*! I WASN'T TALKIN TO YOU! DO IT! *NOW*!" says the perp, with the gun shaking in his hand. He is so hopped up on drugs he can barely stand still.

The cashier is just a kid and he is shaking like a leaf, but starts filling a plastic store bag with the contents of the cash register. He hands the bag to the perp and quickly ducks down behind the register.

At the same time the perp reaches for the bag, Shay notices that he is looking away from him. He moves his head back and, at the same time, elbows the perp, hard.

Ghost picks just that second to land on the perp's back. He goes down with Ghost on top of him.

Shay reaches in his ankle holster and grabs his gun, swinging it around to aim it at the perp on the ground.

The perp pulls off a shot, unintentionally hitting Shay in the chest.

As Shay goes down he pulls off a shot at the guy. He hits the perp in the hand. Then Ghost is at the perp's throat, holding him tightly, warningly, but not puncturing the skin. This all happens in seconds.

Flame feels the shot to Shay, screams, and runs into the store. Ghost keeps his grip on the screaming perp and she yells, "HOLD HIM, GHOST! IF HE MOVES, *AT ALL*, KILL HIM!

Shay raises his head to look at the perp, making sure that Flame is safe. He weakly tells her, "Ghost makes a great partner..." and he looses consciousness.

Flame is sobbing.

The police pick that moment to rush in with their guns drawn. The young cashier raises up, looks around, and points to the perp Ghost has by the throat.

"My God, that's Larson!"

Flame looks up to see Sergeant Marty Diener hovering over Shay. She shouts, "Sergeant Diener! I need to help him, *please*." She still sobs, wanting to help Shay, but not being able to move. Her knees are so shaky she is afraid she will collapse.

"Somebody call off the dog! We have the guy now. Don't worry, Ms. Flame, the ambulance is on its way. We'll help him, I promise." Sergeant Diener tells her, reaching over her and applying pressure to the wound, thinking it looks real bad. He's lost a lot of blood.

She sits up, calling Ghost to her. She knows that she has to pull herself together to help Shay. She grabs Ghost in a huge hug and finds his strength. He is filling her with his only way of helping her, his love. She calms and releases him.

She tells him silently, *Good boy, Ghost. You did well. I have to help Shay now. Go to the car with Sergeant Diener.* She tells Sergeant Diener, "He's mine. He'll go to the van with you now, Sergeant. Please, put him in the back. I'll care for Shay until the ambulance gets here, please."

She knows she has to try to help Shay now, or he will die. He's lost too much blood already. She must keep him from bleeding out. She puts one hand on his wound to apply pressure, and the other hand on his head to guide her thoughts.

Sergeant Diener watches her trying to help Shay, his heart breaking for both of them. He doesn't think Shay is going to make it. He looks down at Ghost, pats him on the head and turns around to take him to the van. Ghost follows him closely. The other officers are here, working the scene. He can hear the ambulance. It's close, but he really doesn't think it will help. He shakes his head and says a prayer for Shay and for Flame.

Flame is in Shay now, her thoughts guiding her to the wound. She sees that the bullet has gone through his chest, lodging behind his lung. It's hit an artery. He is bleeding to death. She has to repair the artery first, though there is so much damage that she won't have time to repair everything before the paramedics force her to stop, but she has to stop the bleeding or he doesn't have a chance.

She immediately sends her healing energy to the artery. She barely begins repairing the damage when the paramedics enter the store and run toward Shay. She will not release him, not yet, she has more to do.

She is still repairing the artery, working as quickly as she can. Finally one of the paramedics break her hold on Shay, pulling her out of the way to let them work on saving him. They go to work on him immediately after making her move away from him. They do not understand that she was actually helping him. They wouldn't, even if she told them.

She believes she has at least repaired the artery, though his lung is now filled with blood, but she has kept him from bleeding to death. She's at least done that. She will stay with him and let the paramedics, then the doctors, do their work. They have a lot to do and she can only pray that he will recover. She has done all they will let her do.

Before she can go with the ambulance though, she has to call someone to come and pick up Ghost. She writes down Joe's phone number and hands it to Sergeant Diener. She asks him, "Sergeant would you please call Joe Wolf? Here's his number. He can come and pick up Shay's van. He'll care for Ghost while I'm at the hospital with Shay."

"Sure, Ms. Flame. I'll call him right now. I'll fill him in and if he needs help getting the van back to Shay's I'll be more than happy to take it for him. By the way, you can call me Marty. I'm beginning to think we should be on a first name basis." he tells her.

Then he adds, "I'm so sorry that you've had so much trouble in our little city."

"Thank you, Marty. And, please, just call me Flame. I must admit, it *has* been a bit hectic. Shay will be okay though. I'll make sure of that."

Sergeant Diener smiles and shakes his head. He thinks she is one amazing woman, though he still doesn't believe Shay will pull through this. He was in a bad way.

She gets inside the ambulance with Shay, riding with him and the paramedics to the emergency room. He starts coming around on the way to the hospital and she takes his hand, gives him a smile, and tells him that he will be fine. The paramedic makes her release his hand, but he braves a small smile for her that quickly turns into a grimace. He is still hurting, terribly. She tries to touch him again, to ease his pain, but she is not allowed to do it. She will help him more once she is able to go into the trance that will direct her energy.

The paramedics insert a tube into his side to drain the blood from his lung. Now he will not drown in his own blood, though he might still be bleeding internally. They give information back and forth to the waiting doctors, but Flame hears none of it. She is praying, silently. She is also sending Grandfather details in hope of his help to save Shay's life.

Grandfather hears her and immediately goes into a deep trance, lending her his strength and power. He knows what this man means to her and he will do all he can to help her *and* her man.

She feels Grandfather's power aiding her own. She directs her energy to Shay, it being harder to do without touching him She can only pray it will be enough to save him with the doctor's help.

Chapter 17

Shay goes straight into surgery after arriving at the hospital. Flame has no chance to speak to him, or to touch him. While waiting on word from his doctor she goes into a trance. Luckily she is alone in the surgical waiting area and is able to concentrate her energy where it is needed. She feels Grandfather with her, giving her his strength and knowledge. She is with Shay, in his body, as the surgeons do their work on him.

They are able to get the bullet out, but he is still critical. They give him a blood transfusion and work to repair the damage the bullet has caused. She aids them, without their knowing, repairing areas that they haven't gotten to yet. She can feel their confusion when they find the artery intact.

A nurse, Janey Parson, comes into the waiting room and sees her sitting there with her eyes wide open, but unblinking. The nurse thinks she is in shock, but when she goes to her and shakes her shoulder, she blinks rapidly and looks up at her in question.

Nurse Parson asks her, "Are you all right, honey?"

"Yes, I'm fine, just very tired. Is Shay okay?" she asks, already knowing he is doing well.

"He's still in surgery, but they should be finishing up with him about now. I bet he's doing fine, though. He's got some great people working on him. I'll be sure the doctor comes in to let you know how it goes." Nurse Parson worries about the look of this woman. Her eyes are glassy and she has huge dark circles under them. She has had a bad shock, but she knows it won't do any good to offer her a place to rest. She will stay here until she hears how Shay is doing.

Flame gives her an appreciative smile as she walks out of the waiting area.

Finally the doctor comes in to tell her how the surgery went. "Miss, I am Dr. Michael Kouri. Shay's a very good friend of mine and he's doing very well. He pulled through the surgery just fine. He'd lost a lot of blood, so we had to give him a transfusion, but he will recover fully. There wasn't as much damage as we had originally thought.

"You can see him when he comes out of recovery. He will probably sleep for quite awhile, but you may sit with him then if you would like to."

She breathes a sigh of relief and says, "Thank you so much, Dr Kouri. My name's Flame. I'm his…uh…girlfriend. And, I've been so worried. I'll sit with him as soon as I you'll let me. I don't want to leave his side." She smiles at him, knowing that Shay truly is going to be fine.

The doctor gives her a smile, saying he has to check on another patient and that he will send a nurse for her when Shay is out of recovery.

Sergeant Diener and several other officers come into the room just after the doctor leaves. He has a grave look on his face, obviously expecting bad news, as do the rest of the officers, so he is very surprised by her brilliant smile.

She happily tells him, "Wipe that frown off your face, Marty. Shay's in recovery and doing as well as can be expected. He pulled through the surgery just fine."

Marty's eyes opened wide and before he can stop the words from coming out, he exclaims, "He isn't dead?! Oh damn, I'm sorry...my mouth gets me in trouble a lot. I seem to say what hits my brain without thinking first. I'm damn glad he's alive, Flame. We all are. Right guys?" And, all of the uniformed officers nod.

He continues, "Let me introduce you to some of our boys. This guy here is Sergeant Mike Hansen and the big guy with the sheepish look is Sergeant Steve Tuttle. This guy on my right is Officer John Johnson and we can't forget our lady here. This beauty is Officer Regina Randall. She may not be a sergeant yet, but she sure does keep us all in line. She's pretty good at making us mind our manners. Her partner, Officer Donna Roberts, is booking your perp, but she said she would be by later.

"We'll all keep Shay company, when we have a few minutes to come by, once he's in a room. In fact, a couple of the other guys are planning to come by later today if he's up to seeing anyone. They have the late shift. We try to take care of our fellow officers. At least to let them know we care."

"It's great meeting ya'll. I know Shay will appreciate your concern and that you came to check on him." she tells them.

She turns to Marty and says, "I know you were worried about Shay, but he's proving to be stronger than anyone anticipated. He's pulling through with flying colors. I'm going to sit with him soon. Did you get in touch with Joe?" She has already *seen* that Joe picked Ghost up. She knows that they are both fine and getting to know each other. Ghost seems particularly taken with Mercedes and she is treating him like a big baby, loving him with all that she has to give. Flame doesn't want to give herself away to Marty, though.

"Yes, he picked up Ghost and he had Mercedes drive Shay's van to his apartment. Do you have a ride home?" he asks.

"No, but I'll be staying here with Shay anyway. I'll have Joe pick me up tomorrow. I want to stay, you know, just to be here with him, for now."

Marty nods and says, "I understand. Please, if we can do anything, anything at all, just call. Any of us will be more than happy to help in any way."

All of the other officers voice their agreement or nod their head.

"We'll go for now, Flame. You need some rest too. You won't be any good to him if you don't, and soon." He has noticed the dark circles under her eyes.

"I will, Marty, and thank you for worrying over me. I've learned that I have more friends, in the short time I've been in this town, than I've ever had in my life. I can't tell you how much that means to me." She has tears in her eyes as she hugs him

He turns quickly away from his fellow officers, as he is tearing up himself. Something about this little lady touches his heart like it hasn't been touched in years. He is almost angry with Shay for getting to her first.

Officer Randall waits until everyone else leaves before hugging Flame. Then she tells her, "Flame, I'm glad to meet you. I used to be Shay's partner until he went solo as a detective. He's a great guy and I can see how much he means to you. If I can help with anything, please let me know. I care for him a lot. We spent many hours together and he's the best cop I've ever had the privilege to know." She smiles at Flame as she leaves.

Flame has a very bad feeling about Officer Randall. During that brief hug she got flashes of jealousy, but not of the scorned woman type, and though she's pretty, blonde, petite, and curvy, Flame just can't see Shay being attracted to her. She thinks this woman wants what Shay has, his position as detective, power over others, and to make a name for herself. There is someone in this woman's life that has changed her and made her into a very nasty person.

It was a brief touch, but Flame will watch this woman closely. She is lying and it comes too easily to her. She is hiding something for some reason that Flame was not able to pick up.

She relaxes, leaning back as far as possible, and closes her eyes. *Just for a moment,* she thinks.

The next thing Flame knows, Nurse Parson is gently shaking her awake. She jerks awake, her eyes opening wide, expecting bad news.

Nurse Parson immediately reassures her, "No, honey, there's nothing to worry about. I'm sorry I woke you, but the first thing Detective Larson did when he woke up was to call for you. You can go and see him now if you'd like."

Flame has slept for a couple of hours. It sure doesn't feel like it though. She is sore all over. She looks up into the kind face of the nurse and tells her, "Thank you, Nurse Parson. I'm glad you woke me. I didn't mean to fall asleep. I'd love to see Shay now."

"You can just call me Janey, honey. He'll love seeing you too. We're putting him in a private room. We can put a cot in there for you too, if you'd like."

"I sure would. I won't leave him now. Not when he needs me." She stands and follows the nurse down the hallway and into a large room. There are other patients recovering from surgery in this room also. The nurse tells her it will only be a short time before they can move him into his private room.

When Flame sees Shay she feels such a strong pull to him that it is almost as if he were tugging on her. She cannot help crying seeing him hooked up to all the medical equipment. She sits in the chair beside his bed and takes his limp hand in hers. He is dreaming and she sees his dream.

The dream is of them, with Ghost. They are in the meadow, sitting in the high grass, with wildflowers all around them. Shay is putting an Indian Paintbrush bloom in her hair and both of them are laughing. Ghost is beside her and another wolf, a dark gray female, is lying beside him.

She thinks, *But how can he see the meadow so clearly. It's perfect in all detail! I can even hear the small brook in the woods!* She realizes that he has stronger psychic abilities than even she knew. She wonders why he never knew of his gift, as it is so strong. He doesn't have the ability to enter other's minds or actually read them, but he has very strong precognitive abilities.

She realizes that he is waking and she watches as his eyes open, that beautifully brilliant smile of hers waiting for him.

He sees her, tries to smile, and weakly tells her, "I'm so sorry...I didn't listen to you...at the store. I heard you, but didn't know you could talk to me like that. I was so surprised. I'm sorry, honey. Is Ghost all right? Did anyone else get hurt?"

His look of worry is heartbreaking for her and she assures him, "Oh, Shay, it's not your fault! I should have told you instead of springing it on you like that. I know that I told you I couldn't talk to people in their minds…well, except Grandfather, but I *can* talk to people like Grandfather and me, ones that carry a gift, like us. I knew you didn't even realize that you have a gift too. You do, and it's very strong.

"You have a gift of precognition. One that tells you something is going to happen before it actually does. That's why I can talk to you. I should have told you sooner, but I just didn't want to add more confusion to all the stuff that's been going on lately. It's something that I thought we would have plenty of time to talk about, but I realize now that I should have told you sooner. I had to warn you though, and I sent Ghost in to help you, but I only got you shot. I'm so sorry.

"I thought you were dying on me. I can't bear to lose you! Please forgive me." She is crying silently with huge tears falling from her enormous emerald eyes and rolling down her face.

He quickly says, "No, honey, please don't cry. It's not your fault. You did help… you sent Ghost. I would have tried to take the guy down anyway and I probably would have been killed doing it my way. Please, never ever blame yourself. I'm just so glad that you and Ghost are okay.

"So, I have a gift, huh? Well...what about that?! When I'm feeling better I want to know all you can tell me about it. I admit that I always knew beforehand if something or someone was going to try to get away, or shoot at someone, but I never thought about it being a gift. I just thought I was very lucky." He gives a short laugh, quickly turning into a cough and a painful grimace. He tells her, "I think we'd better talk about this later, okay? Why don't you go on home to Ghost and get some rest. I'm doing fine, honey."

She exclaims, "No way! You're going into a private room soon and they're putting a cot in there for me. You can't get rid of me that easily! Joe has Ghost, and Mercedes is spoiling him completely rotten. I'll be your roommate tonight buster!"

He just gives her a half smile, half grimace, and goes back to sleep.

Joe calls the hospital and Janey gets Flame for him. He tells her that Ghost is fine and asks her how Shay is doing.

She informs him of all that has transpired and he assures her that Ghost will be fine with him for the night, that he and Mercedes will be by to see Shay in the morning. She thanks him and tells him laughingly to tell Mercedes not to spoil Ghost too much more.

Finally they move Shay to his room and Janey even has a cot all ready for Flame too. She tells her, "Thank you, Janey. This is wonderful. I'm so glad you worked this out for me. You're a doll."

Janey smiles gently and tells her, "You're welcome, honey. You two get some rest now and no playing around in here, mister!" She waggles her finger at Shay.

He grins and crosses his heart.

"Have you got anything else for me, Sergeant?" An irritated, gruff voice asks on the phone. No hello. No how are you. Straight to the point and rudely asked.

"No, boss. She signed that document, but we haven't found out what's in it yet. Should we search her trailer while she's at the hospital?"

"No, not yet. First get the boys ready to take care of the old man. We'll handle that first."

"Yes, boss. Do you want the regular boys to do the job, sir?"

"Yes. Make sure they do the job right and I want you there too, just to make sure. There will be a job for one of the others, under your control, and another one for you alone to handle. Hold off on all of it until I give you a call. I'll give you the details then. I think we'll wait until this wedding is over. Remember this and remember it well, Sergeant...My name had better never come up."

"Yes, boss. I'll be waiting on your call."

This time the Sergeant has a worried frown, not wanting to be involved in this dirty job anymore, but nobody says no to the boss and lives to tell about it.

The next morning Flame groans as she gets up off the very uncomfortable cot. She has not slept well at all. She is stiff, sore, and not very rested.

Shay is wide awake and looking at her knowingly. He says, "See? I told you to go home and rest. You didn't sleep much at all. I heard you moving around on that torture bed all night long." He is wearing a sweet smile, but his words have a bite to them. He is worried and upset with her for not getting enough rest. Those dark circles are still there.

"I'm fine, thank you very much! I just couldn't get comfortable, that's all. And, I'm doing just fine now!" She frowns, stretches, and numerous bones pop. She looks quickly and embarrassingly at him.

He just grins even bigger and asks, "Oh, is that right? It seems your body disagrees with you!" He even has the audacity to laugh.

She cannot help it, she laughs with him. She is just so glad to see him feeling better that her discomfort is worth hearing that laugh. Almost anything is, and she thinks, *Even that damn lumpy cot.*

Nurse Janey Parson and Dr. Kouri come in to check on Shay. Janey changes the bandages while Dr. Kouri checks the wound. He tells Shay, "I think it's healing nicely. You should be able to get out of here in a couple of days. I don't want you going back to work for at least three weeks though. You'll be on pain meds and antibiotics for quite awhile. I'll be back tomorrow to check on you again. Get some rest. I know you Larson, and I mean it. Go to sleep!"

Then he looks at Flame, noting the dark circles under her eyes, and determinedly tells her, "And you, young lady, go home. You need to rest too." He leaves after telling Janey to rewrap the wound.

While Janey cleans and redresses Shay's wound, she smiles and tells him, "You were very lucky, Detective. You really should stay away from guns." She laughs and glances quickly at Flame, "You worried this sweet lady terribly and she must love you very much to sleep on that old cot!"

A couple of hours later Marty Diener walks in carrying a couple of books under his arm. He tells Flame, "You can leave now, cause I'm here to do my duty. I have the day off and I thought I'd relieve you of this sick old man for awhile. The guys that came by last night said that you were with him in recovery, so they left after checking on his status.

"I brought a couple of books for him to pick from. He can tell me which one he wants to read and I'll put him to sleep reading chapter after chapter to him. I remembered how much he loves to read and I can read as many chapters as he can stand." He grins teasingly at Shay.

"Oh, hell. Can't a man get any rest around here?" Shay grimaces, but cannot hold it, and finally grins.

Flame smiles and says, "Thank you, Marty. I do need to check on Ghost and I'm going to go ahead and close up shop at the carnival. I was intending to do that in the next few days anyway, but now would be as good a time as any and I'll be there awhile, telling everyone goodbye. Frankie is going to be hard to console, but I'll be back later. Okay?"

She smiles at them both, leans over Shay, kisses him lightly, and tells him, "I'll be back soon. You be nice to Marty. He's only trying to help you!" She giggles on her way out the door.

She calls Joe, once she is out of Shay's room, and asks him to pick her up and drop her and Ghost at the trailer. She tells him that she will be closing up her booth today and that she will need a place to park her trailer for awhile.

He tells her that he has just the place and that he will leave immediately to pick her up.

Back in Shay's room Marty begins, "Okay, chapter one..."

Shay groans loudly.

Chapter 18

Joe, Mercedes, and Ghost are piled into Joe's new station wagon. He proudly gets out, opens the back door for Flame, letting her sit next to Ghost, and asks her, "Well, how do you like it? I just bought it last night."

Her eyes widen and she tells him, "Joe, it's gorgeous. A family car! I guess you thought seriously about how many kids you're going to have, huh?" She cannot help herself; she has to rib him a bit.

Mercedes grins through it all. She looks very happy this morning and she tells Flame, "I'm so glad that Shay's okay. Joe and I are going to visit him after we drop you off. I think Ghost likes me a bit, cause he keeps giving me all these big wet kisses!"

Flame looks at Ghost, and sure enough, he has that big silly grin on his face. He knows well how to work people. She admits, "Sometimes he can be overly, umm...affectionate."

"Flame, you know that damn wolf is just what the name implies…he's a damn wolf! He wouldn't let me anywhere near Mercedes all night! I had to sleep on the damn couch! I thought, since he liked Mercedes so much, we could just have a sleep over at my place, but it didn't quite work out the way I'd intended." He gives Ghost a sneer.

Ghost, being quite the character he is, gives that "cough, laugh" and even places his foot over his eyes. They burst out laughing.

"Ghost, shame on you, you just had to do it, didn't you? I should have kept a better eye on you from the hospital. I'm warning you, next time I will." Flame scolds him, but has to turn her head to keep him from seeing her silent laugh. He knows her well enough to just laugh again.

"I swear he's more human than any animal I've ever met...well, except, of course, for my own Wolf here." Mercedes throws in.

Joe gives her a showing of his teeth, playfully. Then he asks Flame, "So you're closing shop today? I sure don't want to be around when Frankie gets that news. Do me a favor, will you? Ask him to come to the wedding. I think Mercedes has a friend that will really enjoy meeting him." He winks at Mercedes while he asks, then glances into the rearview mirror at Flame.

"Thank you, both of you. I'm really dreading saying goodbye to everyone, but it hurts most saying goodbye to Frankie. He's been so good to both of us. He's a wonderful person, though I'll admit, he's a bit on the strange side. I think that's why we got so close. He could tell I had a hard time with my gift, yet he always believed me, even when others laughed. It means a lot to me that you would think of him."

Mercedes interjects, "Just you wait… I think Frankie is going to want to hang out around here a bit too after he meets Stephan. They're very much alike, from what Joe's told me, and Stephan's a hunk. If Joe hadn't known that Stephan was gay, he'd never have had the nerve to go out with me." She looks at Joe and he nods while turning his head the other way to grin.

"Here we are, little sister. When you get ready to move the trailer just let me know. I'll come by and we can put it in my garage. I think you'll be staying elsewhere. Right?" He cannot help himself, he has to grin at her in the rearview mirror, and she actually blushes. He can tell things between her and Shay are coming along nicely. He feels a great pride in knowing that he has helped in that. Grandfather will be happy for her too.

"Joe, you know I care so much for Shay that it's embarrassing! I've never felt this way before."

"You're blushing, little sister."

"Oh quit! You and Grandfather are too much alike sometimes! I love you both, you know that don't you?" she says honestly, but a bit tearfully.

"I know, honey. We love you too. So does Mercedes." He looks over at Mercedes and sees she is tearing up too.

Flame and Mercedes share a secret smile, both with tears on their cheeks.

"Women!" Joe throws up his hands. He gets out of the car to open the door for Flame and Ghost. He hugs her and shakes his head at Ghost.

Ghost grins up at him.

Joe gets back into the car muttering about "Damn wolves".

Flame and Ghost walk into her trailer. She looks around and then explains to Ghost, by entering his mind, what is happening. She tries to get the point across to him about Shay.

Ghost is not very happy about sharing her, but he will obey her, no matter what. He even likes Shay and he lets her know that too.

She also tells him about getting to see Grandfather. He barely remembers his own family, he had been so young, but through Flame's memories he remembers Grandfather and the warmth and love of his mother. He is very anxious to see them all again.

When she tries to tell him that they will be leaving the carnival, he surprises her. He actually likes the idea, but he doesn't understand about not seeing his friends anymore though, and when she shows him about saying goodbye to them all, Frankie comes into his mind immediately. This surprises her once more as she never expected him to be so upset, but, after thinking it over, she understands. Frankie has been as much Ghost's friend as he has been hers.

She shows him that they will not be living in the trailer for awhile, that the next couple of nights will be the last, for awhile anyway. That part does not bother him at all. He has never cared for the small confines of the trailer.

She is very pleased that he takes it all so well. Now, she only hopes everyone else will, Frankie, to be specific. She hopes that Mercedes is right and that he will decide to hang around here too. That would solve all her concerns.

Flame and Ghost make their rounds, telling everyone goodbye and letting them all know how to contact her if they ever need to. She gives them Shay's telephone number and, after a moment's thought, she gives them Joe's too.

Gregori smiles and tells her that he is sorry to see her go and that he will miss her terribly. He says he will miss most her help with his horses. He adds, jokingly, that he always thought they would be good together, but smiles and hugs her very tightly. She has cried until her eyes are swollen almost shut from all the goodbyes.

She saves Frankie for last. It breaks her heart to do this. By the time she gets to his booth she knows that he must have heard the news from someone already, because he will barely look at her, but once he does, he bursts into tears.

He grabs her in his big bear of a hug and begs her to stay. "Girlfriend, I cain't lose you's now. You two's all I got. I don't know what I'll do if you both up and leave me. Please say it ain't so!"

"Oh, Frankie, it won't be forever, you know. I just want to stay for the wedding and then go see Grandfather for awhile. Also, after what happened last night to Shay, I feel like I need to be here for him." she admits.

"Flame, you ain't foolin this old boy. I seen what you and your man have. It's gonna be forever, little one. I don't have to have no gift to see that. You know it too, in your heart. I'm happy for you, girlfriend, but lettin you, and my big bad wolf here, go is gonna break my old heart."

Ghost picks that moment to raise himself up and place his front feet on Frankie's shoulders, which is no small feat.

Frankie hugs Ghost, just as he had Flame, and tells him, "My friend, you be in charge of protectin our girl now. You watch over our lady here real good. Aww, I know you will...but it helps me to say it. I love you, too, you big bad-assed wolf."

Ghost gives him a big wet kiss right across the face, gaining laughs from tears.

"Oh! Frankie, will you hang around a bit after the carnival leaves?"

He begins shaking his head, but she holds up her hand, stopping him,

"No, listen to me. Joe and Mercedes are getting married this coming Saturday and they've invited you. Mercedes has a little something up her sleeve for you. I think it would be a good idea if you'd stay for it. I mean, I really do...I have a good feeling about it, Frankie."

"Well...it ain't like this place'll fall apart without me. I guess I could hold up a little while. I'll let Tom take over here a bit. He can take this thing mobile on his truck and I'll catch up later. He's been a good guy. I guess after havin him round the last year or so, he's earned a raise." He looks thoughtful a moment.

"This might be a good thing after all...I need a break anyways!" He grins delightedly. Suddenly he exclaims, "I be damned, I guess you be my lucky lady after all. The first vacation I had in five years!"

She grins, impulsively hugs him again, and says, "Joe and Mercedes will love it. I knew you would hang around! Joe told me there's a small RV Park about a mile out, on the south end of town. I love the idea of you being here. You'll be able to meet Grandfather! He's coming for the wedding and I can hardly wait to see him."

After a bit, she goes to her booth and looks around, realizing that she is really going to miss this little place. She has had many good times and has made some great memories here. She remembers Grandfather telling her once, "Life goes on, Granddaughter, and it moves from time to time." He was so right. This is right. Moving on is a good thing.

As she is looking around, a blonde woman walks up to her and asks, "Excuse me, you are Flame aren't you?" This woman has a friendly face and immediately holds out her hand in greeting.

"Yes, but I'm not open for business right now. I'm actually closing up. I've decided to stay here in town for awhile. Can I help you with something else?" She takes her hand anyway, and shakes it. As soon as she does, she realizes, strangely, she cannot read this woman at all. It is usually an unconscious thing with her, but when she gets nothing she notices right away.

"No, I know you're closing shop. Let me introduce myself, I'm Sandy Casteel and I'm here to see if I can take over for you while you're gone. I have my own trailer and will only need to use your booth. I'll pay you well for the use of it, if you decide to let me use it." She sees Flame's confusion and suddenly realizes why.

Sandy smiles, genuinely, and says, "No, you can't read me. I know how to use a block and, I'm sorry, but it comes naturally for me to use it. Here, let's try this one more time." And she holds out her hand to Flame again.

"I'm sorry, Sandy, but I'm not usually faced with someone who has the knowledge to block others. I even still have a hard time remembering to use a block. I don't usually need to do so, but I wish I could remember to more often. I have to admit, I would very much like to know how you knew I was closing up though. I just decided it myself last night. Let's see what I can see now though, shall we?" And, she takes Sandy's hand in her own once more.

Ghost is calmly watching, giving no indications of not liking the woman. Flame is used to Ghost's reactions to someone they just meet, his opinion usually coming before her own. He knows on sight if someone is not truthful, or if the person has a dishonest intention. She usually relies on touch, so with this knowledge she does not hesitate to test this woman.

As she takes her hand the woman gasps, but otherwise stays quiet. She sees this woman has a strong gift, that she can read others the same as Flame can, but she does not have the gift of entering into the mind of animals. She believes this is the reason the woman gasped, maybe never meeting or knowing of one that can do so.

She sees goodness in this woman. She feels trust and honesty. She also sees that Sandy had found out, through a dream, of her closing up shop here. She sees the woman has recently lost her husband to cancer, has no children, or anything to tie her down anymore. She needs this. It will be a new beginning for her, much like it once was for Flame.

She is also very well qualified for this kind of work. She will be honest with people and not try to take their money on a lie. It seems too good to be true, but there is no doubting what she has felt.

"Well, Flame? Do you know me a bit better now? Am I qualified to run the shop?" Sandy asks.

Flame smiles that sunshine smile and tells her, "Sandy, you are more than qualified. Your gift is a bit different than mine. I don't have dreams like that, but I know of someone else that does.

"You may take over anytime you're ready! Go see Mr. Rice at the office in front, near the ticket booth, and let him know that I've given my booth to you. It's yours, free and clear. No strings. I have a feeling I won't need it any longer." and, she realizes, for the first time, the truth in that statement. She has had her days of traveling and they are over. She will either have a future with Shay, or on the land of the wolf. She hopes for both.

Shay's dream comes back to her fully. She realized, when she saw into Sandy's dream of her, he has the gift of dreams too. They will be in that meadow one day. There is always a way of altering the future, but she will do everything possible to make that dream come true. That is the future she wants, that she has dreamt for all her life. She had just never realized it fully, until now.

"Flame, there are some things I must tell you before I do that. I saw into you too. I need to warn you of something. There's an extreme darkness covering your immediate future. I feel evil surrounding you, and those you love. Please, take extra precautions to keep yourself and those you love safe.

"I also see that, even though there will be sadness and grief, there can also be a lot of happiness for you, if you make it through the darkness. It'll be hard. I don't see if you are going to live through it. This darkness is complete. It will be the hardest trial you have ever faced.

"Believe in your gifts and don't let anyone sway your trust in those you love. Be strong and keep your wolf here," she looks down at Ghost with a wistful smile, "very close to you, always. He loves you, but he's also in grave danger. I feel his love for you, and yours for him.

"You have a very special gift, Flame. If you had dark hair, I'd swear you had to be a Native American. Usually this kind of gift is tied to them. You're very special and I want to thank you for your trust. I won't let you down." Sandy finishes by giving Flame a hug, then bending down and hugging Ghost to her.

Ghost allows the hug, surprising Flame. This woman, Sandy, not only has a gift, she *is* a gift. She has to be very special. Flame knows that what she has warned her of will come to pass, and it sends a shiver up her spine. Though she can read others, she has no ability to read herself, or her own future.

She tells this lovely woman, "Thank you, Sandy. Now I'm sure, more than ever, that you deserve my booth. You can help so many, and I'll heed your advice. I've been having small warnings myself, but I blew it off, thinking it was just because of the many changes I've had in my life in such a short amount of time. I know now that there's more coming and I can't thank you enough for telling me. God bless you, Sandy. I'll always remember your honesty."

A while later she makes a call to Joe's office, takes Ghost, and leaves the carnival for good. She will drive her van for just a bit, so she unhooks the trailer, deciding to stay in it until Shay comes home instead of staying at his apartment without him, but right now it is time to keep a promise, and then she will go visit Shay.

Chapter 19

Flame stops at the huge building that houses Joe's office. She takes Ghost out of the van, putting him on a leash, though unnecessary, it is a law here, just as it is in many places. They take the elevator up to the third floor and when the door opens, two beautiful children run squealing toward Ghost.

Debbie admonishes them, telling them to have some manners. They immediately stop, though they keep their hands on the smiling Ghost, to say hello to Flame.

The older child, Tessa, speaks first, "Hi, Miss Flame. Mom told us that you were going to bring a real wolf to meet us! He's so pretty! I thought wolves were supposed to be mean?"

Before she can answer, the youngest child, Kayla, tells her sister, "Tessa, you know that's not true. Wolves are not mean, they're just wild. This one's not wild, so he's not mean! Right, Miss Flame?"

She smiles at them both, seeing so much of Debbie in them. Debbie is standing behind the children, obviously itching to do just as the children are... touch Ghost. It is obvious that this is very special to them all. She tells them, "Yes, you're both right. Wolves are wild and they can be mean, but only if they, or their pack and cubs, are threatened. They will protect what they love, no matter what, but they won't attack without provocation.

"Ghost has never been in the wild. He's been with me since he was just a little cub, so that makes me his pack. He's very protective of me."

Both children are awe struck by Ghost. Finally Debbie gives in and stoops down to his level too. He is eating it all up, just loving all the attention. Children hold a special place in his heart. They are innocent and love to laugh, just as he does. He plays the part of the playful pup for them and, before long, Debbie and Flame are watching him and the children run all over the office.

Debbie says, "Thank you for bringing Ghost. It means so much to them, and to me. It's such a sweet thing to do after all that has been going on. Shay's okay, right?"

"Yes, thank God, he'll be fine. I'm on my way back to see him now. Can I ask a favor of you?" asks Flame.

Debbie nods, with an eager smile. She already knows what the favor will be.

Flame smiles brightly to the children and Ghost as they all look up expectantly, "Would you mind keeping Ghost with you while I'm gone? He'll obey you, if I tell him to, and I can't take him to the hospital. If you can give me your address, I'll come by later and get him later, if it's okay."

She hates to leave Ghost again, but there is nothing else she can do. She refuses to leave him alone in the van and he is having such fun with the children. He'll enjoy this bit of play as much as they will. He needs the exercise too, since she hasn't been able to give him his regular run in a few days.

The children shout for joy and Debbie grins from ear to ear as she says, "Sure it's okay! I have some paperwork to do here anyway. The kids and Ghost will be fine. Just come back here when you're done, but please tell Shay that he's in my prayers, will you?" She knows the idea of Ghost being here with the girls is a wonderful gift to them. She will *make* work for herself if it means pleasing her girls.

Flame tells her, "Debbie, you're a doll, and I appreciate it so much. Just let me tell Ghost what I'm doing. He'll obey you, I promise." She calls Ghost to her, looks into his eyes, and talks to him with their mind link. *I'm going to see Shay for awhile. They won't allow you at the hospital, so I need you to stay here and keep the girls company. I won't be too long. Be good. I love you.*

He nods his head in understanding, bringing a gasp from Debbie. She knew that Flame had a special relationship with Ghost, but not this. She is delighted, as are the girls. She astonishingly exclaims, "Oh my! He actually said yes! You two are amazing! Nobody would ever believe this! Oh, don't worry though, I won't mention it, and if the girls do, well...who's going to believe *that*?! Besides, I can't tell anybody he's a wolf anyway. The girls won't either, don't worry, we've had a long talk about that."

"Thank you again, Debbie. Girls, keep Ghost company for me and I'll be back in a little while. Okay?"

The girls giggle and in unison say, "*OH BOY*!"

Flame leaves to see Shay. It is close to five o'clock and she is sure that most of the other police officers that were visiting should be gone by now. She wants a little alone time with him.

"Sergeant go to Wolf's office now. I want it searched for those papers. Make it look like a burglary. Take whatever is sitting around that looks valuable. You can do whatever you want with it, just find those papers."

"Yes, boss. I'll send one of the boys now."

"Just let me know when it's done."

And, the phone line goes dead in his hand.

Debbie is in the back room filing away some paperwork. She has sent the children into the empty office to play with Ghost, leaving her free to do her typing and filing. The outer office door is locked, so she doesn't think anything of it when she hears a small noise in the outer room. She closes the drawer, ready to go into the front to let the kids know they were supposed to stay in the empty office.

When she opens the file room door she is greeted by a man with a ski mask over his face. She begins to yell, but he hits her over the head with something hard enough to knock her to the floor.

He pulls her up by her hair, yelling at her, "SHUT UP! NOT ONE WORD OUT OF YOU! If you scream, you die. You're not supposed to be here lady. I'm just going to take a few things and then I'll go." He tapes her mouth shut first, and then ties her hands behind her back.

In the small, empty office everything is quiet. Ghost has heard the man and is now standing in front of the children with his teeth bared and a low, deep growl coming from his throat. The hair on his ruff is standing on end and his tail is held straight out behind him, prepared for attack.

The girls have heard their mother struggling and know to stay quiet. Their mother has cautioned them well in what to do in an emergency situation.

The man decides that since he has to get this lady out of his way before searching the office. He will put her inside the empty office. This makes it obvious to Debbie that this man knows his way around. He does not even check Joe's office, or put her into the file room. He opens the empty office door to throw her inside. He is in front of her when he opens the door. That is his mistake.

Once the door is opened, Ghost springs. He goes straight for the man's throat, taking him down to the floor. The man is having a hard time holding Ghost away from his head and keeping from getting his throat torn out. Ghost is relentless, biting deep on anything that he can. The man's blood now stains his white fur a slick, deep red.

Tessa runs to her mother while the man struggles with Ghost. She pulls the tape off of Debbie's mouth and starts untying her hands.

Debbie yells for Kayla to call 911.

Kayla immediately does as her mother tells her to do.

Flame is walking into the hospital when Ghost enters into her mind. She is able to *see* what is happening. She calms and encourages Ghost to keep holding the man and runs straight into Shay's room. She is now hoping that one of the officers *is* there, or that Shay will know exactly what to do. She runs into the room with a wild look in her eyes.

Officer Regina Randall and another woman, in uniform, are visiting

Shay. Flame assumes she is Officer Donna Roberts and when they see her face they stop talking at once.

She quickly tells them, "Someone go to Joe's office immediately! Someone has broken into the office and Debbie and her girls are there! Please hurry." She is frantic and tears stand in her eyes.

"Uh...how do you know this?" Officer Regina Randall asks, smiling a bit.

"Don't ask her how, just *do* it. DAMN IT! DO IT *NOW*!" Shay shouts at them, raising himself and wincing in pain from yelling and moving too fast.

"Okay...we'll go. Oh yeah, I forgot, she's psychic..." Officer Regina Randall looks at her partner and they share a snide grin.

Flame is furious. "I'll tell you one damned thing, *Officer*; you're a jealous, power hungry bitch. Now...please *do your job*!" She cannot help herself, she doesn't mean to let her anger come out this way, but if she holds it in much longer she will hurt someone, even if she doesn't mean to. It has happened before, when she was little, but she never forgot it. Her extreme tension, intense fear, and even anger, can cause dramatic results.

Regina's partner, Donna, speaks now with her mouth growing tight and her eyes to a squint. "We *will* do our job, lady, but here's a warning for you...watch who you speak to like that. Neither of us will be spoken to that way and especially not by someone like *you*" She exhumes hatefulness, centered directly at Flame.

Regina, doesn't speak this time. She only watches with a slight frown of what seems to be confusion.

Flame realizes she has just made not just one enemy, but two. But right now, she just doesn't give a damn. She directs her words at Donna, but she is actually speaking to them both, "I suggest you do your job then. There are two little girls in that office and my dog will kill this intruder. If Ghost, or those children, is harmed, I promise you, I will hold you both accountable. You don't want to make an enemy of me."

Her fury reaches its limit. She is so angry that the energy she is accumulating comes out, unintentionally. The window of the room cracks and all of the flowers that have been delivered hit the floor with the vases shattering and glass littering the floor.

The officers, Regina and Donna, glance at one another and take off a bit faster than they had been moving earlier.

Shay is open mouthed and wide eyed. He looks at Flame and says, "Remind me never to make you mad, honey!" He bursts into laughter, then quiets realizing that Debbie, her children, and Ghost, are in terrible danger.

Flame could not exactly tell Regina how she knew. That would have been worse than what she'd already told them. She had no way to explain her knowledge of the break in to them except by saying exactly what Regina had said, that she is psychic. Thank God that Shay told them to go; otherwise she doesn't believe they would have.

She says, "I'm sorry, Shay. That hasn't happened since I was a child. I was just so mad. I could feel the power building, but I couldn't control it. Wow...I wish I could do that on command."

She adds, "I didn't like Regina from the moment I met her. I know she was your partner, but I don't like her at all. Now I can see her partner's just as bad as she is. I'm sorry, I know she's your friend, but I can't help how I feel about her.

"Ghost has taken that intruder down, but he hasn't sent me any more information. I need to sit down, and then try to see what's going on again." She is so angry and so worried her knees are shaking. She sits next to Shay's bed, pulling the chair closer to it. She tries to calm down, to check on Ghost and the children. She already knows that Debbie was hurt, she just doesn't know how badly.

"I like the jealous thing, but don't go overboard next time." He says, trying to ease her fears.

He knows exactly what his old partner has become. She is not one of his favorite people, especially lately, and when she teamed up with Donna Roberts she became even worse. That is one pair of bitches, as far as he's concerned. He hates to feel that way, but that's how it is.

Regina hasn't always been this way. She had been treated unfairly, not being promoted when he was. She should have made sergeant, at least. He had been a sergeant when they had been partners. Then, when he was promoted to detective, she was partnered with Donna instead of being promoted like she should have been.

He never understood it, but he wasn't about to buck the authorities that be, not in Munson anyway. The system here is run by a bunch of old men that should have been retired years ago. They still hold to the old standards. They do not even believe a woman should be a cop, let alone in a place of higher authority.

He actually feels sorry for Regina, or at least he used to. She is a beautiful woman, and sure, when they had been partners they had both considered a relationship, but both were honest enough to know it would never work. They were two very different people. Plus, it is never a good idea for partners at work to be partners in any other way. He knew that wasn't why she changed though.

He has a completely different opinion of Donna Roberts. Sure, she is pretty enough, in a rough sort of way, but she is always looking for trouble. She is also always in the middle of every piece of gossip at the station. She seems to be drawn to the wrong sort of men, hell, the wrong sort of people. Since Regina has been teamed up with Donna, she has turned into someone he doesn't want anything to do with and he never thought he would feel this way about her, but he does.

Flame is inside Ghost, seeing what he sees. The man is down, screaming for someone to get the dog off him. Kayla has called 911 so the police are on their way. She is glad, because she is not sure if Regina and Donna will even get there at all.

Debbie grabs both girls and shoves them into the file room, going back for Ghost. She can hear the sirens now. She does not want Ghost to kill the man. She tells him, "Ghost, come here now. Go with the girls! Watch them!

Ghost immediately obeys, but Flame is in his mind now. She tells him, *Back Debbie up into the file room too. Don't leave her alone with that man.*

Ghost obeys.

Debbie sees Ghost stop and turn to look at her. He pushes at her until she goes into the file room too. She locks the door behind her and, as she does, she hears the man run out of the office. Ghost hurt him, but not enough to stop him from running. She will not unlock the door though until help is here.

In just a few moments she hears the police rushing into the office calling out, "Police!"

She yells, "HE'S GONE! WE'RE IN HERE!" She unlocks and opens the door.

Ghost goes out first with Debbie and the girls coming out behind him.

Debbie explains what happened and the officers see the blood on Ghost and on the floor of the office. All of it has come from the man. No one else has been hurt.

Flame sends, *Good boy, Ghost. Stay with Debbie and I'll be there soon.* She comes back into herself and tells Shay, "They're all right. Ghost bit the man, quite a lot. He has to be bleeding quite badly. He got out of the office before the police arrived though. They should be searching for him now, but all of them are okay. Regina and Donna aren't there, Shay."

She doesn't think they had time to get there, but it still makes her angry. She knows she cannot blame them for this, though. She can only hope they catch this man.

"They didn't have time. They're good cops, honey. They can be difficult, to say the least, but they *are* good cops. Maybe Regina or Donna will see the guy leaving as they arrive. We can always hope. I just wonder what he wanted in that office. He must know that the closing time at Joe's is four-thirty. He wanted something though, and I'm curious as to what that something is."

She agrees, "Me too. I hope you're right about your friend, Officer Randall...umm Regina, and her partner, Donna. I just don't like them and that's not a normal feeling for me. I don't trust easily, but I don't usually dislike people so quickly either.

"Did Joe and Mercedes come see you? I need to call him." She starts for the phone and Shay lays his hand on hers.

He says, "Don't, honey. Debbie and the police will take care of all that. You just go and get Ghost. I'm fine, and yes, Joe and Mercedes came. I've had a regular circus of people in here today. I know they all mean well, but they've all worn me out completely."

When she hesitates, he says, "Go, honey. I'm going to sleep anyway. Please, if you and Ghost want to stay at the apartment go ahead. Joe told me about you leaving the carnival and I'd feel much better if you'd stay at my place instead of in your trailer.

"I don't know what's going on in this city lately. I admit, we stay busy at the station, but not like this." He is so tired that his eyes are already closing.

She leans down, kisses him, and says, "Shay, we're going to stay in the trailer tonight, but tomorrow I'll move some of our things to your place. I need to do a few things at the trailer anyway. Plus, I'd like some time with Frankie, but Joe told me he'd store my trailer in his garage when I need him to." She stands.

Then hesitates and asks, "Oh, do you want any books before I go? I can get some at the hospital gift shop for you."

"Oh, God no! I heard so many chapters from Marty today that I thought, if I could only get up out of this bed, I would kill him with my bare hands. He kept reading and at every chapter he'd say the damn chapter number." He closed his eyes, but this time there is a smile on his face.

She leans down and kisses him again, then leaves the room quietly.

He is already asleep.

Chapter 20

Flame gets to Joe's office to find Debbie still there with the girls and Ghost. An officer she has not met is taking Debbie's statement, but Regina and Donna are there too. She feels that she has to talk to Regina first, and stands near her to say, "I'm sorry, Regina. I really am. I didn't mean to say all those awful things. I was just so worried and I didn't want Ghost to kill that man, though it wouldn't have been a big loss." Her feelings about this woman have not really changed, but she doesn't want to make an enemy of her. She knows it would only be harder for her and Shay if she does.

Regina gives her a look of what seems, almost, to be shame and tells her, "Don't worry about it. I guess I can understand how you felt. What I don't understand is how you knew what was going on even before 911 was called, but then I really don't want to know either. I don't want to believe your answer." And, she actually smiles. A real smile this time.

Officer Donna Roberts watches this exchange. She keeps her lips held together tightly. She will not pretend to like this woman, or that damn dog. She has always hated animals. They are dirty, smelly, and she has never known one to have much sense. She especially does not like *this* dog. He is preening around like a king, with everyone getting all gushy about what a good dog he is. It makes her sick.

Flame rushes to Debbie next and, as she does, Ghost comes to her side and looks up at her. She takes the time to hug Debbie before reaching down and holding Ghost to her. She sees all the blood on his fur and it makes her sick. It is almost like it's his, though she knows he is not hurt.

She looks up at Debbie and the girls and tells them, "I'm so glad that ya'll knew just what to do. Ghost's good, but he couldn't have done this without your help. You girls were great. Your mother's taught you how to do all the right things. Listen to her well cause she's one smart lady." She looks into Debbie's eyes, seeing her tears of pride for herself and her daughters now that the fear is gone.

Debbie says, "Ghost is wonderful. I don't know if that man would have hurt us, but thank God that he didn't get the chance. Ghost took care of that. I can't thank either of you enough for it."

Flame smiles, laying her hand on Ghost's head, and says, "You don't have to, Debbie. We both love you. Can't you tell? And girls, when Ghost needs a babysitter I'd be very happy if you would do that for me." She knows this will take the girl's minds off of all that has happened, or at least it will help.

Both girls smile from ear to ear and both nod excitedly. They both hug Ghost first and then Flame.

"Lady, is this your dog?" The Officer taking Debbie's statement asks her.

"Yes, Officer. He was staying here with the kids while I was at the hospital. Why?" Flame asks.

"Well, to tell you truth, I don't like this, but I have to tell you, we have to take him to the shelter. He'll have to stay there for about ten days since he *did* actually bite somebody, even if the guy did deserve it. I'm sorry." says the officer, regrettably.

Her eyes tear up and overflow. She cannot bear this. No way can she stand putting Ghost in a cage.

Then, Debbie and the girls start giving their opinion on the subject, objecting as much, and as strongly, as Flame.

Surprisingly, Regina looks at the Officer and tells him, "Steve, don't take that dog. This is Detective Larson's girlfriend, Flame. She's been through the mill since she's been in Munson. Don't worry, I'll keep checking on the dog. If he's sick, we'll know. Just leave them be."

Flame speaks up too, "Besides, Doctor Butler had Ghost at his home for awhile. He's had all his shots. Doctor Butler can verify that."

Officer Steve Reid looks from Regina to Flame, nods, and says, "I'm sorry. I heard about Shay. I don't know him too well, but I'll go by to see him anyway. I haven't been with the Munson Station too long. I'm still getting to know everyone.

"Okay, I won't take your dog, but please make sure you keep an eye on him. I honestly don't care if that man he attacked dies from blood loss or even rabies, but taking him to the shelter is procedure, even if we don't catch the guy.

"I'm sure he's hurting and I'm glad. He had no right to come in here and scare or threaten these people. I promise we'll search for him. I would say with all the blood he's lost, here alone, that he'll go to the hospital, or at least a doctor. If he does, we'll have him."

"Thank you Officer....." Flame starts to say, Reid, but he stops her.

"Just call me Steve, please."

"Thanks, Steve. I don't like the idea of Ghost being in a cage. He was shot just a few days ago and is still healing. Also, I'm sure Shay would like for you to stop by and say hello. He needs to keep his spirits up."

She smiles brightly and Steve is as awe struck by her smile as most men are. He is as jealous of Shay as Marty was. It seems that Flame could have many suitors here if she wasn't already taken.

Officer Steve Reid also knows that Ghost is no dog. He was raised in the country, and knows a wolf when he sees one. He thinks that Ghost is a wonderful creature and fears that if he had taken him to the shelter, the lovely lady would never get him back. It is illegal to keep a wolf as a pet.

He knows that Ghost was only protecting the kids and their mother, and he just cannot take him from Flame. He is very glad that Officer Randall helped to keep him from having to. It is obvious, though, that Regina Randall and Donna Roberts don't know a wolf when they see one and he is not about to enlighten them.

He doesn't really care for either of the women. They have attitude enough to make their eyes float. Real smart-asses, like they are better cops than he is, just because they have been with the department longer than he has. He is new to Munson, but he had been a cop in New York City for ten years before moving here. He is no rookie.

Joe arrives, rushes to Flame, pulling her into his arms and exclaiming, "Thank God you left Ghost here with Debbie and the girls. I don't know what I'd done if anyone had hurt them. Those kids are like my own. I care very much for them all."

He takes the girls and Debbie in with a glance and a smile, then says, "I bet the girls had a great time playing with Ghost though!" He winks, trying to change the subject.

"We sure did, Uncle Joe!" Kayla speaks up.

Tessa adds, "Yeah, until that man came in. Man, you should have seen Ghost get that guy! It was something! There was blood everywhere! See? It's still there!"

"Yuck, Tessa, that's gross!" Kayla has to add.

"Yeah, it sure *is* gross. I'll have to have that all cleaned up before anyone else sees it. Debbie, do you have any idea what he was looking for?" Joe asks.

"No, Joe. Officer Reid here already asked me that. He didn't have time to look for anything, or to take anything either, before Ghost jumped him. I have no idea what he wanted."

"I don't either. There's nothing here that's worth breaking into the office for. I mean, we don't keep any valuables and I have no idea what else they would want. The furniture's the most expensive thing here and I'd love to see them try to carry it out of here." He turns to Officer Reid and says, "There aren't any papers kept here that anyone could possibly want."

"Thank you, Mr. Wolf. I guess we're done here. I'm sorry about all the trouble and if we get this guy, I'll be sure to let you know." Officer Reid says to all of them.

"Thank you, Steve. I appreciate all you've done. Bye, Regina, Donna.

Maybe we'll run into each other at the hospital again." Flame says and smiles at all of them, gritting her teeth as she says goodbye to Regina Randall and Donna Roberts.

"Bye. Take care of Shay for us. He's the best. You're a lucky lady." Regina says and actually smiles at them all.

Donna stands looking over the room, but never makes eye contact with anyone. She doesn't open her mouth at all.

Steve gives Flame a wink as he pats Ghost on the head before leaving. She has a moment to wonder what that was about.

Joe looks down and says, "Ghost, old boy, I think I owe you an apology. You're a wonderful friend to have. I'm sorry I was a smart ass to you earlier today." He rubs Ghost's head and Ghost gives Joe that silly smile and sneeze-like "shucks".

This brings a tremendous smile to the girl's faces.

Flame grins and says, "We're going now. I'm staying at the trailer tonight, and then tomorrow we're packing up and going to Shay's. Hopefully he'll be out of the hospital in a few days. Soon enough for your wedding!"

"He'd better be. He's still obligated to be my best man, even if he looks like a mummy." Joe hugs her, whispering into her ear, "Thanks, little sister."

She pulls back, looks into his eyes, and smiles.

After much hugging and kissing between the kids and Ghost, she finally gets out of the building. She decides to stop by to see Shay one more time before calling it a night. She misses his laughter and having him close to her. It doesn't seem possible he means this much to her already.

She thinks, *Damn, I've got it bad.* but, grins nonetheless.

Ghost looks over at her and coughs, rolling his eyes at her. He gives her that wolf grin and she cannot help the laughter that bubbles out.

You stop that. You're not supposed to listen to my thoughts unless I let you! "I love you too, you know. I'm so proud of you, Ghost. You and Shay, my men. What would I do without you?"

Ghost's grin grows even larger.

Shay is asleep when she gets into his room. He looks so peaceful. She cannot bring herself to wake him up. She just sits and watches him for a little while. She cannot believe this handsome man is really hers. She loves him so much.

Finally she jots down a note telling him that she had been by and that she loves him. She left Ghost in her van, and she doesn't like doing that. As she is leaving the room the nurse, Janey, stops her.

Motioning for her to come into the hall she tells her, with a bright smile, "Honey, he's doing great. He'll be able to leave in a couple of days. We just want to make sure his wound doesn't get infected. You'll have to keep an eye on him and make him take his antibiotics though, and he might balk, but make him take a pain pill when he needs it. Cops don't like to admit when they're in pain." She winks.

"Thank you so much, Janey. I'm so glad he's doing so well. We're supposed to be in a wedding this coming Saturday and I know he won't want to miss it. He'll be okay to do that, won't he?"

"Sure, honey. He'll be fine. He'll need to be taking his pain medication and if he's careful, he'll be able to do just fine." She leans over and hugs Flame, making Flame like this thoughtful woman even more.

Chapter 21

Flame and Ghost make their way back to the parking lot of the carnival. They both climb out of the van, but Flame decides to wait until morning to hook the hitch back up. It is already dark and she doesn't see any reason to do it tonight.

Just as they start toward the trailer, Sandy, the psychic that took over for her, rushes into the lot, yelling at her, "NO! DON'T!" Stopping them both in their tracks only feet from the trailer.

At precisely that moment a blast comes from the inside of the trailer, knocking both Flame and Ghost back at least ten feet. The trailer is burning and rubble from it falls all over them and the parking lot.

Sandy rushes to them. Ghost whines, raises his head, and crawls to Flame, laying his head on her chest. People are running toward them now and Sandy yells for someone to call an ambulance.

I am coming, Granddaughter. Hold on. I am almost there. Everything will be fine. Just let the doctors work, I am going to fix everything. Grandfather has been driving for almost two hours to get to Flame. He knew she was in danger. He has never had precognition before, only the same gifts she has. He knew this time though. He saw a woman yelling for her to stop, trying to keep her from going into the trailer.

He thanks God for this woman. If she hadn't yelled when she had, Flame and Ghost would both be dead. He is almost at the Munson hospital now. He had *seen* when Joe had taken Ghost to the same vet that had him before, Doctor Butler.

At first the old vet thinks Ghost is hurt badly, seeing all the blood, but Grandfather hears Joe tell him what had just happened at his office. This relieves the Doc's mind. He first washes Ghost, then examines him, finding only a bit of burned and singed fur.

Grandfather goes into Ghost's mind, comforting him and giving him strength. Ghost will heal. He lets Ghost know that he is on his way to Flame. He is reassuring him, as he knows that he is worried for her. Her injuries are much worse than Ghost's.

He arrives at the hospital and goes instantly to Joe, who is now in the emergency room. He sees the woman with Joe and knows that this must be Mercedes. He smiles at her and hugs her to him, letting her know that he knows who she is. Then he exclaims, "Joe, where is Flame? You know I must see her now!"

"I know, Grandfather, but I don't know how to do it. She's being worked on right now. It's her eyes. She has a broken arm and is otherwise fine, except for her eyes. They say that she may never see again." Joe wipes his eyes and continues, "Grandfather, you have to help her. She's still unconscious. Ghost is inconsolable. Doc Butler put him under heavy sedation."

"Yes, Joe, I know. I have talked with Ghost and he knows I am here He will be fine. You must find a way for me to get to Flame. I can help her. You know this."

"I'll talk to the nurse that Flame has befriended. Let me find her. I'll be right back." Joe hurries off to find Janey.

Grandfather says, "Hurry, Joe. We *must* hurry if I am going to be able to help her. They must not do any surgery on her eyes!" He turns to Mercedes, seeing the tears running down her face, and he assures her, "Mercedes, do not worry. I will help her. You have grown close to my granddaughter?" He makes it a question.

"Yes, sir, she's already like a sister to me. I've never had any real family, except my father, and he's not very, uh...lovable. Flame's the greatest. Can you really help her? They said she's going to be blind because of the shrapnel." She has been sobbing, but now looks hopefully at him. He is so much like Joe that she feels an instant love for him.

"Please, Mercedes, call me Grandfather, all my family does. You too are family. Yes, I can help her. They cannot try to remove the shrapnel though. I must push it out from the inside of her eyes. They will not understand. I hope Joe can make this work somehow." He is so worried for Flame that he cannot sit, but paces, waiting and waiting.

Then Frankie storms into the hospital emergency room. He is bawling like a big baby.

Mercedes rushes to him, wrapping her arms around him, her head coming only to mid chest on him.

Frankie demands, "Where be my girl? Who done it? I'll kill the bastard that done hurt my girl! Is she okay, Mercedes? Please tell me she's okay."

"She's okay, Frankie, don't worry. And Grandfather's here. You know he'll take care of her." She tries her best to console him, but there is no consoling Frankie when he is in this state.

Grandfather sees Frankie and instantly knows who he is. He goes to him, placing his hand on Frankie's shoulder. He uses his gift to calm this friend of his granddaughter's. He knows how much Flame and Ghost love this big man.

He tells him, "She will be fine, Frankie. Calm yourself. I might need you to help me to get to her. We must wait on Joe, to see what he can do first. Be ready, Frankie, in case we need your help."

Frankie's huge shoulders are shaking, but he stops crying, looks at Grandfather, and says, "I know you. She done told me 'bout you. You can heal her, right? What be wrong with her? And where's my friend, Ghost?"

Grandfather smiles gently and tells him, "Ghost is fine. Flame's arm is broken and she has shrapnel in her eyes. She is still unconscious and they do not know if she will ever see again. That is why I must get to her. I can remove it without surgery. She has told you of this gift we have?"

"She sure has. She tells me everything. That girl's the best friend this old boy ever had. I'll do anything you need me to. You just tell me when and what!"

Finally, Joe returns with the nurse, Janey. They move to Grandfather's side, and she tells them all, "Come with me. We need to talk."

They follow her into a conference room.

Janey says, "Okay. Now, tell me what you want again? I can't believe I'm even listening to this! I'm a nurse, and a good one. I do care for Flame and I know she's a great person, but I don't understand what it is you want from me!" She looks at each of them.

Grandfather takes her hand in his, using his energy to sway this woman's decision. He says, "Nurse, Flame is my granddaughter."

At the incredulous look he receives, he continues, "No, not by blood, but by our gifts. She has a wonderful gift. A gift of sight and one of healing. Did you know this?"

"No, and I can't believe I'm saying this, but I *do* remember the doctor that operated on Detective Larson was really freaking out because he should have been dead when they operated. The bullet had torn a large hole in his chest and should have hit an artery, though the artery showed no sign of injury, but he'd bled out *so much*, and his lung was so full of blood too… they couldn't understand how the artery was intact… they just couldn't figure it out." She's shaking her head from side to side, not really looking at anyone, or speaking to them directly, but thinking aloud.

She has a thoughtful look on her face, remembering how she had found Flame after the surgery, the glassy look on her face and circles under her eyes. She says quietly and almost reverently, "She did that, *didn't* she?"

Grandfather nods.

Janey continues softly, "I knew she was special, but not this. I've heard of it and to tell you the truth," she looks around the room, her face reddening, "I've always believed in this stuff, but how can you help her?"

"Nurse Parson, I also have this gift. I need to get to her *before* they work on her eyes. If they remove the shrapnel it will cause damage to them. She probably will never be able to see through them again. I can get it out from the inside, but I need your help. Will you help us?"

Janey and Grandfather are quietly talking beside the door to the room that Flame is in. Hearing a great noise from the emergency room waiting area, Janey opens the door and yells, "Doctor! Hurry! In the waiting area! They need you…*now*!"

Frankie is screaming his head off and Mercedes and Joe are acting as if they are trying to calm him. Frankie cannot be held down by any of them. The ER people are screaming for security and he is still running in circles. The doctor rushes in yelling for someone to get him a sedative immediately.

Janey is standing in front of the door to Flame's room watching for anyone trying to enter. She will do everything she can to keep everyone out. Grandfather is with Flame. Janey put her trust in this man. She doesn't really know why, but she usually goes with what her gut tells her is right. This time it's telling her to try to help this woman, and her Grandfather. Her gut has always been right so far. She is praying it's right this time too.

Grandfather takes Flame's limp hand in his. He closes his eyes and enters her body. He goes directly to her eyes. He knows he doesn't have long, so he must work fast, but very thoroughly.

Her eyes are badly damaged. They are burned from the heat of the bomb and damaged by the shrapnel. He compels her to open her eyes and then pushes out the shrapnel. It falls onto her face. He starts to work on the burns, making sure of no nerve damage at the same time.

Janey is getting anxious. It has been long enough. She knows the doctor will be there in the next few minutes. Then she sees the doctor and four orderlies wheeling Frankie into a cubicle. He is out like a light. The doctor is talking to the orderlies and he glances her way. He holds up a finger, letting her know that he will be right there.

Grandfather has finished with Flame's eyes. She will be very sensitive to light for quite some time, but will see again through her own eyes, not just her animals. The shrapnel has also cut into her face, causing deep cuts that will scar if not fixed properly. He goes to work on this, the shrapnel pushing out of her skin and off her face, leaving no mark and no scar behind

He starts working on her broken arm, setting it and healing the break. He is almost through when Janey bursts in whispering loudly, "The doctor's coming! Hurry! Get out now, while he's not looking, or I'll be fired for sure!"

He leaves, quietly walking back into the ER waiting area. Joe and Mercedes look at him hopefully and he smiles. Their relief is obvious. Everyone is so relieved, except Frankie.

"What in the world did that crazy man do in here?!" Grandfather asks, looking around the room and noting that it is a disaster. There are people cleaning and picking up broken chairs everywhere.

Joe and Mercedes stifle their laughter, barely. Their relief for Flame added to Frankie's antics is almost intolerable. Joe, seeing that some of the security people are nearby states, "He went nuts! We think he must have been on some kind of drug. It took almost ten of them to get him still enough for that doctor to give him a shot!" His voice is breaking it is so hard to hold in the relieved laughter.

Grandfather shakes his head, doing everything in his power to keep from laughing out loud. He winks at Joe and Mercedes and says, "I must relieve Ghost's mind. I need to sit awhile. This is the most energy that I have used in a very long time. It is very tiring for an old man."

He enters Ghost's mind to find him heavily sedated, but Grandfather is able to relay to him that Flame will be fine. He feels Ghost's relief as he goes back to sleep. He can rest easy now.

After what seems hours, the doctor, Mike Kouri, comes into the waiting area. Janey is right behind him giving them a thumbs-up and quickly leaving. Dr. Kouri asks who is waiting for news of Miss Flame.

Grandfather, Joe, and Mercedes, stand up and follow him into the same conference room that they had been in earlier with Janey.

Dr. Kouri has a bewildered look on his face as he says, "I don't know how to explain this to you, but she's fine. I can't understand it. Her eyes were badly damaged when she came in. We didn't think she would have use of them again, or at least not too much, they were so badly burned, and the shrapnel in them was astonishing. It alone had done tremendous damage to the optic nerves in both eyes.

"There were shrapnel cuts in her face also, but it had all fallen out of her eyes and face when I went back in the room to prepare her for emergency surgery. I found it lying on her chest! The shrapnel left no scars. Her right arm was broken also, I thought...no, I *know* it was!

"I was called out to sedate another patient and when I returned the shrapnel was lying on her face and her eyes showed no sign of damage. No internal bleeding…nothing but a bit of a burn that will heal, given time.

"Even her broken arm was mended to the point of a fracture. I would never have believed it, but I put both xrays side by side—the one I took when she was first brought in, and the one I took after I walked back into the room—and the first clearly shows that the break was there, that it was fully broken, and then in the second xray it was only a fracture.

"This is the second time this week that I've had this happen. It's the strangest damn thing. I'm sorry, I shouldn't be telling you all this…but the other case was this lady's boyfriend, Shay Larson. He should have been dead when he arrived here. He's doing fine now though.

"I'm happy to tell you that Flame will be fine also. She'll have to wear dark glasses for quite awhile, but she'll make a full recovery. She's still unconscious, but I don't believe that's anything to worry about. I believe the lady was just worn out. She's been here day and night since Shay arrived, but she'll wake soon enough."

Grandfather smiles and says, "Thank you, Doctor Kouri. We are most pleased to hear this wonderful news. You are amazing. We have been so worried. Will you admit her to the hospital?"

"Oh, yes, I meant to ask, should we put her in the same room with Detective Larson? It's not usually done, but if I know Shay, and I do, he will insist on it. I've known him for quite awhile. He's a very stubborn man." The doctor smiles while he says this and adds, "Also, he doesn't know about the accident yet, does he?"

"No, he doesn't. Please give us some time to prepare him, and then, yes, by all means, put her in the same room with him. She's just as stubborn as he is and they'll end up in the same room, no matter what we say." Joe answers this question. Shay will be very upset, to say the least, that he hasn't been informed already.

Dr. Kouri nods, knowing how upset Shay will be. He says, "I'll leave it to you then. Flame will be ready to move soon." And, he leaves.

"Joe, you two go on to Shay's room. I will join you in a few minutes. I think I had better check on our friend, Frankie. I do not want them to put him in the psychiatric ward by mistake!" Grandfather chuckles as he walks to the desk to ask about Frankie.

Grandfather asks one of the attendants if he knows why Mr. Franklin Bell had "gone nuts" in the waiting area.

The attendant tells him there were no drugs in Frankie's system, but they were keeping him overnight for observation.

Grandfather assures them that Frankie was only worried about Flame and has only *lost it* for awhile.

They still insist that they are going to keep Frankie overnight, but if everything goes well they will let him out the next morning.

Grandfather has to agree, but Frankie is going to put up one hell of a fight if they don't let him see Flame.

Chapter 22

Flame is in the same room as Shay. Though unusual, it has been allowed. She is still unconscious, but is otherwise doing fine. Shay insists on being right beside her, so they place the beds close enough for him to hold her hand.

Everyone has gone home, except Grandfather. He will not leave until she is awake. He sits very straight in the barely padded chair on the other side of her bed with his eyes closed.

Shay would think him asleep, but he knows if Flame moves, at all, Grandfather will be wide eyed immediately.

He has called the station to be sure its best detective, Detective Don Clanton, will work the case of the bombing. They have no idea who has set it, but they do know that it was set by remote ignition.

The person that placed the bomb in the trailer had to have been close enough to it to see her going in before they pushed the button to blow it. The trailer's front, near the door, is completely gone. Only the rear of the trailer has anything left of it. The whole of it hardly resembling a camper at all. Someone had tried to kill her, intentionally.

Shay will not allow that to go unchallenged. He will work the case himself, when he is able to do so.

Frankie was kept overnight, but he is going to be released anytime now. It is almost noon of Thursday.

Grandfather knows that Frankie will be in the room soon and he is glad. He owes him a huge debt of gratitude. Because of his actions, Grandfather had been able to save Flame's eyes and keep her face from being scarred.

He has already been in Ghost's mind, reassuring him that Flame is fine and that he will be to see him sometime today. Ghost is sore but it is nothing that will not heal.

Flame should wake soon too. He goes into her mind every hour to check on her. She is dreaming of the forest.

He and Shay have come to know each other quite well over the last few hours. They share laughter over Ghost's antics and tears over Flame's pain. He tells Shay that he knows how much he, Shay, means to Flame. He and

Shay reminisce over Joe's and Shay's college years, and their friendship. He thanks Shay for being such a good friend to both his grandson and his granddaughter.

He also tells Shay of the Will that he had Joe draw up to have Flame sign. He worries that it might have something to do with the trouble that is happening here, to his granddaughter.

Shay is beginning to believe that this has to be the truth. He tells Grandfather about the break in at Joe's office. It is all fitting into place.

❧

"What the hell happened?! Where are those papers I wanted?"

"Boss, our guy got attacked by that damn dog! He's really torn up. We have him being taken care of by a doctor that won't say anything to anyone. The dog was in the office with the secretary and her children. We didn't know that, but we did get the papers."

"I don't give a rat's ass if he dies! He should have been sure that office was empty before going in! If you have the damn papers then get them to me now, Sergeant! They should already be in my hands. *How* did you get them?"

"Boss, we sent Otis on this one. He searched the woman's trailer and he found the papers. It's a Will made by the old Indian. There was a complication though"

"*WHAT*?! Why the hell did you send that idiot in the first place? What did he do this time?"

"He was the only one available and he felt like he owed her for some trouble she caused him once before at the cabin. He set a bomb in the trailer. He waited in the lot for her to come home and then blew it up, but she wasn't inside. He made a mistake and she's in the hospital." The Sergeant pulls the phone from his ear after relaying this, knowing there will be a loud, vile response.

"I TOLD YOU NOT TO DO A DAMNED THING WITHOUT ORDERS FROM ME! WHO THE *HELL* DO YOU THINK YOU ARE? *YOU* WORK FOR *ME*!" Everything is quiet for a moment, then, "Otis will be dealt with *my* way, when the time is right. Can the bomb be traced back to him?"

"No, boss. I'm sorry. He wasn't supposed to do it. He took it on himself. He's getting very impatient too. He says he only did what he thought you wanted."

"*I* WANTED?! *I* don't want any more mistakes. You'd better hear this well… no more mistakes. You wait for *my* orders! That goes for Otis too and you'd better tell him that! Now get me that Will. *NOW*!"

"Yes, boss. Right away."

❧

Flame is waking up. Her eyes are covered in thick bandages and her right arm is in a cast. It will be off soon though, in a week at the most. Grandfather has already healed the fracture, but the doctors don't know it yet. She groans, and calls out for Ghost.

When the realization of what has happened hits her, she bolts upright and screams out, "*GHOST?!*"

"Shh, honey. He's fine. You are too. Don't worry, he's at Doc's again. He's fine, just a little bit of burnt fur. Lay down, honey, don't get so excited. There's someone here to see you." Shay is squeezing her hand, trying to give her consolation and take away her fear for Ghost.

"I should have known, Granddaughter, that you would think first of your Ghost." Grandfather chuckles, laying his hand on her shoulder to comfort her.

"Grandfather?! Oh, thank God you're here! What's happened? Why can't I see?" She is trying her best to get her hand to her eyes and Shay is trying just as hard to keep it away. She asks, "Grandfather? Can I........"

"Do it, Granddaughter. See for yourself." he tells her. He is giving her the permission she asks for.

She enters his mind, seeing herself through his eyes. She sees the bandages on her eyes, sees her face is mildly burned, but no real damage has been done.

Grandfather shows her his memories of what has happened.

She gasps, going back into herself, and says, "You've healed me, Grandfather. How did you know to be here? Why's my arm in a cast? How did you get here so quickly?" She has many questions still bubbling forth when he stops her.

He says, "Hush now. I was warned that something would happen. I do not understand it myself. I dreamed of a woman screaming for you to stop, not to go near your trailer, and then the explosion. This woman saved your life, Granddaughter."

"That was Sandy. She took over my booth, Grandfather. I left the carnival and she wanted to run the booth." she says, smiles and asks, "Where's Frankie?! He did that?!" She has seen the damage Frankie had done in the waiting area while in Grandfather's mind, making her love him all the more. He is such a good friend, but she worries about him. What if they won't release him?

She asks, "He's coming to see me, right?"

"Flame, you know you can't keep that crazy man out of here!" Shay says, and laughs.

"It is good to know, Granddaughter, that you have made such good friends. I think you will need to lean on them for a while. I do not know what is going on here, for sure, but I want you to stay close to those that love you.

Do not go anywhere by yourself. Do you hear me?"

"I hear you, Grandfather, but, what happened? Why did my trailer blow up?"

This time it is Shay that speaks, "We're not sure yet, honey, but I promise you I'll find out who did it, and why it was done. Someone wants something you, and possibly Joe, have. It's no coincidence that his office was broken into and your trailer was bombed. That bomb was no random act. It was set by remote, so they were watching you walk to the trailer. You are *not* leaving my side until we find out what's going on."

"My God, if Sandy hadn't yelled at me, then Ghost and I would be dead! But, I don't have anything that anyone could possibly want, Shay! I haven't done anything to anyone that would cause them to want to kill me! Why's this happening?" she asks, almost tearfully.

"Granddaughter, we think it might have something to do with the Will I had Joe have you to sign. I think it is about the forest. Even the land is not worth your life to me. You have to know that. We must stop this from happening, somehow, some way."

"I don't know what we could do, except to find out who's doing it. I know Shay will do all he can to find these people. He's the best, Grandfather." her voice goes soft.

"I know, Granddaughter, I know." He doesn't know what else to do. He must find out more about the people that have been trying for so long to buy his land. He feels like kicking himself for not ever getting any information on them. The only one he knows is Mr. Stokes, but he doesn't even have a first name for him. He will talk this over with Joe later.

Finally, Frankie bursts into the room with Janey right behind him, telling him, "Slow down, Frankie! She's okay! Slow down or you're going to scare her to death!"

But, he just keeps going until he is right up against her bed, almost pushing Grandfather out of the way. He exclaims loudly, "Girlfriend? You hear me? You really okay? Did your Grandpapy fix you?"

"Yes, Frankie, I'm okay. Really. Yes, Grandfather did it. I really am okay. I just have to be careful with my eyes for awhile. They're very sensitive to light, so I guess I'll need some dark glasses to wear, but really, I'm okay." she answers and smiles brightly for him.

"I'm so happy, girlfriend. That sure do make what happened to me worth it all. I thought you was gone. Damn, girlfriend, don't ever do nothin like gettin hurt on me again. My old heart was just broke, and on top of all that these dumb-assed doctors done put me in a damn crazy room! They even tied me down! Like I was gonna hurt somebody! I thought I'd go nuts and they wouldn't listen to nothin I told em. Said I was outta my head! Me! Outta my head! I tried to tell em you was hurt and I was only tryin to get your

Grandpapy to fix you up, but even that sent em off for more of those damn shots!" He has his head in his hands, shaking it back and forth.

Everyone in the room is shaking with silent laughter. Even Janey has a huge grin on her face. She tells them, "You should have seen him, poor man. I almost *never* got the doctor to release him! I had to tell another little fib to get him out. I told the doctor that I was taking him to see you and that an officer was waiting to take him to the police station from here. Well… it was almost the truth. I felt so sorry for him. He really did try to make them believe him, but they really thought he was nuts, especially when his toxicology screen came up negative!

"I still don't know how you did it, Mr. Wolf, but thank God for you. You and Flame are both miracle workers. If there's ever anything I can do to help you, in any way, please just call me." Janey says, and grins.

Then she adds, "Flame, I'll bring you those glasses and as soon as the doctor comes in and takes off those bandages, you can use them. It'll still be dark, but at least you'll be able to see...something I honestly thought would never happen again." She leaves the room shaking her head and they can all hear her laughter as soon as the door closes.

Grandfather calls Joe to come and pick him up. He is feeling every bit of his ninety-some years this day, and does not think he should be driving. It had been a very long night. Since Joe only has the one bedroom. Shay had insisted that Grandfather go to his apartment and use his guest room. Joe will take Grandfather to pick up Ghost first and Ghost will stay with him.

Flame says, "Frankie… go home Shay's here with me and I promise no one will come in here to do anything to me. Now you go get your sleep and when they let us out of these beds, I promise I'll have Joe tell you. I know you want to be my bodyguard, but really, I'm okay right now, but I love you."

"I love you too, girlfriend. You go on and tell that big bad wolf that I love his mutt-ass too. Bye, girlfriend, Shay." And he is gone.

There are a few moments of blessed silence and then Shay says, "I love you, honey. We'll fix this, somehow, some way. I promise."

"I love you too, Shay, more than I can ever say. I know you'll do everything you can for me, but it's not me that I'm worried about. If it's really over the land then what about Grandfather? What's going to happen to him?"

"I don't know, honey. I honestly don't. We'll take it one step at a time. First we have to convince Dr. Kouri to release us. I'll work on that when he comes in." He squeezes her hand and she entwines her fingers in his.

Within the hour Dr. Kouri comes in, bringing Janey with him. He checks Shay over first, having Janey clean and rebandage his wound. Then he goes to Flame, removes her bandages from her eyes, checks their response to light, and has Janey give her the dark glasses.

Dr. Kouri tells her, "These will help, young lady. I don't know how it's possible that you can see, but I've seen God work miracles before, just not two in the same room. What is it with you, Larson? You always have been one lucky bastard!" He chuckles.

"Mike, I'm lucky to have a good doctor and an even better nurse." Shay winks at Janey and adds, "We both need to get out of here though. There's something going on that I can't talk about right now, Mike, but we really do need to go home. I promise that I'll keep Flame at home, and I'll even try to stay with her as much as possible. Can you release us?"

"No way! Not today, buddy. I tell you what, if you're both doing as well tomorrow, and I'll make it earlier in the morning, I'll release you both. Only because I know you wouldn't ask if it wasn't serious. Flame was unconscious until just a little while ago, Shay. She needs to be observed at least one more night. Deal?"

"Thank you, Mike. We're supposed to be in Joe Wolf's wedding on Saturday. I'm the best man and Flame is the maid of honor. Won't we make a charming surprise for the wedding guests, me in my bandages and Flame in her dark glasses and cast?"

"I think I'm going to take Saturday off and crash that wedding! I'm going to bring my camera and then I'll have my blackmail pictures!" Dr. Kouri laughs as he leaves.

Janey smiles at them both, giving them a thumbs-up once more.

Chapter 23

Joe picks up Shay and Flame the next morning. It is Friday and Flame is worried because she has no personal items of her own. They go home to Shay's apartment and Mercedes surprises her with everything she can possibly need, and more. She hugs her and runs straight to Ghost.

She tells him, *I'm home, my friend. I see you're well. I'm so glad, Ghost. I worried over you so much. I'm fine, and we're going to a wedding!* She gives him a picture, in her head, of what a wedding is and what he will be doing.

When he sees that flowers will be on his head he shakes all over, covering his head with his front paws.

She laughs and explains what she has shown him to everyone.

The room rings with laughter.

Grandfather says, "I think not, my friend. I would not let my granddaughter embarrass you so. There will be no flowers on you, this I promise, Ghost. Shame on you, Granddaughter, do you know what that can do to man's character?" He is shaking with amusement as he adds, "I think he will be your guide wolf instead. You will need to have him close to you, not only to be your sight, but to protect you. There will be nothing to upset this wedding!"

Joe's serious about this too and says, "You're right, Grandfather. It'll be a wonderful day for all of us. I have seen to that already. I hired security for the entire event and we'll take no chances. Mercedes and I have already decided to stay here for awhile after the wedding, instead of taking our honeymoon right away. I think everyone's protection comes first, for now."

Mercedes says, "Flame, I hope you don't mind, but I brought your dress for you. I hope you'll like it. I think it will fit beautifully. Do you want to go into the bedroom with me and see it? I'd like for you to try it on for me.

"Also, Shay, Joe's brought you a tux too. We knew there would be so much going on that you two wouldn't have a chance to do it yourselves. I hope you're pleased with our choices." She takes Flame's hand, pulling her from the room. She knew the men had to talk and she didn't want to overwhelm Flame with the security details. She also did not want to remind her someone was after them for some reason. She has had enough to worry about lately.

"I'm sure we'll both love them, Mercedes, and I guess I'm going to try it on now!" she says, and laughs, letting Mercedes pull her to the bedroom.

Ghost will not leave her side. Grandfather has told him to stay with her and Ghost will not disobey him. He has not forgotten Grandfather, or his love for the wolves and his forest home, especially since Flame has reminded him of them all since he was a cub.

As soon as the women leave the room, the men seat themselves in the living room.

Shay is first to speak, "Okay, Joe, tell me about this security. I don't want to take a chance on anyone getting hurt."

"Don't worry, Shay. I've hired some of the best security people available. I've even talked a few officers from the station into coming without uniforms and sitting close to the front. They'll be carrying, under their jackets. I want everyone protected just as much as you do. Someone wants something from us, but damn if I can figure out what, or who."

"Grandson, Shay and I have discussed this. I believe it has to do with my home land. I believe someone went into your office to search it for the Will you and Flame have signed. When they could not get to it there, they sent someone else to her trailer. We do not know if they found the Will, but they did try to kill her. This is a fact."

"My God, Grandfather! Why haven't you told me this before?! If they're trying to get your land then you, too, are in danger! You must be protected!"

"Do not worry for me, Grandson. I have my own protection, and you know this. I will not change my lifestyle for anyone or anything. No one will come onto my land without me knowing it.

"You have a wedding tomorrow. You should worry about taking care of your new wife. It is a joyous occasion! Enjoy it, Grandson. We will not let anyone take this joy from us." he says, placing his hand on Joe's arm.

"Joe, Grandfather, I understand your concerns. I've talked with a few of my friends at the station and they're doing all they possibly can to figure this out. My friend, Don, is on the case, and I'm sure we'll find something soon. They can't do things like this and get away with it. I'll go back on the job next week even though I'm not supposed to. It'll be unofficial, but I'll find some answers, I promise you that."

"Thank you, Shay. I do feel better knowing all this, but Grandfather please; won't you stay here for awhile? I know you said you must get back home after the wedding, but please just stay here until we can figure some of this out." Joe is so worried about him.

"Grandson, you know me too well. No, I will not let anyone scare me away from my own home. I have protected that land for over ninety years now and I will not stop until I can do it no longer. Please do not scare Flame, or your soon-to-be wife, with any of this talk. They cannot know. Please do this for me…get married and enjoy your new wife. I will be fine."

Reluctantly, Joe looks from his stern expression to Shay's shrugging shoulders and agrees by nodding and saying, "I will honor your wishes, Grandfather, as always, though I don't like it. I love you and I want you to be here to see your great-grandchildren."

Grandfather assures him, "I will, Grandson. Never worry about that. I will see them and they will know me."

Flame enters Shay's bedroom to find a beautiful dark green full length formal gown on Shay's bed. Beside it is a black tux, dark green shirt, and black tie for Shay. She exclaims, "My gosh, Mercedes, they're beautiful! I hate that you had to do all of this without my help, but you did a wonderful job I love it!"

"Then try it on! I can't wait to see it on you! I knew that the green would look great on you. I hope it fits!"

Flame immediately strips down and pulls on the gown, with Mercedes trying to help her get it over the cast. There is no way it will go on over it.

An exasperated Flame exclaims, "*Oh*! We have to take this damn thing off! Will you help me? Come on...let's go into the kitchen. We're getting rid of this damn cast!"

"But, the doctor said you have to leave it on! Your arm was fractured! We can't take it off!" Mercedes looks incredulous.

"Mercedes, do you really think Grandfather would let me have a fracture and not repair it? He's done it already and there's nothing wrong with my arm. The doctors didn't check it again after putting the cast on. He repaired it while I slept." She smiles and pulls Mercedes out of the room.

"Okay...but I wish I could get used to all this magic you two seem to have so much of. I guess, since I'm going to be family now, I'll have to get used to it, won't I?" She giggles, letting Flame pull her into the hallway.

The men watch them laughing their way to the kitchen, and shrug their shoulders, until they hear the sound of a knife cutting something obviously hard. They all three rush into the kitchen to find Mercedes cutting away at the cast while Ghost lays on his back grinning from ear to ear. When he sees the men, he jumps up, looks at the women, coughs loudly while shaking his head, and lies back down.

"What the hell are you doing? You can't take that off!" Shay says, giving them an incredulous look. He turns to Grandfather and tells him, "Tell her to stop that!"

Grandfather laughs and comments, "The dress would not go over it, huh?"

"No! And I want this damn thing off of me now!" she states impatiently, and actually stomps her foot.

Shay's face is red and he looks ready to pull the knife from Mercedes' hand himself. He cannot believe they are doing this.

"It is okay, Shay. I have already healed her. I healed her after they put that thing on her. She knows what she is doing, but I do not think the knife will work so well, Granddaughter." He is laughing so hard by now at Shay, and Flame, that tears are rolling down his wrinkled face.

"Shay, do you have a handsaw? I'll take it off. You'd better get used to this, buddy. It's part of your life now too. I broke my leg when I was a kid, and Grandfather worked on it all night. It healed perfectly, but it's kind of a strange thing to see. Isn't too much fun sometimes, is it?" Joe is having a hard time holding his laughter in, but doesn't want to upset Shay anymore than he already is.

"Damn. I should have known." Shay says, shaking his head. He adds, "I'll never get used to this. How the hell do you do it, Mercedes? Doesn't it freak you out a little too?"

"Well, I guess it does, kind of. I think it's cool though!"

"You would, you're a woman." Shay shakes his head as he walks into the storage room off the kitchen. He is muttering something about "women". He comes back in the room with a handsaw and cautions Joe before handing it to him, "You'd better be damn good with this thing."

After the cast is removed Flame and Mercedes rush off into the bedroom once more and Flame puts on the dress. She exclaims, "It's a perfect fit! Mercedes, you *are* good!"

"Wow, I think you'll be the center of attention tomorrow, not me! That dress looks gorgeous on you! Oh, please don't show it to the men yet! Let's surprise them tomorrow. Shay will flip when he sees you."

"I can't wait, Mercedes, but you're right, I do want to surprise him. I can't wait to see the look on his face when he sees me in it. I swear, it's been one bad thing after another while I've been here. I'm so glad we finally have something to celebrate. By the way, have you found your father a condo yet?"

"Yes, but I don't want to tell him until tomorrow. I'm going to surprise him. It's going to be sort of a wedding gift, but from *us* to *him*. I hope he likes it. I really don't know what his reaction will be. I think Joe and I will stay at his place for at least another week, before moving in to the house. That'll give Daddy time to move out and it'll also give Joe and me a little time off, you know, to ourselves."

"I heard Joe mention that you were putting the honeymoon off, but I thought you were so excited about it. Why have you changed your plans?" She cannot believe they changed their plans, because they had been looking so forward to going to the island.

"We'll still go, just not now. Joe and I have agreed that it'll have to wait for a little while. We want to be here long enough to get moved into the house first. It won't be too long, though." She does not want Flame to know that they are staying because they are worried about her and Grandfather. It wouldn't be fair to tell her. She would insist that they go, and Mercedes knows Joe will not hear of it. She also cannot go off and enjoy herself if she is worried over her best friend the whole time.

Chapter 24

It is a beautiful warm summer day. The sun is shining and the breeze is not too strong. The wedding is being held in the city park. The bride and groom will be in a beautiful white gazebo with the minister. Flame and Shay will be on the steps behind them, with Ghost between them. The guests will be seated on white chairs that stand in front of the gazebo.

Mercedes is so nervous and so excited that she cannot sit still.

Flame exclaims, "*Mercedes*, stay still or you're going to have the wildest hairdo you've ever seen!"

She is braiding Mercedes' hair and pulling it atop her head, with small ringlets falling softly around her face. It will look perfect with the old fashioned wedding dress. The dress had been Mercedes' mother's dress. It is gorgeous. It fits perfectly and has a long train trailing down in the back. The headpiece is a simple ring of white that will fit around the top of her hair.

Finally she is ready.

She looks in the mirror and exclaims, "Oh my gosh, Flame, I look just like my mother! Look, I have to show you her picture." She pulls out a small photo of her mother and father taken at their wedding and adds, "I wanted to carry this with me today. I guess it's my way of making sure that my mom is with me."

"Mercedes, you're right, she *is* with you. You know that no matter where she is, she's with you today. You do look just like her, though. I can't believe how much. It's like looking at a picture of you!"

Mercedes is a beautiful bride. She absolutely radiates happiness.

Flame is so happy for both Mercedes and Joe. They make a beautiful couple.

Joe is just as nervous as Mercedes.

Shay is trying to calm him down and he isn't doing very well at it. He thinks, *How do I calm him down when I can't even calm myself down! I'm not the one getting married, yet I can't even tie my own tie!*

They are pitiful in their efforts until Grandfather steps in. He says, "Boys, you two are going to hang yourselves. Here, let me see that." First he fixes Joe's tie, then Shay's.

Joe's tux is white with a dark green shirt and white tie.

Grandfather says, "You both look great. I cannot wait to see the ladies."

"Thank you, Grandfather. I don't understand why I'm so damned nervous. I love Mercedes, but I hate the thought of getting up there in front of all those people." Joe admits.

Shay laughs and tells him, "Joe, there aren't that many people here. You only invited about twenty people all together. By the way, I saw Frankie earlier. He's already met Stephan and they seem to be getting along just great. I'm glad Stephan is as tall as Frankie is anyway."

All three of them share a laugh over this.

"That man is a bit strange, but I like him. He has been good to my granddaughter and that means a lot to me." Grandfather smiles and tells Joe, "Your young bride will be very proud of you, Grandson."

"God, I hope so, Grandfather. I keep picturing myself falling down, passing out, or doing some other stupid thing."

Shay and Grandfather cannot help but laugh at him, though they understand what he is feeling.

"I cannot really see you doing that, Grandson. You will be fine."

The wedding begins. Joe and the minister are now in the gazebo. Shay and Flame are walking together up the dark green silk runner leading up to the gazebo. Ghost walks on Flame's left with Shay on the right. Flame must still wear the dark glasses, but every once in a while she looks through Ghost's eyes at the crowd.

Shay is in complete awe of Flame. Never has he seen anyone so very beautiful. And, she is his. He still cannot believe he got so lucky. He cannot imagine how Joe must feel, because he feels breathless himself. You would think it was him getting married. He is as proud as he can possibly be walking Flame down the aisle. Luckily the bandages fit well under his tux and he doesn't feel too self-conscious.

Shay, you look amazing. I'm so proud to be here with you. I love you. Flame cannot help but tell Shay how she feels.

He jumps just a little when she whispers into his mind, but he hides it well. He does not know if he will ever get used to it.

He mentally says back, *Flame, don't do that! You scared the crap out of me! I'm getting a bit more used to it though. You can hear me right?* Shay can't help but glance at her when he thinks the last.

Yes, Shay, I can, only when you project it to me though. I can't really read your mind, but sometimes I can see what you see, or what you're thinking, in a picture book sort of way. You can't do that with me though. I don't really understand it all yet myself. Only Grandfather and the animals have ever been able to hear me before. Get used to it, babe. I'm not going anywhere any time soon! She smiles at Shay, enjoying this back and forth banter with him.

Shay smiles brightly back and says, *I love you too, honey.*

Ghost walks proudly beside her. No flowers are on him, but he does have a black silk bow-tie around his neck. He doesn't much like it, but it is much better than flowers.

The three of them take their place on the steps and the wedding march begins. Every head turns, looking for the bride.

Mercedes looks so beautiful and her father is at her side.

He looks down at her and says, "Mercedes, you look so very much like your mother. You're the spitting image of her today. You make me proud."

Flame looks over at Joe to gauge his reaction to his bride. He is grinning from ear to ear, his eyes bright.

Mercedes smiles up at him as they reach his side and the ceremony begins. The vows were written by Joe and Mercedes and they are beautiful.

They even have Shay tearing up, but he is a bit sensitive after seeing the way Flame glows today.

Ghost is giving them his great wolf grin.

When the minister tells Joe he can kiss his bride the guests stand and cheer. Everyone is having a wonderful time. Even S.R. Holst has an honest smile on his face this time

Grandfather is sitting on the other side, the groom's side, with tears shining brightly in his old eyes.

The reception is to be held at the Holst mansion.

❧

"I've read it. Did you? Do you understand what needs to be done, Sergeant?"

"Yes, boss, I have and I do."

"The wedding reception will be over very soon. I want you to begin the show. The old man first. Be there waiting when he gets to his precious land."

"Yes, boss. Who do you want to do it?"

"I want three of your people this time. I have another little job for *you*, but it won't happen until this one is done. I want it done without any mistakes this time. You're to see it through all the way to the end. Do you understand?"

"Yes. I'll take care of it. There will be no mistakes this time."

"You do that, Sergeant. Call me when you take the old man out. And you'd better get it right, this time!"

And the line goes dead.

❧

Flame, Shay, Ghost, and Grandfather, ride in Shay's van, and the bride and groom ride in a huge white limousine. The guests follow behind.

When Flame gets a glimpse of the mansion she gives an audible gasp. It is huge. She cannot imagine living in such a monstrous house. It is not her style. It *is* beautiful, and if that is what makes Mercedes and Joe happy, she is happy for them.

"What do you think of the little old Holst home, honey?" Shay asks, after hearing her gasp and seeing her mouth drop.

"My Lord! I'd get lost going to the bathroom in that thing! Please, Shay, tell me we'll never live like that!" She is very serious about this and makes it known.

"Granddaughter, I do not think your man here would quite fit in to that kind of life. He is made for you; like you in his needs and wants. You will have the forest, and your own home there, one day."

He speaks this with a far-away look in his eyes, giving Shay a chill up his spine as he looks at him in the rearview mirror. He seems to know things that others can only guess at.

Flame, did that sound like a prediction to you? Shay cannot help asking her, silently.

She only smiles a small sad smile and looks back, in the backseat, at Grandfather.

Shay, I can talk with you like this also. When you project your thoughts to my granddaughter, you must *remember that I can hear them too.* sends Grandfather.

Shay is shocked when he actually hears Grandfather's chuckle.

Grandfather adds, *Maybe it* was *a prediction, though I have only done that one other time. That was two nights ago, when Flame was hurt.* He finishes aloud, "I think we should talk openly while we are in the company of these people. I have the strangest feeling we are being watched here. I have felt this ever since the wedding started." He warns them.

"Yes, Grandfather, I think you're right. It was a strange feeling and, though the wedding was beautiful, I felt eyes on me the whole time. I even checked around, using Ghost's eyes, but I saw nothing too strange. I did notice that there were a couple of men in dark suits that were watching us all. They caught my attention because they didn't smile like everyone else did." She frowns at the memory.

"Honey, those were cops that Joe hired for the wedding, as security. I'm sorry I didn't tell you. I should have known that you would notice them." admits Shay.

"I saw someone there that I have a feeling I have seen somewhere before. He was in a dark suit, like my granddaughter said, but I cannot see him being a cop. Not if where I saw him before is where I think it was."

They arrive and the van doors are opened by the valet before anything else can be said between them. When they enter the house the first thing they see is Sadie. She is sitting beside a door off of the foyer. When she sees Ghost she stands and whines, looking to the young man that is holding her on a leash.

Flame knows she wants to greet them both and she sends a thought to her, *We'll come to see you, Sadie. Let us ask permission first. I don't want to cause you to be punished for your, or our, actions.*

Sadie calmly sits back down to wait.

They enter a huge ballroom off the foyer and after a few minutes of conversation with a few of the guests, Flame turns to speak to Grandfather, "Can you keep Mercedes' father occupied a few minutes? His dog, Sadie, has become a friend to Ghost and we'd like to greet her properly. She'll be punished if he sees us. He's not a kind man."

"Granddaughter, you do what you need to do. I will keep him occupied. It is time I have a few words with this man anyway. I have put it off as long as possible. I know he is not a kind man. I too have eyes that still see well." he says, with a grim look on his face as he heads in the direction of Mercedes' father.

Shay has been standing with them and he offers to help too. "I'll try to get the goon away from Sadie for you. Let me come with you and just go along with what I say. Okay?" he asks.

She nods and they leave the huge ballroom and head back toward the foyer.

As they approach the young man holding Sadie, Shay asks, "Excuse me, I hate to ask, but I'm the best man and we left a wedding present in my van for the bride and groom. Could you possibly take me to where they parked my van?"

"Sir, I cannot leave the dog unattended. She's a guard dog and Mr. Holst doesn't want her to scare any of the guests. She must stay here. It's part of her training." He says this with a sad look down at Sadie, obviously thinking it is wrong to treat her this way. He adds, "She's a good dog, but Mr. Holst is very firm about the way her training is done."

"I'm Mercedes' best friend, Flame. I know Sadie and we've been together many times. Maybe I can keep her here for you long enough to show Shay where his van's parked. He'll need you to help him with gift though, it's very heavy."

Shay looks at her with eyes wide. He does not know what she is talking about. He wonders what he is going to do when they get to the van and there is nothing to get?!

He asks silently, *What am I going to tell this guy when there's no present there?!* He hears her laughter.

She silently tells him, *Trust me, Shay. Did you actually look in the back of the van? Go... take him. It* is *heavy.*

She smiles beguilingly at both men.

"Well, since it's a wedding gift, and you're the couple's best friends, I guess it'll be okay. Please, Miss, keep Sadie right here though. I could lose my job if Mr. Holst sees me leave her. He seems busy, but I don't know what I'll do to explain if he sees me leave my post." The young man actually looks frightened when he speaks of Mr. Holst.

"Don't worry. My grandfather has Mr. Holst cornered in there and I promise he'll be there for quite awhile. Grandfather has a lot to tell him." She gives this young man her brightest smile and the guy goes all glassy eyed.

Shay says silently, *Damn, Flame, you do know what you do when you smile at a man like that! I wish you wouldn't do that...it makes me want to throttle the guy!*

The poor man hands the leash to her and starts toward the door without another word.

Shay looks back at Flame and she sticks out her tongue and winks at him, her laughter echoing through his mind.

As soon as they are gone she stoops down to Sadie's level. Ghost and Sadie are nose to nose. She enters Ghost's mind. They are greeting each other and Sadie is very happy to see them both. She shows Ghost the punishment her master had given her on the day they met at Doc's. It was pure cruelty.

Mr. Holst is a very cruel man. Flame is furious that he would treat any animal so cruelly, let alone his own pet, or guard dog.

Ghost is growling deeply.

Flame calms both animals. She sends love and reassurance to Sadie and leaves Ghost's mind and enters Sadie's. She tells her, *Sadie you're a very good girl. Don't let that man make you feel otherwise. I know Mercedes is good to you and that you love her. She loves you too. I'll do everything I can to help you. I promise, but I need a favor from you too. You know I entered your mind...so you can do the same to me, or even Ghost. We now have a mind link and if you ever need me, call on me. I will hear you.*

When she mentions Mercedes' name, flashes of her move through Sadie's mind. She sees Mercedes' father yelling at her, slapping her across face, flashes of cruelty, not only to Sadie and Mercedes, but to other people, people that have crossed Mr. S.R. Holst.

She has to pull out of Sadie's mind. She cannot stand to see anymore without confronting this monster of a man, but first she tells Sadie, *Watch over Mercedes while she's here. If your master ever raises his hand to Mercedes you must tell me immediately! Please do this for me.*

Sadie nuzzles her hand in acknowledgment.

They spend the next few minutes just touching one another. Flame pours love on Sadie's glossy fur with each stroke, and Ghost does the same by rubbing his head on her. Flame knows that Mercedes loves Sadie, but she has always seen her as her father's dog, not having a lot to do with her in his presence.

Sadie is comforted, perhaps more than she has ever been. She will do as Flame tells her. She will do anything for love, but her master has never understood that and probably never will.

Shay and the young man return with a large wrapped package carried between them. There is a small table in the center of the foyer that is covered with packages. They place the gift at the foot of the table and Shay shakes the young man's hand when they return to Flame's side.

"Thank you again for your help. I couldn't have carried it by myself. Here, let me give you a little something for your trouble." Shay reaches for his wallet, but the young man puts his hand up in the air to stop him.

"No, sir, I was glad to help. I'm glad Sadie was able to see her friends too. Thank you for caring for her, Mam. I'm sorry, I don't usually talk about my boss, but I just hate the way he treats her. She tries so hard to please him, but I don't think anyone or anything could actually please that man. I can only ask that you don't repeat what I've said." He reaches out and takes Sadie's leash again, patting her on the head.

"You're a good man. Thank you for trying to help with Sadie. We care very much for her and Mercedes. I know how your boss is and don't worry; we'd never say a word to him about any of it. I hope you'll be able to continue to help Sadie. I wish I knew of something I could do for her." Flame admits.

She looks at Shay and he can tell she has seen something terrible in Sadie's memories. He takes her hand, and squeezes it. It breaks his heart, too, that this beautiful, well mannered animal is cruelly abused.

"Mam, if you don't mind, may I ask you a question?"

"Sure, anything." she answers, as she turns back toward him.

"If you're blind, and using a seeing-eye dog, why's there no leash on him?"

"You'd never believe us if we told you!" Shay can't help saying and he and Flame laugh, turning back to join the party.

He leans closer and asks, "By the way, what's in that huge, heavy box and where did you get it?"

"I had Frankie pick it up for me. He had it wrapped and everything. Can't you even guess what it is?" she asks, getting a crooked grin on her beautiful face.

"I have no earthly idea!"

"Silly man. It's a baby's cradle!" She exclaims, and laughs at Shays open mouth look, and then he laughs with her, thinking what Joe's reaction will be.

He adds, "Well, if what you saw in their future holds true they'll sure need it. Maybe we should buy them another one, just in case!"

Mercedes and Joe are having the time of their lives. They dance, laugh, and enjoy the toasts from all of the guests. The cake is cut and everyone is well fed. Even Ghost is given a piece of cake.

Mercedes takes it upon herself to give Sadie a piece too, though obviously her father does not approve. She knew that he wouldn't, so she didn't even ask him.

Grandfather has spoken to Mercedes' father. They stood uncomfortably together for awhile and he finally ran out of things to talk to this man about. He obviously did not want to talk to Grandfather either. He answers Grandfather's questions but never really looks at him, and completely ignores Grandfather's outstretched hand.

Grandfather wonders why he has agreed to the marriage of his daughter to his grandson. It is obvious, to all that care to see, that this man, this Mr. S.R. Holst, does not approve of Joe's Indian heritage.

He finally gives up trying and returns to Flame's side. She asks how it went and he only smiles slightly. It was painfully obvious they were not doing much talking.

He finally says, "That man is a real pain in the ass. How did Mercedes grow up to be such a bright light with that man for a father?"

"I know what you mean, Grandfather. I get terrible vibes from him. Mercedes was raised in boarding schools." She lowers her voice and says, "She believes her father may have been the cause of her mother's death. Her mother committed suicide when Mercedes was very young and, in her mind, she connects the death to him. I didn't reveal that to anyone else when I read her past."

"Granddaughter, I do not think anything is out of the question when concerning that man. There is not much he would not do. He would not even shake my hand. I offered my hand to him and he acted as though he could not even see it. I do not understand how he agreed so readily to this marriage." He is looking at Mercedes' father with consideration as he adds, "I think there is more to what this man wants than meets the eye."

"Do you believe he only wants to be rid of Mercedes? I mean, he doesn't know it yet, but Mercedes and Joe bought a condo for him, and plan on surprising him with it today. They are going to live here. The house belonged to her mother and it was left to her. I wonder what his reaction to that will be."

"I do not know, Granddaughter, but I want to be sure she is not alone with that man. One of us, or Joe, must be in the room when she gives him this gift. Do not alarm her, but try to do as I say." He is watching Mercedes and Joe now. He is worried that Mercedes' father may do harm to her if someone is not present. He adds, "I do not think that man will willingly leave this house."

Very soon afterward, Mercedes decides that the time is right to give her father their gift. She looks up at Joe, "Honey, let's call Daddy off a minute and give him the keys to his condo, okay?" She looks so happy and excited about this.

Joe looks at her father. He is talking with another man and Joe thinks that Mr. Holst does not look the part of the happy father. He has been dreading this moment, but he cannot put it off any longer.

This house is Mercedes' and she wants to make it their home. He only wants her to be happy and he will do anything to see to that. He glances at Grandfather and then back to Mercedes' happy face, giving her a smile full of love. He says, "Sure, honey. Let's do it."

S.R. Holst sees them coming his way, shakes the man's hand that he is talking to and walks to meet them. His whole face has changed to one of false happiness and fake smiles. He says, "Don't tell me you're already leaving for the honeymoon! You haven't even opened your gifts and there are quite a number of them in the foyer!" He chuckles.

"No, Daddy, this time we have a gift for you. Come into your office with us just a minute, please?" she asks, and takes her father's arm, excitedly pulling him toward his office.

"For me? What in the world could you give to me? This is your day!" he asks and smiles, but Joe sees his eyes darken momentarily.

Joe thinks, almost snidely, *This man believes we're going to announce that he's going to be a grandfather.* He cannot help but grin when this thought crosses his mind. That is yet another conversation that he wishes never to hear with Mercedes' father present.

They walk into his office and Mercedes reaches into the top desk drawer, pulling out a set of keys. She has a tremendous smile on her face, but Joe does not believe it will be there long.

Mr. Holst asks, "What are those, Mercedes, and how did they get into my desk?"

"I put them there, Daddy. If you haven't noticed, I don't really have a pocket to put them in!" Mercedes says and giggles delightedly.

Only Joe notices the slight frown that comes into her father's eyes.

She continues, "Daddy, Joe and I bought you a gift. Here these belong to you. These are the keys to your new condominium in the Forest Oaks Community! Surprise, Daddy!"

Joe watches his father-in-law's face redden in anger.

His mouth tightens as he tries to control it. He says, "Thank you, honey, but why do I need a condo? The thought was wonderful, but this is a huge house and I know it belongs to you, but I'm almost never here anyway. I really don't see the need, right now at least, for me to move." He doesn't take the keys, doesn't even reach for them.

"Uh...I'm sorry, Daddy. I thought you'd be happy with it. I mean, we're not asking you to move right this minute. We aren't even going on a honeymoon right now. We're going to stay at Joe's for as long as you need, to give you time to move into the condo. Oh, *Daddy*, it's not that we don't want you here, you know you're always welcome here, but we...I mean, *I*, really want to start this marriage in our own home. This is *my* home, Daddy." Even Mercedes can see that her father is trying to make her feel bad, to make her feel as if she is kicking him out on the street.

She thinks, *Daddy, you'd better remember that I am your daughter too...I can be just as damn stubborn as you can.*

While Mercedes thinks this, Joe says, "Mr. Holst, please understand Mercedes is only trying to please you. We looked for a place that would be located in a perfect setting for you. It's nearly in downtown, so you can take care of all your business needs. There's a large, spare room for your office. I'll even be happy to help you set it all up there.

"Please don't make her feel like she's done something wrong. You knew she would want to raise her family in her own home." Joe tells him soberly. By this time, he is getting royally pissed. He has never liked this man anyway and after hearing how this man treated his own daughter after her mother died, he has to stand up for her. He has had all he can, or will, take.

"Son, this will always be her home. It's also *my* home and I will *not* move out of it. I'm sorry, Mercedes, but I can't take your offer. I will not be thrown out of my own house!" S.R. Holst is near his boiling point. He turns away from them to walk out of the office.

Mercedes grabs his arm, surprising him, turns him around almost forcefully, and says, deathly soft, "Daddy, this is *my* home! I didn't want us to argue over this, that's why we bought you a condo. We didn't even *have* to do that.

"Joe even paid for the wedding, never asking you for a dime. That was something that the bride's parents are *supposed* to do and I know if my mother were alive she would have insisted on paying for it. You *never even* offered." She takes a deep breath and screams, "AND WE BOUGHT YOU A CONDO AND YOU *WILL* BE MOVING FROM THIS HOUSE, I don't give a damn if you take the condo, or not! I *am* moving in here next week, *with my husband*, and *you* will be moved out of here by that time! Do you understand me, Daddy?!"

Both men are taken aback at this outburst from Mercedes.

Joe has never seen this side of her. But, he likes it. He thinks, with a grin, *That's my little hell cat!* He is so proud of her at this moment. He cannot help but grin as he looks at her father's scowling face. From the way her father looks, he is as surprised by this new Mercedes as Joe is.

This outburst from Mercedes has taken her father completely by surprise. He clenches his jaw and his hands ball into fists. He swallows audibly and looks at Joe with complete loathing, then back to Mercedes. He grits his teeth and says indignantly, "Mercedes, how *dare* you talk to me like that?! I would have gladly paid for the wedding, but I was never asked to do so! I sure would have planned a bigger, better one than this travesty of a wedding, with Indians, dogs, gays, and a damn fake psychic as guests.

"It's a damned shame that I couldn't even invite any of my friends to this thing. I was almost too embarrassed to invite the damn servants, or haven't you even noticed that most of the staff is not here?!

"I will *gladly* be out of this house by the end of the month and I don't want your damned condo. Shit, the building's probably filled with these kind of people." As he says this he looks at Joe with complete loathing and adds, "*I* will find my own place. Now leave me in peace! You can move in here whenever you want."

Mercedes is in tears. She is angry, embarrassed, and completely blindsided by this outburst from her father. She asks, "Daddy, you don't mean that do you? I thought you *liked* Joe? You told me that you would be happy to see me marry such a good man. Why are you saying these awful things?"

Her father, realizing his outburst has given his hate for Joe away, tries to recover his composure by saying, "I'm sorry, honey. Yes, I did say I was happy for you, and I am. I just got angry. Please, both of you, forgive me. I'll leave your home by next week as you've asked, Mercedes." He cannot afford to make an enemy of his daughter now.

Joe has clenched his jaw until it's sore. He wants to bash this bastard in the face so badly he can barely hold it back. This bigot of a man has embarrassed and ruined the happiest day of his daughter's life, and now he is trying to make her feel sorry for him. He begins, "Mr. Holst..."

Her father holds up his hand to stop him, saying, "Please, Joe, I'm sorry. You should call me S.R. now, or even Dad, if you would." S.R. Holst tries to appear humble now.

"Let me finish, *Dad*. I will never forgive you for hurting my wife this way, and on our wedding day! Yes, I am Indian. Sioux Indian. So will your *grandchildren* be! You had better get used to the idea, because nothing you do can change that." He glares at this obnoxious man for a moment.

Then he adds, "We'll be leaving after the reception and I will *not* come back here until you're gone. Mercedes can make up her own mind about how she feels, but I will not forget your words here today. In your anger, you let your true thoughts be known." His face is a mask of anger. It is all he can do to keep his voice at a normal level.

He will not stoop to this terrible man's level. He will try to make Mercedes happy for the rest of her time in her father's presence, to help her to forget the hurt that he has caused her.

Before another word is spoken, Joe wraps his arm around his wife's waist and pulls her from the room, slamming the door in her father's face. He thanks God that no one is standing in the foyer as they burst through the door. The young man with Sadie must have heard the commotion and taken Sadie outside.

"I'm so sorry, honey. I didn't mean to get so mad. Please forgive me." Joe feels so bad for Mercedes. Tears are gathering in her eyes again and he knows she must be angry with him for his words to her father.

She is crying, but not tears of sadness. Tears of anger. She is so furious at her father that she can barely breathe.

She looks up adoringly at Joe and tells him, "I love you and I am not mad at you. Never you. I'm so very angry at my father that I can barely catch my breath. I can't believe he said all those awful things. I'm so embarrassed for *him*. He's shown how ignorant he really is. Please forgive me, Joe, for all he said."

"Honey, I love you so much. You have nothing at all to be sorry for. Don't worry; we'll take care of everything. No one has to know what was said in there. It's all between us. I would never embarrass you by repeating what that man has said, to anyone." He places his hand under her chin, pulling her face up lightly to place a kiss on her lips.

He holds her to him, trying to take away all the things that she has heard. It was a terrible thing to do to such a wonderful, loving woman. He wonders how often things like this have happened to her over her young life. He will never forgive her father for any of this.

Chapter 25

Mercedes' father does not come back to join in the rest of the festivities and Joe does his best to take her mind off of what has happened. She appears happy, but he knows her too well. She is hurting. He will do whatever he can to change it for her.

They rejoin the rest of the party at the large table in the ballroom after the fiasco with her father. Everyone knows right away that something is wrong, but no one mentions it.

Flame helps to lighten the mood by asking Mercedes about baby names, but it is obvious Mercedes doesn't want to do it. She finally gives up, looking at Joe with a sad smile.

Joe tries another approach, saying, "Let's open the gifts now, honey." He smiles down at her as he takes her hand and pulls her gently up from the table.

"Sure, I love presents! Come on you guys, let's see what you gave us!" she announces to the room with a genuine smile this time.

The guests have dwindled down to only a few of their closest friends.

She pokes Flame in her side and whispers, "Did you see Frankie and Stephan? What did I tell you?!"

Flame laughs gaily. She has been quietly watching Frankie for the last half hour. He is openly laughing and talking to Stephan and she knows him better than anyone. He has to really like Stephan or he would not be so open with him. He is loud, big, and funny, but he does not open up to just anyone.

She agrees, and says, "Yes, Mercedes, I love that you did that for him. He's been such a great friend to me and Ghost. He's always been there for us."

She truly loves Frankie and she will miss him more than she cares to think about when he decides to return to the carnival. She knows now that she will never return. She just prays that Frankie will be happy, no matter what he does.

Mercedes tells her, "I love that I met him. He's such a sweet and funny man. He and Stephan are perfect together. Stephan's tall and so handsome, but he's so shy. He's never been comfortable with many people, and Frankie's made him smile so much today. Don't they look good together?"

"Yes, they do. They really do." Flame admits.

Stephan has a dark complexion, his ancestry Latino and he really is very handsome. Flame knows that Frankie is having the time of his life. Watching them she has to wonder if he might just decide to stay in Munson after all. She prays that is so, as she loves the idea that he might hang around too.

The gifts are opened and the happy couple has received everything they can possibly think of getting. It is time for the last gift to be opened.

Mercedes reaches down, picks up the tag, and reads, "With all our love on this most wonderful day, Flame, Shay, and Ghost. My goodness! What in the world did you guys do? This thing's too heavy to move!" Her eyes are gleaming and finally the happiness is back on her face and in her heart.

Joe is so happy to see she has apparently put the things her father said and did behind her. It is great to see her shining with excitement and love. He tells her, with a glare at Shay and Flame, "I don't know what they've done and with those three you never know!" He finally looks down at Ghost and warns, "If it whines I'm going to chase you down, Ghost!"

Ghost presents them all with his cough-laugh and wolf smile to the delight of everyone present.

"Open it up, Mercedes! It's the perfect gift. You'll see!" Flame grins.

She is so excited that she is practically jumping up and down. She has never been around so many people that she loves. She has actually never loved so many people. It is the most wonderful feeling she has ever had, next to what she feels for Shay.

Mercedes and Joe tear the paper off together and open the plain cardboard box, revealing a beautiful, white, hand carved baby cradle. Joe's mouth drops to his chest and Mercedes squeals in delight. Joe turns accusing eyes to Shay and sees that he is grinning mercilessly.

At precisely this moment her father opens his office door, seeing the last gift. He quietly closed the door, sits down in his office chair, and places his hands over his eyes. *What have I done?* he thinks to himself.

"Little sister, I can't believe this! I know it was you that did this! Can't we have the honeymoon before we start filling the cradle?!" Joe laughs as Mercedes gets that far away look on her face, telling everyone where her thoughts are.

"I remember telling you that you were going to fill this house with the sound of little feet. I thought I'd get you started on the right track!" she says and laughs at the look on his face.

Grandfather tells them all, "Now, that, Granddaughter, is a *real* wedding gift! You two can get started right away! I love kids!" And he chuckles right along with the rest of them.

Only Shay notices the way Flame's face closes off for a moment. He sees the scared, child-like fear in her eyes and he knows she is thinking of her own childhood. He wants the smile back in her eyes and on her face.

He whispers, "Honey, before too long I think we need to think about our own little cradle. Wouldn't a beautiful little girl look wonderful in that cradle? She would look just like her mother."

She turns her head around to look at him, her eyes wide. She sees the love on his face and in his eyes. She tells him silently, *I love you, Shay. Thank you. You knew what I was thinking of. I think a little boy that looks just like his daddy would look wonderful in that cradle too.*

He puts his arms around her from behind and pulls her into his embrace.

Grandfather looks at his whole family, seeing happiness and a lot of love. It is nearly palatable. He looks down at Ghost, who is looking back. He smiles gently, knowing Ghost wonders what all the fuss is about. He tells him silently, *Our family is happy, Ghost. They are becoming complete. It is a good thing. Soon it will be your turn to find a mate.*

At Ghost's wide eyed gaze Grandfather cannot help but laugh as he adds, *Not yet, my friend. No, Sadie is not for you. Your mate will be free and able to run with you. I promise you this.*

Ghost seems to have a permanent smile plastered on his wolf face this day.

The reception is over. Everyone says their goodbyes, but Frankie and Stephan inform both Flame and Mercedes that they are going to have a little coffee together.

As they leave together the women look at each other. Mercedes wiggles her eyebrows at Flame and they both burst into laughter, making the men look their way and smile at their happiness.

Grandfather, Joe, and Shay, are busy taking wedding gifts up to a guest room to be stored until the happy couple moves into the house. Joe takes the time alone with them to fill them in a little on what had happened in the office with Mercedes' father. He had promised Mercedes that he wouldn't talk about it, but he feels it is necessary to tell them some of it, for her safety and possibly his.

He tells them, "Mercedes' father refused the condo."

At both Shay and Grandfather's incredulous look he continues, "He said some pretty nasty things to us both, but he really hurt her feelings terribly. She told him the house was hers and that he had to move. At first he refused, but then he apologized and told us both he was sorry, that he'd be out by next week.

"I had some harsh words with him too. I told him I would not set foot in this house again until he's out." Joe looks a bit embarrassed at this admission.

"How did he take that one?" Shay asks.

"I don't really know, I took Mercedes and walked out then. I slammed the door in his face." He looks down at his feet, obviously uncomfortable for being so rude to his wife's father.

Grandfather surprises both men by laughing out loud before he says,

"You did the right thing. If it were me, well, I would have punched his lights out. You have a level head on your shoulders, Grandson. How does Mercedes feel about all of this?"

Joe admits, "She's hurt, obviously. I think he made her feel bad about trying to make him move out of the house, at least that's what he was trying to do, but she stood up to him. I've never seen her get so angry. She was furious, but I'm still scared for her. I don't trust that man and I'm afraid he's going to do something to get back at us for having him leave this house."

Grandfather looks at Shay, noticeably concerned for their safety also. He asks, "Shay, will you check into this man? Please have your friends at the police station watch him for me? I do not trust him either. He was rather rude with me tonight also. I too worry for my Grandson and his new wife."

"I'll do everything I can. I promise you that." Shay replies sternly.

He does not like the sound of what passed between Joe, Mercedes, and her father either. He has heard many stories about S.R. Holst and knows that he is a very cruel and ruthless man. He needs to talk to a few of his friends at the station anyway, so he will just do some checking into S.R. while he is at it.

Grandfather says, "I think I should be getting back to my home tonight, Grandson. I will call you tomorrow to see how married life is treating you." He decides to be totally honest about his worry over his family and adds, "Also, Shay, I want to check around my cabin for anything I might have kept that may have any names on them, such as people who have tried to buy my land.

"The Will I had Joe draw up for me leaves the land to Flame and everything else to Joe. I do not know if she has mentioned any of this to you. I need to see what I can find out and I think I will need your help in this.

"The only name I can remember is the lawyer that last came when Flame was with me. Stokes is the name, but I will let you know if I find anything else."

"Did you say Stokes?" At Grandfather's nod, Shay continues, "This man was a lawyer? Are you sure?"

"No. I only know that he comes in a suit, with a couple of big guys and a briefcase. I only assumed that he is a lawyer for someone else who wants to buy the land." Grandfather looks at Shay quizzically and asks, "Do you know this man?"

"I don't know. I know a Stokes, but it can't possibly be the same man. The one I know works at the station and he's a good cop. At least I've always known him to be. Let me check into a few things and I'll call you tomorrow. I think I'll spend a couple of hours at the station tonight. I want to get Flame settled in at home and I'll just go in for a little while to talk to a few of the guys."

Joe tells him, "Thank you, Shay. You're a great friend, you know. I'm so happy that Flame has you." He hugs Shay, making them both a bit uncomfortable, and Grandfather laughs.

He tells them, "I am glad for all of you. You are all my family now. Shay, you take good care of my granddaughter. She is very, very special. She will not like it that I am leaving tonight, but I think I must." He takes both men's arms and holds them tight, the Sioux way, on the forearm.

Flame, Shay, Grandfather, and Ghost, go to Shay's apartment, while Mercedes and Joe decide to spend their first night as a married couple back at his condo. Flame tries her best to get Grandfather to stay at least another night with them, but he refuses, as she knew he would.

He tells her honestly, "Granddaughter, I must get back home. I have not left my home for this many days in many, many years. I love you and I know you are safe with Shay and Ghost to watch over you. Please understand, I have to go home. I have checked with Prince and he does not understand me not being there, you know this. He has never been without me." He takes her into his arms, giving her a surprisingly strong hug.

"I do understand, and Shay, Ghost, and I, will be coming to see you soon. I've promised Ghost that he'll see his family again very soon and I want to show Shay the meadow. I know he'll love the forest as much as we do. Promise me you'll drive safely?" She worries over him as if he is a child.

"I promise, Granddaughter, and I love you. I will see you soon, all of you." He says, and then leaves with Shay carrying his small case to his truck for him.

On their way to the truck, Shay tells him, "I'm going to the station in a bit, but I think I'll wait until Flame lies down. I don't want her to have too much time on her hands. I haven't mentioned anything to her about Mercedes' father, or Stokes. I want her to think the only reason I'm going in is to check on the bombing. I'll tell her that the detective I need to speak with is there tonight, which won't be a lie. He likes working nights best."

Shay shakes Grandfather's hand, and Grandfather surprises him by pulling him into a hug.

Grandfather tells him, "Be good to her. She loves you."

"I know. I love her too." Shay says, honestly.

"It's time, Sergeant. Is everything in place?"

"Yes, boss. There are three of our people waiting for the old man now. They're staying in a nearby camping area. They are prepared to stay for a few days."

"I want it done tonight. You call me as soon as you know it's been handled. I'll give you further instructions then. You make sure it's done right, Sergeant."

"I will." But, the sergeant hates this more and more. He has no choice but to do as he is told. He had sold his soul to the boss long ago. There is no going back now. He has too much to lose.

Flame and Shay are relaxing on the couch with Ghost at their feet. Shay has turned the TV on to an old monster movie and Flame is very caught up in it. She has never watched too much TV, only leaving hers on when Ghost was alone, so he would not feel lonely. She had never had one as a child. The only time she has really watched TV is at Frankie's, and he only liked the late night talk shows. This is a special treat for her, especially since she can curl up in Shay's arms while watching it.

Shay laughingly says, "I can't believe you've never seen a Dracula movie! Honey, if this has you all curled up around me like this, I'm going out tomorrow to buy all the monster movies at the store!" He is dreading telling her that he has to go to the station in awhile.

"Shh...this is scary! I'm glad you and Ghost are here. I love it and I want to spend a lot of time watching scary movies with you too!" she says and tries to laugh, but it comes out as a Ghost-type cough-laugh, as Dracula appears on the screen.

He smiles and tucks her head under his chin. He will wait a little while before leaving her. He is much too happy having her curled around him right now.

Finally, she is curled up in bed with Ghost lying beside the bed close to her.

Shay makes a phone call, comes into the bedroom and tells her, "Honey, the detective I need to talk to about the bombing is at the station. Will you be all right here with Ghost if I leave for a few hours? I want to go over what he's found so far."

She does not like the idea of going to sleep without him, but if he needs to go she will not stop him. She knows he wants to find out who was behind the bombing. She says, "Sure, Shay. We'll be okay. Ghost will scare off Dracula if he comes calling!" She giggles sleepily and curls her fist under her chin.

"I won't be long, honey. Sweet dreams. Ghost, don't let anyone in here except me. Got it?" Shay looks at Ghost and Ghost gives a slight shake of his head.

He shakes his own head, wondering if he will ever get use to such a smart wolf being a part of the family. He thinks, *I can't imagine making love to Flame with Ghost in the room, shoot, in the damn apartment!*

He kisses her lightly on the head as he leaves her sleeping, with Ghost watching over her, and locks the door behind him. He is going to check into quite a few things tonight. The first is to talk to Don about the bombing, just as he told Flame he would do. He knows Detective Don Clanton is the best person to have on this case, and besides, he is one of Shay's best friends.

Chapter 26

When Shay arrives at the station Detective Don Clanton is not there. He is in the old warehouse where the burned out trailer is being stored until the case is closed. Shay decides to go there and see what he can find out.

The garage is just an old warehouse that belongs to the police station, acquired from a drug bust just last year, but never sold. He finds Don going over the underside of the trailer.

"Found anything useful, Don?" he asks, moving close to the underside himself.

Don is not expecting anyone and Shay has come in so quietly that when he speaks, Don quickly rises up, hitting his head on the underside of the wreckage. He grabs his head, and blood pours over his fingers. He shouts, "OWW! *DAMN*, LARSON! Don't sneak up on a man with a gun! Shit, how bad is it?" He let his hand come off his forehead as he pulls himself out from under the bombed out trailer.

Shay says, "Shit, Don, I'm so sorry! I didn't mean to scare the hell out of you like that. Man, you need stitches in that, at least ten. Here, put this on it and hold it tight. I'll take you to the hospital." He hands him his handkerchief, turning to walk back out of the warehouse with Don trailing behind cursing under his breath.

On the way to the hospital he questions Don about anything he may have found out about Flame's trailer being bombed.

Don tells him, "Larson, whoever did it was good. The explosives were placed right in front, on the inside of the trailer. If your girl had opened that door, or even been any closer to it when it blew, she'd be dead. Does she know anyone who might want her dead?"

"Hell, I can't figure it out. There have been so many things happening over the last week that I haven't really had a chance to ask anyone anything, but her grandfather thinks it may be linked to a Will he's made, leaving her his property in River Valley. People have been trying to buy that land for ages, but her grandfather won't sell it. Someone broke into Joe Wolf's office the same afternoon that Flame's trailer was bombed. He's her brother, well... not biologically, but they have the same grandfather."

When Don gives Shay a quizzical look, he bangs the steering wheel with his open palm and says heatedly, "Hell, anyway, her grandfather mentioned that a man, he thinks may be a lawyer, named Stokes, may be involved." He looks over at Don to get his reaction to this news.

"Stokes? You don't think...? Naw...not Sergeant Stokes, surely. He's a good cop." Don says, but turns thoughtful.

He lets it drop for a moment, both men lost in thought. After a couple of minutes Don says, "You know, Larson, Stokes did have all that trouble a few years back. Remember when his wife was so sick? She needed that liver transplant and he had to take all that time off work. Four kids and a dying wife. Do you remember how bad it got for them? He couldn't work and the bills kept piling up. Then, all of a sudden she gets the transplant and he comes back to work."

Shay tells him thoughtfully, "Yeah, I remember. I already thought that through too. I just wanted to get your view on the whole thing before I mentioned it. If you remember, before he came back to work, after his wife got out of the hospital, the whole family went on that little two week vacation. He never did say where, but wherever it was, it was on the beach somewhere. He has that picture of all of them by the ocean right there on his desk. Then he comes back to work all smiles, like nothing's wrong anymore. I wonder how he paid for all those hospital bills, not to mention that beach vacation."

"Yeah, a sergeant doesn't make that kind of money. You might have something here, Shay. You'd better keep it quiet though, you know he's got a lot of friends in uniform. Let me do some checking too. I know you're not even supposed to be back to work for a few weeks."

"Thanks, Don. I won't *officially* be back, but I will do some checking around of my own."

"I didn't know about Wolf's office being broken into. Sounds like you're right about the Will. I think Judge Baron is still the only judge in River Valley and we both know that she cannot be bought. Maybe she can send some of her uniforms out there to keep an eye on the old man." Don says, as they are getting closer to the hospital.

"Sounds like that may be a good idea. I know it would relieve Flame's mind if she knew he was okay."

Shay pulls into the hospital parking lot, and they walk into the hospital together. He has an idea and, since he is already at the hospital, he will check into it. He walks into the ER with Don.

While Don is filling out his insurance forms, Shay asks the attendant, "Excuse me, but is Nurse Parson working tonight?"

"I think so, I saw her a little while ago. Do you want me to page her?"

"Please. I need to speak to her just a minute if she's not too busy."

The attendant pages Nurse Parson and in a few minutes she walks out to meet him. She says enthusiastically, "Hi, Shay! What have you done now? Are you shot, or is it Flame again?" She looks around the room.

He smiles and tells her, "It's not us this time, Janey. I had to bring my buddy in for a few stitches. While I'm here I have a favor to ask of you."

Her eyes widen and she whispers, "It's nothing to do with all that magic stuff, is it?"

He believes she really wishes it were. She seems excited to be involved in their escapades. He almost feels bad as he says, "No, sorry, Janey. And, Frankie isn't here either, but I do need you to do something for me. Can we step into that conference room for a minute?"

She nods and they go into the room and close the door.

She asks, "Okay, Shay. What's up?"

"Will you do a little check on someone for me? A friend of mine had his wife in here for a liver transplant about two, maybe three, years ago. Last name's Stokes, and I think, but I'm not sure, that her first name is Darla. Will you see how that hospital bill was paid? I need to know how much was covered by insurance and how the rest was paid for too. If it was by check, would the file have a copy of the check?"

"Why do you need this information?"

Shay tilts his head a bit and doesn't answer her, but gives her a little "I can't tell you that" smile.

Janey hesitates just a moment, then says, "Never mind. Yeah, the file should have a copy of all of it. I guess I can do that. It might take a little while. Are you going to be here awhile?"

He says, "I should. We just got here and my buddy has to have stitches, but if you haven't got anything by the time he's done, I'll check back with you tomorrow."

"That's great. I should be able to find something soon. I'll see you in bit."

He goes back into the waiting area and sees that Don has already been taken to the back for his stitches. He spends the next hour waiting for word from either of his friends.

Just as he starts to doze off a bit, Janey shakes his arm. She is carrying a file and motions for him to come with her. They walk back into the conference room.

"Okay, here's her file. It's quite large. She'd been very sick for a long time. Even before the transplant the hospital bill was over a quarter of a million dollars. Insurance covered about seventy-five percent of it, but after the transplant the bill was tremendous, reaching nearly a million dollars. The insurance took care of part of it, but it wasn't the best insurance in the world, if you know what I mean." Janey looks knowingly at him.

"Yes, Janey, I know. It's the same as mine. You're right, her husband's a cop. You should be on the force, you know that don't you?" he asks.

This brings a smile to Janey's face and she continues, "Okay...here's the good part. The bill was paid, in full, just a week after her transplant. Pretty hefty bit of money for a cop. It was paid for by a cashier's check, not a personal check, and every time she's come back for check-ups and all that, the bill is paid for…in cash."

"Thank you, Janey!" he exclaims, grabs her, pulls her into his arms, and kisses her smack on the lips. He adds, "You're the best! I knew I could count on you!"

Shay leaves the room quickly, leaving Janey standing there with her eyes wide and her finger touching her lips.

He walks quickly to an attendant and asks if he can go into the back to see Don.

As soon as the attendant sees him though, she tells him, "Detective Larson, your friend has been asking for you. He's driving the doctor crazy back there because he won't sit still. Will you please go back to cubical three and try to get him to let the doctor do his job?"

"Sure." he says and grins as she buzzes him into the ER door and he walks into cubical three to find Don arguing with the doctor.

"I said *NO*. Not until I see…" And, Don sees Shay standing there smiling.

Shay says, "Don, you look a bit pale there buddy!" He smiles cynically and adds, "Doctor, if you'll leave me alone with my buddy for just a minute I promise he'll be a big boy and get his stitches when you get back."

The doctor is a young intern. He looks at Shay, then back to Don, shakes his head, and says, "I was told cops were the worst patients!" Then he walks out, closing the curtain behind him.

"Shay, I just..." Don says, at the same time Shay says, "Don..."

"Okay, you first, Don. Go ahead."

"Shay, I just remembered something that I think is pretty damn important to the bomb case. Do you remember that case about four or five years ago, the bombing of that drug house in the projects?" At Shay's nod Don continues, "It was done exactly the same way as your girl's trailer, same kind of material and remote device. Do you remember who caught the guy we were looking at?"

"Yep. It was Stokes. What was the guy's name, Owen, no…something like that though. I remember he got off too. The evidence was tampered with."

Don says, "Sure did, and actually, the evidence disappeared. I know, because I was the detective on the case. It just up and walked right out of evidence lock-up. Never did figure out how. And, the guy's name was Otis

Edwards. I wonder if he's still in town."

"I don't know, but I'll bet he was a few days ago. Now, for my news… I had a friend pull up the records on Stoke's wife…" and Shay tells Don all he has learned from Janey.

Don says, "Sounds like we need to have a talk with Sergeant Stokes. I happen to know that he'll be at the station tonight. He's been working second and third shifts lately. I heard him ask the Chief for them myself, about two weeks ago."

"It sounds like he's had something to keep him busy lately, huh? Get your head stitched up and then we'll go feel Stokes out a bit. Maybe ask him to come look at the trailer and see if he thinks it looks like the work of Otis Edwards. Let's see what his reaction will be." says Shay.

"Sounds like a plan to me." Don agrees. Hopefully they will get just what they want from Stokes.

They stop off at the warehouse first as Shay decides it might be best if Don goes to the station alone to get Stokes. He might get spooked if he sees Shay. Shay goes into the warehouse after parking his van down the street a bit.

When Don gets to the station Sergeant Stokes is on the phone. Don walks to Stokes' desk and sits in the chair facing him. Stokes looks at him questioningly, pointing to Don's head.

Don quietly says, "Finish your call first."

Stokes nods and after a moment hangs up the phone and asks, "What the hell did you do to your head? You have blood all over your shirt."

Don gives him an embarrassed look and says, "Oh hell…I forgot all about the damn blood. It's nothing. I slipped down the damn steps outside and cut the hell out of my forehead. Had to go get stitched up, but I got to thinking about something and thought I'd run it by you before I call it a night."

"Sure, what can I do for you, Don?" Stokes is lounging in his chair, feet propped up on the desk, giving Don his ready smile.

Don tells him, "I need you to do something for me, if you will. Remember that trailer that was bombed the other day?"

Stokes looses the smile, and nods.

Don continues, "I'd like for you to come down to the warehouse with me. I have a feeling you'll recognize the handiwork of the bomber. Have you got a minute?" He makes it sound more like a demand than a question, getting another nod from Stokes.

"Sure. I really don't know what I can tell you, but if you want me to take a look, I will. Let me file this away and we can go." He gets up and walks out of the office.

While he is gone Don decides to check something else. He picks up

Stokes' phone and hits re-dial. A man answers immediately and he is not too happy listening to nothing. After a bit of cursing and threats, he hangs up. Don knows that he will remember the man's voice. He replaces the handset and waits on Stokes.

When they arrive at the warehouse and walk inside, Stokes' eyes open wide when he sees Shay, but he says, "Hello, Larson. Glad to see you're doing better. What in the world are you doing here though at this time of the night? Aren't you on medical leave?" Stokes tries to hide his surprise, but he does not quite pull it off.

Shay says, "Hi, Stokes. Yeah, I'm still off duty, but this one hit close to home. Just thought I'd take a look at the trailer. I haven't had a chance to see it yet, so I came in tonight after calling Don. I thought it would be a good idea to see it for myself." He smiles brightly, trying to ease Stokes' mind, and puts out his hand for a shake.

Sergeant Stokes smiles and reaches to shake Shay's hand. Shay notices Stokes' hand is sweaty.

Don says, "Stokes, remember the drug house bombing a few years back?"

At Stokes' nod, Don continues, "I'd just made detective then and you helped me with the case. You worked most of it, well, the arrest and all the damn paperwork anyway. Remember the guy you busted for it? What's his name…Edwards, I think?"

"Sure, I remember it. Can't remember too much about it though, that was when my wife was so sick and that took most of my time. I remember that we couldn't make the case because the evidence up and took off." he says, and doesn't even realize he is nervously running his hand through his hair.

"Do you know if the guy…is it Edwards?" asks Don.

Stokes seems to think about it for a second, then nods.

Don continues, "Do you know if he's still in town?"

Stokes quickly says, "Shit, Clanton, I don't know. I haven't kept up with him. I haven't heard anything about him though. Why?"

Don looks from Stokes, to the burned out trailer, and tells him, "Stokes, this bomb has Edwards' name written all over it. He blew that drug house *exactly* the same way this trailer blew. Same kind of bomb, same materials, set in the same location. Put the bomb right inside the door, and then, when the victim walked for the door, he blew it wide open by remote. That's exactly how this one went down, except in the drug house three people died. In this one the lady lived through it." He points out the area where the bomb went off, showing Stokes the evidence.

"No shit? Sure does look the same, huh? Damn, I don't know why the guy would do that. I mean, what would he get out of it? Did he even know the lady?" Stokes is clearly uncomfortable, but he is covering better now than he was earlier. Seeing Shay had obviously rattled him.

Don tells him, "We don't know yet, but we damn sure will. This time the evidence isn't going anywhere. I got a good fingerprint off of the inside of the door jamb. It doesn't match the girl's, but I bet it'll match this Edwards'. We'll find out by tomorrow." Both he and Shay know this is a lie, but Stokes does not have to know that. Yet.

Stokes looks down at his watch. His hand is noticeably shaking. "Damn, boys, I have to go. I'm supposed to be in on a bust that's going down tonight. I'll check around and see if anyone's seen the guy, but don't get your hopes up." After saying this, Stokes walks very quickly from the warehouse.

Shay and Don share a knowing look as Stokes leaves the warehouse.

Shay says, "Don, it looks like we're on the right track. We have no proof yet. If push comes to shove though, I'll personally make the man talk." He has never meant anything more in his life. He will not take a chance on Flame's life. No way.

Stokes goes back into the station hoping for a call soon. Everything seems to be unraveling in his face. He is to the point of not giving a damn. If he goes down, he will be sure to take every single of them down with him. He does not like what he has been forced to do anyway. He had always been a good cop, until he had made a deal with the devil.

CHAPTER 27

Grandfather drove slowly, but he has finally reached his land. He breathes a sigh of relief. He realizes that he is worn out. There has been too much excitement for his old heart over the last few days and he will be glad to see Prince and to sleep in his own bed.

He smiles when he remembers Flame making him name his friend, Prince, and as he turns onto his long dirt driveway he is hit with a vision from this friend. He slams on the brakes of the truck, not being able to see the road ahead.

Humans are on Grandfather's land. He cannot tell how many. Prince has kept hidden, and the other wolves are in the forest waiting for Grandfather's call.

Prince is hidden under the porch. He will not let anyone enter Grandfather's home. They haven't tried yet, but there are two of them standing on the porch steps.

He is ready for attack. He doesn't understand what Grandfather does; these men have guns with them and hold them at their sides, ready. Grandfather does not want Prince to attack these men by himself. He has no chance against these men with their guns.

He reaches under his seat for his shotgun. As he pulls it up onto his lap, he feels Prince move, knowing that Grandfather is near. He feels that he must protect Grandfather from these men.

Grandfather tells him silently, *Prince! No! I will be there in a moment!* But, he is too late. Prince jumps out from under the porch, springing to attack the closest man. While in mid-leap Prince is shot by the other man. His attack lands him on top of the man that he had been attacking, knocking the man to the ground.

Prince…hold on, I'm coming. But, Grandfather knows he is too late. His friend, Prince, is no more. He is dead. Grandfather's eyes are blinded with tears. Tears of grief. Tears of fury.

He puts his foot down on the accelerator hard and the old truck leaps forward. He will avenge his friend, but for the moment he is too angry to even call for the other wolves.

He pulls right up to his porch, seeing Prince lying on the ground. He does not see the men. He doesn't see the other wolves either. That means the men are close. He breathes a deep, calming breath, trying to relax enough to get his message out.

Finally, he calls to the wolves, *Come to me, my friends, but do not show yourselves yet. Try to get close to the men, but do not let them see you. Show me where they are.*

He feels the wolves moving. He wants so badly to go to Prince, but the best place for him right now is in the truck. He knows he should not show himself, that there is nothing he can do for his friend now. These men are not here only because they want his land. He knows this time they also want his life.

He does not want Flame to know what is going on yet. She will only run to him and he does not want to put her life in jeopardy. He blocks his thoughts and his grief from her, telling the animals to do the same, including Ghost.

She will not understand why he has done it this way, and if there were any way he could tell her without putting her life in danger, he would, but he cannot chance her coming here too quickly because he has no idea how many people are here or how long they will stay.

One of the wolves calls to him. The alpha female, Magic, Prince's own mate, shows Grandfather that the men have separated. One is near her, the other about ten feet away, both in the dense forest.

He tells her, *Wait for my command before taking him. I want no more of you to leave me.*

She already knows that her mate is gone. She is almost uncontrollable. Another female comes alongside to help her.

Grandfather is afraid Magic will risk her life to avenge her mate if he doesn't move quickly. He calls to the others, showing them where to go. They creep upon the other man, quietly, with death in their hearts and on their minds.

Grandfather has lowered his window, listening to the sounds of the forest, waiting for the movement of the men. He has parked facing his cabin with the men behind him in the forest. He may not live through this, but, if possible, one or both of these men will die this night. Wolf's take care of their own.

He sees, through the wolf's eyes, that two of the male wolves have come up behind the other man. They are close enough now to take him down and together they can easily do so. He wants both of these men taken at the same moment. He finally gives them the permission they wait so impatiently for.

All of you take them now!

Then he hears the men screaming, begging for help. Guns go off and Grandfather, deep in the minds of the wolves, knows none of the bullets have hit their mark. The wolves were not injured, but are ferociously tearing at the men.

Suddenly, one of the other females sends an urgent warning to him. There is a third human. A female, and she has been hiding in a tree above all of them. She has been waiting, watching for Grandfather. She is almost upon the truck before he is warned.

The other wolves, the ones not killing the men, jump to defend their keeper, their friend Grandfather brings up his rifle just as the woman puts her gun through the open driver's window right in his face. He has no time to fire his rifle. Even if he had, he would not have hit her. She has placed the gun around from the back of the truck, through the open window, with her body still behind him.

In the split second before the gun goes off, all the wolves in the forest howl, racing toward Grandfather. They are too late. The report of the gun carries throughout the forest Wolf. The wolves cry their song of sorrow to the world. Then they go in for the kill. Death rules the forest this night.

Flame is awakened by Ghost's mournful howl. It is extremely loud in the small apartment. She immediately knows something is wrong. She looks to Shay's side of the bed, finding that he is still gone. She glances at the clock and sees that it is after midnight.

She silently asks him, *What is it Ghost? What's wrong?*

For the first time ever Ghost ignores her and continues to howl, not sharing his mind with her, blocking her, keeping her out. He has never, ever, done this before. Try as she might, she cannot break through the mind block and it terrifies her.

She feels for Shay, for his mind, his thoughts. She finds him, not being able to *see* through their mind link, but she can feel that there is nothing wrong with him. The only other person that could cause this reaction in Ghost is Grandfather.

She gives a mental scream to him, *GRANDFATHER!?* She waits, but gets no answer. Something is wrong with Grandfather, for she does not *feel* him. At all! Even if he does not answer her, she should be able to feel him, to touch on his mind. The first thing she can think to do is to call Joe. She runs from the room and Ghost continues to howl.

By the time she reaches the phone, neighbors are banging on the door, screaming for her to stop the noise and they are threatening to call the police. She must take a moment to calm Ghost, to assure the neighbors that everything is fine. She goes to Ghost, leans down, and places her hands on either side of his large head.

"Ghost, please, I know you're crying for Grandfather. I can't hear him or feel him. Please, you must be silent. I want to scream also, but we can't. Not here. Not now. We'll find Grandfather. I promise you that!"

He looks at her, quieting his mournful howling. He is crying though, with huge tears streaming down his furry face.

She is all the more worried for Grandfather and she tells him, "Ghost, I'm going to call Joe. We'll go with him to Grandfather."

He obeys, though he is still blocking her from his thoughts. She does not understand this and it is breaking her heart. She tries to call for Shay through their mind link, but is so out of control, her mind running so wild, that she cannot touch his mind.

She goes to the door, opening it slightly, and reassures the waiting, angry, neighbors that she is sorry and that everything is fine now. Then she and Ghost go into the living room and she picks up the phone. She is so upset it takes three times for her to get the number right.

Finally, Joe answers sleepily, "Hello?"

She is so scared that she temporarily cannot find her voice. When Joe says his second hello, she is able to tell him, "Joe! It's Grandfather! Something's happened! I can't find him!" She is trying to get the words out, but not making sense to his half asleep filled mind.

"Flame, calm down. Grandfather went back home, remember?" he says, and sits up, rubbing his face wearily.

Mercedes sits up also, knowing that Flame would not call them at this time of the night unless something is terribly wrong. She lays a comforting hand on Joe's arm.

Flame screams, "*NO!* JOE, I CAN'T *FEEL* HIM! DON'T YOU HEAR ME!? WE HAVE TO GO TO GRANDFATHER! *NOW*!"

She is frantic, and now it is her making all the noise. She cannot seem to get through to Joe. Ghost's howling earlier and his whining now, is breaking her heart. She knows it must be really bad for Grandfather, for Ghost to block her like this. He still will not let her in.

She uses tremendous effort to calm herself long enough to tell him, "Joe, we have to go to the forest! Something's wrong. Ghost woke me up howling! Can't you hear him? He's beside me now, whining. He won't stop! He won't let me in his mind! He's blocking me and I can't find Grandfather's thoughts! Please?" she asks, sobbing now. She adds, "Please come and take me to Grandfather. Shay's not here. You and I need to go. Now! I know this is what we need to do. Don't ask why."

She is finally getting through to him. He is wide awake now and shaking all over. He knows their mind link is very strong. Too strong for her not to be able to find him, especially if she is just trying to check on him and not talk to him. He knows that actually transferring thoughts takes a lot more effort.

Mercedes, seeing the look on his face, asks, "Joe, honey, what's wrong?"

But, Joe barely hears her. He knows if Flame cannot feel Grandfather it has to be bad, very bad. He is already up and trying to pull on his pants as he says, "Flame, calm down. I'll be by to get you in a few minutes. Where's Shay?" He is trying to reach the rest of his clothes.

Mercedes is also dressing, quickly.

Flame answers, "He went to the station to talk to a detective friend of his earlier. He's not back yet. Joe, we can't wait. I'll make sure Shay knows. Just get here fast. We must go now!" She slams the phone down and runs to get her clothes on.

She cannot take the time to call Shay and she cannot reach him through the mind link either. She is too overwrought to do it. She will reach him later when she has calmed enough to do so.

She thinks about jotting a quick note to him, but is shaking so badly that she ends up throwing the pen across the room. She dresses, and then she and Ghost leave the apartment, locking the door behind them. They reach the parking lot just minutes before Joe and Mercedes pull in to it, fast.

Joe slams the brakes on right in front of Flame and Ghost. She pulls open the back door and Ghost gets in first, then she jumps in. He doesn't even wait for her to close the door, he just stomps on the accelerator with the door slamming shut from the force of the movement.

He asks, "Have you found out anything?! From Ghost? Grandfather?" He looks quickly into the rearview mirror at her tear stained face.

"No, but I'm so upset and I think that's why I can't get use the link with Shay, but not Ghost, or Grandfather. Ghost is purposefully blocking me. He's never done that before. And, Grandfather is either very effectively blocking me, or he's unconscious, but even then, I should be able to find him, Joe, or at least *feel* him." She sobs while trying to buckle her seat belt.

"We'll find him. I promise you that." he replies, glancing quickly at her again, hoping to calm her fears. She is scaring him to death.

He quickly prays, *Please God. Not Grandfather—not on my wedding day. Not ever. Not like this.*

Realizing that he doesn't know what they may be walking into, he looks over at Mercedes. Deciding on the lesser of two evils, he hopes, he tells her, "Honey, I know you want to go with us to Grandfather's, but you can't."

Seeing her wide eyes and her mouth starting to form words, he demands loudly, "*No*, Mercedes, and no arguing about this either. I am taking you to your father's, I'm sorry, *your* house. You'll get some rest and be protected and there are guards to watch over you there."

"Joe, please? If I can't go with you, please, let me at least stay at your place tonight. I promise I'll be careful." She asks, practically begging.

"No, honey. I want to be sure that you're protected tonight. I can't lose you. Please understand." He has calmed his tone, trying to make her see that it is only for her own good that he is doing this.

"Fine, but I don't have to like it. Please call me as soon as you get to Grandfather's. I won't be able to rest knowing something could be wrong." she asks looking at him beseechingly.

"I will, honey. I promise." And, he means it He will call her as soon as he can. He doesn't like the idea of leaving her with her father, but the house is big enough that her father might not even realize she is there. He is truly concerned when he tells her firmly, "Mercedes, use your key and go straight up to your room and lock your door." He knows she is probably better off there, but he still worries because of her father.

She jerks her head around to look at him. She does not want to believe that her father would harm her, but she understands why he is worried. Her father's earlier words and anger are still fresh in her mind.

"I will and I'll be very careful. Don't worry about me, honey. You just keep your mind on the road and I'll be praying for Grandfather and for you and Flame also."

They can still hear Flame crying quietly in the back seat. Neither is even sure if she has heard anything that they have been saying. Ghost's whines, and added to Flame's cries, it cuts them both to the quick.

As they pull around the long circular driveway of the mansion, Mercedes turns around and places her hand on Flame's arm and says, "Flame, I'm sure you'll find Grandfather and he'll be okay. I'll pray for you all. Please, calm down and help Joe. He needs your strength right now as much as you need his. Do you want me to try to reach Shay?"

Flame sniffs and raises her head to look at Mercedes. She realizes that they are at the mansion and their conversation sinks in. She has a dazed look, but she nods her head and tells them both, "I'll be fine. I'm not worried about myself, Mercedes. I've never been blocked like this. No, don't call Shay. Not yet anyway. Give him a little while to get home. I know he'll be worried when he finds us gone, but I think I can reassure him mentally as soon as I calm down a bit."

Mercedes nods, wondering if she is truly thinking clearly. She thinks, *How will she mentally tell Shay?* But, she squeezes Flame's arm, trying to comfort her. She steps out of the station wagon and opens the back door for her and says, "Flame, ride up here with Joe. You can see better up here." Then she leans down to look at Joe as Flame nods and climbs out of the back seat. She tells him, "I love you, Joe."

"I love you too, honey. Lock up behind yourself when you get inside."

She nods, closes the door, and walks quickly into the house.

~

Shay and Don have gone over every inch of the trailer. They find the metal lockbox that Flame had placed under her bed. It is closed, but not locked. They open the box and inside are the checkbook and additional books of checks she had placed inside. They are the only things in the box. Shay checks the numbers on the checks, making sure that they are all there. They are.

He looks up at Don and says, "Don, old buddy, I think we found the reason this place was broken into first. I think she would have placed her copy of the Will right in here with this. Don't you?"

Don nods and says, "I think you're right on that count. Do you know what the Will says?"

Shay looks up at him with a surprised look and exclaims, "Shit. I know what her Grandfather told me…that she's to inherit the property and house and that Joe gets all the rest, but I don't know the specifics. Damn. Why didn't I ask?!" he says, almost to himself, and shakes his head, running his fingers disgustingly through his hair.

Don says, "Don't worry about it. You can call Joe in the morning and get a copy of the Will. He should have one on file. I would tell you to call him now, but he might kill you himself if you do. I know you were the best man today at his wedding. You don't suppose his new wife would have anything to do with this, do you?"

"Mercedes? No, I don't think she's got a mean bone in her body, but it does make sense to think so. I mean, she would naturally be the one to inherit the land and money if anything were to happen to her husband or Flame. Right?" He knows they need to see that Will as soon as possible.

"Shay, you go on home to Flame. We'll know more when we see that Will. I'll try to keep an eye on Stokes and maybe put a little pressure on his conscience…if he still has one." Don says disgustingly.

"Thank you, Don. I think that would be a good idea. I'm bushed too. I'll feel much better knowing that Flame's okay." he says and smiles as he says, "Though, if anything were wrong I know she'd tell me. Plus, she has Ghost with her."

"Ghost? Is that the huge white Shepherd I've heard so much about?" Don asks, not really hearing the part about Flame *telling* Shay. He is a dog lover, having two of his own Shepherds, one a police trained K-9.

"Uh...yeah. Shit. I have to be honest with you, Don. I haven't told anyone else this, well… Doc Butler knows, but… Ghost is no Shepherd. He's a full blooded wolf, born in the wild. Actually, right there on the property her Grandfather owns." He knows Don would never give this secret away. He trusts this man with his life, and now with Flame's, and Ghost's. He is a good guy though and a good friend.

"Damn! How the hell did that come about? I sure would like to see him. How much does he weigh?" This news excites Don. He has been attracted to wolves all his life. That is why he loves the Shepherds so much, because they look so much like a wolf. He has wolf pictures, books, and statues all over his own home. It drives his wife nuts.

Shay cannot help but chuckle at the look on Don's face and he tells him, "Shit, Don, I didn't know you'd be this excited about it! He's beautiful, solid white, and weighs at least 165 pounds. He's very attached to Flame. I honestly don't think one could exist without the other. I've never seen a bond like they have." He knows the bond between Flame and Ghost is really that strong. He cannot imagine something happening to Ghost. She might not ever be the same if anything were to happen to him.

Don exclaims, "I'd love to see him. Do you think it would be all right if I come by to talk to Flame about the case?" He grins at Shay's knowing look and add, "Yeah, I know. I'd really love to see the damn wolf. I'll admit it!"

Shay laughs and tells him, "You're welcome at my place anytime. I'll go on home and in the morning I'll call Joe. I'll get him to meet me at his office and get a copy of the Will. I'll call you at home as soon as I get it. Maybe you can come by then and talk to Flame." Shay gives Don a light punch to the arm, ribbing him about wanting to see Ghost.

Don has the grace to look a bit embarrassed at his earlier enthusiasm. "Sounds good. Do you think you can drop me at the station as you leave? I walked down here the first time, just thinking I'd get a little exercise. Now I've been to the hospital, come back, walked back to the station, and damn...I don't think I'll make it if I try to walk back." he admits.

Shay laughs, "Sure, buddy. I wish you'd told me that you walked. I wouldn't have had you walk back for Stokes the first time. I take it he drove you here?"

"Yep. And, yes, I checked around his car for anything that might tell us something, in what little time I had, but didn't see anything. Though, it was so dark something could have slapped me in the face and I wouldn't have noticed it."

"I know the feeling. Too damn well lately."

He drops Don off at the station and turns for his apartment. He is relieved to be heading home. He misses Flame. He hadn't meant to be gone so long. He glances at his watch noting in surprise that it's almost two in the morning.

He thinks, *Damn! Flame's going to be upset with me. I didn't realize that I'd been gone so long.* But his body knows he has. He is exhausted.

Don walks into the station expecting to find Sergeant Stokes gone, and is surprised to see him on the phone at his desk.

He thinks, *So, the drug bust either didn't go down or you were lying, Stokes.* He has an idea that it is the latter.

He decides to stand back a bit and watch Stokes a minute before showing himself in the squad room. Stokes' face is red. Angry. His hand keeps nervously running through what little hair is left on his head. He says a few words, writes down something, and hangs up.

Stokes then places his face in his hands, rubbing his face vigorously. Then he picks up the phone and places a call. He has a very heated, very quiet conversation with whoever he is talking to and then abruptly hangs up, jumps out of his seat with his coffee cup, and heads for the break room.

Don does not hesitate. He goes straight to Stokes' desk and copies down the phone number that is written on the paper. He then calmly sits at his own desk and waits for Stokes to return. When he does, Don is looking at him.

Sergeant Stokes has been waiting all night for the phone to ring. Detectives Larson and Clanton have spooked him, real bad. He is anxious to get this over with. He cannot go home until he hears from one of his people.

Then the phone finally rings. He answers at once, "Stokes."

"Stokes, we've got a big problem here. Tuttle and Johnson are both dead."

"*WHAT*?! What the hell happened up there? Is the job done?" he asks. Stokes is becoming frantic. Now he has two dead cops and he knows he is in deeper shit than ever. He does not know what the hell is going to happen now.

"The damned wolves got them! YES…the old man is dead! I would be too if I hadn't pulled his ass out of that damn truck before the wolves got me! As it is I've been bit. My gun hand too. I need help up here and fast! We sure as hell don't want these bodies found." This woman is obviously at the end of her rope. She could fall apart on them at any minute now. If that happens they could all go down.

Stokes doesn't know what to do next, but he tells her, "Give me your location and the phone number there, right now! I have to call the boss and find out what the hell to do. How did you get out of there?"

"I drove the old man's damn truck! How the hell do you think I got out? I couldn't get out of the damn thing with all those wolves after my ass! I'm at the phone booth of the RV Park...River Park Campsites. Get back to me fast!"

Stokes hangs up, laying his head in his hands. The boss isn't going to like this. Not at all. What the hell, he doesn't have much else to lose. He picks up the phone and dials the boss and when the phone is answered he says, "Boss, this is Stokes."

"Yes, Sergeant? I hope you have good news for me. Is it done?"

"Well, yes, but we have complications."

There is deadly silence on the phone for about five seconds and then Stokes says, "Two dead cops. The only one left is female and she's been bit. I need to get a couple more men up there fast. She had to take the old man's truck to get away. It's bad, boss. Do you have any suggestions?"

"*SHIT*! What the hell is wrong with you, Stokes!? Let me call my people in River Valley, and I'll get a couple of guys up there fast. You send out that damn, stupid ass Otis. I want that cabin burnt. AND, if *anyone* shows up, I want them *DEAD*! You got that?! Where's your girl?"

Stokes says, "I'm sorry, boss. She's at River Park, the RV campground, the phone number there is 564-1389. She's waiting on my call to tell her what to do."

"You get out of the station now. You've already been there longer than you should be. I'll call her. I'll get my people in River Valley up there to clean up this mess. You get Otis up there now and *you* go with him!"

This is an order, not a request, and Stokes knows it. He thinks, *Damn. This is all going to blow up in my face*. But, he has no choice but to obey. He says, "Yes, sir. I know where he is right now. I just got off of the phone with him a while ago. I'll get him up there and I'll go with him."

"Get it done. When you get there take Otis to the end of the drive and drop him there. Wait on him, and then go to the dirt track on the other end of the property. I'll have someone come to you, to tell you what to do next."

And the phone goes dead in Stokes' ear.

Stokes jumps up, thinking that he needs a drink bad. There is a bottle of gin hidden in the break room. Sometimes even the best cops need a little shot. He grabs his coffee cup and heads for the break room.

When he gets back to his desk he feels eyes on him. He quickly looks up and around, Detective Don Clanton is at his desk and staring straight at him.

He thinks, *Shit. Now what?!* He nods at Clanton and doesn't even get an acknowledgment in return. He knows he is going down. He had better hurry and try to clean up this mess he has gotten himself into.

He gets up and walks out of the station with Don Clanton's eyes on him the whole time. He knows that there is no evidence they can possibly have on him. *Yet*. But, knows there will be before too much longer. He is done. Burnt out.

Don watches Stokes walk out of the station. When Stokes is out the door, he picks up his phone and dials the number that he had copied off of Stokes' desk. It rings one time and a woman's voice answers.

"Yeah? What? Are you getting me any help up here, or what?"

Don knows that voice. No mistaking it. He hangs up and calls information. He wants the address of that phone number. After finding out that it is in River Valley, he realizes that he should already have called Judge Baron. He hates to wake her up at this time of night, but he has no choice.

He looks up the number for his friend, Erin L. Baron, the only Judge in River Valley. They had worked together, many years ago, before she became the Judge over that area. He knows that she will help him in any way she possibly can. He dials and on the first ring the phone is picked up.

"Yeah, this is Judge Baron. This had better be good."

"Hello to you too, Judge Baron." he says and chuckles, then says, "Sounds like you haven't changed much."

"Damn. I know this voice...Don, is that you? What the hell are you doing calling me at this time of night?"

"Sorry, Erin, I had to. I just wish it were only to say hello. It's been too long. How have you been?"

"I'm fine, Don. Now, please tell me what you want before you really piss me off."

He can picture the impatient look on her face. She likes everything straight up and to the point. He grins and tells her, "Calm down. I just need a bit of a favor. We have a little problem here and I think it's headed your way."

This sits Judge Baron straight up in the bed, pushing her long blonde hair out of her face as she asks, "What?"

Time for business and he explains what they know, then asks, "Erin, can you send someone over to the RV Park and check into what I've told you? Also, if possible, have them check on Mr. Wolf. He's a family member of a close friend of mine and, as you can see, we have reason to be worried about him. You might want to wait until you see what's going on at the RV Park first. I'd hate to wake the old man unnecessarily. He's had a very full last few days and only returned back home this past evening."

Chapter 28

Flame and Joe are getting closer to Grandfather's home. In only a few minutes they will be on the forest land that Flame loves so much. Joe has gone well over the speed limit getting them here and she has cried almost the whole way, close to two hours now.

She has tried repeatedly to enter Ghost's mind, but he still will not let her in. She has also, repeatedly, tried to focus on Grandfather, but is receiving no information. She is ready to scream with frustration.

Joe realizes that he and Flame may very well be walking into something they might not walk out of. He is extremely worried about all of them, with Grandfather uppermost in his mind. He does not know what he will do if something is wrong with him. He is more than happy when he sees the turn off to Grandfather's driveway ahead.

He pulls over to the side of the road, stopping before turning into the driveway. He looks over at Flame seeing that she is still crying, but silently now. He reaches into the glove box and pulls out a small handgun.

She is watching him with her eyes wide.

"I'm sorry, Flame, but I think we had better be prepared for anything. I always carry my gun, but I've never had reason to use it. I hope I don't have to this time either, but it's better to be ready, than not. Just in case."

She has never felt so lost and she realizes that, even as a child, she had not felt this kind of despair. She cannot use her gift. After all the years as a child that she had wished to be like the other kids—normal—now all she wants is to be able to use her gift again. She is not whole without it and she craves the touch of her mind to those she loves.

But, she only nods at Joe, without speaking a word. She has not spoken the whole way here, staying focused on trying to get to Grandfather and using her gift.

Joe is very worried for her, in more ways than one. She is not in control right now and even she knows it. He tells her, "Okay, here we go. If I tell you to get down, don't hesitate. Do it. I mean it. Do you hear me?" He knows she can hear him, but he doesn't know if what he is saying has even registered with her.

She finally looks him in the eyes and says softly, "I hear you, Joe. I'll be as careful as possible. Please, go. I *must* find out what is causing this, in me, and in Ghost."

He rolls both windows down to be able to hear any noise that may be out of place, then he slowly makes his way down the long driveway. He is watching the woods around them, ready to push Flame down if necessary. There is nothing. No sound coming through the open windows. Nothing.

Flame realizes it first, "Joe, the forest is too quiet. There's no noise, no crickets, no birds, nothing. I've tried to call the wolves, but they don't answer. I can feel them here though. They're in hiding. Not only out of sight, but out of mind. Just like Ghost."

Then she realizes that she can identify the wolves, all of the ones that she has known, but not the newer ones, the ones she hasn't met or been inside. They are all here, except Prince.

She says, "Joe, I can tell all of the wolves are here, all of them, except Prince. I can't locate him. He would be with Grandfather." This makes her all the more upset.

As they reach the cabin he slows even more before coming around to the front of the cabin. He does not see Grandfather's ancient truck and he usually keeps it parked in the barn, but the barn doors are wide open with Joe's headlights lighting up the interior. No truck.

Flame exclaims, "Joe, Grandfather's truck is not in the barn, but there are no lights on in the cabin. He always leaves a light on, you know that." She is relieved at the fact that the truck is not visible, thinking that Grandfather may not be home, but she knows in her heart that there is more here they have yet to see.

Joe slowly pulls around to the front of the cabin. At first they see nothing, but then Flame screams and Joe sees Grandfather too. Flame immediately reached for the door handle, but Joe grabs her and pulls her back into her seat.

He screams, "NO, FLAME! You stay right here until I check around first. Get down! Lay in the front seat. No arguing with me!" He forcefully pulls her down on the seat and commands, "You stay right here until I call for you. Do you hear me?!"

She is out of control. She cannot even form the words to tell him yes, so she nods her head.

As Joe steps out of the vehicle, Flame is bombarded by visions from the wolves. They mind link with her now that she has seen Grandfather. Ghost's knowledge is uppermost in her mind. He shows her what has happened here. Now the other wolves come out of the forest, knowing she has arrived. She disobeys Joe's order because she knows what has happened and she is in no immediate danger. Ghost and the others would warn her otherwise.

Joe is bending down at Grandfather's side. He does not hear her come up behind him. She reaches down and places her hand on his shoulder. He immediately brings the gun around, pointing it at her.

When he realizes it is her, he screams, "FLAME, WHAT THE *HELL* ARE YOU DOING?! I TOLD YOU TO STAY DOWN! I COULD HAVE SHOT YOU!" He realizes that Ghost is showing his teeth with a low growl focused on him. He pulls the gun down, laying it at his side.

Now he hears the others. They are surrounding him, teeth bared, ready to spring. There must be at least ten wolves surrounding them. He knows they think he is threatening Flame. The only thing keeping them from springing is Flame's hand on his shoulder.

Flame is lost. Her mind is so numb that she doesn't even realize the peril that Joe is in.

He tells her, quietly now, "Flame, please call off the wolves. Tell them who I am."

She is in shock looking down at Grandfather's body. There is no response from her. None. Nothing.

Joe is afraid to raise his voice now. He pleads with her and then with Ghost, "Flame...Ghost, please tell them I'm no threat. Tell them who I am. Please?!"

Ghost gently takes her hand in his mouth, putting enough pressure on her hand to pull her away from Joe, to make her hear him. She looks at Joe, then around at the snarling wolves.

She realizes then what he has been saying and tells them all, "This is Joe, Grandfather's grandson. He is not here to do harm, like the others. He's grieving with us."

The alpha female of Prince's pack, Magic, his mate, comes to her. She is a beautiful solid black, but there is blood caked in her fur and around her face. She goes from Flame to another body, one they had not noticed yet.

It is Prince. He is lying a few feet from the porch steps.

Flame tells her silently, *I know your mate's with Grandfather. They walk together in the other world. We will both see them again one day. This I promise you.*

Joe has checked Grandfather for any sign of life, but Flame already knows he is gone. She tells Joe, "I know now what's happened here. They blocked me because Grandfather told them to. He didn't want me to know it was happening. He knew I would come to him and he was trying, in the only way he could, to protect me. Us.

"There are two bodies in the woods. It's two of the men who came to kill Grandfather. The wolves got them, but there was another, and *she* killed Grandfather. She took his truck after pulling his body from it. The wolves were going to kill her too, but she got away."

Joe is furious as he says, "Open the door to his home, Flame. I will *not* leave him lying here like this. We have to call the police, but first I want him to be in his home."

She rises, going to the door to the cabin. It is still locked. The intruders did not even go into his home. She takes the hidden key from the fake rock and opens the door.

She is holding the rock in one hand, the key in the other, and she looks down the porch steps at Joe with her tears falling freely, but she smiles as she says, "I remember sending this to Grandfather one Christmas. He was so thrilled about it. He was amazed at how much it resembles the real thing. A real rock."

Joe smiles, too, remembering Grandfather's excitement over the silly gift. He had called Joe to tell him about it.

"He loved it, little sister. I think it was his favorite Christmas gift ever." he says, as the smile leaves his face when he looks down at Grandfather. He reaches down and reverently picks him up, carrying him into his home.

Flame turns on the lights throughout the cabin, trying to keep her hands busy. She notes that nothing has changed in the cabin in the years she has been gone. Only a few more pictures scattered around the room. Pictures of her. Pictures of Ghost and even a few of Prince. He loved his family.

Joe lays Grandfather on his own bed. He had been shot in the head and it is an awful sight, one that neither of them will ever shake. They had not seen the wound while they were outside because it had been too dark.

He covers him with his favorite Indian blanket. The one his wife had made for him before Joe was even born. Then he turns to find Flame standing quietly behind him, her eyes dry. No more tears.

She says, "Joe, bring Prince in and place him beside Grandfather. It's what he would want us to do. Prince was his constant companion for years and will continue to be so." She nods toward the door.

Joe's hesitates to return to the huge pack of wolves, but she tells him, "Go. Magic knows you're coming for Prince. They will protect you now, Joe, just as they would me, and as they did Grandfather. Have no fear of them."

He goes into the large circle of wolves once more. So many wolves, and it is deathly quiet. No sound whatsoever. He sees his gun, lying where he left it. He hesitates to pick it up and Ghost walks to his side, nudging him. He knows Ghost is giving him permission to get it. After picking up the gun and placing it in the small of his back, into his waistband, he kneels and picks up Prince.

As Joe takes Prince inside to lay him with Grandfather, the alpha female, Magic, comes with him. She watches him place Prince beside Grandfather, looks at Joe and then to Flame, and walks back outside.

Flame tells him, "Magic thanks you. She thinks it's a fitting place for her mate to lie."

He goes to the phone now, telling her, "It's time to call the police." When he places the phone to his ear, he finds there is no dial tone.

He curses, "Shit! They've cut the damn line. Come on, we have to go to the police station and let them know what's happened so they can get some people out here. Maybe they'll find something on the guys in the woods."

"I'm not leaving here, Joe. You go. I'll stay right here." she tells him firmly.

Her face tells him there will be no talking her out of this idea, but he has to try. He cannot just leave her here; he would never forgive himself if anything happens to her too.

He says, "Flame, you know you can't stay here. Not after what they did to Grandfather. They'll come back to get their dead. You know that." he pleads with her, but she only gives him a cold smile, one that does not reach her eyes. A look he has never seen on her before.

She is way past tears now. She is furious. This is the forest Wolf. *Her* forest now. She almost wishes they would come for their dead. She will welcome them with all she has, all she is. They have no idea what they have done.

She tells him, "No, Joe. You know I won't leave this home now. Not until the time is right. I have protection. A lot of protection." And, she actually gives a little laugh. One with no humor whatsoever.

She actually scares Joe a bit, and he loves her.

He says, "All right, but I don't like it. Here, you keep the gun. Use it if you have to. Grandfather told me he taught you to shoot. I'll be back as soon as I can. Please, don't let anyone in here. Keep everyone away until I get back, even if you have to use this." He hands her the gun. He does not like leaving her, but he has no choice.

"Joe, take Magic with you. She's ready and waiting on you by the station wagon. She'll help watch over you. I don't need your gun. I know where Grandfather's are, so take yours in case you need it." She goes to the desk drawer and pulls out a small gun. She checks to see if it is loaded, already knowing it will be. She is not disappointed.

"I don't like this, Flame. I'm doing it your way, but we'll talk about who's the big brother here. And, soon." he says, walking to her and kissing her on the cheek.

She pulls him into an embrace, holding him to her. She knows how much he is hurting, but all he worries about now is her. It feel so strange for her to have so much love for him. She had never expected to have a family and she knows that she could not love this family more even if she had been born to it. She misses Grandfather so much already.

He leaves and she is suddenly hit with a vision and it is not from the wolves, but one like she has never had before. She sees that Joe is in danger. Something is going to happen to him and she runs for the door, but the station wagon is already driving away.

She sends a warning to Magic using their mind link, *Magic, Joe's in danger. Watch over him well. Don't let him out of your sight. When he goes in the station you are to go with him. Don't let him leave you for a moment!*

She knows Magic will obey her commands, but that does not ease her mind.

The phone in the booth finally rings and the woman answers immediately. "It's about damned time! Why did you hang up on me dammit?"

"Officer, this is not Stokes. I thought I would call you personally. How the hell did the three of you let that damned old Indian run all over you like that?!" When the young officer tries to speak, he cuts her off, "Never mind. Just listen. No mistakes this time."

"Y...yes, boss. I'm listening."

"There are a couple of my men coming to meet you. They'll help you get this mess cleaned up. You're to go to the far end of the old man's property. There's a small dirt drive there that leads into the woods. Park there and wait for them. DO *NOT* DO ANYTHING WITHOUT THEM. Do you understand me?"

"Yes, sir. I'm on my way now."

And again, the line goes dead in her hand.

Shay finally reaches the apartment. He unlocks the door and goes straight to the bedroom. He is exhausted. He reaches the bedroom, expecting to find Flame asleep, with Ghost guarding her, but she is not there.

He starts calling out loudly for`her, "Flame! *Flame*! Where the hell are you?"

He rushes to check the bathroom, but she is not there either. He searches the whole apartment and, by the time he reaches the living room again, he is frantic.

He thinks, *Where the hell is she?*

He searches the apartment again, looking closer this time, hoping to find a note. Still nothing. He does the only thing he can think of, he calls Joe.

When Shay dials Joe's number the phone just rings and rings with no answer. He does not know what in the hell is going on. He hangs the phone back in its cradle and puts his head down, rubbing his eyes and trying to calm his racing heart. She would not just leave him. Something has to be wrong. Very wrong.

As he stands to go in search of her, the phone rings. He hastily picks it up and immediately asks, "Flame? Where are you? What's wrong?"

"No, Shay, this is Don. What's up? Flame's not there?" he asks, sounding like he was expecting this news.

Shay realizes that it is the middle of the night and Don's voice is too strange combined with Flame being missing. Not to mention Joe. He asks, "What's wrong, Don. I know you know something, so tell me!"

"Hell, Shay, I was only calling to warn you. I had no idea anything would go down before I got to you." Don thinks immediately of Sergeant Stokes. He wonders if he could have Flame already.

"What do you mean by that, Don? Come on, spill it dammit! I'm going nuts here!"

He hesitates momentarily, then admits, "It's Stokes. I think we really spooked him tonight. Then I added to it by seeing him again at the station."

He explains what has gone down with Stokes, and continues, "I traced the number that he had written down. It was in River Valley, Shay, at the River Park campground. I called it, and you'll never guess who picked it up..."

Shay screams, "SPILL IT, DON! I don't have time for this damn chit-chat! Flame's missing, and Joe too! Who? And what's going on?" He is ready to throttle someone.

"Calm down, Shay. We'll have to be calm to get this fixed. It was Officer Donna Roberts. She's in on all this somehow, with Stokes and Otis Edwards too. I think we need to get a few people together and head over there. Something doesn't feel right." He adds, "I called Judge Baron and she said she'd send someone to check the campground and then check on Mr. Wolf too."

"Thanks, Don. I appreciate it. I'm sorry I've been such a bastard, but I don't know where Flame is, and I can't leave until I find out. Can you head on up there until I can locate her?"

"Sure. I'll call in a couple of favors and take a couple of cops with me. I know for a fact that Marty Diener is just getting off duty, so he is the first one I'm calling. I'd trust him with my life and I may just be doing that. You find Flame. You can reach me through the River Valley Police Station. We'll stop there first." Don tells him.

"Thanks buddy. I owe you big." Shay hangs up the phone, not knowing what to do, or where to go first. He has no idea where she might go, but then he thinks of Frankie. He leaves the apartment in a rush and jumps back into his van, racing to the carnival parking lot.

Halfway there he thinks, *Damn...I forgot! They left!*

He remembers that Flame had mentioned the RV Park on the outside of the city and he heads there, praying Frankie will be there and breaking every speed law in the city getting to it.

He reaches the trailer park and has to drive slowly through it, slowing further at each trailer, to locate Frankie's small trailer. While he is doing this a police car comes up behind him and turns on its blue lights. He cannot believe the bad luck he is having tonight. He pulls over as far as he can and gets out, slowly walking toward the police car.

As he steps up to the car, Officer Regina Randall steps out, smiling brightly. She says cheerfully, "What's up, Shay? Doing some detective work around here this time of the morning?"

He knows she is only ribbing him a bit, but he is in no mood for it tonight. "Dammit, Regina, I'm looking for someone. It has been a very long night, and it is going to be an even longer day, so what the hell do you want?"

Regina is taken aback by Shay's tone. Sure she has given him a hard time in the past, but he always knows when she is joking. She knows something has to be very wrong for her to get this reaction from him. She tells him, "Damn, I'm sorry, Shay. I was only joking. Do you need some help?"

"Sorry for biting your head off, Regina. I'm just really worried about Flame and Joe Wolf. I don't have time to go into all of it, but if you're going back to the station, check in with Don Clanton. He's getting a couple of the boys to go down to River Valley. Probably off duty cops. You might have to call his home, or contact Marty Diener. I think Marty is just getting off duty. I don't have time to explain it all right now, but I'm sure he could use your help." He starts to walk away.

Regina stops him, quickly asking, "Did you say River Valley?"

He stops mid-step, remembering what Don had said about the female officer, Donna Roberts. She is Regina's partner. He thinks, *Oh shit. I've really screwed this one up.* but, aloud he says, "Yeah, I did. Why?"

"Well, Donna called in tonight, said she has some family trouble going on down there. Her mother's family lives in that area. She took the night off to go down there earlier. Does that have anything to do with all of this?" Regina is looking at him speculatively.

He can tell, she knows more than she is saying. After a brief hesitation he admits, "I'll tell you the truth, Regina. Shit, I guess I have no choice. Yes, Donna's involved in all of it. I don't know any details, but I know that Don could use your help in all this. Please, radio in, ask for him and tell him to wait for you. Okay? You might even have some information that could help in this whole mess."

Shay knows Regina well, after all, he was her partner, and when you are partners you get to know each other pretty damn well. He hopes she knows something about her new partner that might help them all. He just prays it isn't something that will hurt them.

She immediately says, "I'm on my way, Shay. Oh, and Shay?"

"Yeah?"

"Don't worry. I'll be on the right side this time." With this mysterious statement she gets into her squad car and immediately picks up the radio.

Shay stops and smiles before returning to his van. Now *that* was the old Regina. The one he had really liked.

Once back in the van he continues his search for Frankie's trailer. Toward the end of the park he finally finds it. No mistaking it, "Frankie's Buns" shines brightly.

He rushes out of his van, almost running to the front door of the trailer. He bangs on the door calling out loudly, "Frankie…wake up…it's me, Shay! Come on, Frankie!"

Finally Frankie pulls the door open, almost pulling it off its hinges. He demands, "What?! What the hell's goin on?! Where's Flame? What be wrong?!"

Shay asks, "She's not with you?" He had actually been hoping that she had gotten mad because he was so late coming home and had come to Frankie's to teach him a lesson. He has talked himself into believing it…it being better than any other possibilities he can think of.

When Frankie sees the expression on Shay's face he reaches out the door, literally pulling him into the trailer by his shirtfront, lifting him completely off the ground, over the small steps, and into the trailer. He sets his feet back onto the floor and gets in his face, almost nose to nose, and demands, "What the hell've you done to my girl that she'd up and leave for? Come on…what'd you do?"

"No, Frankie, it's not me. I swear. Come on and get dressed. I'm going to need your help. I'll explain everything in the van. Hurry! I'll be waiting in the van. Oh…and bring that cannon of yours too."

"Damn straight I'm a bringin my gun. Gonna shoot me some white boy ass if you done hurt my girl. If it ain't you then somebody's gettin his ass shot anyway, just for the hell of it." Frankie is furious, but Shay has not heard half of what he has said as he is already running back to the van.

Frankie takes barely five minutes to get dressed and in the van. They take off, not really knowing where to go next. Shay thinks the next place he should check would be Joe's. Maybe there is some clue there as to where they have gone.

While on the way to Joe's, Shay brings Frankie up to date on all that has happened and is still happening. He is furious. He is just as worried about Flame, and the others, as Shay is.

"I done told you I'm gonna kill me somebody. If any of them little assholes has hurt my girl or her family, they got one big, mad black man with a cannon that's gonna pop their asses." he says, angrily.

Shay glances at Frankie, seeing his face set in a grim mask. He knows Frankie means every word of it.

Chapter 29

Mercedes, in her old bedroom, has been fitfully in and out of sleep. She finally gets up, thinking to go into the kitchen for a cup of hot chocolate. It usually helps to calm her nerves.

On her way into the house she did not see anyone. Nobody. She wonders where all the staff is. Usually at least one man is always on guard, on the grounds, or in the large foyer.

Her father's office is right there off the entrance to the home and foyer. She had listened at the closed door when she came in and heard nothing. She thought he was either sleeping, or most likely out. Usually Sadie would alert him to anyone in the house and she had made no noise.

Mercedes goes once more to the office door after fixing her hot chocolate. She sees it is now open and that the light on the desk is turned on. She starts to go inside to tell her father what is going on when the phone rings. She decides to wait until he is off the phone as he gets very angry when interrupted during business calls.

Then she realizes what time it is and she wonders what kind of business it could be for someone to call at this time of the morning. She slips closer to the door to listen, out of curiosity. Though she is usually bored stiff his business deals, she decides to wait. He really should know what is going on with Joe and Flame. Maybe he can help in some way.

She hears her father pick up the phone and say, "Go on, I'm waiting and it had better be good."

He listens for a moment, then says, "Joe Wolf is there at the station? What does he want?"

After a brief moment he says, "Damn. They weren't supposed to be there already." He hesitates for a moment and continues, "I guess it's time to finish it. Cut his brake line while he's inside."

Mercedes' mouth drops. She starts into the office but hesitates, waiting to hear what he says next. She is growing more furious by the moment and soon her temper will get the best of her.

"Yes, *dammit*, I said to cut the damn line. He'll lose control on his way back to the cabin, most likely going off the mountain and into the river. He'll be out of the picture. Then all you have to do is take the damn woman. She's probably at that filthy cabin waiting with that dead old Indian.

"I want it all done tonight. No reason to wait now. It's almost too perfect." He waits another moment, listening, and then says, "Yes, she's a liability. She screwed up real bad earlier with the old man. Now we have two dead cops up there. Take her out too. No mistakes this time."

After a brief quiet, he says, "Yeah, I've got two more men coming up there to help in the cleanup. I want them taken care of, too, once they've cleaned their mess up. They've both screwed up so badly already that it's a wonder they haven't brought all this shit down on our heads. You just remember, if anyone goes down it's going to be all of us going down." And he slams the receiver down.

Mercedes is in such complete shock that the mug she is holding slides from her hands, hits the floor, and crashes into a million pieces.

Sadie jumps up, growling and starts toward the door, but after seeing that it is Mercedes she starts wagging her tail.

Her father shouts, "Who's there? Get your ass in here. *NOW*!"

She walks inside the office, her face ashen, and tears spilling down her face. Once her father sees her, he knows immediately that she has heard everything.

He tells her roughly, "Sit down, Mercedes, before you fall down."

She sits and looks at her father, wishing she were only dreaming, but this is no dream. She knew her father was ruthless, but not this cruel. She cannot believe he would have her own husband killed. She wonders if he could just as easily kill her.

"Daddy, why are you doing this?" she asks, wanting to rush to the phone to call Shay, to call anyone that can help Joe and Flame.

"Oh hell, Mercedes, stop that damn sniveling. You don't have any idea what's going on here." he says, forcefully.

He looks at her like she is a stupid child, still treating her as if she has no mind of her own. He has never accepted the fact that she is a grown woman and a strong willed one.

"Daddy, I *do* know that you've just told someone to kill my husband! Why would you do that? I love, Joe, you know that." Mercedes is pleading with him, wanting to know why he would do this terrible, terrible thing. She had no idea her father was so cold. Ruthless, yes, but nothing like this.

"You don't know what the hell you're talking about." he says and tries to call her bluff, trying to make her believe he would never do such a thing.

"Yes, I *do*, Daddy. I heard it all. Why would you want Joe dead? And, why did you have his Grandfather killed?" Mercedes asks, and she is growing angrier by the minute, tired of being treated as a pawn in his ridiculous games.

"It's business, little girl. Only business. You've never noticed the money you spend and you spend it like it grows on trees. Your mother was the same way, always buying anything that took her fancy. You're just like the bitch." He is past trying to hide anything now, lashing out at her in anger.

"It was *her* money, Daddy! She was the one that had the money, not you. It was all hers and if she wanted to spend it, she could spend it all. I don't spend *your* money either, Daddy. I have my own accounts. My mother saw to that."

"Little girl, you never even check your account statements. Haven't you realized that you have no money? I spent it long ago. I've been trying to keep our heads above water for the past two years! We're *both* broke. If this home wasn't in *your* name it would have already been sold, to pay off some of the debt." He has the nerve to laugh.

"You can't possibly mean you have lost all the money my mother had! Even you couldn't have done that." Mercedes is shocked. She knows that her mother's family had been very wealthy. They had owned many oil fields all over the state, and even a few in others. It is next to impossible for him to have lost *all* of it.

He says, in a dismissing tone, "It's all gone, girl. Now I'm trying to make sure we get it all back."

He no longer even looks at her, but down at a paper on his desk. He says almost consolingly, "Thanks to my efforts we can get most of it back, with all the oil that your *Indian stud* is leaving to you."

"What's that, Daddy?" She asks quietly.

She walks around the desk to see what he is looking at. As she reaches the edge of the desk, she sees, in large black print the words, Last Will And Testament, on the header and she exclaims, "Oh my God! Daddy! Are you completely mad?"

"*SHUT UP*! Don't you *ever* talk to me like that again! I'm your father, and I'm trying to bail *your* ass out of all this mess. Why the hell do you think I let you marry that damned Indian in the first place?! Surely you know I hate the man. I wouldn't have allowed you to even sit at the same table with him if it weren't for all the money he has. Even as stupid as you are, you must have known that!" His face is an angry red, with spittle flying off his mouth with every word. He continues angrily, "Don't you realize all that money will be yours, *ours,* when they're all dead?"

"You *are* mad, Daddy. Completely mad. I won't let you hurt the man I love *or* the rest of his family. You've done enough damage already. And, even if that were true I would never, I repeat, *never,* allow you to get your hands on even a penny of it! I'm calling the cops now. It's over, *Daddy*!" She reaches for the phone and when she does her father pulls the line from the wall. She looks at him incredulously.

He stands and slaps her face so hard that she falls to the floor. He screams, "YOU WILL *NEVER* DISOBEY ME AGAIN, LITTLE GIRL! You slept with that damn dirty Indian and you expect me to just sit back and smile? You're just like your mother! Maybe I can arrange for the same thing to happen to you that happened to her. It's not so hard to do, you know?!"

She is sobbing, staring at father, realizing that he has lost his mind. She knows now that he has always been this way. Mad. Not the angry kind, but completely loony.

She ask quietly, "You killed her didn't you, Daddy? I knew it then, even as young as I was, I knew it. Admit it, Daddy."

She has suddenly remembered what she had blocked so long ago. She sees her father with the razor in his hands. His hands bloody, telling her that her mother did it to herself, but she knew, even then, that *he* had done it. She had blocked it out, not wanting to remember something so horrifying.

He admits, shouting, "HELL, YES, I KILLED THAT BITCH! I warned her not to interfere in my business, but she kept sticking her nose in anyway. Threatening to do the same thing you just did! Call the police on me. I can't kill you, little girl, the money would then go to some damned *Indian Institute*, whatever the hell that's supposed to be!

"Like the damn Indians would know what to do with anything that large. That damn old man didn't even know how to write a Will! No, I can't kill you, but I *can* put you in an institution. One for the insane…how would like that, little girl?"

She has heard enough and she stands up to run from the room, but her father grabs her by her long auburn hair, ripping hands full from her head. She is screaming, but now her father has her in hand. He slaps her over and over. Not realizing, in his rage, that she is already unconscious.

Flame is sitting in Grandfather's favorite chair at the cabin, looking out the window at the dark forest. She is waiting for Joe to come with the police. Suddenly she is hit with a very strong vision.

It is Sadie. Flame is shocked at what Sadie is showing her.

Mercedes' father is doing the unimaginable. He has a handful of her hair in one hand, holding her head up, while slapping her with the other. Mercedes is unconscious, but he is still hitting her!

Flame gives Sadie a command, *Stop him, Sadie! Don't let him harm her anymore! Attack him* now*!*

She watches, through her mind link with Sadie, as she attacks Mr. Holst. She knocks him back, off Mercedes, and pins him to the floor. She goes for his throat. He is screaming, but Sadie has him in her control now.

Flame gives her another command, *Don't kill him, Sadie. I'm sending*

Shay to you. Keep him pinned down and don't let him get up! Don't let him hurt Mercedes, or you, ever again!

She releases Sadie from the mind link. It is time to summon Shay. He will have to go to Mercedes' aid and then he needs to come here. She needs him now too.

She searches, then enters Shay's mind. He is at Joe's home, trying to get someone to answer the door. He has been searching frantically for her. She feels terrible that she has let him worry over her so much. She should have already contacted him to let him know where she is and why. There has just been so much going on that she has not thought to link with him. Her grief over Grandfather and her worry over the vision of Joe, clouding her thoughts.

She links with him and says, *Shay! Listen to me, Shay!*

He stops banging on Joe's door and looks quickly at Frankie.

She continues, *You must go to Mercedes immediately! She's at the mansion! Her father has beaten her and she's unconscious. Sadie has Holst pinned to the floor! Hurry, Shay! I don't know how badly she's hurt, or how long Sadie can keep him down!*

Frankie is looking at Shay like he has gone mad.

Shay is holding both hands to his head with a wild look in his eyes.

"Shay, what the hell's wrong with you? SHAY! Tell me what be wrong!" Frankie demands, frantically.

Shay looks at Frankie, shaking his head from side to side, but, finally, he tells him, "It's Flame! She's talking to me! Hush a minute!"

Frankie thinks he has really lost it. Flame is not even here. The man is losing his mind. He says, "Shay, she ain't here! You be losin it buddy!" His eyes are wide, the white glowing completely around them in the dim light. Shay is really freaking him out.

"No, Frankie, she's in my mind! Hush!" Shay is listening carefully to Flame.

She tells him, *Go to Mercedes, Shay! Now!*

He is so overwhelmed and so relieved that she has contacted him that he does not realize he is speaking out loud, instead of silently, as he says, "Flame! Where the hell are you? I've been worried sick! I couldn't find you and now Joe's gone too! Where *are* you?!"

She can hear him this way too, as she is in his mind. She answers, *I'm at Grandfather's. Someone has killed him, Shay. I had to come to him. I wasn't able to use the mind link. I'd been blocked. I* had *to call Joe. We dropped Mercedes at her father's. You must go to her. Call the police and get that man arrested! Make sure she is okay and then come up here, to Grandfather's. Joe's in danger and I can't reach him, the phone's out here. HURRY, SHAY!*

He does not hesitate, but runs to the van, screaming at Frankie, "Come on, Frankie! We have to make a stop at the Holst mansion. Mercedes' father has beaten her really bad! We have to stop him from hurting her worse, or even killing her. I wouldn't put anything past him. Let's *go*!" He is in the seat with the van running before Frankie is even inside the van.

"Damn, Shay, my girl can talk to you like that? Like with Ghost? *How?*! How come she don't talk to me that way?" Frankie asks, hurt, not understanding why, if she could do this with Shay, she has never talked to him that way.

"Frankie, you must have some psychic ability for her to do it with you. I didn't even know I did. The first time she talked to me was when that man shot me. It freaked the crap out of me! I'm just so glad to hear from her!" He is relieved, but very anxious to get to Flame. First he must save Mercedes though. He adds, "Frankie, hand me that police ban radio right there."

"You got it!" Frankie says, and grabs the handheld radio, giving it quickly to Shay.

"Dispatch...dispatch?" Shay speaks into the mike.

"Dispatch here. What's up?" It is Kaitlyn, one of Shay's favorite dispatchers.

"Kaitlyn, this is Larson. Who's nearest to the Holst mansion?"

"Did you say the Holst mansion? No *shit?*!"

"Come on, Kaitlyn! It's an emergency! I need a couple of guys out there fast! If I'm not there when they get there tell them to wait on me in the driveway!"

"You got it, Shay. I'll send the word out now."

Shay hands Frankie the radio, noting that he is holding on to the dash with both hands, eyes wide. He tells him, "Frankie, take this and stop freaking on me! I need you, buddy. Calm down."

"Damn, sorry, Shay, but I never been this fast in no car before! Damn boy, you sure can drive!" And, Frankie grins widely.

Shay shakes his head, thinking that Frankie is a force all his own.

When they arrive at the Holst mansion the patrol car Shay had requested is already there. Officers Reid and Hansen are waiting outside their car for Shay. He is glad they are two officers he knows he can trust. He would really like to have Marty Diener here, but he knows that Marty is helping Don in River Valley.

"Thanks, guys. I'm glad you got here so fast. There's a problem here. Mr. Holst has beaten his daughter and we need to get to her. She is unconscious and the dog has Holst pinned to the floor. If we don't get in there fast she'll kill him." he tells them, not thinking how to explain how he knows.

Officer Reid looks from Shay to Officer Hansen and asks, "Uh...Detective Larson, how do you know all this?"

Both officers are hesitant to go into the Holst mansion without the reason being a very substantial one. Holst is well known in Munson. He is no one to mess with. Everything has to be by the book or their asses are on the line.

Shay realizes what he has said and he looks at Frankie, and Frankie takes matters into his own very large hands.

He nods at Shay and tells the officers, "Here's how we know…see, I was in there, working in the kitchen when it all happened. I'm real scared of that damn dog, so I wasn't 'bout to go in that damn office to help em none, 'sides, if I'd tried to stop him from beatin his own daughter, he'd of fired me on the spot, so I called Shay here, cause he's a friend of mine."

Shay notices that Frankie has made nearly the whole explanation one long, nearly indecipherable, sentence, probably to keep the officers from asking more questions. He thanks God for Frankie, yet again. He gives him a wink.

Officer Hansen speaks this time, "Okay...if you were in there, how come you were just in that van with Detective Larson?"

Frankie's had enough, and says bluntly, "Oh hell. Just follow me. Damn smart ass five-oh's." And, before anyone can stop him, Frankie runs to the big front door, hitting it hard with his shoulder. The officers rush to try to stop him.

Shay stops them with a yell, "*NO*! Let him bust it down. It's all on me if I'm wrong!"

The officers stop mid-stride. They both look from Shay, then to Frankie. Officer Reid shrugs his shoulders and Officer Hansen nods.

The door does not give, but there is a loud cracking noise when he hits it the first time. He gets knocked back a few feet, shouts, "DAMN!" and kicks it, hard, with his large booted foot. This time the door bursts inward. All four of them rush inside.

Then they hear Holst's frantic cries for help. He screams, "In here! Get this damn dog off of me! She's killing me! Hurry!"

They all rush into the office where the voice is coming from, to find Mercedes on the floor and Sadie standing over S.R. Holst, teeth bared and growling.

Officer Hansen pulls out his gun pointing it toward Sadie, and Shay yells, "NO, HANSEN!"

This outburst takes the two officers by surprise, both of them looking wide eyed at Shay.

Officer Hansen quickly says, "We have to get that damn dog off of him!"

Shay says, "I'll take care of Sadie. Frankie, get Mercedes!"

Shay walks over to Sadie and she stops growling, looking up at Shay expectantly. "Come on, Sadie. You're a good girl and you did the right thing."

The two officers are awed when Sadie steps away from Holst and goes directly to Shay, tail wagging.

Holst stands, yelling, "I want that damned dog killed and if you won't do then I'll do it myself."

He reaches into his desk and Shay, seeing what he is doing, grabs him, yelling, "Officer Reid, cuff this man. He is under arrest. Read him his rights."

Reid grabs the struggling Mr. Holst, doing just what Shay tells him to do. It feels so good to put him in cuffs, especially after seeing Mercedes' face, that Reid turns a grinning face to Hansen and grins as he says to Holst, "You're under arrest. You have the right…"

Holst interrupts him with, "Larson, I'll have your damn job for this! What are you arresting me for?" He has a wild-eyed look on his blood red face.

At that moment Mercedes, who has come to in Frankie's large embrace, tells her father, "I'll tell you what for! I'll tell you *all* what for!"

Holst turns his head quickly toward Mercedes, giving her a blank look. He had not even realized she was still in the room, until then. She looks terrible, but he screams, "SHUT UP YOU STUPID LITTLE BITCH! I SHOULD HAVE KILLED YOU JUST LIKE I KILLED YOUR BITCH OF A MOTHER!"

Shay smiles at Mercedes, and then at the other officers, and says, "I think that's one reason for your arrest Mr. Holst. You just admitted to killing your wife. You also beat your own daughter, almost to death. Is there more, Mercedes?"

She is awake fully now and very mad. She looks at Frankie and nods. He sets her on her feet, keeping his hands on her shoulders as she is not too steady. Then she tells Shay, "There's much, much more. Shay, take a look at that paper on the desk, and that should tell you everything. I think, *Daddy*, that you'll be leaving for a very long time. I just wish we'd known sooner."

Shay steps behind the desk, seeing the Will that belonged to Grandfather. He picks it up and quickly reads it. He looks at Mercedes, his eyes wide, and asks, "Mercedes, what do you know about this?"

She never takes her eyes off of her father and gets a triumphant look on her face as she says, "I know everything about it. My *father* had Joe's grandfather killed. I don't know who all is involved, but I heard him on the phone with someone in River Valley. He told the person on the phone to cut Joe's brake line and then to go to the cabin and take care of Flame.

"He was planning to get me committed to an insane asylum, so he would have control of the money once they were all dead. He's insane! He killed my mother because he couldn't control her. He spent all of *her* money and all of the money in *my* accounts."

Shay wishes he were alone with this girl's father, Mr. Holst, right now. He would kill him himself, but it is Frankie that can hold his tongue no longer, "I ought to tear your damn fool head right off your shoulders. I swear, if these boys wasn't here I'd kill you with one hand wrapped right round your scrawny chicken-ass neck! You done messed with the wrong people this time, you white-assed son of a bitch."

He takes a step toward Holst and Shay hurriedly steps between them saying, "No, Frankie, let the law take care of him this time. I swear to you, if he somehow gets off, I'll help you kill the bastard myself."

Frankie looks at him and, seeing the determined look in his eyes, nods.

"Mercedes, is there more?" Shay asks gently. He knows she is in as much of a hurry to reach Joe as he is to reach Flame.

"Yes, there's more. He had three people go kill Grandfather. Two are dead. All three of them were cops. The one who got away is a woman. He told someone in River Valley to kill her too. Then, he told this person that there are two more people from here that are on the way down to River Valley, to clean up the first mess. He told the person to kill them once their clean-up job is done.

"That about covers it, huh, Daddy?" Mercedes concludes, a cold look in her tear filled eyes.

Holst's face has gone white as a sheet. He refuses to look at anyone, or acknowledge anything. He is not struggling now, but is almost cowed in the officer's grip, though he shows no sign of remorse.

Shay tells the officers, "Get that piece of shit out of here. I don't think you'll ever have to worry about him living in your house again, Mercedes." Shay cannot help but tell her.

"Thank you, Shay. Let's go. We have to get down to River Valley quickly. They're going to kill them if we don't hurry." Mercedes starts walking out of the office, heading for the front door.

"Uh...honey...I think you best go on up and get you some clothes on first. I sure wouldn't want to get down there with you in your nightie." Frankie says, turning red faced.

She looks down, realizing she only has her thin nightgown on, and nods, heading straight for the stairs. Her right eye is swollen shut and bruises are already blackening on her beautiful face.

Shay calls out to her, "I'm going to call the Judge in River Valley and fill her in on what's going down. She'll be able to help us."

She stops, turns, and tells him, "You'll have to use the kitchen phone. Daddy pulled that one out of the wall." Then she turns and walks back up the steps.

Frankie looks at Shay, "Damn that man. He done hurt that pretty little thing real bad. I cain't believe he beat his own girl so bad." His hands are balled into huge ham-like fists.

Shay nods in agreement, "I know. The bastard. I should have guessed he was behind all of this. *Dammit.* Frankie, you stay here and wait for Mercedes while I go call the judge."

Frankie nods, and Shay looks down at Sadie, patting her huge head and telling her, "Sadie, you did a very good thing. You go on up and stay with Mercedes. You'll never have to be with that awful man again."

She wags her tail and rushes up to Mercedes room.

Shay reaches Judge Baron and informs her of all that has happened. She tells him she has one of her detectives going to the RV Park and then to the Wolf property. She also tells him that she will have some of the state police sent there too, since the River Valley Station only has a few officers.

Shay thanks her for all that she has done and hangs up the phone. He hopes Mercedes is ready to go, because he cannot stand thinking something could happen to Flame or Joe. It breaks his heart to know they weren't in time to save Grandfather. They need to hurry.

Chapter 30

Joe arrives at the River Valley Police Station and, when he starts to go inside, Magic jumps out behind him. He tells her to get back into the wagon, but she will not do it. Finally he gives up and takes her with him.

When he gets inside, an officer rushes up to him saying firmly, "Sir, you can't bring that dog in here. It's not even on a leash and what the hell is that in its fur? Is that *blood*?"

Joe has reached the end of his rope and he exclaims loudly, "YES, it *is* blood. And, there's plenty more where that came from. Do you want to tell her that she can't come in here? I tried, and she wouldn't listen to me!"

The officer is new to the force and he backs up a step, not quite knowing what to do, let alone what to say. Another officer, standing close by, is watching the scene.

He walks forward and says, "Where *did* the blood come from?"

"About damn time somebody with a bit of sense says something!" Joe is very frustrated and it is beginning to show. He says, "It came from the people that killed my grandfather. Two of them are dead and so is my grandfather. I tried to call you after finding him, but they've cut the phone lines. I came to get someone to follow me back to the house."

At that moment a woman in uniform comes into the room. She takes in the scene and then looks at Joe with a smile brightening her face. She says enthusiastically, "Well hell, Joe Wolf! I haven't seen you since high school!" When she sees the wolf, noticing the blood coating its fur, she looks quickly back at Joe and says, "What's all this about, Joe?!"

The older officer says skeptically, "He says that someone has murdered his grandfather and two other people. That's supposed to be blood all over that dog."

"Thank God it's you, Cheryl! I didn't know you'd become a cop, but I'm damn glad you are. I need someone to come out to Grandfather's land. What this man has said is true. Some people came to Grandfather's cabin and murdered him. The wolves got to two of the murderers, but one of them got away." He is trying to rush through this to make them understand he must hurry. He adds, "I've left my little sister there. She may be in danger and I need to get back there quickly."

The young officer looks down at the wolf and says loudly, "DID YOU SAY *WOLF*?! THAT'S A *WOLF*?!" This is too much for him and he takes off into the other room slamming the door.

The older officer tells Cheryl, "This is your job. You're the detective around here." And, he heads back to his desk, sitting and propping his feet up on the desk.

At that moment the phone rings and the same, older officer, Wallace, answers. He says, "Detective, it's for you! It's Judge Baron."

Cheryl, on her way out the door, looks at Joe with raised brows, motioning him to another door. Her name is on the front of this door. It says, Detective Cheryl Hendrickson. Joe, with the wolf right beside him, follows her inside the office.

"I'm sorry, Joe. I'll make it fast. Come in and let me take this call. It must be important for Judge Baron to call me at this time of the night, or should I say morning?" She impatiently grabs up the phone.

Cheryl holds the phone in a white knuckled grip, looking at Joe the whole time. Finally, she says, "Judge, Joe Wolf is here now. He says that his grandfather is dead." She continues to listen for another minute, hangs up, turns to Joe and says, "I need to talk to you for just a minute."

Joe cannot believe this, and he says, "Cheryl, I don't have time for this! I have to get back to my sister! She's all alone up there!"

"Joe, I just got word from Judge Baron to go out and check on all of this. I'm sorry. I was hoping that it was all a bad joke. I see I was wrong." she says and hesitates momentarily, then tells him the full truth, "I'm supposed to go to the RV Park up that way and check into a lady cop being there. I was told to bring her in and keep her here, in lock-up, for questioning by a detective from Munson. She's an officer out of there too."

Then she asks, "Isn't that where your practice is?" She looks concerned for Joe's state of mind.

"Yes, that's where I live. If you know all of this. Cheryl, then what are we waiting for?" He cannot even sit down. He is moving from foot to foot.

Cheryl eyes him warily, "Joe, you don't have a little sister. Who's up there that you're so worried about?"

"Cheryl, her name is Flame. Grandfather adopted her, unofficially, into our family years ago. To me, she *is* my little sister. Please, can we go now?"

"Yes...I'll follow you in the squad car. You can go on to the cabin while I see if I can get this lady cop in cuffs. Do me a favor, will you?"

At his quick nod, she says, "Keep all the wolves in the woods. I can't afford to have any more bodies on my hands. I'm going to get the old man out there to go on up to your cabin. He'll be in front of us, just in case there's anything you don't need to drive into. The state police should be there soon too." She starts for the door.

"Fine, Cheryl, let's go!" Joe turns and heads back out of the office with the wolf right on his heels.

When they reach the squad room once more, Cheryl places her hand on Joe's arm. "Joe, hold up. Wait outside for me. I'll pull around from the back of the building. I want to be in front of you on the way up. Got it?"

Joe nods once again.

Cheryl glances toward the squad room. "First I need to talk to the old crank over there."

Joe walks out as Cheryl walks toward the older cop. After a brief conversation the older cop grabs his hat and quickly heads out the door. Joe sees him rush by him, heading for the marked police car. It is a small town and there are only two marked cars in the whole of it. Most of the police work in the rural section is handled by the state police.

Joe and the wolf are waiting, engine running, when Cheryl pulls up around him in an unmarked car. She blows her horn in a short blast letting him know it is a go. He immediately hits the accelerator, foot to the floor, keeping up with Cheryl's lead foot.

Detective Don Clanton, along with Officers Marty Diener and Regina Randall, are finally at the River Valley Station. They all get out of the unmarked police car and rush into the station. They do not see a soul when they get inside.

Don yells, "Anyone here?!"

A door opens and a young officer sticks his head out of the door looking wide eyed around the room. He asks, "Is that damn wolf gone?"

The three Munson cops look at one another and then back to the young cop.

Don tells him, "Boy, there's no wolf out here. Just three pissed off cops. Get your ass out here now!"

The young officer comes slowly out, looking around the room quickly.

Don is getting truly pissed off and he yells, "HEY KID! Get your head out of your ass and listen up!"

This gets the kid's attention quickly and he apologizes, "I'm sorry, sir. Can I help you with something?"

"You damned well better. I talked to Judge Baron very early this morning and she told me that I'd have some help waiting on me here. Where the hell is everybody?" He looks around the room, seeing nothing but empty desks.

"Sir, a man just came in here yelling about a murder and dead cops, and he had a big damn wolf with him that had blood all over it! Next thing I know, I hear everyone slamming out the door and cars starting up. I'm the only one left on duty." This poor kid is wide eyed and scared shitless.

"Then it's going to be you who shows us the way to the Wolf property. You know where it is?" Don does not like the idea of this kid being in the middle of all this mess, but he has no choice.

"Y...yes s...sir, I know where it is. I've heard stories about that old Indian and his wolves all my life. Never been there, but everyone in this town knows where that land starts and ends. Nobody goes there!" This kid is ready to crap his pants.

"There's always a first, isn't there son. Do you have a squad car?" Don asks.

"Yes, sir, but I don't think I can drive. I really don't. This is my first week on the job and I've never driven one by myself." The young boy answers.

Marty and Regina both say, in unison, "Oh shit!" They turn to each other and grin.

Don looks at them, shrugs, and says, "Marty, you go with the kid. We'll be right behind you. Kid, you let my officer drive."

"Yes, sir. Thank you, sir." He runs toward the back to get the keys to the squad car.

Don looks at the grinning officers with him, and tells them, "Don't you two say a damn word. Poor kid. Keep him in the car, Marty. Don't let him get out for anything, you got that?"

Marty chuckles, and says, "Hell, I don't think I could pry his hands off the dashboard if I tried!"

Regina cracks up and even Don cannot wipe the grin from his face.

Once they are in their separate cars, Marty and the young officer in front and Don and Regina following behind, Regina turns to Don and tells him, "Don, I just want to thank you for letting me come with you. I'm so sorry I didn't see this coming with Donna. I should have known. I saw her whispering with Stokes so many times. I knew Stokes was bad news, but I turned a blind eye to it. I'm sorry it went this far."

Don glances at her, seeing that she is truly sorry, and tells her, "Regina, it's not your fault. You can't baby-sit your partner all the time. At least you didn't fall in with her. I'm glad you're with us on this. You might be able to help talk her down for us."

"Thanks, Don, but I doubt anybody can talk Donna down now. Do you believe what that kid said about the wolf, and the wolves on Joe's grandfather's property?" Don takes another quick look at Regina, seeing her knowing smile.

"Shit, Regina, you know it's the truth. You know about Ghost don't you?" He asks and grins, showing his excitement at the thought of being around the wolves.

"Well hell, Detective...what'd you think, that I'm just another dumb blonde?" She asks and laughs.

Don joins in the laughter a moment, and after a moment's silence, he asks, "Is he as beautiful as Shay says he is? I'm so excited about seeing them all…but I hate that it's because of all this shit. You know?"

"Yes, I *do* know. I feel the same way. Don…Ghost is gorgeous. I knew the first time I saw him. I just couldn't let on. You know they would have taken him away from Flame if anyone found out. Especially Donna. She *hates* animals. I mean, she's downright cruel when it comes to them. I wouldn't be surprised if she didn't kill kittens and puppies as a child. When we were on patrol, I learned very fast that I had to drive. She would actually go out of her way to hit any animal in the road, shit, even *close* to the road. When I said anything about it she would laugh at me. I had to turn *bitch* just to be able to take her."

Don feels sorry for her, never thinking he would feel sorry for this lady. She had always been cold, unfeeling, as far as he had seen. This was a completely different woman. Shay had told him that Regina was not really the bitch she put on as, but he didn't really believe him.

He says, "I'm sorry that I've given you such a hard time, Regina. I know it must be awful to be partnered up with someone like that. I don't think I could have done it."

Shay, Frankie, Mercedes, and Sadie are all piled into Shay's van. Shay has a vague idea where the land in River Valley is, but he is not sure of the exact location. He needs to link with Flame, to let her know they are coming and to get the directions right.

He starts the van, then looks at the broken down front door of the mansion. He turns to Mercedes and says, "I should have thought about it, but we need to get someone out here to fix that door. I'd hate for someone to rob the house."

She looks at the door, then looks at him and says, "Shay, there's nothing in that house that I would give a damn about if Joe's not here. I don't care about the house. I've finally realized that. It's only a house."

She is sitting in the long back seat with Sadie's head lying on her lap. She has a cloth and bag of ice on her right eye.

It makes Shay mad again every time he looks at her, but he nods in understanding and tells them, "Okay, you guys, I have to talk to Flame now, so don't interrupt."

At Frankie's nod, Mercedes looks from one to the other, and says, "Frankie, what's he talking about?"

Frankie says, "Hell, Mercedes, don't ask me. I ain't no damn psychic!" And, he grins at Shay.

Shay gives Frankie a small, grim smile and shakes his head. He does not need everyone knowing about this, though after thinking about it, Mercedes and Joe would soon know anyway. Plus, they are family.

Mercedes has already made the connection though. She realizes this is what Flame had been talking about. She watches Shay in fascination.

He tries out the link, saying, *Flame? Flame… answer me.*

I'm here, Shay. Is Mercedes all right?

He answers, *Yes, honey. She and Sadie are in the van with me and Frankie.*

She asks, *Frankie too? Thank God. We need ya'll here. Joe's in trouble…I don't know what will happen, but I know it will.*

He says, *I know he is, honey. It's been Mercedes' father all along. He's the one behind it all. I'll explain it all to you when we get there.*

Shit, Shay! He killed Grandfather? It was Mr. Holst?

Shay tells her, *Flame, honey, calm down…I need you to listen to me. Yes, he was behind it, but there's more trouble coming. I can't go into it all, but there should be someone there for you in a little while. Detective Don Clanton, my friend, is bringing a couple of Munson officers with him. They can all be trusted, honey I promise you that. Trust me?*

She answers immediately, *Of course I trust you, Shay. I must tell the wolves though. They won't let them on the property. They're guarding me, and the land.*

He says, *Okay, honey, you do that, but be sure who you open the door to. Yes, Joe's in danger. Mercedes heard her father tell someone, over the phone, to cut his brake line. Can you reach him in any way?*

No, Shay, I don't think so. I sent Prince's mate, Magic, with him, to guard him, but she can't tell him what's wrong. It's been long enough that he should already be coming back here, but I'll try!

Do that, honey. Tell me now how to find the property.

Flame relays the directions to Shay, as best she can. Her thoughts are on Joe now and as soon as she breaks her mind link with him, she goes into a mind link with the alpha female, Magic. She tells her, *Magic, if you can, warn Joe. His brake line has been cut.*

She tries to give Magic an image of what she is talking about, but says, *I know you don't understand that, but Magic, both of you could die if he loses control of the wagon. If you can't warn him, try to push him from the wagon before it crashes. Please, Magic, he's Grandfather's grandson. Grandfather would want you to do this, so would your own Prince.*

Flame feels Magic's acknowledgment, but she worries that it will do no good. Magic just does not understand what it means. She then sends out a call to the wolves and the birds. She tells them silently, *My friends, there are many people coming this way. I can't tell you which are the good ones and which are not. You'll have to wait and watch. Don't attack until you get my command to do so. Relay any information to me though.*

Flame has done all she can. Now all she can do is wait.

Officer Donna Roberts is getting tired of waiting. She has been here, in the forest, close to two hours now. She gets out of the old truck to stretch her legs. Suddenly she sees headlights coming her way. She crouches in the bushes next to the truck, not willing to take a chance that it is not the right people. The vehicle slows when it reaches the old truck.

The vehicle pulls over next to the truck and a deeply accented voice calls out to her, "You can come out now, senorita. We are here to help you. You follow my orders now. Jeno will ride with you. He can drive."

Donna does not like the sound of this. She is still hidden in the bushes so they cannot possibly see her. She has a feeling if she follows this man's orders she will not live to tell it. She keeps quiet.

He calls for her again, "Senorita Donna, you come out now. I do not want Jeno to have to come for you. The boss will not like this, disobeying his order. You *will* come out."

She continues to stay covered. She has her gun with her and will use it if she has to. She does not trust these men anymore than she does the so called boss.

Finally, after several minutes of calling for her, she hears the man tell this, Jeno, to take the truck. They will dispose of it and then come back for her.

Jeno gets into the truck. The keys are still in it and he starts it up, turning around on the dirt track. The headlights pass right over Donna's head as he turns around and she lays flat on the ground, waiting until they are far down the road before standing and running.

She has no idea where to go now and she knows those men were sent to get rid of her, along with the truck. She stays to the inside of the tree line on the Wolf property and jogs back toward its driveway. She will wait there until she can figure out what to do next.

She reaches the driveway just in time to see another car coming up the road. She lies flat in the brush once again, waiting to see who this will be. As the car gets closer it slows, starting to turn into the driveway. Donna recognizes the car. It belongs to Sergeant Stokes. It is her only chance of survival. She stands, running in front of the car.

Stokes is so shocked at seeing Donna run in front of his car that he almost hits her before he can stop. He slams on the brakes. Donna runs to the rear door of the car, pulls it open, and jumps in. Stokes is so surprised that for a moment he cannot even say anything.

Otis is the first to speak. He asks, "What the hell are you doing here? Stokes, I thought you said the boss was sending someone to help the lady?" Otis leers in the backseat at Donna.

Donna pulls out her gun, putting it in Otis' face, and says, "SHUT THE HELL UP YOU LITTLE PRICK! I'll kill you, just like I did the old man, if you so much as speak to me again! Do you understand me?"

Otis nods his head, never taking his eyes off of the barrel of the gun pointed at his forehead.

Donna risks a glance at Stokes, asking warily, "What's going on here, Stokes? Why were those men sent after me?"

Stokes sees that Donna is shaken to the point of blowing Otis' brains out and he is afraid she will not stop there. He tries placating her, "I don't know what men you're talking about, Donna. The boss only told me that he was going to get us some help up here to clean up this mess. He said that Otis is to set fire to the cabin. That's all I know! I swear!" Stokes turns around and looks Donna in the eyes, trying to make her see that he is telling the truth.

Donna thinks about this for a minute, pulling the gun to her side, she says, "Stokes, those men aren't here to help us clean up anything. They were sent to clean *us* up. The boss has put out a hit on us now. He wants us all killed." Donna looks at Stokes while relaying this tidbit of information.

Donna then turns to Otis, giving him a hate filled look and saying, "I don't really give damn if they kill this asshole, but I don't want to be with him."

Otis imagines his hands around her throat, choking her, while he has his way with her, just like he has dreamed of doing to the woman called Flame. She made the mistake of crossing him once, right here on this land.

She embarrassed him in front of his buddies and he took his revenge. He blew her damn trailer all to hell. It was just too damn bad that she wasn't in it, like she was supposed to be. Next time he would have it his way and she would be dead. He will even have her, no matter if she is alive, or dead.

Stokes speaks to Donna again, "Have the men been here yet? Are the bodies still out there?"

"I think they're still there. The men came up on me up the road, where there's a little dirt track into the woods. I hid until they left. They took the old man's truck and I ran."

Stokes thinks for a moment, then tells them both, "That would be the way for us to go. We need to go in through the back side. I believe that track leads all the way through the property to the cabin. Where did you and the boys park Otis' jeep, Donna?"

She answers, "It's sitting behind the barn, hidden from anyone, unless they go all the way around it. I think going in the back way would be a good idea. Those damn wolves are crazy. There are about fifteen of them and they're damned smart." This is something she hates to admit, but she has never seen an animal smarter than they are.

"Otis, you get out here and take the gas can out of the trunk. Make your way to the cabin and start the fire. Then get your jeep and meet us back here. Hopefully we can get in and out of here quickly. If you see anyone, use your gun. Man or animal, kill it. No chances."

Chapter 31

Flame is warned that there is a car coming onto the driveway and heading for the cabin. She sees through the eyes of the wolves that it is a police car. She tells the wolves to let it come. Not to show themselves. This is no enemy.

As the squad car pulls up she opens the door to the cabin and walks onto the porch, glad to have someone with her. An older man gets out, one she does not recognize, and he strides purposefully up the steps.

He says, "Morning, mam. I'm Officer Wallace. I was told that you've had a murder up here. Can you show me the body please?" This man is straight to the point.

She answers, "Yes. Come with me please. Where's my brother? I thought he would be with you."

She starts into the cabin and Ghost comes onto the porch. He will not leave her alone with this man, no matter who he claims to be. She waits for Ghost to come to her, and then asks Officer Wallace inside. She takes him to the bedroom, showing him Grandfather's body.

The officer tells her, "He's following the detective up here. They should be here any minute now."

"Thanks and I'm sorry, but I'll have to wait out here. I can't bear seeing him like this again." she says, and starts into the living room.

The officer stops her, asking, "Mam, was his body here when you found him or has it been moved?" This officer is looking at her with suspicion and adds, "And, another thing…why's this wolf lying here with him?"

"Yes, Officer, he was moved. Joe and I found him in front of the cabin and we moved him in here. We couldn't leave him on the ground. He's our grandfather and he deserves our respect. He deserves yours too, please." she answers.

Then she tells him with a note of impatience in her voice, "The wolf was his friend and he died trying to protect him. He's in this place because it's where he belongs."

She is getting angry again. This man has no sympathy and no manners.

He hooks his thumbs in his suspenders and says, "Mam, you've tampered with a crime scene. You shouldn't have moved the body. The detective working this case won't be happy that you've done this. Will you point me in the direction of the other bodies?" Officer Wallace is getting pretty angry now, himself. Surely these people know better than to move the body, and as for this girl being Joe's sister *or* the old man's granddaughter, it isn't possible.

He adds, "I also need to ask you to stay inside the cabin. You will have to make a statement as soon as Detective Hendrickson gets here."

She tells him, a note of anger beginning to show, "Sir, I don't know where the other bodies are. I think they're in the woods in front of the cabin. You'll have to find them yourself, since *I'm* not allowed out of the cabin." She turns around and stomps back into the living area.

She has had enough of this man. She will not help him find the bodies or help him further in any way. He can search for the bodies himself. The wolves are not going to let him see them unless she gives them permission and she is thinking of not doing so.

Joe is behind his friend, the River Valley Detective, Cheryl Hendrickson, and she waves as she turns off into the RV Park. He waves and continues on, coming to Grandfather's land.

When he gets to the large downhill incline, he taps his brakes. Nothing happens. Instead of slowing down he is going even faster. There is a very bad curve coming up and, he knows, without brakes he will never make the curve.

Magic has been trying to get through to him, but she does not know how. She has nudged and whined, but he has not paid any attention to her. Finally, as they come closer to the curve, she reaches over him, causing him to lose control of the car. She pulls on the handle to the car, nudging his door until she is sure it will open.

He is trying very hard to keep control of the car and, when the wolf lunges over him, he can do nothing except let go of the wheel. He screams. Then she grabs the door handle in her teeth, pulling it into the open position. When she does this his arm pulls the steering wheel, causing the car to swerve radically to the right. She pushes him with her whole body, shoving him out of the unlatched door and throwing him clear of the car.

The car hits the guardrail with enough speed that it goes through the railing and over the huge embankment, rolling over and over. It lands in the river far below with the female wolf, Magic, going with it.

Joe is knocked unconscious when he hits the pavement. He rolls over and over, like the car, but lands in the tall grass on the other side of the road. He is hurt badly, and bleeding from cuts on his face and body. If he is not found soon he may also die, just like Magic has.

Flame is watching out the window, following with her eyes the soft glow of Officer Wallace's flashlight moving over the dense forest. She could tell him he should go farther into the woods to find the bodies, but she doesn't. She is past the point of caring what this man does.

Her eyes go blank, a blinding vision before her. Magic has mind linked with her, showing her the fight that Joe is having trying to control the large car. She sees that he is not going to make the curve ahead and tells Magic to do what she must to save him.

She sees Magic lunge over him and then sees him lose control of the car. She sees Magic pushing Joe from the vehicle and then all she sees and feels is the car rolling over and over. Then, Magic's eyes can show her no more. Magic is with her Prince.

Flame comes back into her own mind knowing she must reach Joe. The quickest way to him would be over the track that runs through the forest and to the meadow. She has to go. Now.

She quickly grabs the small handgun, placing it in the small of her back and into her waistband. She slips out the door in back of the cabin and rushes to the barn. It will be dark outside for a little while longer. The old officer will not see her until the horse runs past him.

As Ghost tries to follow her, she tells him silently, *No, Ghost. I must go myself. The horses are afraid of you and the other wolves. I must do this to save Joe. You stay here and wait for Shay. He'll know what to do. Keep him safe, my friend.*

Ghost whines, not liking the idea of letting her do this alone, but he will obey her. He will know if she is in danger and then nothing will keep him from her.

She hastily bridles one of the horses, not taking the time for a saddle. She bolts on to its back, kicking hard, pushing the horse straight into a fast gallop. As she gets to the front of the cabin she never slows, not even as she hears the old officer yell for her to stop as the horse runs past him. He would never understand, much less believe her.

Two cars pull onto the Wolf land. Officer Marty Diener behind the wheel of the first, and Detective Don Clanton driving the other. As they reach the end of the driveway they see Officer Wallace running toward his squad car.

Don jumps out of his car, yelling to the officer, "What's the problem, Officer?!"

Everyone, except the young, scared officer with them, gets out of their cars, pulling their guns from their holsters.

The older officer, Wallace, looks at them, seeing their guns drawn, and asks, "Just who the hell are you and why have you drawn your guns on me?!"

Don replies angrily, "We're here to help protect some people here. We drew our guns because you're racing toward your damn car!"

Officer Wallace gives them a skeptical look, telling them, "Only one that needed protecting here were those two cops in the woods! They're dead and the damn woman that was here just took off on a damn horse! Now, can I do my job and get someone to help me catch that red-headed murderer?"

The young officer surprises them all by opening his door and shouting, "YOU OLD DAMN COOT, THEY'RE HERE TO PROTECT THAT WOMAN! IT'S THOSE COPS THAT WERE THE MURDERERS! GET OUT OF THEIR WAY!"

This takes everyone so much by surprise that nobody speaks a word for a moment, but just stare at him open mouthed.

Then Officer Wallace states, "Boy, you'd best get your ass back in that car. You have no idea what these people have done. Detective Hendrickson should be along shortly and then she can figure this out. I ain't letting these three inside that cabin, or near the other bodies! Right now this is *my* crime scene. Not theirs!"

The three Munson cops look at one another. Don shrugs, and Marty walks calmly over to Wallace, never putting his gun down. He reaches out and takes Wallace's gun from its holster and throws it to Don. Marty calls to the kid, "Hey kid, come on over here and bring your cuffs."

The young officer's eyes are wide, but he does as he has been told and comes to Marty and Wallace, taking his cuffs off of his belt on the way.

Marty tells him, "Cuff him to that porch rail right there, son."

"You can't do that, boy! You cuff me and I'll be sure that badge is ripped off your damn uniform!" Wallace warns.

"Shut up, old man. I've heard enough shit from you that it won't make a damn to me what they do! I'm going to cuff your old ass, just like this officer told me to!" And, the young cop does, grinning widely at the three Munson cops as he adds, "Can I help you now?"

Don shakes his head, grinning, and looks at Marty, "Did you tell him *everything*?"

Marty grins and says, "Yep. Figured he should know, since he's going to be here to see it for himself."

Don looks to the kid and asks, "You sure you're going to be okay with the wolves?"

The young cop looks around, wide eyed, swallows hard, but looks back at Don and nods.

Don tells him, "Okay then, we can always use some good help, son."

The young cop grins widely and walks to Marty, who tells them, "Don, Regina, this is Anthony. He doesn't like to be called son too much. I think old Wallace over there has rubbed his face in so much bullshit that he's ready to be a man now."

Regina walks up to the young Anthony. She holds out her hand, and says, "Nice meeting you, Officer." She grins, and Anthony grins back, shaking her hand with enthusiasm.

Don too shakes Anthony's hand, then slaps him on the back. He says, "Let's go. We'll check out the cabin first."

Officer Wallace just continues cursing every one of them.

They reach the porch and Ghost is waiting for them. He walks to Don, smells him, then steps back, walks to the door and opens it with his mouth.

Don looks at Ghost, turns to the three cops with him, and says, "Regina, is this Ghost?"

Regina is grinning from ear to ear as she says, "Yep. That's him all right. I've never seen an animal as smart as this one. He's inviting you in. He must smell Shay on you."

Don realizes that she is right. He looks at young Anthony and tells him, "Anthony, I want you to meet Ghost. He's one of the wolves you've been so scared of."

Anthony's eyes go wide and Ghost, smelling the boy's fear, walks to him. He looks up at the young cop and gives his best smile, holding out his front paw for Anthony to take.

Anthony exclaims, "Well, I'll be damned. That wolf's smiling at me!" He takes Ghost's paw, shakes it and turns to the Munson cops, grinning from ear to ear.

Don smiles and tells him, "Marty, you stay out here and keep an eye out for anything wrong. Come on you two."

And, they walk into the cabin.

Don goes into the open bedroom door, calling to the others, "I've found Mr. Wolf. Come on in here."

After searching the rest of the cabin they go into the barn. They find two obviously used stalls, but only one horse. Don realizes that Wallace had been right. Flame must have taken the other horse, but he has no idea why.

Anthony tells them, "That old man's grandson came and got Detective Hendrickson and she was going to follow him up here. I don't understand why they aren't here yet. He was worried that someone was going to hurt his little sister, but Wallace said the woman that took off was a red-head. How can she be his little sister?"

"You don't have to share blood to be related. That old man in there loved her, and so does Joe, his grandson." Marty, having come around the cabin and into the barn, relays this to Anthony. Then he adds, "I've known Joe and his grandfather most of my life and when Flame came into their lives they became one family. She's real special. She has a real gift."

"Gift? What do you mean? I've always heard that the old Indian man, Grandfather Wolf, could do magic. All the kids around here, and most of their parents, have known about him and his wolves for as long as I can remember. Is she like him?" Anthony asks.

This time it is Regina who answers, "Yes. She's real special. She knows things that nobody should know and she's beautiful too. If I've ever met anyone with real magic, it's her."

As shouts from outside the barn reach their ears the four of them rush to the front of the cabin. Smoke is coming from the back of the cabin and Officer Wallace, cuffed to the porch, is screaming his head off. "Fire! Get these damned cuffs off me now! Hurry!"

Anthony rushes to Wallace and unlocks the cuffs. Don, Marty, and Regina rush to where the fire seems to be centered to find a gas can lying on its side. The whole back end of the cabin is in flames. This fire has been set intentionally.

Officer Wallace yells, "I saw a man in fatigues run into the woods back there!"

Ghost rushes by them, his hair raised all along his back, teeth bared, and deep growls coming from his throat. They can all hear someone running through the brush with Ghost on his heels.

Don yells, "Anthony, get on your radio and call for assistance from the fire department. Marty, you and Regina head out after Ghost. He'll catch whoever did this and if you can keep him from killing the man, do it! If you can't, then remember where the body is."

Detective Cheryl Hendrickson has looked over the RV Park and she has found nothing that will help to catch this woman cop. She has found one empty tent that has obviously been abandoned. She searches the tent, finding nothing except empty food cans and sleeping bags.

She decides to go on to the Wolf cabin. She needs to check in with Wallace and make sure Joe and his sister are okay. She knows that it will take the state police a while to arrive.

She leaves the campground, turning back onto the main road. As she comes to the steep incline she sees the guardrail down. She pulls to the side, gets out and rushes to the drop-off. Joe's wagon is laying half in the river with only its upturned back end sticking up.

Cheryl calls out loudly, "JOE? JOE CAN YOU HEAR ME? I'M ON MY WAY TO YOU!"

She knows that there is, most likely, no way he could have survived this accident, but she has to go see. She slowly makes her way down the steep incline, tearing her uniform and getting cut on the sharp rocks and sticks, as she makes her way down. She finally reaches the car and looks inside the rear window. Joe is not inside, but the poor wolf is and she is obviously dead.

Cheryl does not know where Joe is. The driver's door is open, so he could have been pulled into the swift current of the river. If so, there is no help for him now. She knows that he is not a careless driver. She had spent a lot of her teen years riding back and forth to school with him. She cannot figure out how this has happened to him.

Just before she turns to make her way back up the incline, to call for search and rescue, she notices something on the underside of the car. She steps closer to the mangled vehicle getting a better view. The brake line has been cut completely in half. A clean cut. This is yet another murder.

This time it is personal for Cheryl. Joe was one of her closest friends during their school years. She, too, is Sioux and Joe had been one of her best protectors, never letting anyone bully her because of her Indian heritage. Someone is going to pay for this and pay big.

Chapter 32

Shay, Frankie, and Mercedes, have finally arrived to the entrance of Grandfather's land. Shay checks the name on the mailbox to make sure and they turn into the driveway. Almost as soon as they turn in they hear yelling and actual screams coming from the left side of the woods.

He slams on the brakes, telling Mercedes to stay in the van. Shay, Frankie, and Sadie get out with both Shay and Frankie carrying their guns in their hands, prepared for anything. Sadie runs into the woods and Shay and Frankie decide it is best to follow where she leads. As they come about thirty yards into the woods they are surprised by a sight they will never forget.

Ghost has a man on the ground and the man is screaming for mercy.

Shay says firmly, "Don't kill him, Ghost!" and Ghost backs off, still growling deeply. Sadie rushes to Ghost's side, joining him in watching this man, both daring him to move, their teeth showing and their ruffs raised. They do not see his hand behind him, reaching for his gun.

Suddenly Marty and Regina run up on the man from behind. Regina has her gun drawn and pointed at the man. She says, "I wouldn't do that if I were you. Roll over onto your stomach and put your hands behind your head, *NOW*! You're under arrest."

Marty reads the man his rights.

Shay now notices the smoke coming from the area ahead of them. He looks at Marty questioningly.

Marty tells him, "This guy started the cabin on fire. It's burning fast. Ghost took off after him and we followed. He was trying to circle around to the barn, probably to set it on fire too."

Regina pulls the man up, takes his gun from the back of his pants, and hands it to Marty. When she turns him around to cuff him, Shay sees who he is.

He says, "This is one of the people we're looking for, Otis Edwards. He's the one who bombed Flame's trailer."

Otis gives Shay a killing look, telling them all, "Yeah, I bombed that little bitch out. She set those wolves of hers on me once, right here. I took what I wanted from her place though before I bombed it, but I just wish that bitch would've been in it when it blew."

Frankie steps forward, cannon in hand. He places the barrel of the gun right up against Otis' forehead, saying quietly, "You be the little asshole that done tried to kill my girl. I wish Ghost would of killed you. Since he didn't I think I will."

Otis' eyes go wide and he does not dare to move.

Shay says unemotionally, "Frankie, don't kill the bastard yet. I want to hear what he tells us before we decide if we want to let Ghost and Sadie have another go at him."

He takes Frankie's arm trying to pull him back, but it is like trying to move a two ton rock. No way. Ghost steps up to Frankie, stands on his rear legs, and lays his huge head on his shoulder.

Frankie, regrettably says, "Awww hell, Ghost. All right. Not now, but if he don't tell us somethin that'll help us put em all away, I'm gonna help you tear him limb from limb, okay?"

Ghost is eye to eye with Frankie and he nods.

"Damn. Regina, I know you said he was the smartest animal you've ever seen, but shit!" Marty Diener is awestruck by Ghost's intelligence.

Shay tells them, "We're going back to the van, but we'll meet you at the cabin. Has the fire department been called? Is Flame okay? And Joe?"

Regina looks at Marty, and he hangs his head, not able to look at Shay. Finally he says, "Shay, Joe had left to go get the police because the phone line was cut. He hasn't made it back yet. Flame was seen taking off on one of the horses just as we got here. I don't know where she is. We haven't had time to look for her. We hadn't been here very long when this guy showed up."

Shay looks at all of them. He looks at Otis one more time and asks sternly, "Edwards, do you know where she went? If you do, you'd better tell me now."

Otis just shakes his head from side to side.

"I swear, Edwards, if I find out later you know something and aren't telling me, I'll let Frankie have his way, and I'll watch. Hell, I'll cheer him on!" Shay says, meaning every word of it.

Frankie looks at Otis too, baring his teeth in an expression much like Ghost's.

Otis admits, "Only thing I know is Stokes and that bitch cop went in the woods down the road aways. They thought they could find a way in here that way."

Shay cannot help himself, he punches Otis as hard as he can in the face, knocking him out cold. He says, "Sorry. Couldn't help myself. We'll put him in the back of my van. It's right over here. He's going to be helping us if he's awake later."

Frankie picks up Otis Edwards' legs and drags him roughly all the way to the van. Nobody dares to interfere.

❧

The two goons who Holst had sent to take care of Donna Roberts, Stokes, and Otis Edwards, have finally gotten rid of the truck, but they still have a lot to do. They head back to the track leading onto the land to look for the lady cop, Donna.

The goons pull over and while they are looking for Donna an unmarked police car pulls in front of their car, headlights pointed right at them. They stand straight, putting their guns behind them, waiting for whoever it is to get out. They do not realize this is one pissed off detective.

Cheryl pulls out her revolver, aims at the tallest one, and shoots his knee out before they can move, not even waiting to get out of her car, but shooting him from the driver's side window.

He falls to the ground, dropping his gun. The other goon runs into the woods.

She gets out of her car, rushes to the fallen man, and yells at him, "SHUT UP, ROLL OVER, AND PUT YOUR HANDS ABOVE YOUR HEAD! MOVE ANYTHING ELSE AND I'LL KILL YOU. YOU GOT IT?!"

The man does as she tells him and she cuffs him, takes him to the back of her car, and shoves him in. She gets in the car, turns facing the man, the fenced divide between them. She waits, not speaking a word.

"Hey…I'm hurt here…please, Senorita?! I'm bleeding all over da place!" the man begs.

"I don't give a rat's patooty what happens to you. I want to know why you're out here and what the hell you're doing in my jurisdiction?" she asks him.

"We were only looking for someting that fell outta our window! You shot me for nothing!"

She tells him calmly, "Juan Velez, I didn't shoot you for nothing. I have warrants on you and your so called friend, Jeno Menendez. You're wanted for more charges than I can count. I could've killed you and nobody would have said a damn word. You also had guns with you. In fact, I could still kill you and nobody would give a rat's ass. Wanna talk now, Juan?" Cheryl is one tough lady and she is pissed enough to do just as she says.

Juan knows it too and he does not want to die, even if it means he goes to jail for the rest of his life. He has spent more than half his life in prison as it is, and prison is more home to him than his life outside prison.

He says, "I tell you everything, Senorita. We suppose to kill some people. Jeno cut the brake line on the Indian man's car. Then we suppose to find da lady cop with old truck and kill her. We find the truck and drive it in the river, but we no find the woman."

"Glad you're in a talkative mood now, Juan. Anyone else you're supposed to kill?" she asks.

"Yes. Senorita with red-hair. Boss say we can have her to do with what we want, then kill her We were going to sell her, no kill her. They pay big for red haired, white girl in Mexico. Then we suppose to kill man name Stokes and man name Otis. That is it, I swear." he tells her and actually makes the sign of the cross on his chest.

Cheryl cannot believe this stroke of luck. This guy is a regular jabber machine. Now she has to get to Joe's sister. She has to take her away from the cabin before anyone else finds her.

As she heads back out of the dirt track and onto the driveway, she notices the smoke coming from the area of the cabin. She turns on her siren and stomps the accelerator.

Flame is riding as fast as she can. She has been riding through the land for, what seems to her, hours. The sun is now coming up, with the sky turning a light pink in the East.

She holds the horse's mane tightly, rushing to find Joe. When she gets in the meadow she sees a large sedan parked there. She slows, moving more cautiously. She tries to go around the sedan, on the far side, when two people step out of the woods. It spooks the horse, causing it to throw her to the ground. She stands and realizes that one of these people is Officer Donna Roberts.

She believes these to be two of the cops Shay had told her were coming to help her and Joe. She does not realize that Donna is the cop that killed Grandfather.

"Officer Roberts, thank God! We have to hurry, Joe's in trouble! He's had a car accident and he's hurt badly. Come with me please, help me!" she cries out.

"Oh, we'll help you all right." Stokes says, pulls his gun and grabs her by the upper arm. He continues, "We've been looking for you. How nice of you to run into us this way." And he laughs madly.

This is Flame's first indication that this man has completely lost his mind. She turns to Donna, hoping that she might help her in some way, and pleads, "Please, Officer, will you go to Joe? Help him! He's going to die if someone doesn't help him soon!"

Donna looks seriously at her, "Sure, I'll help him. Where is he?"

She is shaken, and blurts out, "He's on the side of the road! He's had a car accident! Please help him now, before he dies!" Huge tears are running down her face.

"I'll go right now, little Indian princess. I'll go to him now and put a bullet in his head. Maybe it'll put him out of his misery." Donna cackles, looks at Stokes, and asks sarcastically, "Should I help him out, Stokes?"

"Sure, Donna, just like you helped the old man. Go on. I'll take care of the little lady here." He pushes Flame toward the woods on the other side of the meadow.

At the mention of this woman killing Grandfather, Flame realizes what she has done. Then, Donna calls this man Stokes. She thinks, *Stokes. I should have known.*

Flame is back. No more tears. It is time for her form of retribution.

~

Shay pulls up behind the patrol cars and they all pile out, leaving the unconscious and banged up Otis cuffed to the rear seat of the van. He sees two bodies lying on the ground covered with Indian blankets. His breath leaves his body in a great rush.

He and Frankie stagger their way to the bodies, Shay, shaking, reaches down and pulls the blanket off the first body. It is Grandfather, and as he steps to the other body a young man in a River Valley Police uniform runs out of the burning home. He is carrying a load of everything he could grab.

He says, "Sir, that's the wolf. Not a person."

Shay breathes a sigh of relief and Frankie runs his hands over his tear streaked face.

The two River Valley cops have been running in and out of the burning cabin, bringing first the body of Grandfather out. Then, young Anthony had brought out the body of the wolf, Prince, staggering under his weight. They have tried to get everything out that will mean the most to the family.

Officer Wallace has been doing his part, finally deciding that he should help, not hinder. He carries out another load, bumping into young Anthony.

He shouts, "Damn, move your ass, boy!" He then looks up, seeing why Anthony has stopped moving and he asks bluntly, "And, just who the hell are you? More damn people around here than at the grocery store!"

Don sees what is happening and rushes from the back of the barn, introducing Shay to Wallace and Anthony.

Shay thanks the men for saving all that they can from the burning cabin. He knows what this will mean to Flame and Joe. Both Wallace and Anthony redden at the thanks.

Wallace says, "I'd want somebody to do it for me."

Anthony nods his head in agreement.

Shay looks at Don pleadingly, "Anything yet, Don?" Then he sees the regretful look on Don's face and hangs his head. He cannot bear the thought that anything might have happened to his Flame. He feels like crying.

Frankie lays his ham-like hand on his shoulder with tears rolling down his face and tells him, "We'll find her, Shay." He looks over to find Mercedes standing there, her enormous amber eyes full and overflowing and he tells her, "Don't you worry none, Mercedes. I promise we'll find em both. I ain't gonna let no one take them from us. You hear me?"

Don sees Mercedes' face, all bruised and swollen, and looks quickly at Shay.

Shay shakes his head and Don tells Mercedes to sit down in any one of the cars she wants to. She goes to sit in the first patrol car, leaving the door open. Sadie goes to her and climbs in beside her, keeping her company.

Ghost stays by Shay's side. He knows that he is to protect him, just like he is to protect Flame.

Don asks Shay to follow him a moment and Frankie follows them to the back of the barn. They find a jeep parked there.

Don tells them, "This jeep is registered to Otis Edwards. We've found explosive material and fingerprints all over it. I think this will put Donna Roberts, Stokes, and Otis Edwards, away for a long time. We've also located the bodies of Tuttle and Johnson. They were torn to pieces. If they hadn't had identification we would never have known who they were unless we used fingerprints or DNA Now, will you tell me what happened to that little lady out there?"

Shay fills him in on all that has happened.

Don shakes his head, saying, "I'll be damned glad to see that crazy old bastard go to jail. I just wish we could have caught them before all this happened, before the old man was killed."

Shay tells him, "The man was crazy as a damn loon. I wouldn't be surprised if he's committed instead of going to prison, but I have to say, honestly, I would believe the defense of insanity. I just pray he never gets a chance to walk free again."

They hear the sirens of the fire truck coming down the driveway now and they all rush back toward the cabin. First to pull in is Detective Cheryl Hendrickson and behind her is the fire truck. After a brief introduction, and quick handshakes all around, Cheryl pulls Don and Shay off to the side. They pass information back and forth between them.

When they return to the rest of the party, the firemen tell them they cannot do anything to save the cabin. They will be able to keep the barn from burning though. They go to work doing just that. The cabin is nearly gone already. Shay knows that when Flame sees it again, all that will be left is a smoldering shell.

Cheryl asks Frankie for his assistance. They go to the back of Shay's van, and Cheryl unlocks the cuffs as Frankie pulls the now struggling Otis out of it and places him in the back of Cheryl's patrol car. Now, Otis and Juan will be able to get to know each other.

Cheryl grins at Frankie, saying, "I can't wait to play that voice recorder back and hear what Otis says when he finds out that Juan is the one sent to kill him. I already have Juan on tape telling me everything."

Frankie shakes his head, "Damn woman. You be one crafty little lady. I like that. Damn, if I wasn't gay I think I'd ask you out."

This stops Cheryl mid-step with her chin hitting her chest.

Frankie never notices. He just keeps on walking.

Cheryl yells to Wallace, "Stay with the prisoners and keep your gun drawn. Don't let anyone near that car!"

Wallace nods and nearly runs to her patrol car, pulling his gun out and holding it at his side

After learning of Joe's accident, Mercedes wants to see the site where he went off the road. She asks Cheryl tearfully, "Detective, would it be okay if Anthony takes me to the place that Joe had his accident?"

Cheryl looks quickly at Anthony, noting his facial expression has now taken on more of a man's look than a young boy's. She nods and tells him, "Anthony, take the lady to the U curve. You know where it is. The guardrail's down. Don't let her go down the embankment. I've already been down there and there's nothing to see but the wolf."

He takes Mercedes' arm, escorting her around the patrol car and opening the door for her. She hears whining behind her and turns to find Sadie looking at her expectantly. She asks Anthony if Sadie can come too and he opens the back door for her. He then climbs into the driver's seat, expertly turning the patrol car around and racing down the driveway.

"Okay…which one of you made that boy grow up?" Cheryl quickly asks all of them.

Wallace has the grace to hang his head.

Don notes Wallace's shamefaced look and he says, "Well, Cheryl, I think it was mostly Officer Wallace here. He gave the boy a little bit of confidence this morning. He showed him how to be a man."

Wallace quickly looks at Don with his eyebrows raised.

Don only nods and turns away.

Wallace smiles at Cheryl, then looks in at the prisoners, who are now shouting their heads off at one another.

Cheryl says under her breath, to no one in particular, "Well I'll be damned."

Suddenly Ghost howls, his hackles rise, and his tail is held straight out behind him as he looks down the dirt track. He growls low in his throat, looks at Shay, and starts running down the old track, turning once more to look to Shay and then he is off again at a fast run.

Now all the people at the cabin hear the howls of wolves all around them, all heading away from them. Huge birds of prey fly from the trees, all flying in the same direction, down the old dirt track.

Then up the track runs the horse that Flame had ridden out on. It has been running so hard that it looks ready to drop, foam falling from its otherwise glossy coat. It runs straight into the barn, heading for its own stall. All of them know that Flame is out there somewhere down the dirt track.

Shay shouts to all of them, "HE KNOWS WHERE FLAME IS! HURRY! GRAB YOUR GUNS AND LET'S GO!"

Cheryl jumps behind the wheel of the other River Valley Patrol car, taking Marty and Regina with her and Don gets behind the wheel of his unmarked car, taking Shay and Frankie with him. They leave Wallace to keep watch over the two prisoners and barrel down the track, seeing the wolves running and the birds flying in the same direction.

Marty cannot help himself, he has to ask, "Uh...mam, why are we chasing all those wolves? And, what's with the birds?"

Cheryl looks at him incredulously, "Damn, don't you white boys know anything?" She grins jokingly, "Sorry, couldn't help myself. I'm Sioux, just like Joe and Grandfather. If this woman has been adopted into the family of Wolf, well...let's just say, she has certain gifts."

Marty is still puzzled, but he sure will not open his mouth to ask again.

Regina, grinning, slaps Marty in the back of the head and tells him, "Marty, when we get back home I'm going to take you out and show you what a woman knows that a man can only guess at!" She giggles.

Marty turns his head so quickly to look at her that his neck pops, audibly. He stares at Regina, open mouthed and red faced.

"Now that's what I'm talkin 'bout girlfriend!" Cheryl adds with a womanly grin.

Chapter 33

Flame is past anger and she calls to the forest animals, to them all, *Come to me now! Come to me and rid this land of these interlopers! All of you come. Bring your power. Give me your strength! It is time to avenge Grandfather!*

Stokes has Flame by the arm and is pulling her into the forest. As they round a huge oak, another man, this one dark with eyes like death, steps out from behind a tree.

He looks at Flame, smirks, and then he turns to Stokes to say, "You must be the one that the boss say to look for…Stokes. I am Jeno. The boss, he tell me to help you here."

Stokes looks at him and then turns to face Flame. He tells him angrily, "I don't need any help here, boy. You go on and tell the boss that it's done. I'm still in charge of this operation, *Jeno*. I *know* what you're here for and I ain't planning on dying just yet." Stokes turns once more to look at Jeno.

Both men have their guns drawn and are now pointing them at each other.

With their attention turned toward each other, Flame jerks away and runs as fast as she can, away from Stokes and Jeno and back into the meadow. Her meadow. Her only thought is to get to Joe, to try to heal him before he dies.

Mercedes, Sadie, and young Anthony, pull over where Joe's car has gone off the embankment. He helps Mercedes out of the car, holding her up, as she looks down and sees Joe's new car lying on its top, half in the rushing river. She lets loose a heart wrenching sob and Anthony cannot help but cry too, for *her*.

Something breaks through Mercedes sobs. She hears Sadie. She looks around, but Sadie is not at her side, and she is barking continuously. Both Mercedes and Anthony look around for her, finally seeing her on the other side of the road standing in the tall grass looking at them. She barks again and looks down.

Mercedes runs toward Sadie with Anthony right behind her. They reach Sadie and they find Joe, lying in a pool of blood. His leg is turned at an awkward angle, obviously broken.

Mercedes screams, "OH MY GOD, *JOE*! JOE!" She bends down to him, but Anthony pulls her away. He does not want her to find that this man, her husband, is dead.

He tells her, "Just stay back a bit, mam. Let me, please." As she moves to the side he bends to feel for a pulse and he finds a faint one. He smiles at her and says, "He's alive, mam. We can't move him though. We have to radio for the rescue squad."

"*GO*! DO IT BEFORE HE DIES!" Mercedes shouts.

Anthony runs back to the squad car and picks up the radio. He radios for the rescue squad to come to the U curve on Wolf Mountain. He looks back at Mercedes and sees that she is down on her knees, talking to her husband. Suddenly he notices the dog's head jerk up.

Sadie growls and lowers her head.

Anthony looks in the direction that she is looking and he sees a woman moving slowly forward. The woman is disheveled and has a mad look on her face with a gun held straight out in front of her.

Donna has finally found the damn Indian and as a bonus she gets to kill the boss' own daughter. She laughs manically before saying, "Now don't this just make my day! I get to finish off that damn Indian, the boss' precious daughter, and his biggest pride, that stinky assed dog of his! And to beat it all, it was your own screaming that helped me find you!" She smiles snidely and aims her gun at Sadie saying, "Guess I'll take out the biggest threat first!" She cackles, her laughter sounding like it has come right out of the wicked witch of the west's mouth.

Her own confidence is her downfall. She never even sees the young cop, Anthony, as he slips around behind her. Mercedes has not taken her eyes off Donna and her gun. Anthony slips up behind Donna and he quickly brings his gun down, clipping her right on the back of her head, knocking her out in an instant.

He cuffs her and then turns to Mercedes and asks her, "Will you be okay here if I leave you? I saw her come from the little track running right back here. She may have left Flame back there somewhere. I need to put her in the back of the car and see what she was doing back there."

"You go on, Anthony. You're a hero, you know. I'll be fine here. I'm with Joe." she says, and sits at Joe's side, stroking his long black hair.

Sadie stays on alert for danger.

"I'll have someone right back with you, mam. Until I get back you take this gun," he tosses her Donna's pistol, "and if you see anything that doesn't look right don't take a chance. Shoot it." He then picks up the woman, takes her to his patrol car, and places her on the caged in back seat.

He starts the car and, instead of heading back toward the driveway, he turns on the small dirt track. When he gets further into the woods he sees the clearing and the meadow. He also sees the sedan parked there. He pulls up behind the sedan and gets out.

The other patrol cars have now reached the meadow, but they came from the direction of the cabin, down the old dirt track that runs from the meadow to the cabin. They pull around to the sedan and patrol car. Everyone piles out.

Anthony pulls the now half conscious Donna out of the back seat and walks her to the group of officers. She is mumbling something about animals and Indians. She doesn't seem to notice she is in handcuffs.

Cheryl looks at Anthony with her eyes wide and asks, "Where did you get her, Officer? And, where's Mercedes?"

Before Anthony can answer, they all hear the sound of the rescue squad on the road behind them. The siren stops, reaching its destination.

Anthony looks Cheryl straight in the eyes and tells her, "Detective, we found Joe Wolf. Mercedes is with him, but he's hurt bad. I called the rescue squad and I imagine that's who we just heard, but this woman came up behind Mercedes and she had her gun drawn, threatening to kill them, starting with the dog first. I slipped in behind her and now here she is."

Cheryl looks proudly at Anthony, nodding her head, and telling him, "Officer, you're turning out to be a wonderful addition to our ranks."

Anthony reddens, but grins all the same.

Regina walks up to the scene, taking in Donna's appearance. Regina looks her dead in the eye, jerking Donna's head up to do so as she says, "You bitch. I've wanted to tell you how I feel about you for a long time and now I have the chance. You are nothing. You are an empty, pitiful, little *bitch*, that has to take her vengeance out on animals to make yourself feel like you have some kind of power over something. I used to feel sorry for you. Now I wish we were alone, so I could *show* you just how I feel."

Donna spits in Regina's face and Regina slaps her face so hard that she falls to the ground. Regina tells her, "Do that again and I'll beat the shit out of you before we take your sorry ass to jail! You hear me, bitch?"

Cheryl takes Regina by the arm and says, "She isn't worth it, Regina. She's going to find that prison is much worse for her kind than death is."

Thinking about this for a minute and remembering how cruel this woman has been to so many of the people she has arrested, brings a smile to Regina's face. She smiles and nods in perfect understanding.

"I hope you heard that, Donna." Regina smiles, knowing that prisoners do not take well to cops, especially cops like Donna.

They all see the state police coming down the dirt track from the direction of the cabin. They pull up to the same area as the rest of them. All of the police officers from the various stations group together to relay information.

The sun has risen to the point of turning the sky a deep red in the East, lighting to a pink, then clear blue. Now they can all see the wolves stalking through the tall grass.

Shay stands alone, apart from the rest. He is looking for Flame. He can feel that she is near, but she hasn't answered any of his calls. The hawks and eagles circle the meadow in continuous motion.

Frankie joins Shay and he tells him, "Our girl, she's out here. I can tell. See them wolves? They know she's comin. They're gonna tear apart whoever done hurt her and her family."

"I sure do hope you're right, Frankie. I can't stand the thought of losing her now."

Jeno and Stokes are at a stand off. Stokes tells Jeno, "I think we'd best get to the girl. The boss wants her dead. It won't do us any good to shoot each other if we lose the girl. Put the gun down, Jeno." Stokes slowly lowers his own gun, knowing that Jeno will do the same.

Jeno, not being quite as stupid as Juan, knows that this job is over. He knows he is going back to prison soon. Too much has happened here. He will wait and watch. Maybe he will get off easy, since he hasn't hurt anyone.

He lowers his gun and tells Stokes, "Go on. We will search for her first. She cannot get very far yet." Not bothering to tell this man that he will not be joining him.

Stokes runs in the same direction he saw Flame go. He never notices that Jeno has turned to go back into the woods. As he enters the clearing, the meadow, wolves converge on him from all sides. He takes aim and hits one, killing her instantly. The others temporarily back off. They are waiting for the command from Flame to kill this man.

Suddenly, from the woods behind Stokes, he hears screaming. Jeno is screaming his head off. He is screaming for his life and begging for Stokes to come and help him. The screaming lasts for close to thirty seconds, then the woods are silent once more.

All of the officers hear the man screaming. They rush toward the sound of the screams, on the other side of the meadow. The birds, all hawks and eagles, swoop down in front of the officers, blocking them from going further. They are forced to stop or get torn to bits by the talons and large beaks.

Shay sees Flame come into the meadow and then he sees Stokes coming after her. As Stokes get closer to her, she stops, turning toward him, not running away. She is surrounded by her wolves. They can all see her face as she turns on Stokes.

Seeing this, all the people searching for her begin to run toward her, Shay included. Then Shay plainly hears Grandfather in his mind.

He says, *Shay, keep them back now. Flame cannot stop the killing here. Do not let them move. Stand still and watch the power of your woman. It is all her. As I have said, wolves take care of their own!*

Shay yells to all of them, "NO! DON'T MOVE...STAND STILL AND WATCH!"

Cheryl yells at him, "Shay, that man is going to kill her! We have to get to her!"

He tells her and the rest, calmly, almost whispering it, "Don't move. Stand still and watch. This is Wolf land, remember?"

Cheryl looks at Shay like he has lost his mind and then she hears someone whisper to her, *Ho kay hey! It is a good day to die!*

Now, she nods too. She puts her hand out stopping them all from moving and tells them all, "He's right. Everyone hold your positions. Don't distract her."

These statements have surprised everyone else, even Frankie, and he knows Flame well. He can barely contain himself, wanting to go to her, but if Shay says be still, he will do so. They are all watching expectantly.

Flame hears the shot go off with Stokes killing one of her wolves. Actually feeling the death herself. She turns, seeing Stokes, watching her with a smile. She smiles back, erasing the smile from his face immediately.

She calls to the wolves and to the birds of prey. *Now it's time for our form of retribution! Birds, my friends, go for his head. Take his attention from the wolves.*

The large birds of prey have been circling the meadow, keeping the police back. They now converge on this man.

Flame sees Stokes trying to fight them off.

She raises her hands high, reaching toward the heavens. Her waist length, red hair blows around her like the flames of a fire. Her large eyes are hard green emeralds and her hair continues to whip wildly around her, but yet, there is no wind. The wolves surround her, all facing this man. The birds continue their dives toward the man's head.

Stokes, ignoring the beating of wings and razor sharp talons, brings his arm up, pointing straight at Flame. Suddenly, the large, white, glossy body of a wolf jumps high into the air, going straight for Stokes' neck. He fires his gun, hitting the wolf squarely in the chest.

Flame screams, "*NO*!"

Stokes, pulls the trigger once more, blowing a large hole in the middle of her chest. Blood gushes from the wound. She falls to the ground, hitting it hard. The wolves howl in unison.

Now Flame hears Grandfather calling to her. She turns her head and he is with her. He has Prince on one side of him and Magic on the other.

She tells him, *Grandfather, I tried to find you. I couldn't, but here you are! Oh, Grandfather, I've missed you so! I need you, Grandfather, and now I've found you!*

He answers, *Yes, Granddaughter, you have found me, but you are not ready to go with me now, daughter of my heart. It is not your time for the path that I now must walk. You must stay with Shay. He needs you. You have much more living to do, my child.*

I do love Shay, Grandfather, but I don't want to leave you! Please, let me stay with you?

He says, *No, little one. Not yet. I will be with you again, one day, many, many years from now. You must protect the land now, and the wolves. They need you, Granddaughter. Go back. Go back for them.*

She admits, *I hear them calling me. The wolves and the birds. I hear Shay and Frankie. They're crying for me, Grandfather. I must find Joe too, Grandfather! He's been hurt.*

Granddaughter, Joe is going to be with you again. Do not worry. Nothing has happened that cannot be undone. Go back. It is not your time. Go back, Flame.

I love you, Grandfather.

I know, and I love you also I will always be with you. I was granted one more wish, and that was to heal you, Granddaughter. Go back…

She feels her body tugging at her, pulling her back into the pain. Suddenly she feels the wound closing, the arteries and muscles mending. Grandfather is working on her from the inside out, even after his death. The bullet falls onto her lap as she sits up. There is no more pain. No more blood.

She opens her eyes and sees the evil man standing before her. He is surrounded by the wolves, which stand snarling at him. She stands, facing her enemy, whole and unhurt. She gives him a smile with her head held high.

She feels Shay and the others running toward her. She turns her head and looks at them. They see her face and stop. Her eyes glow with a bright green light and her hair continues to whip, wildly around her, almost transcendent in her beauty and power.

She quickly sends a message to Shay, *STAY BACK, SHAY! KEEP THEM ALL BACK! THERE HAS BEEN TOO MUCH DEATH HERE TODAY! HE HAS TAKEN GHOST FROM ME AND NOW HE WILL DIE FOR IT!*

She raises her hands high into the air, facing this man. She feels the power, Grandfather's, hers, the wolves and even the birds. All of it focused on this one man, Stokes. The wolves surround her, all facing him. The eagles and hawks are flying in the air all around her, circling her, waiting for her command.

Seeing this frightening miracle, Stokes turns to run. Bullets will not help him now and he knows it. He has nowhere to go. He cannot outrun her vengeance this day. He owes his life for his deeds done here, on the wolves' land. This Wolf land.

Flame slowly lowers her arms and the wolves and birds seek their prey.

Stokes falls, screaming under the double pack of wolves and birds fighting alongside them, until there are no more screams. Nothing more than a carcass. The carcasses left here, in these woods, are so diseased that even the crows will not touch them.

A single hawk flies to Flame, landing on her outstretched arm. The hawk carries something in her mouth and she drops it into Flame's open palm. It is the necklace that Grandfather said would one day be hers. The wolves tooth necklace. She slowly walks to the fallen white wolf, bends and strokes its fur, her tears blinding her.

But, she immediately thinks, *Wait! This is not my Ghost! This is a female!*

She stands and yells, "GHOST!"

He rushes to her. He has been with her, with the other wolves, and she has not even noticed! After the white wolf went down, she had paid no attention to anything except to kill the man, Stokes.

She bends and hugs Ghost to her.

Then she hears her name called softly, *Flame...*She stands facing back toward the woods, her hair blowing wildly, with Ghost at her side. There is Grandfather standing in the trees, Prince, and Magic standing with him.

He smiles at her, saying, *Put on the necklace, dear Granddaughter. You have more than earned it this day. I love you, my child. Ho kay hey! It is a good day to die!*

She turns back again, toward Shay. She smiles that sunshine filled smile, standing there looking like a goddess. *His* goddess, with Ghost by her side.

Shay sees Grandfather watching her for just a moment, but when he blinks, Grandfather is gone.

They are all watching her, every man and woman present. She is captivating in her beauty and power.

Flame knows Grandfather will continue to watch over his land and his family. Wolves protect their own.

Epilogue

It is now spring in the meadow. The birds are singing and flowers are blooming in abundance. More than a hundred people are sitting in white chairs facing Shay, who is standing in his white tux, red shirt, and white tie. In front of him stands Judge Erin L. Baron. They are looking expectantly toward the woods, waiting.

Just when Shay thinks he cannot wait any longer, he sees Mercedes and Joe coming toward him. She has on a beautiful flame-red formal gown. It has many yards of extra material to cover the large bulge of her stomach. Joe, in a black tux, red shirt, and black tie, walks on her right. Sadie walks on her left with flowers on her huge head in a woven circle. Mercedes smiles brightly at Joe and then at Shay.

Someone starts the taped wedding march. All stand and turn expectantly, seeing the most amazingly beautiful woman they have ever seen. She glides through the grass, wearing a gorgeous white, beaded wedding gown. It fits her womanly form like a silk glove.

Her hair is worn loose and blowing freely. She wears a wreath of Indian Paintbrush in her hair. She smiles that sun-filled smile and you can hear the gasps and appreciative mumbles throughout the crowd. There has never been a more beautiful bride.

Ghost walks beside her, proud and smiling. He keeps step with her perfectly. As they step up to Shay, Ghost moves to Sadie's side. He turns and smiles at Sadie and the whole crowd gives a small laugh.

When Judge Baron asks for the rings, Ghost opens his mouth and puts out his tongue, surprising everyone. Two rings of gold lay on it.

"Flame...did you make him do that?" Shay whispers.

"No, Shay. Joe was supposed to have the rings!"

They turn to look at Joe, who is grinning from ear to ear as he says, "Sorry...I couldn't help myself."

And, laughter runs through the crowd, including the wedding party.

As Judge Baron pronounces them man and wife, they kiss, and turn toward the guests. Flame nudges Shay, looking out over the crowd to the woods.

Shay nudges Joe, and Joe says, "You had to know he would be here."

Flame's brilliant smile could outshine the sun. Grandfather, Prince, and Magic, are standing in the shadow of the forest. Grandfather with his beautifully, wrinkled smile, glowing for only them to see.

The reception is being held on the site of the old cabin. There is now a huge ranch style house there, completed only a short month ago. It has four bedrooms, three full baths, a huge kitchen, large formal living room, and large den. There is also a large dining area. The large dining table is laden with food of every kind imaginable.

This is where the guests fill their plates, taking them into the den, living room, or large kitchen. Everyone that Shay, Flame, Joe, and Mercedes, cares about have come to the wedding. Even Flame's friends from the carnival have taken this weekend off to attend.

Frankie and Stephan are here. Frankie has given up the carnival, letting Tom, who had at one time worked for Frankie, buy him out. Frankie and Stephan have moved closer to Flame, here in River Valley. They have opened their own small family restaurant and it is doing wonderfully.

Surprisingly, Regina and Marty are here also. They have been dating for some time now. Both have been promoted. Regina to sergeant and Marty has taken over Shay's position as detective.

Mercedes and Joe are standing with Flame and Shay. Their small daughter, Sasha, who looks so much like her mother, is playing in the corner with Ghost and Sadie.

Joe turns to Shay and says, "Buddy, when do you hang your sign out at your new office?"

"I'm waiting until after the honeymoon, which is going to be spent right here, in our new home." he replies proudly.

"Do you think you're going to be all right with being a lawyer and out of all the action of being a cop?" Joe cannot help but ask.

"Buddy, I've had enough action to last me, *and my wife*, a lifetime!"

Flame smiles, turning to ask Mercedes, "Mercedes, are you sure you're not due until fall? I swear, if you get much bigger Joe will have to wheel you around!"

They all laugh.

"Yes, Dr. Darling swears they'll be born in September. I don't know if I can hold these two that long!" Mercedes admits.

Joe adds, "Just wait until the boys are born! Then you'll really have your hands full!"

"Uh...Joe, I hate to break it to you, buddy, but I think you'll find your hands will be just as full!" Shay says and grins, and they all chime in their agreement.

"Okay, you two...it be time to open your presents! Come on into the living room!" Frankie is as excited as a kid at Christmas, dying to see what they have gotten.

"I think we'd better listen to him, honey. He's liable to open them himself if we don't!" Flame says, laughing delightedly.

They all gather into the living room, fitting as many of them as possible into the large space. Flame and Shay take turns opening the gifts. Everyone has been so generous and they have everything they need to help furnish their huge new kitchen, bathrooms, and more.

Then, they get to a very large package wrapped in gaily colored red paper. Flame knows this one must have come from Joe and Mercedes. She looks at them and says, "Let me guess…" and she laughs, telling Shay, "You open this one."

Shay tears the paper off revealing a beautiful, hand carved baby cradle. He pulls it out of the box and sets it in front of Flame. She traces the edge of the cradle with her fingers. Then she notices the head of the cradle is carved with a wolf's head on it.

"Oh, Joe, I know you did this, didn't you?"

"Of course, little sister. I want my nephew to know he's one of us!" he says as he laughs.

"Joe, it's beautiful. Thank you both so much!" Flame looks up at them with tears in her eyes.

Shay has to ask, "What makes you so sure we'll have a boy, Joe?"

Joe looks at Flame, she places a hand over her slightly bulging belly, and answers for him, "Honey, some things are just a given."

"You mean…? *Really?* We *are*? OHMYGOSH! I'm gonna be a Daddy!" Shay shouts, grinning brightly and hugging Flame to him.

It is now later in the day and most of the guests have left. Only Mercedes, Joe, little Sasha, Frankie, and Stephan have stayed behind. Flame looks at Shay and he nods.

She opens the door to the house, telling Ghost, "It's time for your gift, my friend."

Ghost goes out and gives a short cough-like bark. In only a brief moment Ghost's mate, a beautiful dark gray female, Smoke, comes into the house. She is carrying a small, wiggling, dark gray cub by its scruff. She lays it at Flame's feet.

Flame bends and rubs the female, Smoke, on the head. She picks up the cub, and says, "Frankie, Ghost has a gift for you and Stephan. As you know, Ghost is now the alpha male of the newest pack. This beauty, Smoke, is his mate. He very much wants you to have his son and he wants you to name him."

Frankie looks at Flame, then to Ghost, with huge tears rolling down his large face. He takes the cub and hugs it to him as he says tearfully, "Ghost, I cain't think of a better gift in the world. You knows how much I'll love him. Stephan will too." He looks at Stephan, and he nods, tears building in his own eyes. Frankie says, "I'll name him after his mother. Smoky."

Ghost grins, laying his large head on his mate, Smoke's, back.

All is well in the forest Wolf.

About the Author

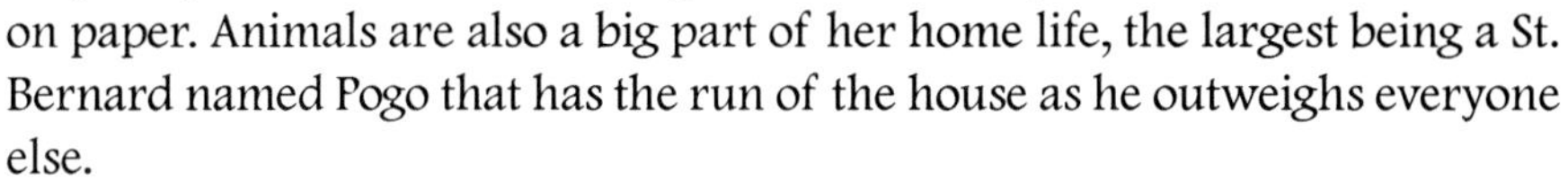

Cynthia Cantrell lives in the Smoky Mountains of Tennessee. She has a special affinity for animals and includes them in all of her novels.

Cynthia has lived in many places, growing up in a military family. She graduated high school on Guam, USA in the late 70's, spent many years near the beaches of South Carolina, and will be visiting many of these childhood stomping grounds in future books.

Cynthia has a daughter and niece that keep her very busy when she's not creating an altered reality on paper. Animals are also a big part of her home life, the largest being a St. Bernard named Pogo that has the run of the house as he outweighs everyone else.

Printed in the United States
115233LV00005B/238-306/P

9 781594 26709